OPEN

SEASON

OPEN SEASON

CASSIE WERBER

First published in Great Britain in 2024 by Trapeze
an imprint of The Orion Publishing Group Ltd
Carmelite House, 50 Victoria Embankment
London EC4Y 0DZ

An Hachette UK Company

1 3 5 7 9 10 8 6 4 2

A CIP catalogue record for this book is
available from the British Library.

ISBN (Hardback) 978 1 3987 1490 8
ISBN (eBook) 978 1 3987 1492 2
ISBN (Audio) 978 1 3987 1493 9

Typeset by Input Data Services Ltd, Bridgwater, Somerset

Printed in Great Britain by Clays Ltd, Elcograf S.p.A.

MIX
Paper | Supporting
responsible forestry
FSC
www.fsc.org FSC® C104740

www.orionbooks.co.uk

To our bodies turn we then, that so
Weak men on love reveal'd may look;
Love's mysteries in souls do grow,
But yet the body is his book.

John Donne, 'The Ecstasy'

To Val and Lawrie, of course

Chapter One

The palm of his hand is a battleground. The war is a war with himself.

James Alston registers a sensation like whispering at the back of his neck, cold lips moving from collar to nape and into his hair. There is nothing there, not yet, but he shudders and the convulsion ripples his shoulders, impossible to hide.

'I can go first if you prefer,' the woman beside him says. James shakes himself, inhales hard.

'No, I can do it.'

There was a moment, earlier, when he had felt profoundly calm; the hypnosis sessions had done their work. Now they have moved deeper into the zoo, and this room is hot, the air jungle-damp. The lighting is dim, with shadows deep and black in every corner. James shuts his eyes for a moment, and tries to reconstruct the safe place he had envisioned in the guided meditation: his grandparents' greenhouse, a tiny sub-tropical cube embedded in the sharp northern spring. Warm, full of light, smelling of earth and tomato stalks. A wicker seat, and an old water butt for a table. On the rough wood, a blue china cup and saucer, and in the cup – make it detailed, the coach had said – tepid tea with a thick silt of sugar.

He opens his eyes and stares straight ahead.

A young, dark-haired woman, one of the keepers, is carrying a small opaque box towards him. She sets it down on the table be-tween them, and looks up to meet his eyes.

'Ready?'

James wills himself, a child again, to stay on that wicker seat, to smell tomatoes ripening, to taste wet sugar on a fingertip. He looks down at his arm like it's some unfamiliar limb. A brave man's arm. He nods once, tells himself to reach forward, palm flat. The woman dips both hands into the box and lifts them back out, gently cradling their new occupant.

Tarantula. A beautiful word. This, James knows, is a Mexican Red-Knee. He knows because he has read the website, the day's information pack, obsessively, again and again, as if repetition could blunt the sting of the word 'spider' and all words associated with it. A red-knee. A spider with knees. Cute, he says to himself. Who could be afraid of anything with knees?

And yet here it is: fear, a bully in the playground of his brain. His heart knocks hard. Panic looms.

The keeper holds the spider over his outstretched hand. Wonkily affixed to the material below her right collarbone is a white sticker on which she has written her name, Pilar, and added the two dots and upcurving line of a smiling face. James looks at the dots and fails to see eyes, but keeps on looking anyway, in order not to look anywhere else.

'Remember, she is very fragile, like an egg,' Pilar says. 'If you drop her, she will break.'

Deftly she opens her fingers. The other participant, standing beside him, muffles a gasp. And now the spider sits on James's skin.

He looks at it. In the close room, sweat pours down the back of his neck, down the sides of his body, but James barely notices. He is marvelling at the spider's weight; its delicacy. He had imagined a sickening meatiness. But this thing is feathery, mouse-like, balanced on tiny, still feet. The spider doesn't scuttle, as he had deeply feared. It is motionless. It is calm. James feels a rush of blood to the head, so hard that his vision blackens at the edges, his ears burn, and he seems to feel the presence of every hair on his scalp.

And then, unexpectedly, awkwardly, his eyes are overflowing with tears. The spider lifts one foot, and puts it down again. On the other side of the table, James senses that Pilar is smiling.

In a moment, James thinks, he may be able to look at her. For now, he looks at the spider, and his tears fall and fall in a steady, silent stream.

Six miles east, Hura Holmes lies very still on the floor of her living room. Nearby, Casimir – part husky, part Alsatian, part, they always say, human – rests his head on his forepaws. He's an old dog now, with grey around the muzzle, and patient as a stone. If there's one thing he knows, it's that however long Hura seems to disappear, into herself, or into the big world outside these walls, she always returns in the end. She always comes back to him.

Hura's family and friends were surprised when, at twenty-one and just out of university, she came home with a puppy, wrapped in a towel and small as a lump of flint. Her mother Aisha sat her down and told her it was no time for such a big commitment; to be tied down, whether to a man or a dog or anything else. Hura had laughed at her mother's prescription for freedom, though eventually had to admit to herself that she hadn't understood the commitment she was taking on. This is the reward, though: companionship through these terrible weekdays on which she has nowhere to be. Hura lost her teaching job a month ago. Her thoughts are running through a short, worried cycle, and every time they hit the memory of that day – roughly every ninety seconds – the room seems to tip. As though the building itself has come unmoored, and is drifting out to sea.

Hura's phone is cradled on her belly, and her eyes are closed. Now she opens them and sees the white of the ceiling, like an empty page. She checks one last time to make sure that she hasn't somehow missed a call. The agency hasn't phoned. No one has phoned. The day and all its hours unspool before her, blank and anxious.

Making a decision, Hura propels herself up, shoves her wallet and keys, a book, an apple, and a bottle of water into her backpack. Her jacket and shoes, and Casimir's lead, are by the door. Sensing an impending journey, the dog unfolds himself and trots towards them.

3

'Good boy Caz,' Hura says, stroking his black back and brindled chest as she slips on the lead. 'Where shall we go?'

Cillian is thinking about fucking someone other than his wife. They discussed it, he and Hura, the night before, the latest in a series of many conversations spread over years, which have intensified in recent months. Now, sitting at his desk, the thoughts won't leave him alone. A door opened, a chink of light, and then the realisation that on the other side are rolling, golden fields of opportunity.

He has been at his computer only an hour but he can't sit still. When he left for work, Hura was still in bed, and he wonders whether she'll have made it out for a walk, the only thing that seems to help her through these empty days. The morning is one of the most beautiful in weeks, one of those late-March days where spring goes singing through the streets that it's coming, coming, it's here, now. His fingers tap out a brief message to the team that he will be back in five minutes, then he rises and takes his jacket and heads to the coffee shop round the corner. As he crosses the street he notices, as if for the first time, a row of silver birch trees just coming into leaf. The flicker of green in what, over the winter, had become a world of wet greys and sodium glows and the darkness of dark afternoon.

The café he always goes to, Cup, is warm, and its windows are fogged. The place is tiny, and self-consciously utilitarian: chipboard counter, shelves of brushed steel, a gleaming Gaggia machine, a cashless payment system. Cillian thinks of the staff here as self-consciously cool; he never imagines that anyone would put him in the same bracket, but today, like most days, he fits it: wearing blocks of colour, tattoos visible at neck and wrist, blond hair long to his shoulders. Today the person taking orders is a tall woman with dark skin and bleached hair. She gives him a familiar smile, clocking him as a regular, and as he returns it Cillian feels a powerful rush: possibility; a high tide held back by a sea wall.

Waiting for his drink, he texts Hura quickly, a series of emojis that he knows she'll be able to interpret: sun (it's a nice day), dog

(Casimir will enjoy it), snake (bad people/things), explosion (will be/have been destroyed), fire (by the flame that is you), hand applying varnish to nails (easily). She replies almost immediately with a laughing face, a blown kiss. He relaxes: a good day.

The coffee arrives in a reusable glass cup with cork insulation, which the café lends to regulars. As the tall barista hands it to him, Cillian says:

'I've got a stack of these at the office.'

Few people can truly raise one eyebrow, but this woman can. She doesn't smile back this time, but one brow hikes far up at the outer corner. Cillian feels himself flush, and grins his wide and apologetic smile.

'I'll bring them back then.'

'You better had.'

He takes the drink and ducks out into the morning. His blood is on fire, and from what? Potential, nothing more, but that alone is awesome and seductive. He tastes the coffee, bitter and sweet and strong enough to turn his head for a moment.

He and Hura had been together for years before they began sharing fantasies of other lovers. First they told each other stories from their distant pasts. Sudden kisses and how they had felt. Particularly wild encounters. The dancer at a rave he had sex with, even though they never spoke a single word to each other. The man she met in a white-out halfway down a French mountain, who had skied with her carefully all the way to the village, then taken her to his hotel for restorative brandy and a very hot sauna.

One night, in bed, they began a new whispered thread. What if it wasn't just the two of them there? The idea was a depth-charge, shifting and intensifying their sex life after years, re-drawing all its patterns.

That stage, exciting, satisfying in itself, had lasted a long time, during which they organised a raucous wedding about which their friends still reminisced. But the thought of opening up their relationship never went away. In some ways, marriage solidified it, since they had now committed to one another publicly, and for the long term. They floated the idea of meeting others in real life, not knowing how to go about it. When he suggested the internet, she wrinkled her nose.

'Urgh, really? It just makes me think of chat rooms where everyone's called BigDick2000 or PrincessPussy.'

'I wasn't really thinking of chatrooms.'

'And those terrible profiles: "I have always loved writing." "I'm looking for great banter and a partner in crime."'

'Come on, it's not like that any more.'

'Isn't it? What's it like?'

'It's not weird any more. It's just what people do. It's more normal now than meeting someone in a bar.'

'But it's not sexy, is it?'

Cillian finds it sexy. The extraordinary breadth, and the chance to see strangers' desires carefully typed out like a shopping list; to share intimate moments with them in the vast non-space of the internet. Cillian suggested that he create profiles on some of the apps and see what happened. Hura didn't object, on two conditions: that he tell everyone he chatted to that he was married; and that they'd discuss it again before he actually arranged a meeting. They were just testing the waters.

But then came the conversation last night. Cillian, tired from long days of work and a base-level of worry about how to manage on one salary, had been sinking quickly into sleep when Hura murmured something he didn't quite catch.

'What was that?'

'I said let's do it. Meet some other people.'

Cillian turned to her, very much awake.

'*Now?*'

'Why not? I haven't got much else on.'

He settled his head on his arm; picked up a strand of her hair with the other hand.

'Are you sure it's the right timing? Maybe it's not what you need right now, with everything . . .' He stroked the hair with his thumb; he'd always loved her hair.

'I think it's great timing. I need to not be moping around,

stressing. I want to do something. I've been so careful and sensible and . . . *nice*. I need to be in my life, in my body.'

'It is an excellent body.' Cillian smiled. 'But just . . . there's no pressure, ok? Not from me.'

'Ok.'

'It's been a hard few weeks.'

'Shh, don't remind me. But you still want to?'

She looked at him, saw the dim glow of his smile: 'Hell yeah.'

Made strange to one another by the idea of strangeness, they made love.

Roses needs a seat, and when the Tube doors open in front of her, she identifies one and makes straight for it. From the other direction, another woman has also spotted the space, and they arrive at it simultaneously. In the less-than-a-second before the decision is made, Roses has made an appraisal: the woman is older than her but not old enough to require deference. She isn't obviously pregnant, nor is she wearing one of the 'Baby on Board' badges that Roses finds insipid – like a declaration to the world of weakness, or privilege, or both. She has large sunglasses and a loose silk headscarf and a perfect manicure. Roses smiles the smile of a person who wants to sit down, and the woman, with an inclination of her head, concedes.

Now, as the rickety Circle Line jolts its way over- and underground east from Sloane Square, Roses transforms. Her hair is pinned up with Kirby grips, her face bare of make-up, and she is dressed in something closely resembling a school uniform: white shirt, black skirt, tights, sensible shoes. She unbuttons the shirt and slips it off, revealing a black singlet underneath. She takes a thin green sweater from a bag at her feet, pulls it on, then takes out a stick of deodorant and applies it to her armpits under the sweater. The woman with the manicure pointedly looks away. Roses slips off her shoes and peels the tights down from under the skirt, replacing them with a pair of black jeans. Wriggling out of the skirt, she stuffs it into the bag, and slips her shoes back on. She takes the grips rapidly out of her black, bobbed hair, runs a brush through it. Out of a make-up bag she draws three items – eye pencil, liner, mascara – which she holds with one hand, and a small mirror, which she holds in the other. She waits until the train stops at Monument, and while the doors open and close she outlines one eye. At Tower Hill she starts the other, and finishes it at Aldgate.

Finally, she fishes out a necklace with a Mexican Day of the Dead pendant, one long silver earring and several rings, slipping them on as the train rattles into Barbican. On her wrist, a chunky plastic Casio, which she now checks. On time, just. She shrugs on her leather jacket, shoulders her bag, and slips on headphones. As the doors open, her ears fill with a woman's voice, singing in layered, sixfold melody.

Roses emerges from the station into sudden hard sunlight, which is almost immediately cut off as she crosses the road and heads down the tunnel that runs beneath the Barbican complex. She aims for the stage door. Now that she is in her own clothes and close to the rehearsal room, there is almost no trace left on her consciousness of the morning's work, pouring Bellinis and carrying canapés at an art gallery breakfast; just an ache in her shoulders from the fucking slates. The warm-up will help: she'll lead the performers physically. Today is a group audition for a project starting in May, her first at the Barbican. The show she plans to create, which centres on the life and work of the poet John Donne, will be her highest-profile so far. The company she brings together will devise much of the material. The money comes from a prestigious competition. The final piece will play in the Pit, one of her favourite theatres. She feels sick and stunned with excitement whenever she thinks about that looming first night.

Her phone, back above ground, buzzes in her pocket, and she takes it out and sees the name, swipes open the message as she walks.

'Holy shit,' Roses says aloud.

The screen is filled with a picture of a huge spider, and behind it James's slightly blurred face, grinning in triumph. She laughs quietly, texts back in capitals as she walks: *A-FUCKING-MAZING.*

Roses has been encouraging James to face this fear; she even found today's course for him. Now that he has conquered it he can fulfil another ambition: months of travel in the Amazon rainforest, planned for years and put off, in part, because of the jungle's preponderance of spiders. Rehearsal starts in three minutes. Her heart had leapt when she saw the picture, but after the split-second of euphoria there is a rush of cold; a sense of open air, yawning and empty, beneath her feet.

Chapter Two

As the train pulls in to Tring – a few miles outside the M25, chosen because Hura liked the word – she leans down and clips Casimir's lead to his collar, keeping him close on platform and road. Once they find a footpath she undoes the clasp and lets him walk freely beside her. She knows he won't leave her unless she gives him the word, so while they cross arable land she watches out for other walkers – seeing none – and Casimir trots at her heels.

At home she's painfully aware of every petty task that needs to be done, each one taking up a grain of her attention: the buttercup-coloured bedroom that needs painting, emails to answer, a broken lamp she plans to glue, an insurance claim to make, the car's MOT. Only when she's away from home can she really think.

The path leads them into a small wood, fenced off from the fields.

'Ok, Cazi, go running,' she says, and the dog stretches his legs and lopes away, scanning and scenting his way around the feet of the young trees. Hura takes a deep breath, lets it out, and listens. There it is: silence. Not the dead silence of a vacuum, but the living silence of the outdoors, which is not silence at all. Just the absence of traffic or voices, the white noises of the city. Hura hears the hustle of leaves as Casimir turns over a stick. The small calls of early-year birds. She hears the breeze weave between the tree trunks. She lets her mind come to rest. And there, finally, is an answer.

Her teaching career is over. Hura stands very still, too cold in her spring jacket, but feeling the chill sharpen her mind.

She has struggled so hard, for so long, to make teaching her identity. For years she's defended her choice against the subtle scorn of her overachieving family – *what could be* more *ambitious than working with knowledge itself?* – but at the same time, she's felt herself dragged down by daily compromise. The private versus state debate, the carousel of leaders with top-down plans, replaced a few years later by other leaders, other plans.

Working for a decade to get *where*, exactly? Sticking with it through a mixture of stubbornness and belief, hope and insecurity. Maybe, she now thinks, the idea of not teaching has been creeping gradually closer over the last months. But still she's stunned to find it here, in these woods, fully formed, waiting. It is more than an idea, she realises. It is a fact. She is no longer a teacher. She repeats the phrase in her mind, feeling its impact. Marvelling at the fact that she can bear it.

The change began last summer when Hura, instead of returning to the elite private school where she'd been due to resume in September, had found herself on the phone to her head of department, quitting. She'd started by expressing doubts and ended without a job to go back to when term began. The man had been annoyed, hostile; there was no way, once the conversation had taken its unexpected turn, that Hura could backtrack. Since then she's been supply teaching across London for six long, wearying months, the last three at a school so similar to the one she'd left – girls, blazers, lacrosse – that she had disorienting moments of forgetting where she was.

And then, last month, the scene: the one she's been replaying in her head to see if – this time, or this time – it would make her feel less wretched. The head teacher, a woman named Lena Shah with a marked fondness for purple clothes, had called her in for a chat. Hura wasn't surprised when the conversation turned to a particular group of girls in her GCSE class. The group, which orbited around a very beautiful and keenly bright 16-year-old called Jenna Petrovich, had taken an instant dislike to Hura when she took over from their regular geography teacher just after Christmas. They sat at the back of her classes and whispered. When she asked them to stop, they turned on her, eyes full of boredom and disdain. They raised their hands and asked irrelevant questions to fluster her. More recently, they had begun passing comment on her clothes, her hair, her figure. And then, last week, most mortifying of all, Jenna had touched her. It was so subtle she couldn't pull the girl up on it. But passing her on the way out of class, Jenna had brushed Hura's buttock with her hand. Just a graze. Hura had felt dizzy in the seconds after it happened, and had stared after the receding group with incredulous fury. Before they left the room, Jenna had looked straight back at her, raised her eyebrows, and smiled. Then they'd all disappeared laughing into the corridor.

Sitting across the tidy desk, Hura nodded as Lena Shah – violet jacket, lilac blouse – brought the subject round to the group. She felt relieved, assuming Lena was going to ask about her mental health in a difficult situation. How had Lena noticed, she wondered, without ever coming to observe a class?

'I'm afraid that all complaints need to be investigated,' Lena said.

Hura smiled. 'I'm sorry, I think I missed something.'

'I said that there's been a complaint.' Lena was trying, Hura realised, to be gentle.

'From one of the girls?' Hura felt her polite smile freeze; her own voice came out high with incredulity.

Lena Shah's response was a redoubled calm.

'From the parents, in fact,' she said. 'The parents of . . . more than one.'

Hura's mouth was dry. She wished Lena had offered her water or tea, and it suddenly seemed significant that she hadn't. A punishment.

'I'm sorry,' Hura managed, 'I don't understand. *They've* complained about *me*?'

She should have told someone. About the nastiness; about the touch. Someone at the school. Of course, she'd told Cillian, exhausted and tense in the evenings, and that had been sufficient, to make her feel strong enough to face them the next day, and the next. She was the adult in the situation; they couldn't really hurt her.

'I'm afraid so,' Lena was saying. 'It's unfortunate. We have such a good relationship between staff and students at this school.'

Hura spoke over the rushing of her heart. She tried to keep her voice steady.

'What are the nature of these . . . complaints?'

Lena's fine forehead was creased in a frown. 'I'm afraid more than one of the girls has, it seems, told her parents that you have "belittled" them, been sarcastic towards them, commented on their appearance . . .'

'Wait,' Hura said. She was finding it hard to believe what she was hearing, finding it hard to breathe. 'Before we go any further can I tell you my side of the story?'

'Of course,' Lena said. She put her head on one side like a concerned bird.

'So, it's certainly been a difficult dynamic,' Hura said. She wanted to rage at the injustice, but things could still be salvaged. 'But the fact is, from my perspective, they've been a very difficult group. Disruptive to the class, in a very subtle way, but constantly. And cruel. Very personal. I mean, supply teaching can be like that, I'm not thin-skinned . . .' Hura realised she was going to cry. She tried to carry on regardless.

'They have been very unkind, though. That group. Jenna Petrovich particularly. In fact . . .' she tried to stem the tears, to claw back some gravitas. 'In fact, and I should have said it at the time, but Jenna actually *touched* me. It was very slight. But it was aggressive; I mean, I believe it was meant to undermine me.'

'Right,' Lena Shah said, her frown deepening. 'In what way did she "touch" you?'

Embarrassed, Hura looked into her lap. 'On the backside, with her hand,' she said. It felt oddly like a confession; like something she had done. 'It was very brief.'

She looked up and saw Lena Shah's still-tilted head, her drawn brow. Something was wrong with her reaction. Hura, a deep believer in natural justice, couldn't seem to compute what was going on.

'This is very difficult, very difficult,' Lena said. 'Because, you see, there have also been some . . . accusations. From the girls.'

She was going to be sick. Hura held herself very still until the nausea passed. Very quietly she heard herself say: 'What?'

'One of the girls' parents said their daughter came home distraught. She showed them a test, a mock exam paper, on which she had scored a low mark. They reassured her, of course. But, the parents say, that's when the real source of their daughter's unhappiness emerged.'

Lena looked down at a piece of paper in front of her, a printed email. It was very long: a dense page of A4, and another page beneath.

'*After giving her the low mark, Ms Holmes asked our daughter to stay back after class,*' Lena read. '*When they were alone in the classroom, Ms Holmes said she could ensure our daughter got better marks. She said that our daughter would need to "help her out" in return. Ms Holmes then put her hand on our daughter's back, making her feel extremely uncomfortable.*' Lena Shah looked up at Hura.

'That did happen,' Hura said. 'Though I put a hand on her shoulder, not her back, in, in reassurance. Jenna did very badly on the test – I'm sure she just picked answers at random. I thought, maybe, that one-to-one I could help her see I was human, that I wanted to get on with her . . .'

'Did you say she needed to "help you out"?'

'I might have. Yes. I think I did use those words. I meant that I needed her to treat me fairly.'

Lena looked down at the printed email. She read: '*The inappropriate and non-consensual touch was the latest in a series of attempts to intimidate and embarrass our daughter, which included commenting on her weight and heritage.*'

Lena sat back in her chair. The room was too hot. The whole school was wastefully, uncomfortably overheated. Hura wanted to get up, go to one of the firmly closed windows, and punch a hole in it. Her voice was dry as charred paper.

'I talked to them about eating disorders. That's what she's referring to, with the weight comment. I didn't mention anyone in the class, of course. I just said being thin wasn't always something to be proud of or, or, aspire to. And the . . .'

Hura ran out of breath, coughed, tried to fill her lungs to continue.

'The comment about heritage, I assume, refers to a class discussion of Russian politics. Kleptocracy. Oligarchs. It wasn't about her. It was about an entire country.'

'Sounds a little more like a history lesson, perhaps, than a geography lesson,' said Lena Shah, not quite smiling.

'Human geography,' Hura said. But her mind was spinning, and the words came out almost in a whisper. Last month they opened the school's new sports complex; the Petrovich Centre. Already, everyone referred to it as the Pet.

'It's very unfortunate,' Lena repeated. 'As I said, all complaints have to be investigated. It won't be appropriate for you to teach that class in the meantime, so best not come in next week. Then it's Easter, of course. After the holiday we can review. But perhaps, in light of what's happened, you'll decide that finding another position makes more sense.'

The subsequent weeks have been a jumble of rage, paranoia, anxiety about paying the rent – thank god, she thinks, for Cillian's steady income – and a waterlogged sadness.

But here in the woods, this morning, she sees something clearly for the first time: a school, at its most fundamental level, is a place of learning; a place to tell the truth. When Jenna's lie succeeded so completely, it finally uprooted the pure thing that had kept Hura teaching for so long.

The sexual element of the accusation, meanwhile, had frightened and cowed her. But now, at last, Hura understands exactly why it was so painful. Ever since she became a teacher, in her early twenties, she's felt a pressure to make herself neutral. To dress professionally. To act with decorum, not just at school, but all the time. It's changed, de-sexualised, the way she sees herself, she realises. She gasps aloud with the power of the thought: it's probably changed the way she acts in her own bedroom, with her own husband.

*

15

Now, through the fury and bewilderment of the last weeks, something is bubbling up. Something rebellious, and new.

'Ok,' Hura says out loud. 'It's over. That's all over.'

There's a distant bark in the wood and Hura turns to the direction from which the sound came. Softly she calls Casimir to her and he comes, but looking over his shoulder, excited. She crouches, strokes his head.

'What is it?'

Then a flurry of barking and another dog comes hurtling through the trees at full speed. It's big and glossy, a red setter, and it pulls up short when it reaches them, turns in a circle, leaps forward, barks, leaps away. A call comes after it, still some way off: 'Barry! Barry!'

Hura stands, Casimir contained but inquisitive beside her, and the setter leaps up towards her face, planting its paws on her chest and trying to lick her cheek.

'Barry, you idiot, stop it. Heel. Heel!'

A young man in white trainers and T-shirt runs up, crouches and grabs at the dog's collar, misses, and eventually manages to attach a lead while the setter tumbles all over him. Finally, he stands.

'Sorry about that. She's a puppy.'

'She?' Hura asks.

'Oh, yeah, she's got a pedigree, her name's Baroness Something Something; I just call her Barry. That's why she's so daft.'

He smiles, and Hura takes him in: cheeks flushed from running, curly brown hair, a bright grin. They look one another in the eye.

'She's beautiful,' Hura says.

'Thanks. Who's this?'

'Casimir. He's not a puppy. I've had him for fourteen years.'

'Wow. Lucky dog.'

There's a beat and Hura laughs, embarrassed, and stoops down to pat Casimir's sides. This man is probably ten years younger than her, handsome in the way 25-year-olds look handsome to her now.

'I'd better get on,' she says, though she has nowhere to be.

'Yeah, right,' he smiles. He wraps the lead around his hand and readies himself to run again. 'See you again, maybe.'

In what world would that happen, two strangers in a wood near a rural station she picked at random?

'Yes, maybe,' she says. He smiles again and they both turn away.

Now, as Hura walks, she remembers the conversation she and Cillian had last night, in the dark, skin to skin.

'Do you think you'll feel jealous?' she asked him. They'd been moving towards the idea gradually, together, but still this crossover into reality felt electric and surreal.

'Maybe. I don't know. Do you?'

Hura nestled even closer to her husband, pressing the length of her body against his.

'I think I might like it. Seeing you with someone else,' she said quietly. They kissed.

It's an extraordinary feeling, that they might really do this, transgressive enough to make her catch her breath here in the woods as she thinks about it. The freedom of it. The wildness, after so many devoted, faithful years.

On the train back to London, her mother calls.

'How are the kids today?' Aisha asks.

'No kids. I'm not in school.'

'You're not working?'

'Not . . . every day.'

Hura's father knows about the 'incident' but somehow she hasn't managed to tell Aisha yet.

'It's good, I'm glad. There's more to life than work.'

'Mum!'

'What?'

'You're a doctor. You love your job. You always told me how important it was to be independent.'

'Independent, yes; a wage slave, no.'

'I'm not a wage slave.'

'You need to earn your freedom, but you also need to use it.'

'By having a baby.'

'Who said anything about a baby?'

'I know what you're thinking! You don't have to say it.' Hura is already annoyed with her mother, and annoyed by her own annoyance.

'You don't have unlimited time. It gets harder, you know.'

'I do know! I know. You don't have to tell me.'

'You're thirty-four already.'

'I know!'

'After thirty-five—'

'Please, Mum. Please.'

'Ok, I know; you know.'

'Just, please. I don't need reminding.'

'I'm sorry. Tell me, when are you coming to see us?'

'Soon,' Hura says, trying to keep the exasperation out of her voice. Of course she knows her own age, even though, when she looks in the mirror, she still sees the same face – or almost the same – as the one that looked back at her at twenty. People often comment that she looks young. She gets her ID checked in bars. It's been a genuine problem in the teaching profession.

'Amin was here.'

'How is he?' Hura asks, a little too eagerly, aware of how long it's been since she called her brother.

'Oh, they're busy busy. He says the boys are great, in the football teams, doing the memes, you know.' Amin has three sons and a good hospital job, a stay-at-home wife and a detached house and a hybrid Lexus. He's less than two years older than Hura.

'That's great.' She hears the flat note in her own voice; the familiar sense that, somehow, she and Amin grew up into animals of different species.

If she does have a clock somewhere inside, it's quiet, tucked away down a corridor or muffled by some door. Partly, she knows, having Casimir has taken the place of a child. He is her dependent, looking to her for comfort and bringing it as well. He is the recipient of her longest and most faithful love. And then there is Cillian. Knowing that she has met the future father of her children has allowed her to relax. They have talked often about kids and are sure they'll make some one day. So why do it yet? There are so many reasons to delay. They've taken wry note when friends with children have dropped out of their shared social world, turning up only occasionally, tired and edgy with the need for enjoyment. We don't have to worry about it yet, they've said silently, eyes meeting across the room. And when we do it, we'll do it differently. Her recent work catastrophe has further blurred any vision of a potential future.

'Is everything ok? With Cillian?' Sensing her daughter's reticence without knowing all its causes, Aisha delves.

'Yes, great,' Hura says, happy to answer a question with unmixed feelings. 'He's great. Things between us are better than ever.'

After they hang up Hura stares out of the window, as the buildings begin to thicken around the train, and thinks about how much she loves and respects her mother, and how infuriating it is that such an intelligent woman can harp on about exactly the same things – babies, security – as any village grandmother of the last five centuries.

Hura's parents were Liberals from different cultures – he a lawyer from Kent, she a medical student from Pakistan – who had met when they were just twenty and travelled together for years before finally marrying, setting up home in a small Essex town and having four children in quick succession. Hura knows that she and her three brothers – Mir, Haris, and Amin – all grew up believing that freedom was the most fundamental right. They saw their mother face the casual racism of provincial England. Felt, through her, the fiery opposition of her family. Sensed from their father's parents a more subdued and complicated mistrust. Their parents taught them to be whoever they wanted to be. So why do some of their choices feel more acceptable than others?

The light changes as the train enters the station. Hura gathers her things and Casimir patters onto the platform. Commuters finishing their weeks are already streaming towards the turnstiles. The volume on the concourse is up by two notches with the approaching weekend, dissolving the bubble of silence around the woman and her dog; looping them into the city's familiar song.

★

The empty cup sits beside Cillian's laptop. On the screen, a menu design. He works through a list of tweaks quickly, flicking his eyes often to the clock. He's promised to get it done by the end of the day; but if he's faster, he'll gain some precious minutes to spend on something else.

Back in college, Cillian knows, he could devote hours, days, to a single drawing. But the truth is that nothing holds his attention like that here, nor in any of his previous design jobs. While he works, a part of his mind is always running restless elsewhere. He imagines a quiet room, an easel, a piece of soft charcoal between his fingers. Pushes the thought out of his mind. He's covering the whole rent and still trying to put some money away. Right now, Hura's career, and consequently her sense of self, is collapsing and re-forming around her. She needs him to be steady.

For a few seconds, Cillian's hands go still over the keyboard. He's allowing himself to picture something else: the child he wants to have with his wife. He's never really been able to see them with a newborn, other than a fuzzy image, like a photo of other people, in which the baby is nothing but a frown and a little nose surrounded by swaddling. What he imagines is a 3-year-old, with Hura's green eyes and – he indulges himself – his broad smile. Sometimes the child is a girl, sometimes a boy, but always with tousled hair and a strong hot hand in his. He imagines tears too; imagines soothing them away, rocking the child into calmness, into sleep, whispering his love into their curls.

This could be the perfect time, he thinks, with Hura on a break from the work that's held her so fast all these years. Then again, given the way she's had the wind knocked out of her, it might be exactly the wrong time to divert her energy into motherhood. No way is he going to pressure her. He re-focuses his eyes on the fonts in front of him. The child's hand relaxes its grip and slips from his.

Ten more minutes and he's finished, giving him almost an hour to switch tasks. Most people do this, he thinks: carve small holes in company time for their own work and creativity. What he's doing isn't exactly a passion project, but he needs to get it finished because he promised to.

Cillian opens up the file and his screen fills with a painting: swimmers entering a frigid sea. The figures are lumpen and life-like, the water thick and choppy, textured and cold-looking even though the oil paint is filtered through digital photography and screen. Text across it reads *Joy Swift* and, on another line, *paintings*. He's spent so many hours working on this site, addressed so many unexpected problems arising from his mother's clear taste but unclear communication skills, that it's hard for him to see it. He glances around the office, sees no one nearby, and calls her. Joy answers on the tenth or eleventh ring, shouting over wind in the background.

'Cillian, love. Hello? Hello? Is that you? I can't—'

'Mum, hi, are you outside?'

'—the beach. I can't hear you very well. Is it about the thing?'

'Yes, I emailed you the latest version. But if you're out it can wait.'

'It's great, apart from that colour, what is it? Taupe maybe, it's everywhere! And, also, the letters look a bit square, Daniel thought. But it's really good apart from those tiny—'

Cillian closes his eyes.

'Let's talk about it when you're home, when we can go through it together,' he says.

'—hear you. I'll call you back from home, shall I? Also, I think I do prefer it with the little pictures down the side.'

'Ok, well, that was a different template, so—'

'Oh, you know all about that, I don't understand it. You're so— I'd be lost without you.'

'Yeah, ok. I'd just love to get this finished.'

'I hope it's not taking up too much time?' A note of alarm in Joy's voice '—much more important things to do.'

'No, absolutely not, it's fine.'

'You mustn't waste— me, petal.'

'Don't be silly, Mum, you know I love helping you.' He makes his voice light, laughing. 'This stuff takes me about five minutes.'

When he was a child, Cillian thought he could hold Joy in the world, stop her falling away; he tried, ferociously, to batten her down with his love. She's more stable now, and has anchors other than him. But still: immediate, total reassurance is a reflex. A lie that might make her happy is always the right choice over a truth that could cause pain.

He checks the clock again: almost five. The days are getting longer. Joy and Daniel will probably stay out for hours more. Resigned to not finishing the site again, Cillian closes it. The idea of Daniel makes his hackles rise, but he knows it's just that same old protective streak and he needs to try and ignore it. From the age of six he'd been his mother's closest confidant; he's delighted she's finally doing the things with her life that she used to talk about as if they were impossible dreams – living by the sea, having a boyfriend. That last word makes Cillian squirm, but it's ridiculous. Joy was eighteen when she got pregnant with him; she's barely fifty now.

Cillian stands up without meaning to, unable to sit still. He wants to move, really move, ideally to music. In pockets of time throughout the day he's been researching a whole host of activities Hura and he could do together, maybe even this weekend, and he can't quite contain his excitement until he gets home and can talk to her about them: club nights, dating sites, meet-ups. Over towards the office kitchen, some of his colleagues are gathering; at this time on a Friday someone usually suggests they all head out for drinks. He likes the people he works with, but tonight he wants to go home. He won't get caught up in it. Not for long anyway. He's going to cook Hura something delicious. He picks up his phone and texts her again: *Are you home yet? I'm leaving soon.*

On impulse he adds: *I'm bringing champagne.*

He hears his name called, and looks up to see two of his colleagues signalling for him to join them by waving bottles of office beer in the air. He taps *send,* and lopes over to join them.

James is arriving home, earlier than normal: he swapped some easy shifts at the hospital for a series of nights he'll have to do in a couple of weeks. This was an uneven trade, but had left the whole day free for the course at the zoo. Now, in the late afternoon light, he looks around at the large shared kitchen and living room. The building, once a box factory, has huge, multi-paned windows that reach from ceiling to floor all along the western wall. The cold is murder in the winter. But it will be April soon.

His bedroom faithfully preserves the building's industrial feel, Roses has said, dryly. The walls are bare brick. A dark-blue rug relieves only part of the coldness of the concrete floor. The bed is a mattress, also on the floor. The rest of the furniture, sourced from skips and sales, comprises a chest of drawers with patterns of inlaid wood, battered and missing a leg; a couple of chairs; a table. The whole ensemble, the boyish discomfort, is a signal to himself and to everyone else of the temporary nature of his life here. Though a junior doctor's salary might not stretch far in London, it could have stretched to furniture. But the idea of furniture is quietly appalling to James: the mass of it, the dead weight. Anything he couldn't take with him in a backpack or, at most, a small car, feels extraneous and wrong.

He's never painted the walls because, though the feeling certainly isn't conscious and has never been articulated, paint would leave a trace. A mark of himself and the colour he chose.

The exception to this asceticism is the plants, some of which James has been tending for years, carting them carefully from place to place in high-sided cardboard boxes carried on trains, in the backs of cabs. They are hardy jungle or desert plants: red-veined Marantas, cacti, creepers, and succulents. There is one huge cheese plant, its green-black leaves large and glossy as dinner plates. He knows when to water each and when to hold off. The containers, though mostly made of cheap plastic, are clean and of adequate size.

Once, a well-meaning friend had given James a spider plant. Taking the pot in his hands he'd been amazed, and ashamed, to feel the back of his throat tighten. Fear. He was afraid of a fucking plant now. Determined to override it, he placed the plant prominently on the chest of drawers, giving its leaves (*legs*, his mind called them, but he angrily tried to quash the thought) room to bow outwards in every direction. But it was no good. Every time he came into the room, every time he woke and opened his eyes, the same small, sick shock. He slept exclusively at Roses' place for a week and then, late one night, he returned to the flat, collected the plant, and took it outside. He headed for the big industrial bins and then, changing his mind at the last minute, turned and walked down the road. On a street of affluent Victorian homes, he selected a house with a well-kept front garden. Guilty as a thief, he slipped silently up the path and placed the spider plant on the doorstep. Then he walked away into the night.

James undresses in his room and, relishing the rare freedom of an empty house, walks naked to the bathroom, which is large like all the rooms. One of the other tenants has constructed a surprisingly beautiful shower. A broad copper head descends from a curved pipe; around it, a curtain rail forms a perfect circle, and sloping, patterned tiles channel the falling water into a drain.

James steps into the stream and lets it soak his hair and his shoulders. He still has a swimmer's build, though not his former smoothness: his arms, chest, and legs are covered in dark hair. Across one scapula runs a date in Roman numerals, inked when he was seventeen: the day he lost his best friend, another promising swimmer called Gull. The two of them had been out, uncharacteristically, at a club. They'd both become rapidly and badly drunk – their tolerance low with all the training, the abstinence – and had parted late to walk home, James to Gateshead and Gull to a richer part of Newcastle. But Gull never made it home. His body was found in the Tyne three days later. No one could establish if he'd been pushed, or had fallen, or had decided, drunk as he was, to go for a swim. If it was the latter, he'd done so in his clothes. His shoes were never found. The inquest returned a verdict of death by misadventure and when anyone talked about it after that they almost invariably called his death a 'tragic accident'.

This is the story that has always been told. It has been told for so long that, even to James, it has begun to ring true.

More time has now elapsed since Gull died than time he spent alive. The tattooed date is so much a part of James he barely sees it;

he has to use a mirror to do so anyway. But now, with the water all around him and the stillness of the empty flat beyond, he thinks of Raymond Gulliver. Lithe as an otter, it was Gull, James thinks, who was truly gifted. What James retains of him is not exactly memory, which has faded and lost its edges with time and avoidance. He retains a palpable sense that death is close. That surviving from one day to the next is a matter, not of inevitability, nor of prudence, but of luck.

The water is as hot as he can bear, filling the unheated room with steam. Gull is in his mind today, James knows, because of the zoo; because of the stalking fears he's lived with for so long. Today he has conquered one of those terrors. But what about the others? In this cathartic moment, James's arachnophobia seems eminently manageable in comparison with his fear of discovery. Of intimacy. Of disappearing without trace. Of staying in one place and being known, absolutely, and fixed by that knowledge like a beetle with a pin through its heart.

He raises his face, then covers it with his hands as the heat on his eyelids and lips becomes too much. Enough for today. His body and mind feel deeply tired, as though he's finished a long race, and there's a thirst at the back of his throat that he wants only to slake with something cold and alcoholic.

James wills his thoughts now down a different route. He thinks about Roses, focusing on an image he has of the last time they made love: her on top with her hands up in her wet black hair. He's hard now, holding himself, drummed by the raining water. He remembers the eyes of the Spanish researcher from the zoo. He didn't register noticing them at the time. But now he knows that they were myrtle-dark and full of encouragement, steady on him as his own eyes had filled with tears.

In the aftermath, with the water still drenching him, he has a moment of absolute clarity, a combination of today's triumph and the blankness of orgasm. He is falling in love with Roses.

As a consequence of this revelation, and what it powerfully recalls, another knowledge follows quick in its wake: that their relationship will have to end.

★

Roses' audition finishes at 8 p.m., by which time she has been working – with a break to travel in between – for thirteen hours. She doesn't feel tired. Workshops and rehearsals always fill her with energy, part nervousness and part elation, and the adrenaline takes time to wear off.

'Come for a drink,' Stefan, her German producer, says. 'We'll Uber to Soho.'

'I'm heading home. It's been a long day,' she says.

'Bullcrap,' says Stefan. 'You're going to see Dr Love.'

She smiles, doesn't answer, kisses Stefan on the cheek, heads out of the building and northwards up Whitecross Street. The air now has a jagged edge; she always forgets how cold England can be at the beginning of spring. Her breath makes clouds. She checks her phone – the reception at the theatre is lousy – then digs her hands into her pockets and her chin into her collar.

The Tube would be the fastest way to James's. Instead she walks, using an innate sense of direction honed through years in the city. She walks at pace, staying mainly on track while avoiding major traffic arteries. Roses' self-sufficiency is one of her great sources of pride; until now, she's always been able to find a clean, clear kind of happiness in solitude. She passes St Luke's, skirts the swimming pool, crosses the canal. Keeps walking.

This play is going to be good, she thinks; it might be the best thing she's ever worked on. The endless knock-backs that constitute a life in the performing arts have taught Roses not to count on anything, but still: the competition win means funding, publicity. The calibre of performers and technicians she's been meeting is gratifying. Stefan, thank the lord, is Stefan. And the idea, her idea, its oppositions and intensities, is great. It's great. She needs to not count her chickens. But it's great. Still, of course, there is no promise of anything: not ticket sales, not the alchemy of creation, not a future. She hugs herself against the cold and smiles.

As she heads further from the centre, the buildings dwindle in size, and Roses finds herself traversing streets of plush townhouses. At some point she'll need to text James and let him know when to expect her. Angel is somewhere nearby, over to the west. She doesn't turn towards it. Her feet are beginning to ache, and the moon is waxing. Roses thinks: I have never loved anyone the way that I love James Alston.

This feeling arose too quickly to be trusted. Roses was aware of it just weeks into their relationship, a hiss like the gas left on, barely at the level of hearing. That it has lasted, and grown remorselessly stronger, thrills and worries her. She is off balance, and doesn't trust herself like she did in her previous, pre-love existence. She suspects she is not as strong, or stoical, or focused, as she used to believe. She hasn't told anyone how she feels. She most certainly hasn't told James.

Without pausing, Roses takes out a bottle of water and drinks, which mostly serves to remind her how hungry she is. She wonders if James will have eaten, or waited; how he will look at her when she arrives. When I get to Highbury Fields, she thinks, I'll text. Some insistent stars defy the light pollution. Lines of poetry from the day's work chink against an after-image of endless polished glasses lined up on a long, white tablecloth. A spider stalks on silent feet through her mind.

Chapter Three

Spring, 1995

She drops her shoulder bag onto the parquet and her keys onto the bag, goes back into the hallway and drags the suitcase over the threshold. It's too full and Roses hasn't eaten enough to give her the energy to carry it. She feels faint with hunger and apprehension and adolescence. It's the first day of her period, the heavy and irregular bleeding surprising her every time it comes. She sits down on the ornate hall couch, gold-painted wood upholstered in shiny striped fabric. Maybe she's bleeding onto the white and gold, but she's too tired to move. She kicks off her trainers and listens to the apartment. There is the muffled sound of cars and Vespas from the street below, indicating that the windows are closed but the shutters open. There is a very faint shush from the pipes, the sound of the building breathing. From the atrium, a dim mechanical clanking as the tiny lift, which just brought her up to the fourth floor, moves up and down its shaft. The flat is empty. Roses breathes a little deeper, and lets herself lean back against the bolstered backrest.

But then the lift doors clack, there is the sound of heels on wood and a key in the lock, and Ghislaine enters.

'Darling! You're here already!'

Roses stands and they kiss one another, cheek to cheek and back again. Ghislaine is tanned and carefully made up; she smells of orange blossom and cigarettes and liquid foundation. She puts her arms around Roses for a hug but it's careful and patting, a hug once removed.

'How was the plane?'

'Ok. Same as usual.'

'So disgusting, the planes, always full of the germs of others. You must have a shower.'

'Yeah.'

'You're hungry?'

'Not particularly,' Roses lies. The last thing she wants is to discuss food with Ghislaine.

'You must be! Look at you, a little stick!'

It's meant to be a compliment.

Roses smiles and frowns at the same time. 'I'm not.'

'Don't make this expression, you don't want wrinkles. Now come along, you'll drink something at least. A tisane. I have some brioche, you can manage one of those.'

'Mum—'

'What?'

'When did you ever eat brioche?'

'I bought them for you!'

'So you can watch me eat them.'

'Please, Rosie, don't be like this.'

'Like what?'

So it goes.

That evening, Roses has showered and unpacked and been out to refamiliarise herself with the sixteenth arrondissement, and lain on her bed watching the day disappear across the walls of the high, childish room. To please her mother she did eat a brioche, but has since punished herself by eating nothing else. It's getting towards 10 p.m. when she finally emerges into the small kitchen, so diminutive compared to the other opulent spaces. Ghislaine is there, pouring a delicate glass of rosé.

'There you are, were you hiding?'

She was. 'No,' Roses says.

'I don't know where the day has gone,' Ghislaine says. She sits at the table and lights a cigarette. She still looks exactly as she did when she arrived home: perfect make-up, pressed white slacks and white heels, a navy and white shirt, gold jewellery. Her hair, Roses thinks, is if anything more carefully styled than earlier. There is no sign of dinner and no mention made of it. Ghislaine smokes beautifully, tapping ash into a seashell on the table. Roses feels a familiar sadness settle in her stomach.

'So, tell me about your schooldays. Are you having a most wonderful time?' Ghislaine asks.

'It's fine,' Roses says.

'These are the best days of your life, you know,' Ghislaine says. 'You must enjoy them. So carefree. It gets much harder, believe me.'

'I believe you.' She does not.

'You are doing brilliantly well, of course.' It's not a question. 'And what about your friends? Tell me about them.'

Roses has no idea where to begin. Who are her friends? The group she spends time with, which she essentially owns and runs, is a tossed salad of leaf-thin girls and their fragile egos, gritty with fear of isolation and hurt. She knows them all so well, Aradia and Francesca, Bea and Boaty, and yet if she never saw them again, would it matter?

'There's a girl called Janice,' she says instead.

'Janice?'

'Janice Sheldrake.'

Ghislaine laughs a puff of smoke. 'What a strange name!'

'It's not very strange,' Roses says, defensive and confused by it.

'*Janice Sheldrake*,' Ghislaine says in a mock upper-class English accent.

'Forget it,' Roses says.

'What? I'm just making a joke!'

'That's not a joke,' Roses says. It's always like this between them now.

The phone begins to ring.

Roses stiffens: it's too early and she hasn't explained yet.

'That could be Dad,' she says.

'Don't answer it.'

'But—'

'He knows not to ring here.'

'I should have said before, but I need to talk to him, and he said—'

'Not here, not in my home.'

The phone rings loud through the rooms.

'It's my home too.'

'Your father does not have the *right* to phone here.' Ghislaine is furious already, immediately. Her English gets worse when she's angry and it now becomes plain this isn't her first glass of wine. 'I have to lie down and take it from him? No. Not in my home. He doesn't take you out of my home.' The phone rings on.

'I just need to arrange something with him. I can make sure he doesn't call here again but I need to . . .'

Ghislaine is crying now and feeling the tears fuels her anger.

'Ok. This is what you want? Go to him then. Go to America.'

'Mum—'

'Go and pick up the phone and talk to your precious Daddy and not to me.'

The phone stops. In the silence it leaves behind Ghislaine gets up, opens the fridge, pours another glass of wine, sits down, lights another cigarette. Roses thinks she might hate her. But then why does she feel the urge to do something to make her happier, happy even for a moment? She sits down at the table.

'I'm sorry,' she says.

Ghislaine makes a shrugging movement, either accepting or not accepting the apology. Roses is thirteen. Soon she will cease to conciliate, and the arguments will rage fiery in that apartment, and then will freeze into long, painful standoffs. But not yet. Now she is still a child casting about for anything that will bring her mother back to her.

'Maman,' she says. She reaches a hand across the table. 'Can we make crêpes?'

Through the tears and smoke, Ghislaine smiles.

'Are you out of your mind?'

Zahra is half-joking, but only half. Her strong brows are high, her face a picture of mock horror. Hura laughs, leans back, looks away across the lake. She met Zahra in their first term at university, and they know each other as well as she has ever known anyone, other than Cillian. But it seems they can still surprise each other. Zahra is genuinely shocked, though her desire not to judge is battling with the emotion. Hura, for her part, is surprised at the extremity of Zahra's reaction. She had hoped for a more intrigued questioning complicity.

'Does it sound that bad?'

'It sounds fucking dangerous, that's how it sounds.'

'Dangerous how?'

'For your marriage, obviously!' Zahra nearly shouts. Hura looks self-consciously around at the rest of the café's clientele. She is the shyer of the two, quieter, stepped-back, while Zahra is a self-defined loudmouth, a woman with a naturally deep, carrying voice like an actress, and an abandoned way of swearing. Now, seeing Hura's discomfort, she drops into a stage whisper.

'You can't just fuck a load of strangers and expect your marriage to be fine!' She grins, but the grin isn't joyful.

Hura leans forward, hands around her cup, smiling too.

'They're not strangers! And it's not a "load"; it might be . . . a few.'

'A few! "Darling, why are you upset? I only had sex with *a few* other people"!'

'Cillian isn't going to be upset. He's going to be there.'

'God, really? Every time?'

'Well, maybe not every time. We haven't completely set the boundaries—'

'That's so kinky.'

'. . . the rules.'

'You know what happens, don't you? People are all "this is mutual" but then: boom, you find out Cillian's actually into your sister—'

'I don't have a sister.'

'. . . or your best friend, not to flatter myself, and then the shit hits the fan. Bye bye, happy marriage, hello inner "what was I thinking?" monologue forever.'

Hura laughs tensely. She takes a sip of fast-cooling coffee, squeezes her shoulders up to her ears and then drops them. She had thought that Zahra would be more of an ally, someone she could share her excitement with, but also her apprehension.

'Anyway,' says Zahra, 'isn't free love for the young people?'

'I am young!' Hura says indignantly. Then, quieter, 'And I never said the words "free love". I don't even know what that means.'

'So what are these rules then?'

'Like I said, we haven't set them all yet. We're new to this too. We're just finding our way. But some of them are really clear: we're not going to spend whole nights apart, we'll always come home to each other. We'll always use protection. We'll never lie to each other. That's the big one. We have to be able to trust each other completely.'

Zahra is picking at a fingernail, a habit that makes Hura's skin tingle in sympathy. Hura knows her friend is particularly prone to this small self-laceration when she's stressed, or unhappy. Now Zahra makes the unfortunate finger bleed, and puts it in her mouth. Hura glances at the park's small lake, reflecting willows.

Zahra removes the finger and looks at it.

'Trust each other? How can you trust him when you know he's lusting after someone else?'

'Everyone lusts after people who aren't their partner.'

'Yeah, but you're not allowed to fuck them! That's what holds things together! Otherwise no relationships would last. You buy into a partnership, and you pay for what you get. You get someone to bring you toast and tea when you're ill, to tell you you look nice in your pyjamas. But if you need tea and toast, and your partner is fucking some twenty-year-old in a shower somewhere – I'm sorry, but that's the problem, right? – then what? Do you still believe he thinks you look great in leggings? Don't you suspect he's thinking about her in . . . suspenders, or whatever?'

'That's so depressing!' Hura says. 'The idea that it's all a bartering system. People don't only stay together out of duty. At least, Cillian and I don't. You're saying that, if they could, people would betray each other all the time, but they don't because they're scared of what they'll lose. I don't want Cillian to live in fear. I want him to tell me about stuff. I want him to explore.'

'So it's all about him?' Zahra's eyes glitter with challenge.

'No! I want to explore too. I'm curious. Ok, maybe it doesn't come as naturally to me, but I'm interested. I'm excited. It feels like . . .' she leans forward, trying hard to bridge what feels like an increasing gap. 'It feels like something special is happening. Like the night before Christmas, or when you're about to go on holiday.'

Zahra now looks out over the water. There are ducks, swans. A moorhen is building a precarious nest. The early-spring light is already inclining towards evening, lifting a scent of blossom from the trees and of wet twigs from the lake itself. Swans always recall to Zahra the phrase, 'mate for life'.

'I actually hate the night before holidays,' Zahra says. 'You're supposed to be excited but actually you feel sick with fear. I can never sleep because I think I'll miss the flight. I wonder why I ever booked the fucking thing.'

Hura laughs. 'Yeah, all right, I'm the same. And this is a bit similar: I'm excited and scared too.'

Zahra looks triumphant, so Hura quickly continues: 'But then what? You go away and discover a whole world elsewhere. You're so glad you made the trip, you forget the fear.'

There's a pause. Then Zahra really smiles, throws up her hands.

'God, Hura, you have a nice-looking guy like Cillian and now you're going to hoover up a load of others as well. It's not fair! Who'll be left for the single people?'

They look at each other and now they both grin, warmly this time. The tension has passed.

'I'm not going to hoover up anyone!'

Zahra makes a whooshing, machine-like noise with her mouth and performs a complex mime of spotting a man, using a vacuum cleaner to drag him towards her, then kissing him. By the end of it Hura is in fits of laughter and other people in the café are looking round.

Zahra's mimed kiss turns into a mime of consuming the imaginary man like a praying mantis eating its mate. She swallows the last bite and sucks each finger clean. Hura, convulsed, puts her head in her arms on the table.

'I'm wasted as a fucking GP, you know that?' Zahra says. 'I should have been born in the days of vaudeville.'

'Fatimah-Zahra Van Hallenberg.'

'Exactly! No more boring Dr Hall. I'm wasted in so many ways.' Her voice one shade darker.

'God, I know. I'm sorry. Anything exciting happening on the man front?'

'Nothing since the horror story that was Lucas.'

'The last you told me he'd gone away for the weekend and said he'd call when he got back.'

'Yep. And did he call? No, he fucking didn't.'

'Did you try him?'

Zahra, her mirth gone, looks angrily down at her hands, scratching at the cuticle of one thumb.

'Yes. Eventually. I left it for ages. Then finally I cracked. I sent him a really nice message, just chatty, asking how he was. Nothing. Then I sent another one asking if he got the first one. Not a peep.'

'Maybe something happened to him,' Hura suggests, though she doesn't think it's likely even as the words leave her mouth. Neither does Zahra. She looks up grimly.

'Maybe, but I doubt it. In the end I called him. Phone rang, went through to voicemail. I didn't leave one.' She picks at the nail. 'Then I rang again. I left a message asking him to call me back.'

Hura puts her own hand over her friend's, partly in reassurance, partly to stop the horrible sight of the skin being so gradually torn away.

'Oh, Zahra.'

'And then I called *again*.' Zahra says it as though the telling were a necessary penance. 'And this time I was drunk. I'd been out with you actually, it was last weekend. I got home and sat down and I was just so angry, so boiling with fury. I thought, how can I let him do this to me? Just disappear, just act like I don't even fucking exist? So I called him then. It must have been 2 a.m., but the phone was on, it rang, it went through to voicemail again. And I – oh god, Hura, I can't even remember. Correction: I don't want to remember. I let rip. I called him every name I could think of. I just ... It was a flood, a tirade. I must have sounded absolutely fucking mental.'

'Oh, man.' Hura pats her hand, holds it.

Zahra's eyes are just on the brink of tears but she won't let them fall. She squeezes the lids shut and sniffs and smiles brightly.

'So that's the end of that. He deleted me from everything after that, blocked my calls. I'll never know what happened.'

There's a minute of silence where they both look out over the water.

'How long was it, in the end?' Hura asks after a moment.

'On and off? A year. A motherfucking year.'

'We need to talk about the rules,' Hura says. Ever since she got home from seeing Zahra she's been feeling raw and edgy.

'What rules?' Cillian has just walked through the door, kissed her, gone to change.

'The rules for this ... experiment. With other people.'

'Can I have a shower first?'

'I think it's really important we talk about it.'

'Sure. But ... I mean, does it have to be right now, this second?'

'I just don't want to avoid it.'

'No, course.'

Cillian, who has been taking off his shoes and shirt in the bedroom while she leans in the doorway, passes her and heads towards the fridge. He opens it, peers in, takes out a box of leftover pasta and eats some of it with his hands.

'I thought you wanted a shower.'

'I'm on the way, just really hungry. What shall we have for dinner?'

'I don't know. I just really want to talk about this.'

Hura, trying hard to control her voice, hears it crack. Cillian puts the pasta back in the fridge, closes it, and leans against the door. As his bare skin touches the cold surface, goosebumps rise on Hura's arms.

'Ok. Let's talk.'

'Don't you want a shower?'

'It'll wait.'

They're both silent for a moment, Cillian because he's waiting for her to speak, Hura because she's trying to get a grip on her emotions.

'Sorry,' she manages. 'I've just been stressing out a bit.'

'We don't have to do anything you don't want to. We don't have to do anything at all.'

He smiles, his eyes clear and steady. She knows he's hers. She hears Zahra's challenge ringing in her ears but it sounds hollow now, with Cillian so familiar, so close.

'I know,' she says. She presses her fingers to the inner corners of her eyes. 'I want to try it. I do. It's just . . . I had this chat with Zahra today and it's made me feel a bit weird.'

'What did Zahra say?'

'It wasn't what she said. It's that I didn't know – I don't know what we've decided exactly. Don't do that.'

'What?'

'You folded your arms. You're feeling defensive.'

'I'm feeling chilly.'

'Have a shower. Put a sweater on.'

'Holmes, come on.' He takes a couple of steps and puts his arms around her.

'Sorry,' she mutters, head to his chest, where an anatomically correct snake curls its way around an anatomically correct heart. Without letting go of her he leans sideways, tipping them both to a forty-five-degree angle, and by stretching manages to pull a rust-coloured sweater from a nearby chair. He keeps hold of her with one arm while putting the sweater on the other, swaps arms, and pulls it down over both his torso and her head.

'Hey,' she laughs, pulling her head out from under the sweater, 'you'll stretch it.'

'I'll knit you a new one.'

'Great, thanks, since when can you knit?'

'A man can learn.'

He sits in one of the kitchen chairs and draws her down by the wrist to sit on another.

'Hit me,' he says.

Hura takes a deep breath. 'When Zahra asked me what the rules were it just made me feel like maybe we don't know what we're getting ourselves into.'

'What would you like the rules to be?'

'No love.' She looks him in the eye. 'I don't want you to fall in love with anyone else.'

'That's great! I don't want to fall in love with anyone else either. And I don't want you to fall in love with anyone else. I love you. I want to stay married to you forever and have kids together, and get the kids a puppy and live in a cottage in the middle of a field.'

'A puppy! What about Cazi?'

'Ok, no puppy. No field, yet. But one day.'

'Do you think you can stop yourself falling in love?'

'Of course you can.'

'How?'

'Love doesn't just happen to people,' he says. 'It grows. It's a relationship, not a disease. It's not a secret you one day discover, oh, I'm in love with that person. You have to let it in. I'm not going to let it in. I promise.'

'I'm not going to let it in either,' she says. She thinks for a moment. 'What about when I'm not there?'

'Like, seeing other people alone?'

'Yes.'

'How do you feel about it?'

She thinks. 'I'm ok with it so long as I know what you're doing. I don't even mean you have to tell me every time you see a particular person. I just mean, I don't want to think you're at the shops and then run into you having sex with someone in the park.'

He laughs. 'Sex in the park isn't really my scene.'

'You know what I mean.'

'I do. And what about you. Do you want to see people without me there?'

Again she thinks. 'I don't know. Maybe. I'm kind of more into the idea of . . . groups.' She says it quietly, examining the grain in the tabletop with the tip of her index finger; she feels shy admitting it even to Cillian, even though she knows he's the last person who would be shocked.

He grins: 'Hot.' There's a pause.

'It would be ok with me, though,' he says. 'If you wanted to see other people without me.'

'Are you just saying that because it's what you want, and you know if you let me, then I'll be more likely to let you?'

'Um, maybe? No. I don't think so. I want you to be happy. I want you to do whatever you want to do. To not feel trapped by anything. I just want you to always come home to me.'

She looks at him, her young husband. She always thinks of him as young, though he's only a couple of years younger than her. She looks and sees him: his candid gaze, that slender muscularity all done over with ink. Cillian's tattoo craze came in his early twenties, not long before they met. She has never seen his body without the network of designs and she regrets, just a little, that he coloured in so much skin before she had a chance to see it naked. The conversation they are having feels to her fresh, raw, radically new. People do this all the time, she knows; she just spent an hour convincing Zahra how ordinary it is. But still, in the private world of their marriage it feels like they're feeding a bright flame together, burning through normality.

Yet she's also aware of what she's not saying. For Hura, sex is sensual, an extension of the kind of pleasure she takes in massage. She likes slowness, music, soft caresses. Cillian's kinkier and more interested in power: asserting it, but also swapping, being overpowered. Their sex together, therefore, tends to occupy a middle ground. It is good. It is a compromise. Neither has ever felt there to be a 'problem', exactly. Hura had assumed that, once she was married, this was just how her sex life was going to be.

Cillian says: 'Ultimately it's you, us, that matters.'

'You're only supposed to blow the bloody doors off!' she says, in a terrible Michael Caine voice. Bad impressions is a game they play.

He laughs aloud. 'Meaning?'

'We're blowing the doors off the marriage. But we have to be careful not to explode it completely.'

He kisses her. 'Let's both be careful then.'

She kisses him back. 'Yes.' Then: 'I could make tortilla.'

'That would be amazing. I'm starving.'

'Have a shower.'

'I love you.'

'I love you too.'

Clean and in his own clothes, he comes back into the kitchen to find a bowl of gleaming leaves on the table, warmed plates, and tumblers of Spanish wine. Scratchy jazz is coming from the record player they usually forget to use. The air is buttery.

'Fancy,' he says.

'It's the weekend,' Hura says. 'I love the weekend.'

Cillian sips the wine and watches Hura's movements. He can tell she's happy now, by the way she stands at the stove, the way she picks up a spatula and scatters a handful of parsley. It settles his heart, seeing her this way. In the weeks since she lost her job he's become even more attuned to her moods than usual: trying to hide a brittle morning under brightness; the defeated set of her shoulders after a day of introspection. Then again, maybe it's not just these weeks, but the months before, when Jenna's gang was making her life a misery. *Jenna.* The name makes Cillian's jaw tense and he indulges in a quick fantasy of pushing this teenager he's never met in front of a train. Shakes himself, sips the wine, lets it go. Maybe Hura hasn't been truly happy for years, as teaching became more and more of a grind: the pay, the cuts, the workload, a mounting sense of futility. Cillian's willing to believe that this, shocking though it may feel right now, is the best thing that could have happened.

'It's ready,' she says, upending the heavy pan over a big plate and bringing it to the table. 'Sit down.'

'Can we have the—'

'Cillian, you're a monster.'

She puts the tortilla down, turns round and takes a bottle of ketchup out of a cupboard: 'There.'

Cillian finishes the washing up and joins Hura, who is reading on one of the sofas with Casimir asleep beside her. He takes the other sofa and opens his laptop. The arrangement suits his purpose, because sitting in this way she can't see his screen. For weeks he's been working on a project for her birthday, a photo essay about their life together with contributions from friends that has spiralled into a more and more intricate piece of work. It's essentially now an entire book designed with increasingly obsessive detail. After ten minutes she gets up and stretches.

'Do you feel like watching a film?'

'Sure.'

'That German one?' She comes over to him on her way to the bathroom.

'Yeah, want me to set it up?'

'Ok.'

As she pads away, there's a moment where Hura wonders why he shut the laptop like that as she approached. Then she sees her face in the mirror over the sink and shakes her head with a half-smile, and tells herself to forget about it.

Chapter Four

The next morning March bares its teeth again, a bitter wind flinging hail at the long windows on the west side of James's building. He wakes early with a subtle hangover, closes his eyes against light the milky grey of cold coffee. Roses has one arm under her cheek. Her body exudes sleep, her face in repose is clear of troubling dreams. Looking at her dark mop of hair, her mouth slightly open, James experiences a wave of desperation: he must protect her. But from what?

His resolution of Friday, that he'll have to end this soon, is a knotted rope behind his ribs. Perhaps it's from himself that she needs protection: from the pain he's eventually going to inflict on her. By that logic he should break up with her now, this morning. Minimise the damage. He should wake her and do it. He looks at the sleeping face. She snuffles lightly and the rope twists.

He gets up to make tea.

In the big communal kitchen, the detritus of last night covers the surfaces. Pans, plates, bottles with cigarettes stubbed out in them, pieces of paper torn up for a game. James, naturally fastidious, has learned through years of communal living to avert his thoughts from domestic chaos. As he moves between kettle and sink and cupboard he is, in his mind, exploring an Inca city. The idea of being away, gone, far from London with its rain-smacked glass and its panicky warren of underground walkways and railways calms him. He steeps the tea — mint for Roses, black with milk for himself — and carries it back to the bedroom. She's changed position, facing the window now. He gets back into bed behind her and shapes his body to hers, and she moves to accommodate his contours.

'I made you tea,' he whispers.

'You're a fucking prince among men.'

'You look beautiful when you're asleep.'

'Is that a compliment?'

'It is yeah. Smell great too.'

'Like a really great ashtray. It's in my hair. Why did you let me smoke?'

'Wild horses couldn't have stopped you from smoking.'

'Wild horses won't have to nurse me when I'm dying of lung cancer.'

'Hush, pet.'

She's naked under the duvet, her body burning hot against his cooler skin. He kisses a shoulder, and she murmurs some version of the word 'early', her eyes still closed. He peels himself away and sits up higher in the bed, sips the tea and picks up a book from the wooden box that serves as a bedside table: a history of humanity that suggests a slightly updated theory of evolution. James devoured the first third but has slowed. He often finds himself reading the same passage several times, or finishing a page and realising he wasn't concentrating. Did the author just suggest that humans are less similar to apes than to termites? He turns on the bedside lamp.

'Do we have to be awake?' Roses' question is thickened by the pillow.

'You don't have to be.'

'Come back to sleep with me.'

She puts her lips against his arm, her arm across his waist. For a moment, James indulges in the fantasy that he could catch sleep from her like a fever, dream away the morning and reality. Then he re-starts the page. Roses turns onto her side, and after a few minutes he can tell from her breathing that she's fallen back asleep.

Roses is not asleep. Her mind is playing blended loops of fantasy and moments from the night before. James opening the door, the way he shies his head down and away, a movement she loves without being able to articulate why. The too-long wait for him to touch her, the way his knuckles brushing her cheek sent her stomach south like she'd lurched towards a crevasse and caught herself just in time. The sex they had. God the sex.

She senses him close behind her, and the space between them, especially the space. The tea steams nearby, perfuming the air like the courtyard of the hammam in Paris, with its blue-leaved olive trees. In this gorgeous halfway state she can kiss James again and again without it being too much. Her unspooling imagination turns him into a horse that spooks easily. She's the rider. But now she's thrown and winded, and he's away, into a distance of blue curling trees and smoke.

Then, suddenly, a fully conscious thought: there is a way to grapple back some of her power.

Roses opens her eyes. James is reading. She checks her phone for the time but on the screen is a text from Clare, part of their permanent, ongoing conversation:

So does he know your views on monogamy?

Roses reaches for the tea and is surprised to find it cold; she must have slept after all.

Does he know?

She takes a sip of the cold tea and looks up at James, who finishes the paragraph he's on before looking down to meet her eyes.

'Hi,' she says.

'Hi. I was just thinking I might need to resuscitate you.'

'Please do.'

'Can't now; talking means you no longer fulfil the criteria.'

'I have an idea,' she says, before she can change her mind.

Ever since her early twenties, when she first met Clare in one of several exploitative plays after drama school, Roses has been rejecting the concept of the long-term, exclusive relationship: over glasses of Pastis in their aniseed phase, over coffee, over Sunday lunch with Clare's wide-eyed parents. Clare plays devil's advocate: you'll settle down one day and get John Lewis curtains, she says. You're only saying this because you want to shag everything that moves. You only get to say this because you're beautiful. Everyone thinks their friends are beautiful, Roses replies; it's a reassuring trick of the mind.

And so Clare's text this morning is a challenge: it means, is *this* the person who will make you see the error of your ways? Roses now knows she's been harbouring a similar thought. For James, it seems, monogamy is the default. Does she want to settle into something like that with him, something safe? Does she want to share herself, still? Does she want to share him?

This morning, this moment, something clicked. She needs to stop gripping so tight.

'Last night was so great,' she says, sitting up so they're eye to eye.

'Yeah, it was that.'

She settles her shoulders against the pillow. 'Do you think it might be good to try involving some more people?' She tries to keep her voice light. Feels him become stiller beside her.

'How'd you mean?'

'I mean, sometimes it can also be good to ... mix things up a bit.'

'Are you seeing someone else, then?'

'I'm not trying to tell you something new,' she says, not sure whether that's completely true. She takes his hand, fingers in between his. 'I always said I had more open things before this, right?'

'You want to have a threesome, like?'

She laughs. She can't tell whether he's about to storm out of the bedroom or initiate sex. She can never tell.

'Or something. I'm just saying it's a possibility. Something we could try.'

'Other girls or other guys?'

'Whichever. Or both.'

James puts his hands behind his head, which means letting go of her hand, and looks up at the ceiling. He's silent for what feels like a long time.

Then: 'Yeah, ok, if you want to. But I need another cup of tea first and maybe a bacon sandwich, all right?'

★

An hour later, half dressed and with empty plates and mugs on the floor beside the bed, Roses is scrolling through pictures.

'How about this one?' she asks. She shows him a photo on the phone screen: the two of them in Barcelona, a selfie with them both glowering, a wedge of Catalan architecture in the background.

'Nah, we look up ourselves.'

She scrolls for a few more moments. There aren't many of them together.

'This?'

A wedding, James in a borrowed tux, Roses wearing a long red dress.

'Bit James Bond.'

'This?' A soulful cow in the Lake District.

'Yes.'

She scrolls again.

'This. This.' She shows him a picture of the two of them sitting on a rock in the Lakes. In the morning, after taking down the tent, they had balanced the phone on a stump. In the picture they're in waterproofs, with happy smiles and the tanned legs of late summer.

'Yeah, that one.'

'Yes! I'm doing it.'

They've spent the last half-hour filling in the questions on an app, and a profile picture is the final step. OpenDoor markets itself as a way for 'open-minded' couples and singles to meet.

'I've added the picture,' she says. 'I'll make it live?'

'Why not.'

Roses taps the screen a few more times. She glances from it into James's eyes, holds his gaze a moment. Looks back and taps once more. Then she shoves the phone under the pillow, buries her head in it, and quietly screams. The photos have acted on James's mind like a series of flashcards designed to communicate the phrase: *This is getting serious.* Looking down at the nape of her neck, the prominent vertebra there, he has an urge to touch it, which he resists.

She rolls onto her back and smiles up at him, stretching her arms above her head.

'This is the best bit. Now anything's possible.'

'Really? This is the best bit?'

A wickeder look comes into her eyes.

'Ok, no, meeting some insanely hot new person is actually the best bit.'

He's been turned on ever since they started the questionnaire. Now, leaning beside her on an elbow, he uses the other hand to stroke her face, the side of her body, all the way down to her knee. She reaches her arms up around his neck, and pulls him down towards her.

Afterwards, James falls asleep again and, knowing it's rare, Roses goes to shower. Hair wrapped in a towel and barefoot, she makes coffee, hoping neither of James's flatmates will appear and try to strike up a conversation. She wants to savour the high she's on.

She takes her cup to the sofas in the big communal space, crosses her legs on the rusty velvet, and clears space on the coffee table by gently pushing back a litter of books and glasses. She and her housemate keep their own flat, a couple of miles away in Clapton, tidy and ordered. But part of Roses enjoys this mess; like the set for a play about hedonists on the verge of self-destruction.

She replies to Clare, describing the picturesque ruin of the living room, then stops, sipping her coffee and staring into the middle distance, the phone and its eager screen temporarily forgotten. Putting her feelings for James into words is hard. Clare is funny, cynical; they have long been funny and cynical together. Now Roses isn't sure she wants cynicism, or even humour.

She writes a second text, about joining the app. Clare is also typing, and as she hits *send* Clare's message appears: *You didn't answer my question.*

Roses smiles. Having received her message at the same moment, Clare texts again: *Good ol' telepathy.*

Clare has been to stay in Paris and met both Roses' mother and her father on their separate trips to London. Since Roses doesn't have friends from school, Clare is privy to more of her background than almost anyone she now knows.

Roses' parents had been a spectacularly bad match. She came to realise it only gradually, of course, as hope-filled children do, growing up in the no-man's land between them. Watching them shred each other slowly like cats at the furniture. Her father had affairs; her mother lacerated herself with diets, prescription drugs, rosé, and cigarettes. Trapped in lovelessness, she focused on Roses, a little girl with big eyes and a neat fringe and perfect, maternally orchestrated clothing.

Her dad bought Roses soft toys until she was a teenager and had to ask him to stop. Otherwise, he was too careful with her, as if she was part of a problem he had to deal with. Ghislaine bought her jewellery and two-piece swimsuits. As Roses grew tall, Ghislaine compared the length of their legs. Roses had less wayward hair, her mother said, fuller lips. She was a colt who couldn't put on weight, and on and on the comparative compliments went until Roses' body was, to her, little more than a walking, talking rebuke to her mother. Her lovely mother.

By the time Roses was ten, her parents were both broken in different ways: he like an old shoe, worn and scuffed. She, shattered like a vase, each chip exposing more surface area to pain. Her father moved out, asked for a divorce. He moved back to America. He married a woman with love to give and no very obvious opinions. Ghislaine drank and smoked and excelled in her work and complained about Paris. Roses went to a girls' boarding school in England and swore she'd rather die than climb into the iron maiden of marriage.

She's been non-monogamous in every relationship. Some have been happy, ethical, exploratory couplings. In others, there's been a painful imbalance: Roses pulling for freedom while the man – it's been a man in all her longer relationships – resists, or pulls in another direction. Worst have been the ones (Chris, notably) who pretended to be easy with everything while all the time finding the situation hurtful and burying the pain, until eventually it clawed its way out.

She had loved Chris, she thought. Until the night she came home late from an innocuous dinner with friends to his white-faced fury. He didn't believe her account of the evening. He smashed a phone on the kitchen floor – his own; he wasn't physically violent towards her. He called her a whore. Roses, shocked and dry-eyed, felt her tenderness for him evaporate with the word; with everything it meant about him.

Roses toys with the phone in her hand, thinking through ways she might frame her feelings to Clare. She types: *I never quite know what he's thinking.* Erases it. She types: *Maybe this is the test we need.* She erases it. She types: *I have no fucking CLUE what's going on in his head but this is me and.* She erases it and sips her coffee. Sometimes, a crack opens up in the wall around James and light spills out, and she wants to drink the light. Close as she is with Clare, that makes too weird a text message.

She writes: *It's new for him but he's into it. I think he gets that no one belongs to anyone else.*

She sends the text, watches the phone and sees Clare's reply arrive, using the pet name she often employs:

Bollocks, Bunchie. You belong to me, and you know it.

Back in the bedroom, James wakes to find Roses gone. He listens, hoping he'll hear a sound that confirms she hasn't left the flat. Then he spots her sweater on the back of a chair and relaxes back into the pillow. She's still here. But the sweater reminds him of the dress. What's he going to do about the bloody dress?

Ever since he bought it for Roses on a whim – was it two weeks ago, or three? – it's been stuffed in its carrier bag at the bottom of a drawer. The dress is black with a low back, a material he has no idea how to name and can't really even describe. Is it silky or heavy, or both? And more to the point, why did he think it was a good idea to guess her size and take out his credit card and buy the thing which cost – he didn't have to think about it to know – more than his dad used to make in a month. It wasn't just an extravagance. It was like he'd gone mad for about ten minutes during his lunch break.

The thing is, he hasn't taken it back. He's embarrassed to, that'll be why. But giving it to her seems equally impossible. He might as well buy her a solitaire and get down on one knee.

He gets up, pulls on boxer shorts and a hoodie, jogging trousers and socks. The concrete floor seems to breathe cold up at him. He drags the bag from the drawer and takes out a handful of dress. It slips over his fingers like water.

This new thing, the app, the idea of others. He can't tell if it makes him feel more nervous about his relationship with Roses, or more relaxed. A weird combination of both. Watching her deftly fill in the questions – so sure, so at ease with herself – he'd felt something close to pride.

'What's that?'

Roses is at the door wearing far too little given the freezing temperatures inside the flat and also that the flat is shared.

James stuffs the dress back into the bag and the bag into the drawer.

'I'll show you later. You look like the cat that got the cream. What you been up to?'

She wanders into the room.

'Oh, you know. Washing my hair. Drinking coffee. Texting Clare.'

'Telling her your secrets.'

Roses looks at him with serious eyes.

'Clare and I have no secrets.'

By dinner time Roses still hasn't left. She and James open a bottle of wine and cook stew, making large quantities so that the other housemates, who pass through on their way in or out, can share it. With the dark, a new mood comes over them. They become giddy, laughing at themselves and each other, drunk suddenly and happy. Maybe they'll go out later, there's a house party down in Elephant, but it feels a long way. Clare and her boyfriend are at a bar in Camden from which Clare is sending pictures of laughing, hugging people and their various drinks.

At 8 p.m. James picks up his phone.

'Look at this.'

The new app, which both have left resolutely unchecked, is alive with messages. They leave the stew simmering (half of it will be gone when they eventually return) and retreat to his room with their glasses of wine.

Most of the messages are from people they quickly discount – single men who have sent them stock one-liners or winking faces; couples whose appearance makes them guffaw and hide behind one another's shoulders. When they like a profile they read it aloud to one another, scanning the text for meanings hidden and explicit. They pore over photos, comparing a person's appearance in one with their look in another, trying to construct as accurate an impression as possible.

There is also a record of people who have looked at their profile but made no attempt to communicate.

'Whoa,' says Roses, clicking through the pictures of those who viewed them.

'What?' James, pouring more wine, glances over her shoulder.

'Just that person looked familiar. Like someone I went to school with.'

'Didn't you go to a girls' school?'

'Yeah,' she says. She's already moved on. There's a quiet ping, and a rose-coloured icon appears in one corner.

'New message,' says James.

Roses opens it: 'Wow.'

'They're . . . good looking.'

'Yes. They. Are.'

The message is from a couple who call themselves Holmes & Watson. (Roses and James also have a joint pseudonym, 'The Flea'. A reference to one of the Donne poems from Roses' play, it seems weirder every time they look at it.)

The pictures attached to the couple's profile show a woman with brown skin, darker brown hair, and large eyes. The man is pale and tattooed, with blond hair; long in most of the pictures, sometimes shaved on one side or tied into a ponytail. More than one shot shows the couple with a dog, sleek and black on top, tawny underneath.

The message they have sent is short and to the point:

'You look like a nice pair. Want to meet?'

Chapter Five

James tries to be late, but isn't.

After a slow journey – he chose not to cycle, which would have been reliably fast, deciding instead on an inefficient combination of Overground and bus – he walks towards the pub confident that he won't be the first. Inside, he looks around, but there is no one who looks like the couple. He already knows Roses won't be there on time. She is punctual when it comes to work, but regularly turned up for their early dates twenty minutes after the allotted time. He's still not sure if it was an accident or a technique. It unsettled him, but he has to admit to himself that it worked: by the time she got there, the expectation had always made her arrival very sweet.

Now he goes to the bar and orders a drink and looks at his phone because that's what people waiting at bars do. A minute later he feels a presence at his elbow and turns. Beside him at the counter is a woman much less tall than Roses and more than a foot shorter than him. There is nothing diminutive about her, though. Her presence is vivid, her face wide-eyed and small-nosed and open. She has curly brown hair in a deliberately messy bun, large hoop earrings, and a dog. She looks up at him, feeling his glance.

'James.' It's a confirmation, not a question.

'That's us. Hi.' He diverts focus to the dog: 'Who's this?'

'Oh, yes, I should have mentioned. This is Casimir. Do you hate dogs?'

Her eyes are hopeful and, he now notices, green. A line of black make-up traces the lids and continues into a flick at the outer corners.

'Nah. No. I don't think so. Maybe I'm more of a cat person.'

He says it because he has begun to think of her as catlike and wants, obscurely, to compliment her.

'Oh, cat people, dog people, I don't really get that thing,' she says. 'Since when did we have to choose just one other species to like? I'm a fish person!' She tries it out to prove that the sentence sounds absurd. 'Nice wallaby, but I'm more of a kangaroo person?'

'Everyone's into order, I guess. Clear categories.'

'Well, maybe not everyone,' she says, and looks him in the eye. James feels a rush of heat through his legs that might be embarrassment or desire, or might be the first flush of alcohol from the long sips he's been taking from his pint. It might be all of those things.

He says: 'What are you drinking?'

'What are *you* drinking?'

'Broon. Newkie brown.'

She wrinkles her nose.

'I'll have a white wine.'

He buys her a glass of wine. Even that act feels subversive. They wait at the bar and maintain a decorous distance, though they do turn their bodies to face one another while the dog stretches out at their feet and closes its eyes.

'Roses is on her way,' he says in case she's worrying, but she doesn't seem to be worrying. She seems relaxed. His palms are damp, and he hopes the deep-blue shirt he's wearing won't show sweat stains at the armpits.

'Cillian just texted. He's always late. I think it's really rude, so I'm sorry. I can't be late, don't seem to be capable of it,' she says.

The sense of affinity makes James happy but he chooses not to share it, feeling somehow that to claim a similarity between them would seem over-eager, puppy-ish. He takes her in, while she talks about how spending so much time in schools has made her weirdly obsessed with punctuality. He can't really see her as a teacher; he'd more easily believe she was in the sixth form herself. She's wearing an outsize sweatshirt with a design like large black handwriting, patterned leggings, a gold watch and chains. Her trainers are gold. He wants to touch her. Then the door swings open and Roses stalks in.

James sees her, for a moment, through the other woman's eyes: impressive, elegant, moody. She's wearing sunglasses even though it's dark, and when she spots them he can't see the expression in her eyes. She takes them off as she walks over, and he realises she's more nervous than she's pretending to be.

'You must be Hura?' She has to lean down to kiss the other woman on the cheek.

Roses turns and kisses James briefly on the lips, takes off her coat.

'Hi, yes, and this is Casimir. I hope you don't mind dogs.'

'Hura Holmes?' Roses asks, glancing at the dog.

'You got it. My mum is from Pakistan and my dad's English. Which means I have the weirdest name: Hura Evelyn Holmes.'

'Like the detective?' says James.

'Like Evelyn Waugh?' says Roses.

'Exactly. Old white guys, both.'

'At least you're not named after a bunch of flowers,' Roses says. James laughs. Roses dares anyone to mock her name; he finds it endearing to hear her mock it herself. 'I like Hura Holmes, it's got a ring to it,' she adds.

'Yeah, I don't mind it,' Hura says. 'But Evelyn makes me think of a bat with folded green wings.'

'Nothing wrong with bats,' says James.

'I'm a bat person!' Hura says and they smile; already they have a shared joke. Roses looks between them, eyebrows raised. She says:

'Shall we get a table?'

They have almost finished a first round of drinks when Cillian arrives. He throws himself into the booth beside Hura, bringing the cold and the scent of the spring night in the folds of his jacket. He's already apologising and Hura batters him with mock-angry hands.

'I'm so sorry! This thing happened just as I was leaving work, and then I did leave but I forgot my wallet and had to go back and then—'

'I don't want to hear it! Cillian, seriously. Apologise to them! They think you're a total loser!'

Cillian puts both hands flat on the table like a boy and looks across at the others. 'I'm really sorry. I'm a loser.'

They reassure him that they don't think he's a loser, that they've been having a great time.

'See,' she says, changing the angle of her teasing. 'If you can't be on time you needn't have come at all. We were getting on just fine!'

There's the briefest of pauses while each of the four feels that this may have taken things too far: that suggesting a scenario in which not everyone is present comes too soon and seems too extreme. Then the moment passes.

'I'm getting the next round, what does everyone want?' Cillian says. As he gets up, Roses also stands.

'I'll help you,' she says.

Hura and James are alone for the second time.

'I was nervous,' Hura says.

'You didn't seem nervous.'

'I know. Teaching: it makes you very good at hiding your feelings.'

'I had a bit of nerves too, I guess,' James says.

'Where did you learn to hide it?'

James smiles. 'I don't know,' he says, though he does.

'Most people are surprisingly good at keeping parts of themselves secret. Don't you think?' she says. 'The difficult things. The dirty, shameful things. The things they don't like about themselves. The things they do like, but think no one else will tolerate. Like a ledger of mistakes we all carry around with us.'

'Do we?'

'I do. I still cringe sometimes when I think about things I did years ago: a car I once damaged. Things I said to people.' She looks at him. 'You're not plagued by anything?'

James thinks about the great mistake of his life. Huge, irreparable, still hidden, it looms like an obelisk in his past and the shadow it casts reaches across him and into the future. Oh, yes, he has regrets.

'This lad at work had a stag do. In Budapest or Riga or somewhere. I said I had a funeral. Actually I stayed home all weekend and watched TV. I just didn't want to go. But I felt bad about it.'

She laughs. 'Well, I think that's commendable,' she says. 'That you felt bad.'

He smiles, eyes down on his pint. The shades of honesty are many and various.

'Where are you from?' she asks. 'The accent.'

'Oh, right. Newcastle. Up there they think I sound like a right southerner.' Home is another subject he doesn't want to touch. 'So, you like teaching, do you?' he asks.

Hura finishes her wine before replying, and glances away as if thirsty for more.

'That's a very long story.'

At the bar, Roses watches the man beside her as he tries to gain the attention of the staff and then orders drinks. He's about her height and slim, with long-ish, dark-blond hair pushed back from his face. He left his jacket in the booth and one arm, the one closest to her, is blue with tattoos that emerge from the sleeve of his T-shirt and flow down to his wrist. In a gesture that seems unconscious, he rubs the top of that arm, gathering the sleeve and revealing that the shoulder, also, is damasked with designs. His T-shirt is pink. Where James is substantial, dark, cut clean – she thinks – from good strong cloth, this creature is mercurial and light. She has no idea if she finds him attractive.

He places the order, then turns to smile at her.

'Sorry again I was late.'

'Where do you work?'

'Fitzrovia. It's a design studio. But actually, I didn't forget my wallet. I was working on this thing for Hura. A birthday thing. Don't tell her.'

He turns back to pay.

'What's the thing?' She feels jumpy, but then these first moments are bound to be awkward.

'Oh, it's a kind of book. Photographs and stuff. It's taking ages.'

He knits his fingers together behind his back, tilts his head back, and stretches both arms towards the ceiling.

'What kind of design do you do?' she asks.

'Graphic design. Flyers, posters, that kind of thing. It's not that interesting.' He unstretches, notices her watching him, drops his head and actually puts his forehead on the bar.

'Sorry,' he says again. 'Shoulders. From sitting at a desk all day.'

'You move a lot, don't you?' She smiles, to indicate it's not a criticism.

'When I can. I don't think I was built for an office job.'

'Me neither. That's why I don't have one.' After she's said it she realises it sounds like an implicit judgement of his choice.

One of their drinks arrives, and he passes it to her. 'Was that one yours?'

'Thanks.'

'You're a director, right? Theatre.'

'Yes, how did you know?'

He smiles almost shyly, looks down at his feet, which are clad in white basketball boots. He cycles slowly from one foot to the other. 'I googled you. After we messaged to arrange this. You mentioned your name.'

Now he looks up at her from under his fair brows. 'Didn't you? Research us at all?'

She frowns. 'I didn't actually.'

'We might be psychos.'

'If you were, would an internet search have saved me?'

'Depends how many people we've preyed on before. Set up a date, lure them home, chop them up, put them in the freezer.'

She looks at him.

'I mean, god, sorry, that's not what we're going to do.'

'Phew.'

All the drinks have now arrived.

'Sorry,' he says.

'Stop saying sorry.'

'Can you manage those?'

He hands her another drink and she's about to say that of course she can manage to carry two glasses halfway across a room. But at that point they're fully face to face for the first time, and she sees that his eyes are not the same colour. What she'd taken at first for a trick of light and shadow is in fact a marked difference in the irises, one of which is glacier blue, the other dark brown. The effect is so startling that Roses forgets to speak at all. They look at each other, and he smiles.

'The eyes, right?'

'Yeah, sorry. I just noticed. Sorry.'

'Now who needs to stop apologising?' He flashes her a smile and leads the way from the bar towards the table.

When they arrive with the drinks, the interlocutors naturally change, so it's to Roses that Hura explains the strange month she's having. She glosses over the reason for her teaching job abruptly stopping, framing it instead as taking time out to decide what she wants to do.

'Why did you pick teaching in the first place?' Roses asks.

'Good question,' Hura says. This flinty, cold second glass of wine is disappearing quickly, and going to her head. In comparison to the woman beside her she feels small, and somehow girlish, even though she suspects she's older by a couple of years. Roses is intent, tall, her dark eyebrows drawn together in concentration. Hura feels she is smiling too much, perspiring and inarticulate. It's a sensation she's familiar with but from long ago – trying to impress someone new, trying to make them like you and at the same time find you attractive. A date feeling.

'A few reasons. Because it was the last thing anyone expected, maybe. My mum wanted me to do something "impressive", I think. The pressure sent me off the rails for a bit; or something did. And, like everyone, I wanted to "change the world" and "save the planet". You know – back when we thought it could be saved by everyone recycling. I wasn't a natural campaigner. But I thought

I could educate. I trained as a geography teacher because that was the closest you could get to ecology, land use, weather systems. I thought I could help rear a generation of better stewards.'

'And did you?'

Hura sighs. She thinks about Jenna and her friends, their passionate commitment to skincare routines and social media. But there are others, earnest kids who she's pretty sure are thinking hard about the future; or lack of it.

'I don't know. It started to feel . . . useless. It's like the world is a cinema that's on fire, and we keep telling the audience, but they just mill around getting their coats and buying popcorn and chatting about celebrities. The building's on fire! And what am I doing as a teacher? Lecturing some bored teenagers about playing with matches.'

Roses' wine is red. She swirls it in her glass.

'Do you think any individual can make a difference?'

'Some people do. I always thought, you just need to take care of your patch and the rest will take care of itself. But that's not happening. We need leaders committed to real change . . .' She stops; she sounds like a teacher, and she hates it.

'Right. So the logical next step is . . .?'

'Become a leader.'

Roses looks at her. 'Is that what you want?'

Hura pauses. A month ago the answer would have been no. But everything is changing quickly. And maybe, she now thinks, it has been there for a long time, amorphous, almost undetectable: a new purpose, growing for months inside her. She can still feel the clarity of that morning in the woods.

'It seems so weird to say it out loud,' Hura says. 'I don't even know what I'm talking about. But maybe. I've been micro, micro, micro. This child. This class, this school. I think I'm ready for something macro. Something big.'

Roses holds out her glass. 'Here's to your prime ministerial campaign,' she says, and drinks. 'I'd vote for you.'

Hura laughs. 'You don't even know me.'

'I don't know any of the wankers who run this country. I have to vote for them anyway, even though usually my vote doesn't count. I'd prefer you any day of the week. At least you're not a craven liar or a sociopath.'

'Are you sure?'

'Cillian already reassured me that you're not planning to murder us.'

'Oh god, did he?'

She glances across the table but Cillian is explaining something animatedly using his hands. It's James who glances back, gives her a reassuring smile.

'You'd make a great politician,' Roses says, emphatic. Something about the endorsement of a stranger makes Hura feel more confident than she ever has before about the nascent plan.

'Also,' adds Roses, 'you're gorgeous. Maybe that's shallow, but it's not going to hurt.'

The unexpected compliment almost makes Hura choke on the sip of wine she's taking. Hot and embarrassed and pleased, she ignores it.

'Anyway, that got a bit heavy,' she says. 'Being unemployed is weird. Today I spent the entire day falling down holes on the internet. I only managed to leave the house because we'd run out of milk. What did you do?'

It's a Monday; the low commitment date night. A good night for Roses, since many theatres close. Her day, like most of her days, has been long and packed: a six o'clock start for a corporate breakfast at which she served Eggs Benedict to suits and tried to avert her mind from the actions her body was taking; a quick swim during which she tried to get her mind back again; and then several hours on a hardcore grant application for her next project. She'd spent the afternoon with Stefan, crafting and sending emails to the influential people they always invited to shows and who almost never came.

As she sat on the train from Liverpool Street to London Fields, the first free minutes of her day, she'd opened the app, flicked through the profile pictures of people who had viewed them. There. She stopped and looked for a long time at the solitary picture. Dark cropped hair showing a tattoo on the side of the head, dark eyes that looked up towards the camera. A face familiar and yet strange; a book of memories blown open like a photograph album by the wind. Roses closed the app, and looked at her reflection in the glass, and then looked through it at the gasometers and the sky.

Cillian is hungry. He worked through lunch on the book for Hura, which now involves an entire visual chapter for each year of their relationship. He ran out of time to snack on the way and cycled fast, felt close to fainting on arrival, but has been fortified, temporarily, by the drinks. He feels hyped-up and untethered. He's talking fast to James but isn't sure what he's saying. He's intensely excited, he realises, by the newness of the situation.

He finishes a story and tries to take a deep breath, to slow himself down. He should stop gabbling, get James talking. He casts about for a question to ask, then panics at the thought that maybe he hasn't asked any yet. What does he know about James?

'So being a doctor must be interesting,' he tries.

James looks down at Casimir, puts out a hand to the dog, and smiles with just one side of his mouth.

'Interesting,' he repeats. His tone gives nothing away, other than suggesting he might find the question banal.

'My mum would have loved me to be a doctor,' Cillian says, wincing inside as he notices he's turned the conversation back to himself.

'Yeah, it was my mam's idea too,' James offers.

'Not yours?' Cillian asks, and when James doesn't immediately respond: 'What did you want to do?'

James examines the label on his bottle like he's never seen ale before.

'I was a swimmer,' he says, clears his throat. 'Competitive. But there's a time limit on that.'

'What happened?' Cillian asks.

'I ran out of time.'

He looks up and across the bar. Cillian ploughs on because he's friendly and intrigued, and really does want to get to know these people, to make the evening a success, whatever that means.

'What about your dad?'

James looks him right in the eye for what feels like the first time with a heat that might be anger, or something else. 'What about him?'

'Was he pleased you went into medicine?'

James half laughs, takes a swig of his drink.

'Not exactly.'

James's manner is so far from inviting confidences that Cillian can't immediately think of a way to probe into this possible affinity – to find out if James, like him, is fatherless, or if something else is going on. He stretches both arms above his head. 'Fuck, I wish this place did food.'

James seems so relieved it almost reads as delight.

'Will I get some crisps then?' he asks, already on his feet.

At the bar James keeps his back squarely to the room, to the table he's left behind, sure that a deep blush has suffused his face and neck. On the app he thought Cillian seemed vaguely familiar, and now he knows why: they're both regulars at a coffee shop that's near University College Hospital, but not so near that James is likely to run into any of his colleagues there. Especially not Emma, a consultant who has taken a particular interest in his career. He's never talked to the other man before, and James is pretty sure Cillian won't make the connection. But he's noticed Cillian: the hair, the tattoos, the distinctive way he moves. He's noticed him and thought – what? James himself doesn't put it into words. He feels extremely awkward and, at the same time, the fact that one of the people they've met tonight turns out to be *this* man seems strangely predestined.

James orders another round of drinks, four packets of crisps, and a bowl of overpriced wasabi bullets. When he gets back to the table the others raise their eyebrows at the amount.

'Staying for a while, are we?' Roses says.

'Oh my god, yes,' Cillian says, opening one of the packets and tearing it down the side so that the contents lie open on the table. James, watching him make five crisps into a neat pile and eat them at once, can't help but smile.

Roses glances over at them. She watches Cillian duck down to soothe Casimir, straighten, and lean his shoulders against the bench, each of his movements precise and somehow elongated, as though he's not just completing necessary actions, but almost dancing them. She sees James notice, and wonders what he makes of the other man. She realises she wants to look at Cillian's surprising eyes one more time.

She notices that James seems to be suppressing a grin, catches his eye. His look at her is one of veiled, conspiratorial glee.

Back at his place at the end of the night, James puts his hands on Roses' shoulders.

'Close your eyes,' he says.

'What?' But she does it.

'Keep them closed.'

She keeps them closed and her lips are parted now and she's not exactly smiling. He opens a drawer and pulls out something very black, and tries to smooth the creases out of it.

'Hold out your hands.' Before he lays the dress over her outstretched palms, he tears off and crumples the price tag, and shoves it into his back pocket.

Chapter Six

Cillian got to the club alone, and he's alone still. The friends – can he call them that? – who said they'd join him had been vague, and he'd half known they wouldn't show. He's standing near a stack of speakers with a bottle of Beck's in one hand and the other in his pocket, where his fingers gently touch the ID card that always gets checked. Cillian is nineteen but no one ever believes it. His hair is matt black, his eyes dark with kohl. On his left arm a new tattoo – his first, a human skull he will later regret – itches.

A part of him is enjoying the crash and rip of the music, the way it seems to shiver through to the centre of himself, to places nothing else ever touches. It kneads and shreds at something there, like firm hands on a muscle in spasm. It hurts. It feels good, healing. The rest of his energy is focused on not looking lonely. He sets his shoulders just so, his weight over one leg, his head slightly back. He holds the bottle of beer loosely by the neck and wills his arm to relax. He tunes in to the music's soothing frenzy and tries, tries, not to see himself through the eyes of others.

The night isn't busy yet and dancing is scant. The crowd, mainly dressed in black like Cillian, is milling, drinking fast. He scans it, picking out faces and forms, noticing how the pervading darkness is punctuated now and then by a shock of dyed hair. He watches a young man – sleeveless top, wrists wound with leather and friendship bracelets – walk across the room to the toilets. Another guy with a mohawk gelled into white spikes. Then Cillian's eyes light on a girl standing at the bar waiting to be served. Her hair is cherry red, and she wears black glasses as well as her leather jacket and boots; the contrast attracts him. Cillian takes her in, the size and shape of her, then looks away and imagines them having sex. It has to be this way. If he got stuck on the preliminaries, even in his mind, the desperate shyness that always stymies him in real life would ruin even the fantasy. He doesn't imagine approaching her; he can't. He imagines that has already taken place, and somehow they are in a room – hers, he supposes – where she has just thrown her jacket onto a chair and turned to him in the act of removing her top.

He looks back to the bar. She's finally been served. She turns away with her own bottle of Beck's and looks across the room to where he stands. Their eyes meet and she raises the bottle, cheers. He feels himself blushing and, to his own mortification, looks away. In his fantasy she's wearing a bra that matches her hair and she walks towards him in just that and jeans and boots. He's leaning against the wall and she reaches him and presses her body against his. In the fantasy he puts one hand on the small of her back and the other on the nape of her neck and kisses her, and she lets out a sigh of pleasure and desire. He looks back at the bar, and the girl is gone.

Later. He is moshing. A group, mainly topless young men, has gathered near the front of the dance floor and is roiling, the members throwing themselves bodily towards the centre, crashing into one another, bouncing away. Cillian is caught by the bodies around the edge, gathers himself, and plunges back in. Shoulders strike shoulders, chests buffet and bruise. He's seeking the right mixture of self-protecting tension and relaxation, and as he finds it he's rolled around in the group like a stone in a stream, then ejected again. He's breathless and high. He jumps in again, is hit hard enough to hurt, is pushed out, returns. The next time he launches himself into the melee he collides with a form smaller than the others, and realises it's the girl with red hair. She pushes him hard with both hands, and disappears. He sees her again, pinging through the thrashing group like a bright ball-bearing in a pinball machine. Then he loses her.

Sweaty and exhilarated, he goes to find his jacket on a low sofa at the room's edge. He sits to catch his breath and looks around for his drink, but it's gone, spilled or stolen or cleared away. Someone throws themselves onto the sofa close beside him and he turns ready for the challenge, but it's her.

'Hi,' she says.

'Hi,' he replies.

'Want some?' She's offering him a glass of water.

'Sure.' He takes it and swallows a big mouthful. It's vodka. 'Shit!' he splutters.

'I'm Alice,' she says, taking the vodka back and drinking some.

'Cillian,' he tries to say, hoarse with liquor.

'Kill what?' she shouts.

'Cillian,' he shouts back.

In a lithe single movement she swivels herself so that she's straddling his lap. Stunned, he is still, then collects himself enough to put his hands on her hips.

She pushes the glasses onto her head and peers at him.

'Your eyes are fucking crazy,' she says.

'Heterochromia,' he says.

'What?'

'Never mind.'

'More?' she asks. She swigs and holds the vodka in her mouth, raises her eyebrows.

He smiles, then, and rests his head back, and opens his mouth.

Alice Black is her name, and it doesn't last, and that doesn't matter. She is his first in many ways: first woman to approach him and show him he could be desired. First lover. First, brief, love.

They fuck all weekend. On the Sunday morning he wakes while she's sleeping, and lies still in her tiny, clothes-strewn room. He stares up at the Anaglypta ceiling and feels the slow-motion exploding of himself, his sense of self. He is not small, unlikeable. He is not a mean slice of humanity. Sex with Alice Black – the want satisfied, and the being wanted, and the ability to satisfy – makes him feel huge. He is a great cloud-stack lit by the sun. He is a bear rearing up on its hind legs in a river, scattering drops of glory. This, this, is what he was made for. She stirs and he kisses her, and they fuck again. He makes a vow without knowing it: forever to pursue this feeling, and the clarity it lends to the world and his place within it.

Ten on a Tuesday morning, Hura has decided, is the worst time to be unemployed. All her friends are at work; of course they are. Her parents and brothers and their partners are at work (except for Amin's wife, but what would Hura say to her?). Cillian left for work with a spring in his step.

'Do you think I can text Roses?' she'd asked him over breakfast. She gets up and dresses and eats when he does; the days she hasn't have been some of the very worst.

'Of course you can.'

'But should I?'

'*Should* you?'

'I mean, does that seem too keen?'

'How keen are you?' Smiling, looking at her from under his lashes.

'I don't know. I want to text her.'

'Definitely text her.'

Hura sips her tea.

'Can I text James?'

'*Can* you?'

'You know what I mean!'

'Holmes, honey, text them both as much or as little as you want. Don't overthink it.'

Easy to say. Easy, when 'overthinking' isn't your day job. Hura has taken Caz out and tidied the flat and done some distracted yoga. She's opened her laptop and stared at her email, at various websites. Throughout it all she's been thinking more or less constantly about the previous evening. The word 'gorgeous' on Roses' lips, and the particular shape of those lips. James's hair, dark with a salting of grey. She imagines him in a white coat, appearing by her bedside with some soothing words in that accent . . . stops herself.

Eventually, after many drafts, she settles on a short text and sends the same one to both of them, not wanting to pick, imagining they'll compare notes as she and Cillian would certainly do:

So nice to meet you last night . . .

Roses replies almost immediately.

James does not.

Roses' phone beeps just as she arrives at the theatre. She smiles when she sees Hura's name, taps out a quick reply, knowing that otherwise it will be hours. As she's finishing, Stefan arrives, scarf on, hands in the pockets of his black jacket, bag crossways, unsmiling.

They kiss on the cheek.

'Why it's so cold?' he asks.

'Good morning. You smell nice.' They start to walk into the theatre together.

'Preparing for the Oliviers?' The dress is over her arm.

'A gift.'

She's taken two paces before she realises Stefan has stopped. She turns back to find him standing completely still, mouth open.

'Shut. The. Front. Door.'

'Stop it,' she laughs, 'come on. It's not that big a deal.'

'Oh, no. Of course. Dr Love bought you a dress but it's not a big deal, silly me.'

'It's not.'

'I am agreeing.'

'It's really not.'

'They all said yes, by the way. The performers we offered to.'

Now she stops.

'They all said yes. They *all said yes* and you're only just telling me?'

'We only just arrived.'

She's already hugging him and jumping around the atrium with joy.

Chapter Seven

That evening James begins his rotation of nights. Such weeks necessitate disciplined daytime sleep. For James, who can't sleep at the best of times, they start with the cloud-step of adrenaline and descend into a tortured front crawl through treacle.

He goes to bed on the morning after the first night shift, wakes, realises it's only midday, groans, and hides his face back in the duvet. The glass bricks in his wall are glaring with daylight outside, and images from work are only just below the surface of consciousness.

James searches for the safety of sleep, its muffled sounds and warm folds. Oblivion shifts sideways and melts away. Claws of wakefulness snag him: the clatter of opening doors, a twisted limb. He casts about for something distracting, finds himself picturing the pub two nights before. Sitting across from the women, their faces turned towards each other and smiling. The line of Roses' jaw just below her hair. A checkerboard tattoo on Cillian's arm that moved with the muscles underneath, and the naked place on the inside of his elbow where the veins showed blue like faded ink. James slides a hand under the waistband of his thin cotton trousers.

There's a knock at the door of his room. He whips his hand away, embarrassed though the door is still shut.

'Yeah?'

'Are you asleep?' His housemate Steve's voice from the other side of the wood.

'No.'

Steve takes it as an invitation to open the door and lean in. He's wearing a puffa jacket and a hat.

'You don't usually sleep this late.'

'Yeah, well, I'm on nights.' James rubs his eyes with a hand.

'Oh, right, nice,' Steve says, missing the point and coming fully into the room. 'So are you around today for a bit?'

'Hmmm, maybe,' James says. He can guess what's coming and, though he wants to help Steve – a chaotic friend as well as a housemate – he was enjoying the prospect of a day without plans and the chance to rest, even if sleep was elusive.

'Cool, amazing. I've just got a few bits of wood that need moving. Would you be up for giving me a hand?'

Steve holds up a blue plastic bag from the local shop. 'I can pay you in beer and hot cross buns.'

'That sounds disgusting. And I can't drink before a shift.'

'Hot cross buns and speed?'

'Just the buns is fine.'

'Brilliant, thanks, you're a legend.'

'Give me ten minutes.'

'No problem mate, whenever you're ready.'

They drink china mugs of tea and eat buns in the big, battered van that Steve uses for jobs and, during the summer, as a mobile work-shop and occasional home. As they drive out towards the North Circular, James becomes suspicious.

'Where are we going?'

'Enfield.'

'Ah, fuck man.'

'It's only twenty minutes away, don't worry.'

An hour of bad traffic later they're standing in front of a huge pile of railway sleepers.

'Look at these!' Steve enthuses. 'Beautiful! And they just want to get rid of them. One of these babies in central London, you're paying twenty quid and they wouldn't even be as good as this.'

'So how many are we taking?'

'As many as we can fit in the van. We'd be mad not to.'

After fifteen minutes they're so hot they strip to the waist. The sharp wind immediately cools their sweat but it's a pleasure, as they keep building more heat from the stooping and hefting. James, who has been edgy since they got stuck in tailbacks, starts to loosen up. The sleepers are heavy but manageable, and he feels strong. They stop to drink water, long swallows from a bottle Steve produces from the van and which tastes of engine oil. Then they start lifting again. When the van is full they step back and look at its well-packed interior.

'Shame we can't take more,' Steve says, casting a regretful look at the remaining pile.

'Another day, maybe,' James says. He checks his watch and feels his heart sink. It's past three. Work is closing in on him.

As they drive back, Steve opens the windows and turns on the radio, happy with the day's haul.

'You love your work, don't you?' James asks him as Steve checks a mirror and switches lane fast and dangerously.

'I don't know. I guess so, yeah. Sometimes.'

'Being outside. Actually making stuff. I'd like to do something like that.'

'You must be raking it in. Plus, women love doctors.'

Steve switches lane again, puts a hand out of the window in merry apology for cutting someone up.

'You're living the dream,' he adds.

'Not my dream, though,' James says.

Steve lets that pass without comment.

'Roses not around this week?' he asks instead.

'Not while I'm on nights, probably.'

'How's the thing going, the open relationship thing?'

James probably wouldn't have shared the development with his housemates but Roses blithely did, as soon as it happened.

'Yeah, ok. We've met a few people.'

'Met as in boned?'

'No!' James almost shouts. Then quieter, rubbing the back of his neck: 'Not yet.'

'You dirty dawg,' Steve says in an exaggerated American drawl. 'So is Roses seeing other people then?'

'She can do.'

'And you don't care?'

James is silent for a minute, looking out of the window as north London streams by.

'Roses is different. To other girls. They always, you know. Like you said. They love doctors. Dating one's like a prize or something. They say it when they introduce you to their friends and then hold on tight like someone might snatch us, you know what I mean? And it's all: where are you tonight, this weekend, I miss you. Roses doesn't give a fuck. She's got her own stuff going on. She's not . . . she doesn't need me.'

'And you don't get jealous?'

'I don't know. Not so far.'

'So can I have her number?' Steve's looking at the road and his voice is light. James has no idea whether or not he's joking. He lets a few seconds slide by before answering.

'She's round all the time. You don't need me to give you her number.'

'Yeah, but—' Steve accelerates past another van on the inside '—would you mind? If I called her?'

'Depends what you say.'

'Mate. If I asked her out.'

'You want to?'

'She's fit, you know.'

'I do know, yeah.'

'So . . .?'

'Look, if you want to ask Roses out it's her bloody choice, isn't it? What do you want me to do, text her and ask her if she fancies you like in school?' James has his phone in his hand and realises his voice is a fraction too loud.

'All right all right, keep your hair on, I'm only messing with you,' Steve says. His smile is unreadable.

A red light slows and stops the traffic. The radio is playing a dance tune and Steve taps the wheel in time and sings, *'turn it up, up, up, up.'*

'You're really into her, aren't you,' he adds to the end of the line, a question without a question mark.

'What?'

'You don't want to admit it, *but you are, are, are, are,'* he sings.

James laughs softly: 'Getaway, man.'

The lights turn green.

'Chips!' shouts Steve, throwing the wheel to the left, and sailing across two lanes of traffic. He brakes and there is the sound of sleepers sliding and clunking into the partition behind them.

'I'm starving,' Steve says, double-parking the van and pointing to a chip shop. 'What do you want?'

'Large, loads of salt and vinegar,' James says and then, opening the window to shout after Steve as he runs towards the shop, 'and a Fanta!'

Steve waves without turning. He calls something from the doorway, about pickled eggs maybe, but the detail is drowned by the traffic.

James rests back in the seat and closes his eyes. His arms ache pleasantly. He can manage it, he knows, five twelve-hour shifts in a row with the prospect of very little sleep in between. He's done it before. He can do it again.

By the weekend James senses that he's losing his grip on reality. Each of the nights he's worked so far has been more intense than the last. Each morning he's returned home wired, and taken hours to wind down. Once in bed, with all the sounds of daytime around him, he's lain awake worrying about decisions made during the shift. He hasn't answered a message from Roses since Thursday and, feeling guilty, is putting her to the back of his mind. He never answered Hura's text either. Now it feels far too late.

On Sunday, he wakes with a start after two hours of sleep. His heart is thrumming. He had a dream. He was running from something, but the shoes he was wearing belonged to a patient. A dead man. They were broken and painful and he tripped, fell, picked himself up to run, and fell again. He thinks: *I can't do this any more.* He thinks about his escape plan: to quit his job and go to Argentina and never come back.

Usually just thinking about the plan calms him down, but this time, in his sleep-deprived post-dream state, it doesn't have the required effect. He picks up his laptop from the floor beside the bed. He searches for flights. He needs to take decisive action, he thinks. Knowing there's an end point, a true deadline, will make him take the steps he's been putting off for years. He will finally have to address the practicalities of quitting in the midst of a medical career, working out whether he will ever be able to get back in (though half of him knows that once he's left medicine he'll never return). He'll finally have to give notice on the flat, put his belongings into storage. Tell his mother. Tell Roses.

Clicking swiftly through dates on a comparison site, he finds a flight to Buenos Aires that's bizarrely cheap. It's half the price of everything else; it's probably a scam or a mistake. To check, he selects it and begins the process of choosing seats, refusing add-ons. The flight is just over six months away. The further he gets through the selection process, the more inevitable buying the flight seems to become. The price hasn't yet been increased by hidden taxes or charges. Below the date and time, a line of bright-blue text tells him there's *Just one seat available at this price!*

He thinks about Roses; he doesn't want to leave her. But he's always got one excuse or another; at some point he'll just have to make the leap. He reaches for his jacket, slung over the back of a chair, and rummages in the pockets for his wallet.

His pulse is still racing. Last night a woman died on the table under his hands. A young woman, younger than him, hit by a car near Oxford Circus. She had red hair, made fiery by the unnatural pallor of her skin. Now that she is in his mind he can't get her out. Probably she'd crossed the road at just the wrong moment: a matter of seconds later and the car would have swished safely past. Between kerbside and deathbed, she had never regained consciousness. It happens all the time: life ending in sudden silence.

Everything changing except the world, which marches on without a backward glance. When James told her partner, the man had cried out, then clapped a hand over his open mouth.

His credit card in hand, James clicks *Proceed to payment*. He enters the string of numbers, familiar but not quite known. He imagines Roses dead on a hospital trolley; himself in the waiting room. Would his response be appropriate? He is so tired his body seems to be humming; a low, uncomfortable electric burr. He is hungry, incredibly hungry. But he's come this far, he needs to get this thing done and then he'll feel better. The payment completes.

On the box beside the bed, his phone vibrates. It's Roses, the screen says. She'll be calling him from bed, her voice raspy with sleep, sexy, a wary edge because he's been so unresponsive these last days. *You're going to Buenos Aires!* blazoned across his screen. He leaves the phone shivering and goes to shower.

A couple of weeks after the first date, and they're going to a club. Roses, who has been before, suggested the night and booked the tickets. James has very little idea what to expect. Hura, on the group chat they've created, seemed excited about the costume element, and James has placed himself in her hands.

Now that they're getting ready, together at Roses' flat, he's surprised to find out how seriously Hura has taken the commission. She's shopped for him, Cillian, and herself – Roses has plenty of appropriate outfits – trawling a mixture of charity shops, pound shops, and market stalls. She has employed a sewing machine. She presents him with clothes – if you can call them that, these scanty bits of fabric – and he pulls them on. When he emerges from changing in the tiny bathroom she laughs and claps her hands, then directs him to a chair in front of her so that she can work on his make-up. Standing in front of him, she tousles his black-and-grey hair out of its habitual neat shape, studies him thoughtfully.

She's half ready, a loose dress thrown over her outfit. Above her extra-long leg warmers, her thigh is bare. James lets his eyes brush over the skin there for a moment, then looks up to her face.

Her eyes looking evenly down into his are leaf-green, false-lashed, smiling.

'Don't distract the artist,' she says. 'Now close your eyes.'

Lids closed, he hears the make-up bag opened, the clunk of little objects against one another. She begins to touch his face, and the smell of the cosmetics is reminiscent of every girlfriend he's ever had, and also, confusingly, of his mother and the inside of her handbag: pencil shavings, wax, ink, powder, mingled in that intimate interior with the metal tang of pennies, chewing gum stuck to a scrap of paper, lint. The smell of first dates, of one-night stands, of intimacy.

Every part of Hura feels close. Her fingertips are cold against his eyelids, and he thinks of her sensing the eyeball through the skin. Her breath is warm, Prosecco-scented. Her body is a shadow between him and the lamp. He imagines touching that thigh, how firm or soft it might feel, cool below the hem of her dress. He opens his eyes.

'No! Dammit, James, shut them!'

'Sorry. Sorry. Reflex.'

'You've smudged it, you wally.'

'Sorry.'

'I've got to do this eye again.'

'It's hard, I'm not used to sitting still like this.'

'Be quiet.'

He can hear a smile in her voice. Then there is a cold squelch across his right eye as she drags a cotton wool pad loaded with cleanser over it.

'Urgh. What was that?'

'God, it's like putting sunblock on a toddler. Stop complaining. In fact, no talking at all. And stop screwing your face up. Just relax.'

James feels a hand stroke the side of his neck and settle on his shoulder, then squeeze.

He raises his hand and makes a zipping movement across his own mouth. Hura hasn't let him look in a mirror since they started. The others are dressing next door. With an effort, James keeps his eyes closed and his face as still as he can, picturing himself as a mannequin in a shop being dressed by a saleswoman. He imagines himself in a window, posed with one wrist turned to look at a watch.

'What time is it?'

'Almost done.'

She presses and brushes for a few more minutes, then the movements stop. There is a moment of silence.

'Ok, open your eyes.'

James opens his eyes and looks into hers. A long moment, long enough to remember that the iris is a muscle and the pupil is a hole, black as the outer reaches of space and also unknowable. Then she steps to the side, and behind her is the mirror.

The woman on the door looks them up and down. She's seen too much, her eyes suggest. She's tired, and yet she is compelled to stay, her face set to indicate that smiling will not be happening tonight. She has worked on this look, James is sure, but that doesn't make it any less withering.

'No cotton, no black trousers, no denim. Did you even read the dress code?'

A low smoker's voice, beautiful and broken. She is the weariest woman in the world. She did not ask for this job. She is doomed to it, to stand here like Charon and question those who come to the underworld.

'The costume's underneath. I'm just wearing this because it's cold.'

The woman looks up at James's face – she isn't tall – with a look that could melt glass. She doesn't even speak. James unzips the hooded top he's wearing, drops the black jeans. She makes a silent survey: the feathered shoulders, the latex-encased torso, the rubber shorts, the long legs.

'Shoes?'

He opens his backpack and shows her the boots Hura found, improbably his size.

Finally the woman's facial barometer inches one degree closer to warm. She gives a slight nod, inclining her head to the right:

you shall pass. Feeling awkward as a schoolboy James pulls up the jeans and they all head into the foyer, and beyond it into Eden.

Inside they laugh and pat each other's shoulders: they passed a test; they are together. They find a corner in one of the down-stairs bars and peel off outer clothes. Around the club, others are disrobing and augmenting, and the whole floor has a half-ready, expectant, tense atmosphere, as if the audience has been allowed backstage at a play. James sits, threads the jeans off and feeds his feet into the boots. He wants a drink, or some drugs, or both. His underarms prickle with sweat even though down here it's cold. He looks up and catches Roses' eyes with a look that asks, *Why are we doing this?*

She comes over to sit beside him, leans against his shoulder.

'I know this bit's weird,' she whispers. 'Everyone's uncomfortable at the beginning. You'll get into the swing of it.'

Roses does not look uncomfortable. Her costume is simple and effective: a red rubber dress, slick as wet paint. Huge white platforms, white stockings, a white wig. Her make-up is massive and theatrical, and James has never seen her look like this and it slightly blows his mind. Certain aspects of her image hit certain receptors in his brain and he feels them fire, and it's strange to sense that mechanism kick in over someone he knows intimately. She looks like a comic-book illustration, and like a stranger, and part of James, a big part, wants her back to normal. The rest of him wants something else.

Hura is attending to a detail of Cillian's regalia. He's dressed entirely in white, his fair hair and skin further emphasised by the pale clothes and make-up. The effect is of a fantasy Snow King, all faux fur and flashing scales that now recall armour, now an albino trout. When he turns his eyes on them, James sees that he is wearing contact lenses that retain the black outer ring of the iris and the pupil, but turn the rest – the parts which are so strikingly dissimilar in Cillian's real face – white too. He has antlers. But it is the change in the eyes that makes him seem particularly other. Not the man they have been getting to know; not even quite human.

James watches him stretch his arms wide, ribs visible like ridges in snow. James has a powerful urge to put out a hand and touch the fine fingers of bone.

He turns away and looks across the room to where some women dressed as cats are drinking gin from small plastic glasses and teasing each other noncommittally with a riding crop.

Cillian and Hura finish, and he turns to the others, and notices their appreciation.

'Magic under the UV,' he says, flicking at the white lycra in a way that diffuses some of the power of his altered state. For a moment he is familiar again, before he turns away from them with a lithe twist and moves into the gathering crowd.

Hura is the only one of the four to wear a mask as part of her costume. Sometimes, for moments of the night, she removes it, but then she slips it back on – the chance to retreat, to be unseeable.

Now she is dancing; they all are. So are scores of others, the bodies closely packed and moving rhythmically, the air between them hot and dense. In front of Hura is her own group: Roses in her red sheath, Cillian in white and James, seeming huge and – she has to admit – somewhat clumsy in his platforms, in black. It's only now that she realises the men's costumes, both designed by her, are opposites; the dark and the light. Her design had not meant to accentuate the differences, but rather to identify and emphasise the physical characteristics of each man. Only now does she see them as archetypes, which she has enhanced.

Hura herself is dressed as a mermaid with long green extensions in her hair, a shell bikini, iridescent scales affixed to a thin chain and draped around her hips, completed by the shiny mask covering her eyes. She got so fascinated by planning the other costumes that her own was almost an afterthought and doesn't make her feel powerful in the way she can see Roses' does. The evening has two distinct flavours: anticipation, high and citric, which she tasted when applying James's make-up and watching Cillian and Roses, downstairs, peeling off their outdoor clothes. And something else, cloudier and felt at the back of the mouth; of worry, of loneliness, even – fleetingly – of dread. The alcohol and MDMA in her system have had the effect of heightening both, and she oscillates between them, euphoric one minute, paranoid the next. Dancing, she moves her body fast, arms overhead, as if the music and dancing to it could drive away demons.

Her back is now to the others. A tall woman dancing in huge-heeled shoes turns and smiles at her. Then Hura is not sure whether the smile is for her or not. Someone, solid and square-shaped, wears a full suit of black rubber with a tight hood covering the whole head and face except for eyeholes and a mouth opening. A man dances, topless and sweat-drenched, in rubber sailor trousers and a white captain's hat. To their left a person is clad entirely in fishnet, topped by a large, realistic rabbit head.

She turns again, as the beats intensify, back to Cillian and the others. They are bound together by something, but it's still not clear what – attraction, or a shared sense of transgression. Neither her and Cillian's dissection of their previous date, nor their playful group texts, have clarified exactly where everyone stands, or what anyone wants. She was most nervous to see James again; he never did answer her message the day after the date. This evening, though, she thinks something has been building, as it did in the first meeting, between the two of them. That moment when she noticed his eyes on her thigh, and the look on his face when he glanced up at her a second later, had held an erotic charge that could have exploded lightbulbs. Since then, he's been friendly but much more aloof. And what about the others? Whispered or shouted conversations, looks, the game of buying one another shots, and downing them, and discreetly offering or taking little bumps and lines. Nothing is explicit, and yet this whole thing – being here at all – is one of the most explicit things she's ever done.

The electronic music is cycling towards a crescendo, ramping up the energy in the moving crowd, taking them with it. Hands in the air and feet off the ground, or in James's case one foot at a time off the ground; the poor guy really hasn't got much rhythm. But it doesn't matter. They're together and they're coming up, and the music is carrying them to the brink of something and then it will fling them off. Hura, exuberant, holds out her arms to embrace all three of the others, and they come close to be embraced. She throws her head back as the music pulses harder, and then the beat finally drops, and as it does so Roses kisses her.

It's been a long time since Hura kissed another woman and besides, every kiss is different, each one revealing. Roses' kiss is confident and puzzling: it feels to Hura like she is wanted, but simultaneously she isn't sure whether the wanting is a performance. Roses tastes of lipstick and rum and lime juice, and the softness of her skin and her lips is startling after years of kissing Cillian. Hura kisses back, using her tongue, closing her eyes. And she isn't sure in this moment whether the kiss comes naturally, or whether her side too is performative. The crowd surges, hugs them tighter, releases its grip. They pull back, and Hura seeks out Cillian's gaze, the lighthouse of her home port. He is smiling, which is reassuring, though she'd forgotten his strange white eyes and they briefly freak her out. Then she looks at James, and he and Roses are kissing one another and she feels, distinct and impossible to attribute to one of them or the other, a tiny jolt of jealousy.

Chapter Eight

It's 3.30 a.m. when Cillian finds himself alone. Roses and Hura disappeared to the loos and haven't yet reappeared. James said he was going outside for air and went off to the packed smoking yard. Cillian realises he's near the playroom, an area of the club reserved for people who want to engage in actual sex acts. It's screened off from public view by heavy black drapes and there's plenty of signage about not interrupting, including not watching, unless invited. He glances around to see if Hura is anywhere in sight. Instead he sees a woman approaching in a bodystocking and a turquoise beehive. She struts up to him on precarious-looking shoes and jabs him in the chest with a cigarette holder.

'You look *incredible*, I think I might actually love you. Do you get that a lot?' she says. She's drunk, he thinks, but he can't tell how drunk.

'Thanks. My wife's concept.'

'Well, she's a freaking genius. I was going for Amy Winehouse meets Wilma Flintstone, what do you think?'

She gives him a twirl, which takes a couple of seconds longer than it would take a completely sober person to execute.

'Gorgeous.'

'Can I kiss you?' she asks.

'Um.'

'Too fast for you? Wife not ok with that?'

'Maybe we could have a drink?'

'Do you know what time it is? Club's closing in an hour, this is last chance fucking saloon.' She's smiling. He places her accent as

Scottish, blurred by London and, judging by the glass she's waving, Southern Comfort and Coke.

'What's your name?'

Without answering she comes closer to him and looks into his eyes from very close range. She's smaller than him and has to tilt her head back.

'The things I could do to you, if you'd let me,' she says, and now her voice is quieter there's a different energy to it, less raucous, more intense.

'Could you?'

'Oh, yes. I really, really could.' She puts her hands on his waist and bites her lip.

Cillian swallows. The woman uses her hands to position her hips against his and presses.

For a moment Cillian stays where he is, pelvis to pelvis, lips an inch from hers.

Then he grins and tips his head back.

'Ah, I'd love to. Another night. Tell me your name.'

She's stepped away and turned sideways, a hand up to her hair. When she looks back at him she's careful to keep the playful smile but something's gone from her eyes, the depth of interest she allowed herself to show replaced by a generic, social look.

'Shame, sugar,' she says. She spots, or seems to spot, someone she knows at the bar nearby. Gives Cillian a finger wave, leaves.

Cillian swallows again, wishes he had some water, sits down on a nearby bench to wait for his body to subside. He feels lightheaded, like all the blood has rushed away from his brain, which it probably has. The woman has melted into the crowd or maybe gone to the playroom with someone less married. Cillian laughs softly to himself and goes to look for Hura.

He finds the other three together and when Hura spots him she frowns in relief.

'You ok?' he asks her quietly.

'Yeah, I'm all right, but I feel weird, I want to go home, is that all right?'

'Weird like upset?'

'No, just, I don't know, I've just had enough. Do you mind?'

'Course not.'

'Can you explain to them? I'll get the coats.' Hura gives the others a smile and heads for the cloakroom.

James and Roses look at him questioningly; up to this point it hasn't been clear how the evening will end.

'Hura's tired, I think we're going to head,' he says. Although no one wants to make anyone else feel bad, there's a moment when they all think about how none of them is at all tired. How nights like this can morph into even-more-extraordinary mornings. How nothing has to stop.

James asks Roses: 'Do you want to head then?'

'Not quite yet. Another dance, or . . .?'

He nods, and they both hug Cillian and no one talks about whether they'll see each other again.

By the time they're out on the street it's light and the first buses are running. Hura has wrapped a fluffy coat round herself and gone quiet, burying her chin in the fur. Cillian steers them towards a bus and helps her up the steps because she's half-shutting her eyes while she walks. On the top deck she lies down and puts her head in his lap.

'Hey, are you ok? Did anything happen?'

'No, fine,' she mumbles into his leg. 'Had fun. Just drugs or something. Got really tired.'

Cillian watches the early cyclists and street sweepers out of the window while Hura seems to sleep. He navigates them onto an-other bus and then down the streets to their flat, taking some of Hura's weight on his arm as she walks. Inside the flat – silent, since Casimir is with a friend of theirs – Hura lies down on the bed in all her clothes.

Cillian takes off her shoes. He goes to the kitchen and fills a glass with water, carries it back to her and pops two Paracetamol tablets from their foil. She's already asleep but he scoops her into a sitting position.

'Can you drink this?'

She drinks it and swallows the tablets. When she lies down again he takes off her coat, and unclasps her bra so that it won't cut into her while she sleeps. He covers her and closes the blinds, and goes out into the main room.

He opens the window to let in the dawn light and air. Of course, all that's happened is that he and his wife have been to a new club night. But Cillian has the sense of something enormous unfolding, the existence and nearness of other worlds into which he's barely stepped. Growing up in a too-small, too-quiet household, Cillian dreamed of creating something different: bigger, noisier, full of life and joy and people. He's always pictured kids, pets, a large family. But maybe that's not the only way. There is something about tonight, going there with Hura and Roses and James, that tapped directly into the desire for a rich, vibrant, loving tumble of communal life.

He wonders what James and Roses are doing right now. Both of them seem to him powerful in different ways. James because of his reticence, his apparent ability to hold himself aloof. Roses, because she's au fait with this scene, its language and its workings. He imagines her teaching him; his mind enjoyably reels.

Hura, when he checks on her, is resolutely asleep. He wishes Casimir were here for company, or that any of his friends might be awake at 5 a.m. on a Saturday. He takes off most of his clothes and, for lack of a better idea, starts doing some press-ups. He does them until his arms tremble. He eats some toast and showers and plays video games until, eventually, he thinks he might be able to rest.

Back at the club, Roses and James dance. She's high, at home here and happy they're together, still a bit bruised from the week when she barely heard from him. Nights are weird, he'd said, shrugging. Who can argue with a doctor who has to spend long hours saving lives?

Now she leans into him and whispers in his ear: 'Let me show you something.'

She takes him by the hand and they weave through the dancing bodies, past the bar, up a staircase. The black drapes of the playroom are ahead of them. An attendant stops them on the way in, checks if they understand the rules, whether they have a safe word.

'I don't think we're going to be needing that,' James half laughs.

'It's up to you, but we advise it,' the room attendant says. Their hair is in braids to their waist and they have a nose-ring and wings.

'Let's just see what it's like,' Roses says to James. She pushes back one of the drapes and they step inside.

James has never even imagined such a place. Neither when they planned to come, nor when he checked Eden's website, full of suggestive pictures of non-specific body parts, did his mind create a clear picture of what a playroom might be; he's not even sure he believed they existed. The room is large and very dark, with several pieces of equipment – a big wooden cross, not cruciform but X-shaped, to which someone wearing very few clothes is tied; a cage made of metal bars. Most of the furniture seems to consist of raised, black, padded squares, bigger than beds, so that several people – four, five, six – can occupy each. Everywhere are bodies. Everywhere, sounds and sights that he knows from his own intimate life, and from pornography, but has never witnessed in reality.

'Right then,' he says.

'Do you want to stay for a while?' Roses checks.

'I don't know where to look.'

'Look at me.'

She takes his face in her hands and kisses him. In their platforms they both seem huge. He slides his hands around her waist, glass-smooth the texture of the PVC. She takes his hand and guides it under the hem, between her legs, against the lace there, and deeper. The hot wax of a burning candle, fingers close to the flame.

On Sunday evening, James and Roses meet at a bar in Dalston, and then move on to a Turkish restaurant where they order far too much food, dazed by that first drink on an empty stomach, and by what they're doing, and allowing each other to do.

Friday night at Eden kicked off a weekend of partying and experimentation. They hadn't got home until well into Saturday morning, and then slept most of the day. In the late afternoon, with their phones and cups of tea on the sofa, they both organised separate dates with new people for the evening, showing each other the profiles they liked, crafting one another's initial messages and responses. James, it turns out, is surprisingly good at this linguistic kiss-chase. Roses thought she was the creative one, but jokes that he should go into playwriting. (It's also not a joke. He's never shown much interest in the theatre but she's acutely aware that his job makes him unhappy, that he needs something totally new.)

'So what was she like?' Roses asks.

They each have a cold glass of beer in front of them. James drinks before he answers, then traces patterns in the condensation.

'She was sweet,' he says.

'Ach, the death knell!'

'What?'

'She was sweet means: she was boring.'

'She wasn't boring.'

Roses grins, sits back with her drink.

'I'm sorry. What was she like?'

'Ok, maybe she was a bit boring.'

Roses laughs. She takes a small black olive from the dish between them and eats around the stone. The hard hit of salt, smoothed over by the beer's softer bitterness. Her finger-ends, her skin, seem to tingle with pleasure.

'Tell me everything.'

James describes the date in detail: where they met and what the woman – Heather, a physiotherapist – looked like, and what she wore. How they talked for a while in the street and dithered about where to go, how he bought her a drink and how, as she took it from him, she touched his hand as if by accident.

'Oh, man, she liked you!' Roses says, definitive.

'She didn't "like" me.'

'She must have thought Christmas had come early.'

'Why?'

'Look at you.'

'You're biased.'

'That's true.'

A huge platter of dips and salads arrives, a basket of flatbread, a dish of surprisingly delicious onions.

'What was she looking for?'

'Hm, yeah. She said she wanted something casual, like. That she was over trying to find The One and was ready for something else. That's what she said.'

'You didn't believe her?'

'I got the feeling she might mean "casual until it gets serious".' He stops to eat a long, green, marinated chilli.

'Then again, you do think every woman you talk to is going to fall for you so hard she loses her mind . . .'

James swallows wrong, coughs, chilli and vinegar making his eyes and throat smart.

'Sorry, sweetheart,' says Roses, patting his hand. 'It must be so hard being irresistible.'

James is laughing, coughing at the same time. Unable to speak. Roses waves to a passing waiter and asks for water.

'You're funny,' James says, once he can. She's nailed the fact that he's scared of making people love him; just not the reason why.

'I know.' Roses eats some salad, lemon-soaked. 'It's true though. To Hamlet, every woman looks like an Ophelia.'

James shakes his head, smiles at his plate. His knowledge of *Hamlet* is limited to a school trip when he was fourteen, fighting on the coach and sitting, stunned with boredom, through the impenetrable, interminable hours of the play. Sometimes he gets this sense, that Roses has stepped a few paces away from him, somewhere he can't follow. He remembers a young blonde with flowers in her hair; remembers her because he'd masturbated to thoughts of her for months afterwards.

'You don't look like an Ophelia to me,' he tries.

Roses smiles, pleased. 'You've got me. I'm more of a Clytemnestra.'

There's a pause. James has no idea who Clytemnestra is, and Roses knows it. She doesn't want to make him feel stupid – he's one of the most intelligent people she's ever met – but nor does she want to change her references because of their different backgrounds. The sense of elation is greater than ever, fizzing in her blood, and she knows what the feeling is, and at the same time she tries not to know.

After a moment she says: 'So . . . What did you feel?'

James eats and thinks. 'I liked her.'

'Did you want to sleep with her?'

'Yes.'

She narrows her eyes. 'Is that because you'd want to sleep with anyone?'

'No. She was nice. And pretty. I'd be up for it, definitely.'

'So . . . Are you going to?'

'I don't know. What do you think?'

She dips bread into hummus, bites into it, thinks. She looks at him. He has become so familiar to her, with all the time they've spent together in the past months, that for brief moments she experiences the uncanny sensation that they are somehow the same person. And yet, when she sees him afresh – when James wears a new colour, or, as now, when she sees him suddenly through someone else's eyes – he's breathtaking.

After her own date finished last night she went to a party where she kissed a very beautiful man with an undercut, and hasn't mentioned it yet. Maybe she won't. She feels close to James, having this conversation. But the undertow is still there; as though he is turning away from her even as he smiles at her from the other side of the mixed mezze. She grins.

'I think you should if you want to.'

Now they're eating big chunks of meat seared black at the edges from the coals they've been cooked over.

'Your turn,' James says. 'Tell us about Max, or whatever his name was.'

'It's Max,' she says dryly. 'Do you want the short version or the long version?'

'How long's the long version?'

'Shut up, that's so dirty.'

'You said it.'

'Ok,' Roses says, 'I'll give you the five-word summary.'

'Go.'

'No way in hell.'

'That's four words.'

'No way in hell, ever.'

'That bad?'

'No, actually,' she says more thoughtfully. 'He was a nice guy. Funny, intelligent. But there just wasn't any of that *thing,* you know what I mean? That taste in the air. That *bite.*'

'Are we talking about . . . oral?'

'Shut *up,* James, I'm trying to explain how it felt. How attraction actually feels. What it's made up of.'

'Sorry, go on.'

'It's just weird, isn't it? He was nice: nice face, nice clothes, attentive, good-looking. But nothing could induce me to sleep with him, not in a hundred years.'

'Poor bastard.'

'Whereas this Heather . . . Sounds like she was pretty similar, but you'd be happy to fuck her just to see what it was like.'

They look at each other. James likes hearing her use these phrases in relation to him and another person: sleep with. Fuck. It's strange, and it gives him a twinge of something like guilt, but it also has a nice abandoned freshness to it. The receiving and giving of freedom. It's intoxicating.

'I'd like to know what it was like, yeah,' he says. 'That's the excitement, right? Not knowing someone, then being really intimate.'

'For me it's got to be: bang! Before I want to sleep with someone. I have to be, like, winded by how badly I want them. It's got to be like getting knocked over by a wave in the sea.'

'And you've felt that, have you? Recently.'

'You mean apart from with you?' she says, her tone teasing.

'Yeah.'

'No,' she says, though her mind, as she says it, forms an image of white eyes and antlers. 'Have you?'

James is sawing off a forkful of lamb, which he dredges through yogurt and puts in his mouth, allowing him to take his time before answering. He thinks of Hura's thigh, Cillian's ribcage; the play-room and what they did there.

Chewing, half-smiling, 'Nah,' he says.

They go back to Roses' place. The talk of other people, the fact that each of them has gone out into the world and let the world touch them, has charged the air between them as they walk down Shacklewell Lane and along the edge of Hackney Downs. It's a warmer evening than any in the previous weeks, with a green smell in the air. Grass is pushing up from the winter churn of mud, the lime trees and plane trees are unfolding soft leaves. The moon is a clean white slice in the sky.

James takes Roses' hand and holds it as they walk. He has not told her about the flight he booked. He has barely let himself think about it.

Roses' flatmate is home, her door closed. They're quiet as they make their way to Roses' room, then silent as they turn to each other, as James presses her back against the wall. The curtains are open, the lights off. She wraps her arms tightly around his neck. They speak in whispers, eyes locked in the dim room. When it's over they lie down side by side, hands touching lightly, their bodies separately subsiding.

'We didn't talk about Eden,' Roses says.

'Mmmm. Late. Tired. Work tomorrow.'

'Do you want to see those guys again?'

James's eyes are closed. He says: 'Hura and Cillian?'

'Mm hm.'

'Do you?'

'Yes.'

'Yeah, so do I.'

'And what about Heather?'

'Honestly? No. Not really. I'm not that interested in one-to-ones.'

'Me neither,' she says.

There's a long silence during which they don't fall asleep.

James thinks: I am leaving. The words are there, ready to be spoken. The hurt ready to inflict. In sudden panic he searches his mind for a powerful image to sweep them away, and there it is: Cillian. Pale and uncanny, like an ancient spirit, the antlered man prowling in the half–light.

'I keep feeling like we're as close as we're going to get,' Roses says quietly. 'And then something happens, and I feel closer to you than before.'

He opens his eyes and can see that her eyes are open, but nothing of her expression. A wild thought passes through his mind: he should ask her to marry him.

'Goodnight,' she murmurs, and turns away to sleep.

He lies still. In a few minutes, Roses' breathing becomes regular and light. Her uncovered shoulder is pale as whalebone. James turns on his side and drapes an arm lightly around her. He puts his lips against the vertebra at the base of her neck and breathes in the scent that is her and the day she's had combined: charcoal and burnt sugar, grapefruit and sweat. Slowly, he feels the small cords that connect him to the waking world loosen and, one by one, release.

—◦◦◦—

Winter, 1997

James stares down and sees the black water covered in shattered light. He tries to move his hands but they have frozen to the parapet. How long has he been standing here? What, oh god, has he done? His heart turns over inside his chest; it feels like he will die of the pain there. But, after all, perhaps that agony is nothing more than the cold burning his lungs. He should get inside; he should get warm. Gasping, he peels the raw skin of his palms away from the metal and stuffs them into his armpits. Later he will smell the iron on them. He takes a step or two, but then finds that he has stopped again. Though he now feels utterly, horribly sober, it is not clear to him how he will ever leave this place. It's not clear that he should.

The Tyne is in flood. Whatever falls into it will be tumbled soon away, sucked out eastwards to the sea. Its surface is closed; for all anyone can see, the current carries nothing of value. James knows water. He knows cold. Often, he and Gull have leapt whooping into the estuary; into the plunge pool of a waterfall from banks ankle-deep in snow. And he knows the river at this time of year; its power is relentless and it is blind.

James is wearing slacks, a shirt. The wind seems to be blowing through his clothes and through his skin and into him, as if it has jaws and can bite. His shoes are borrowed – all the clubs have a 'no trainers' policy – and they are rubbing the skin away from his Achilles. He takes another few steps for home, turns back and runs to the spot he just left. He crumples against the parapet, folds both arms around his head, and screams.

The horn of a passing car screams back. As it goes by, the young driver and his teenage passengers lean out of the windows and jeer incoherently. They're high and they've seen another drunk stumbling back and forth on the Tyne Bridge like a clown. Their interruption silences him. He bites the material of his sleeve and his arm through it. He has to leave. The instinct towards self-preservation is pulling him away and its strength makes him ashamed. He is seventeen and has to live, somehow, with everything that he has done, and everything that he is. This thought, the need to survive, cuts through the churning in his mind. Poised on the edge of the high bridge, loss and terror sluicing through him, he realises he is not ready for the ending of another life.

There's a big holdall on the ground beside him. He picks it up. He walks away while the river rushes on, drowned with stars.

Chapter Nine

The last of the actors leaves. Stefan has been sitting quietly in a corner. Now he comes over.

'What do you think of her – Evita?' he asks.

Roses glances at the door through which Evita McNeish, the youngest and most volatile of the performers, has just left. In the last few months, 22-year-old Evita has become a household name because of her part in a suddenly popular television series. It's a coup that she's appearing onstage; her effect on pre-sales is already evident.

'It's early days. I think she'll be good,' Roses says, guarded. They've been rehearsing just a couple of days, but she knows Stefan well and he clearly has an opinion. 'What do *you* think of her?'

Stefan shrugs. 'She looks pretty ok. Her acting is bullcrap. She sells a lot of tickets.'

Roses squeezes her eyes closed. 'Bullshit,' she says. 'Bullshit, not bullcrap.'

'So you agree,' Stefan says.

'I didn't say that. She's young, she's inexperienced. I think there are flashes of brilliance. I think she'll be good,' Roses insists.

'Maybe. With you she has some hope.' Stefan's terse, Germanic assessment is a compliment, but not delivered like one. 'Terrible attitude, though. These *young people*. Urgh.' Stefan, who is not yet out of his twenties, theatrically shivers.

'She does need a lot of maintenance, yes,' Roses says.

She's walking a tightrope with Evita, pushing her to work hard but at the same time aware that the younger woman has a lot of power. If she doesn't want to work, and doesn't want to be pushed, she can walk. Everyone knows that would be disastrous. Roses doesn't like it, though. She saw several wonderful young women who could have played this part. She chose Evita because Evita was marketable. The transaction leaves a bitter taste in her mouth.

Two weeks into rehearsals, Roses knows exactly why she was apprehensive.

Evita McNeish is smoking a cigarette, sheltering from a light rain under the parapet of the Barbican's stage door. Her hood is up, her phone in her hand. Roses pushes open the doors, takes a deep breath, walks over to her.

'Hey, Ev,' Roses says. The big eyes flick up to her, then back to the screen.

'Oh hey.' She's writing rapid messages with both thumbs, her cigarette curling smoke from between two fingers.

'It would be great to get on with the rehearsal once you're done.'

'Yeah, I'm just having a cigarette?'

'Yes, I see that. It's just, you know, rehearsal time is precious. You did say five minutes.'

'Ok, *okay*.' The young woman puts her phone in her pocket, drags hard on the cigarette and makes a face like she dislikes the taste. 'I need a coffee.'

'You've been out here for half an hour. We break for lunch in forty minutes. Can you wait?'

Evita looks at her, incredulous.

'Do you know how much pressure I'm under?'

'Yes, of course, I'm not trying to stress you out.'

Roses is struggling to keep her voice level. She should have asked Stefan to go in search of Evita, then at least she could have carried on working with the other performers. But truthfully, it's getting harder and harder to rehearse around Evita's constant absences: calls she has to take, doctors' appointments, other 'appointments' that Roses suspects are auditions, cigarettes, more cigarettes. The scenes that don't involve her are becoming highly polished. Those that do feel frayed and amateurish by comparison.

When Roses is not in the rehearsal room, she's working on publicity; with the set, lighting, and costume designers; with the puppet-makers. She is writing and proofing programme copy, picking publicity photographs and sending them out to the media. This past week, after a supplier fell through, she and Stefan spent hours on the phone looking for a particular kind of gauze. None of it is her job, except it's all her job. As is this: managing Evita back into the room.

'The others were just saying how great you were in that last scene,' she says. 'I think you found something new there.' Ego massage. She's sinking lower every day.

'Yeah?' Evita finishes smoking and throws the butt onto the wet ground, grinds it with a heel. She puts her hand in her pocket and brings out her phone, like she hasn't even noticed she's doing it.

'So shall we get back to it? Find some more of those great moments?' Roses says. She sounds like an idiot. Evita's phone rings.

'Ev . . .' Roses says. But the young women has already swiped a thumb across the screen to answer.

'Mark?' Evita holds up a hand to Roses, all the fingers extended: five minutes. She turns away: 'So what did they say . . .?' Muffled by the hood.

Roses bites a lip, and heads back inside.

Ten minutes before lunch Evita crashes back into the room. The phone call has obviously not made her any happier. She sits in a plastic chair with her coat on while the others finish a scene. When Roses directs them back to the last place they were at that involves Evita, she can feel a prickly energy from all the performers. Those working hard and with dedication are annoyed by the exception being made for a 'star'. Evita is pissed off, her acting colourless and quiet. Roses is relieved when one o'clock comes and she can send them all off to eat.

She walks to the centre of the silent room. These spaces, tatty and still, have an energy of their own. They are the places where creation happens, where the nothingness at the start of a project becomes *something*. Roses kneels down. She doesn't have a god to pray to, but she raises her eyes up and speaks aloud, quietly, to the universe.

'Please don't let this fail,' she says. 'Somehow, please, let this all come together.' And then, stronger, surer: 'It's not going to fail. It's coming together.'

She smiles at herself, mocking, gets up. Success, failure, she's pretty sure, will come down to her: her ability to reassure and spur on, her instinct, her stamina. She's worked hard for this, for years. She just needs to keep working hard, to make sure it doesn't all collapse into ash.

Sweeping diced onions into a pan, Hura wishes she had let Cillian cook. His food is inventive and confident. Hers, she feels, is homely by comparison. It makes no statements. This whisper of anxiety is present under the music playing in the kitchen, the whir of the extractor fan, the spit of hot oil. Her hands smell of ginger and garlic; she'll need to scrub them. Her hair must be catching the scent of the spices. Because she is already showered and dressed for dinner, she's wearing an apron. Tending the food, she's forced to turn her back often to the room. Somehow this feels weak and makes her apprehensive; she would like to survey the space instead, check the set of the objects around her. She wishes she had chosen to cook something less pungent; that they'd ordered takeaway, or bought sushi. Some restrained, quiet, sexy food that could be presented on cool plates under soft light. Instead, the big open-plan kitchen and living room is filling with steam. Mirrors mist over and become unreflective.

'Candles?' Cillian asks. He is laying the table. They look at each other for a moment.

'It seems a bit . . .'

'. . . try hard,' he finishes.

'Yeah.'

'Yeah, ok, no candles.'

'But the light is so flattering . . .'

Cillian stands, the long white candles in his hands, surveying the table.

'For all they know, we have candles every night,' Hura says.

'True. Candles then?'

'Yes. I think so.'

He places three into holders and doesn't light them.

Hura stirs another pan, replaces the lid, takes a step back and smoothes the strands away from her forehead with the heels of her hands.

'Cillian?'

'Yes?'

'Do I look ok?'

He looks up briefly from laying plates and grins. 'Course, you look great.'

'But . . . really.'

Now he stops. He comes to her and puts his arms loosely around her shoulders.

'You're more beautiful than anyone else in the world. And not just to me. You're stunningly hot. Really.'

She smiles and kisses him quickly on the lips.

'Thanks. You're hot too.' She turns back to the cooking. 'I'm actually really *hot*,' she says. 'Why did I think curry was a good idea?'

'Because you make amazing curry?'

'Thanks, I don't need any more compliments now.'

'Do you need a drink?'

'Can I have a gin and tonic?'

He mixes it for her, places it on a small table by the sofa. 'Come and sit down for a minute.'

She adds a pile of spinach to a pot, wipes her hands, and goes to sit. Casimir, lying on the rug, lifts his head and she strokes it instinctively, the fine skull under her fingers so wholly known it's like an extension of her own self.

Cillian hands her the drink and she takes a sip and closes her eyes.

'Are you ok?' he asks.

'I think so. Yes. I'm nervous.'

'In a good way?'

'I think so.'

He puts an arm around her. 'We don't have to do anything, you know.'

'I know. I want to. I'm excited, too. But maybe I should have made pasta or something?'

'Because that would be . . .?'

'I don't know. More suave.'

He laughs and kisses her. 'Don't worry, Holmes. You're the master of suave.'

They clink glasses and drink and Hura feels the alcohol straight away, in her blood, in her arms, her legs. She leans close and whispers in his ear: 'What are you looking forward to?'

He whispers back, and as he does so his hand falls to her knee and traces its way up the leg and under her dress, and she closes her eyes. The rice, left on too high a heat, catches and burns.

Dinner is just dinner. Four friends, two couples, normal talk about work, the city, the fallout from the general election earlier in May. There is a shyness about them all, almost an insistence on keeping the conversation decorous. There is no innuendo. There is no touching, except if Roses places a hand over James's as she talks, or Cillian strokes Hura's shoulder to get her attention before clearing plates. Once they are cleared, everyone carries their wine over to the sofas. Roses sits on the rug, stretching her legs out in front of her.

'There's space for us all,' Hura says, shifting along.

'I'm comfortable on the floor,' she insists. 'From being in a rehearsal room. It's very democratic, the floor.'

What she doesn't say is that she feels too powerful sitting in a chair. She doesn't want to overbear. Hura waits, Roses has noticed, until she's heard the opinions of the room before sharing her own. Cillian is a chatterbox by comparison and Roses has found herself bristling a few times when he's crashed in with an opinion before anyone else – his wife, especially – has had a chance to speak.

Roses looks across at him now without turning her full gaze or giving him as much attention as he seems to crave, and which she is therefore disinclined to give. Here in his own home he is stiller, seems more relaxed, than the other times she has met him. Up until this moment he has appeared as a composite of clothes, tattoos, hair, as well of course as the idiosyncratic eyes and the distinctive way he uses his body. Now she sees him more clearly. The side of his face turned to her is the one with the blue eye, which is downcast and pensive while he listens to something James is saying. His fair skin is flushed slightly over the cheekbone and the ear. There are fine lines at the corner of his eye, but despite those signs of age he looks very young. In that instant there is something about him that recalls a sensation from long ago – teenagehood, or before – some chord struck inside her and still vibrating. It is in that moment that she becomes certain she wants the evening to progress to another stage. Then he looks up and says something and the moment is over. His assertions are a bit too loud, she thinks; his London accent sounds affected. She finds herself compelled to contradict him; to put him in his place.

Cillian is talking, but his mind is elsewhere. It's run ahead to the possibilities of the latter part of the night, and even to other imagined nights to come. Later, he would struggle to recall what they ate or talked about, but he'd remember that Roses wore a cream silk shirt buttoned to the top. That James took her coat from her and hung it; that there was something classic and detailed in their attentions to one another that mesmerised him as he watched them. He noticed the gold bracelet Hura wore high up on her arm, which touched him because he read it as a sign of effort to please.

He is talking, but suddenly he realises that a change in atmosphere is imminent, if only he would stop and let there be silence. He stops. His eyes meet Hura's, and she laughs quietly and touches her neck and looks away. Then he glances at James. The other man, so self-contained and large and dark, seems finally to have relaxed. Roses, sitting at James's feet, has draped an arm over his knees, and he has leant back and his shirt collar is open and his eyes are calm, the lids almost heavy. Watching them, Cillian reaches out a hand towards Hura, smoothing back her hair. He remembers how, before dinner, he had touched her. He leans forward and kisses her, and the act of kissing his own wife is changed by the context. The quiet non-aloneness.

Cillian draws Hura towards him on the sofa, and she slides a leg over one of his. Over her shoulder, he is aware of the others moving. If he has judged the moment wrong they will be gathering their coats to leave. He steals a glance: no. Roses has moved to sit beside James and they have intertwined their hands. His face is in her short glossy hair, whispering in her ear or kissing her neck, perhaps. For a while it remains this way. The restrained atmosphere of dinner still hangs between them like lace.

Now a sense of exaltation rises in him, a slow and silent mushroom cloud of joy. This is his home. He feels a shudder of desire through his skin so extreme it ought to be visible, as horses shiver flies away. He picks Hura up and carries her to the other sofa, and places her down beside the couple there. The women's bodies move to accommodate one another, then to touch more purposefully. Like in the club, it is Roses that initiates. She takes Hura's face between her hands and kisses her on the lips. Cillian is acutely aware of James on the other side of the two women, and is trying to read the other man's pensive, almost passive energy. The men look at one another. James's eyes seem navy blue tonight, and they are steady on him, but there is something in them, something Cillian will not be able to place for a long time.

Surprising him, James raises his right hand and touches the left side of Cillian's face with the back of it, knuckles to cheekbone and to jaw. It is the first contact between them, and up until that moment Cillian hasn't known how much he wanted it. Art school hadn't been the sexually liberated hotbed he might have hoped for, and anyway he'd spent it battling chronic awkwardness; he's barely experimented with other guys. Now, reticence and excitement fire contradictory messages through his nervous system. James puts the palm of the same hand against Cillian's other cheek and then, lightly, uses his thumb to trace the line of Cillian's lower lip. Cillian turns his face into the other man's palm, and kisses it.

James, in order for his mind not to be blown, switches it off. It's a skill he has. When emotion or sensation gets too intense, like during an argument, he simply uncouples his brain from his body. He can still act and talk, making coherent movements and sentences. But his mind is elsewhere, thinking its own thoughts, observing. The notable exceptions have been around his most visceral fears – spiders, for example – although now, with the new self-hypnosis techniques he learnt at the zoo, he feels confident he can also distance himself from some of those terrors. He's not certain it's healthy, but it's effective.

The situation he finds himself in tonight is therefore a puzzle. Its extremity and its nature call for absolute presence: this is happening, he tells himself, feeling the light stubble of Cillian's cheek against his hand. This is real, as he watches Roses unbutton her shirt and slip it off, here in this living room, an act that seems, somehow, more public and intimate than undressing in the street. And yet, like a man swimming underwater, he feels absolutely separate, as if he existed in another element. Most strange of all, perhaps, is that it's not unpleasant. He watches himself, and enjoys what he sees. Here are his arms, long and strong, circling Hura, whose torso, though she has also removed her top, is partly obscured by the fall of soft hair released from its clip. Her skin has a dewy smoothness that's very different from Roses' cooler, dryer touch; her lips when she kissed him were full. He has an erection. Last time he went to the bathroom he swallowed a small blue Viagra, effectively quashing the fear of underperformance that would otherwise have dogged him.

Hura leans back to look at him, searching his face with her eyes. He gives her a smile of reassurance. If he was to think about what is happening, he could not account for the consequences. There is a deep well inside him covered over. It is full of memory, of fear, of other things he doesn't want to name. He is dimly aware of its presence, and averts his mind absolutely from its contents. Hura begins to unfasten his belt. This is now, he tells himself; but only his body believes it. He delivers his body into the hands of this woman who he is only beginning to know, who seems very sure of what she is doing.

Hura is not sure what she is doing. A kind of breathless surprise is carrying her forward. She feels compelled to act by something in herself, some effervescing desire, but the desire is not the opposite of revulsion; rather, the two are either side of a fine line. She walks it like the apex of a roof, and could easily tumble down one slope or the other. Fascination with the moment, and her place in it, impels her. The world has narrowed to this room, and the four bodies in it (Casimir, a distracting innocent, has been confined to the office).

It is years since she has been with another man. Before Cillian, she had a series of longish monogamous relationships and has rarely been interested in one-night stands. She can count the number of men she's slept with on her fingers. (The number of women, as yet, is zero.) Yet here she is with another man's body under her hands: a chest with pectoral muscles and a covering of dark hair, a trail of hair down towards the navel and lower still. James's shoulders, which are obviously broad when he is dressed, are startlingly so uncovered: she struggles to pull the material of his shirt back from them. After the two previous meetings when they have barely touched, after the unanswered text, this closeness seems extraordinary. The scent of him is warm and animal, soothing. She feels a hand stroke her back and knows it is Cillian's. She feels the silkiness of her own loose hair against her skin, and is turned on by it, and feels James's desire under her thighs and her hands. Sensations of scent and weight, fingers and lips, skin and sweat, move together and over one another like overlapping plates.

Roses sits beside James. He turns his head to kiss her. Now the three of them are sharing a moment, and Cillian is not involved, though she knows he is next to them, watching. She pauses: the intimacy between two lovers exposed to observation for the first time, its tenderness and its own specific rhythm. She leans closer. James and Roses each put an arm around her. Their three mouths are close, are touching. Hura feels it as a flood of heat coursing through her body from head to toe.

This is so easy, she thinks to herself. You'd have thought it would be almost impossible, but it's not, it's simple.

And then, behind that thought and pressing through it, a sense of terrible strangeness. She looks again to her husband and again he's there. I trust him completely, she thinks.

She feels intoxicated by great inhalations of their shared liberty.

If Roses were to describe the evening to a friend (as she does later describe it, in minute detail, to Clare), she would say that the director in her caused problems. These things, she will say, should be fluid. But is true fluidity possible? Or is someone always, in fact, in charge of where the flow goes?

Dinner is pleasant, but the preamble of eating and conversation seems long, almost as though they are performing a dinner party instead of having one. She reminds herself: this is new for all of them. Except for her kissing Hura at Eden, none of them has really touched one another yet. But as soon as the date was arranged she began to imagine the moves that might be made, then to re-imagine and make changes to their order, their intensity and intention. This scripting and mental rehearsing is deep in her erotic makeup. It's how she has fantasised for as long as she can remember, since puberty and, though in a different form, long before. Real interactions don't follow scripts, of course, and in sex she can usually let go, allow the reality of the moment its primacy. But with the dynamic of two, which encourages constant engagement, increased to four, she finds herself stepping back. Her sexual imagination becomes mingled with her daily experience of choreographing words and movement acted out in real space and time.

'It was like, work brain meets sex brain,' she tells Clare, in the post hoc analysis.

'Hot, or not hot?'

'Hot like a campfire,' she says. 'Maybe not a towering inferno. Yet.'

On the night itself she experiences the powerful desire for certain things: to touch Hura; to see James touch people other than her. She knows this will turn her on, make her glad, and doesn't ask herself why. With Cillian, it's blurred: she's not sure how much she really likes him. His volubility reads as a kind of preening. He's lightweight, where James is solid and massy. If she sometimes associates James with a horse, Cillian is more of a cockatoo.

After she, James, and Hura share a kiss, Roses breaks off, moves slightly away, watches. She is aware of Cillian close to her but doesn't make eye contact. She is waiting for something. She reaches for her glass from a side table and takes a sip of wine, and then she looks up and into Cillian's eyes. He is perched on the edge of the coffee table. His gaze, always so surprising because of his unusual eyes, is more direct than she has ever known it. It doesn't waver. It isn't ironic. He doesn't smile. She feels wholly looked-at for the first time, and it's not just a scan of her body; it scoops straight through her. The way he gazes at her then is as eloquent as words, as strong as a slap. This is the memory she will replay again and again. Each time, it will give her an echo of the deep erotic kick she feels at the instant of it happening. For her, this – a look, a matter of seconds – is the most important event of the evening. She will not even try to describe it to Clare.

He stands. She stands. He puts his hand on the back of her neck and they kiss, maintaining eye contact almost to the last. When they have to break it she closes her eyes, experiences the utterly different feel of lips that aren't James's. Cillian tastes of white wine, his scent is of something green and light, grass, plants in spring, dew. He kisses her, and then uses one hand to turn her face away from him. He bends his head, and she expects gentle kisses to the neck like those James gave her a few minutes before. Instead, he sinks his teeth into the top of her shoulder and bites.

The bite is hard; harder than in normal foreplay. She almost screams, mostly with surprise; she takes the in-breath. But now Cillian's hand is over her mouth, stopping her. She bites the hand. Both let go and pull back, shocked. Their look at one another is the circling of beasts. Then they kiss again, hard, and Roses runs her fingers up into his long hair and grips it, his hand is on her throat and his thigh presses between her legs. Her body is flooded with desire, her legs weak with it.

She lets herself lean into the pressure of him for a moment. But something in her still resists. This is more than she bargained for. She breaks off and picks up her glass of wine and downs it. She turns back to the others.

From then on things are more communal. They take care not to allow it to devolve into twosomes. Roses takes care. The eye contact she makes with Cillian for the rest of the night is brief, little more than social. A portal spiralled open between them, but she has closed it, and decided to keep it closed.

Chapter Ten

Summer, 1992

It is high summer and Hura has turned twelve. The hot months have sent all the kids a little crazy. There is a feeling in the air of storms close to breaking, of endless possibility. It's a time of dangerous dares, small fires, of long evenings and short hot nights.

Hura, with her three older brothers, gets more license than most 12-year-olds. She's always held her own with them and her wiry strength and audacity bely her looks. Being small and called pretty drives her to be more boyish: she ties her hair up, wears jeans and T-shirts and backward caps and trainers. She rides a BMX. Ben has taught her to drive, practising slow circles on the abandoned runway of a small disused airport. He will soon regret it.

They are a gang, Hura and her brothers, but only sometimes. She is happy, so deeply happy, when the four of them watch TV together, commenting on the characters, or when they play one of the garden or street games that periodically become popular amongst them and their friends: Swingball or hackysack or French cricket. There are other moments she feels left out and furious. Increasingly this is the case with Mir, the oldest at seventeen, whom she idolises. He has new friends; even, she suspects, a girlfriend. She hangs around his door and he shoos her away, and she goes away and lies on her bed with clenched fists pressed to her eyes. But there are times he invites her in, lets her sit on the bed, plays her riffs on the guitar. He calls her Sparrow, and when he says it – rarely now – she's filled with delight and pride.

The night of the Great Lie starts like many others. Aisha and Ben have gone out for the evening: Hura and Amin, the closest of her brothers in age at thirteen and a half, are now deemed old enough to be left together. Mir, and Haris, who is fifteen, are off somewhere with their friends. It's the holidays and weeks more stretch ahead, but Hura feels left out of everything and burns with injustice. She doesn't plan to steal anything, nor to cause irreparable damage. It just happens: a series of events, of ideas that seemed fine at the time. The lie doesn't just happen, though. It's conscious; it comes from her mind. It changes her.

Amin is playing Nintendo, but it's too hot to be indoors. Hura kicks about the garden, then the street. She walks down as far as a neighbour's drive, to look at a beautiful car parked there. Canary yellow, an old-fashioned low-slung sports car. Like a toy, she thinks. She thinks, it's about my size.

She moves closer to the car and rests her fingertips on the glossy paint of the driver's side door. They live in a quiet suburb and it's the early nineties, but still, when she tries the handle, she expects the car to be locked. It's not. Opening the door, she sees that a key is hanging in the ignition. Hura glances at the house outside which the car is parked and sees no lights in the windows; but then, it's barely dark yet. They may be home.

She slips into the leather driver's seat. Her disproportionately long, thin legs just reach the pedals. She presses down the clutch like Ben taught her, covers the brake, turns the key. There are two realities playing in her head. In one she is Holly Golightly and can bend the world's rules and be saved from censure by luminous eyes and a fawn-like psychopathy. In another she is sick with terror and driven by forces she doesn't understand to make the situation worse. To push, push at the edges of things, and see what breaks.

Much later that night, Hura sits on her bed and looks at those long, undamaged legs. Ben is standing in front of her, the person she loves and respects most in the world (Mir is a god to her, but her dad has, until this point, been a truer friend). The forces of chaos are surging still. They are telling her that she can't change what's done, but must still try to escape. Ben is talking, picking words carefully and leaving large gaps. Her mind, as he talks and in the gaps, is performing a desperate reconnaissance, thoughts sent in every direction to try and find some way out of the thing she has done. She could wail and cry and beg forgiveness. Feign madness. Calmly apologise. Ah, there is a way.

Ben is looking at her with beseeching eyes.

'It was Amin,' she says.

The evening plays on a loop, in the coming days, in saturated colour. She backs the car out of the neighbours' drive, inch by inch, holding her breath. When its nose is facing up the cul-de-sac she waits, expecting to be stopped, but no one stops her. She presses her foot gently and drives slowly up to her own house. She sounds the horn, and its volume and old-fashioned tone sends her into a fit of laughter. Amin comes to the window, then out of the front door, his eyes black and awed. When he sees her giggling he laughs too, nervous, cautiously opening the passenger door.

'What are you doing?'

'Get in.'

'They'll kill you.'

'Come on.'

She found a bottle of bourbon in Mir's room earlier, took one big gulp and was nearly sick, the taste like a hatchet to the throat. She took another gulp, put it back, went to the bathroom and drank water from the tap. She searched his drawers like a thief and found the end of what she guessed was a spliff. She took it to the garden and lit it and tried to inhale, her poor ravaged throat contracting, fighting.

They turn a slow half circle at the end of the street, return, passing their house and the house, still dark, where the car's owners live.

'What are you doing?' Amin asks. They're approaching the end of the street.

'Dare me to drive round the block.'

'No.'

'You're scared.'

'You're an idiot.'

She pulls out into another road, drives slowly to the end. She knows these streets well, but then she's normally on a bike or on foot. She stops and winds down the window because she feels so enclosed and cut off from the world, and a horn blares behind her. Of course, there's a car there and she forgot to check the mirror. She turns left, into a steadier flow of traffic, puts her foot down to keep pace.

'Whoa!' Amin says as the car leaps.

'Shhhhh,' she says, her heart leaping too. She needs to concentrate.

The gathering speed. The misjudgement rounding an offside wall. The long, long, endless sound of metal in pain.

'I just want to know how it happened,' Ben has been saying. 'So I can understand why. After all we've taught you.'

Hura doesn't know why. Because the night was hot. Because chemicals in her brain ceased temporarily to balance one another out. 'Why' sounds to her now like a faraway country. She raises her eyes to Ben's and channels Golightly innocence.

'It was Amin. He wanted to take it. I said we shouldn't. He was upset cos you taught me to drive, not him, and he's older. He made me do it.'

She hears herself and is appalled, but also fascinated. Could this work? Is this what people do? Then Ben's face crumples at the corners and she knows that no, this is not the right course; but words are so much easier to say than unsay.

Ben, who has been squatting, stands and turns away so that his daughter doesn't see his expression. One of his children is lying to him. Ben is bad at being angry. He leaves it to Aisha. Now the emotion that wells up contains fury, which rocks him like a man trying to close the door on a storm. Intermixed with it are dread and sadness and loss. His baby daughter sits behind him on the bed looking like a young woman and lying, probably, like a snake. He feels his heart might break. He says, half turned away: 'That's not how Amin tells it.'

He's giving her a chance and she doesn't take it. She thinks about the long raw dent down the car's beautiful flank, metal showing through the paint. She imagines she didn't do it, and imagining that she didn't has such seductive power.

She wakes in her clothes, on top of the covers. She fell asleep dressed and no one came to check on her or tuck her in. She wonders whether Amin slept; last night she heard him shouting, then crying. She feels sick. She already knows she can't continue the pretence. When she appears in the kitchen the atmosphere is freezing cold, despite the sunshine and the cheery cereals. Her brothers are all there. They eat and avoid her eyes. She looks at the clock and is stunned to see the time is after 11 a.m.; she has never slept so late before. Aisha is at the sink and doesn't look at her either.

Ben comes in from outside and as soon as she sees him she bursts into tears. She feels her face contract, her mouth open, her eyes scrunch up: she can't control it. Aisha and the boys let her cry, but Ben can't, he comes to her, pulls her body against his. His touch releases words: 'I'm sorry, it was me, I didn't mean to, I didn't mean to, I'm sorry, I'm sorry, it wasn't Amin, it was me.'

Her parents punish and forgive her: the pet that she had been promised for her next birthday is the sacrifice. She cries and mourns for it, her dearest wish, but not having the kitten also frees her from the worst feelings of guilt. Ben loves her still, Aisha loves her as she always did. But Amin. When he looked up at her across his bowl of Golden Grahams, as she cried in her father's arms, she saw a depth of betrayal she had never known. She apologises, more than once. She tells herself, even as the child she still is, that this is just a phase children go through. But part of her wonders if she broke something that day that can never be healed. She reads the knowledge of that betrayal into Mir's coolnesses, into the moments when all her brothers leave her out for shoot-'em-up console games or discussions of the weaponry pertaining to them. She thinks: they will always remember.

This is just the beginning: three rebellious years that strain her relationship with all her brothers and, more than anyone, Aisha. Ben is the only one who can pacify her, and then only sometimes. How she became so angry, so suddenly, is a question she often asks herself in quiet moments at the time, and wonders at once it fades. But even through the worst of it, she retains a secret code that she formed on the day she stole that car: she doesn't lie. The decision makes every contravention of a rule, every fight – about homework, or clothes, or where she's been – more painful, but it's a challenge she sets herself, a habit she doesn't break. Trying to shift blame to Amin acts as a fork in her private road. After it, she takes the path of lacerating truth, developing a deep and mostly unconscious horror of anyone who lies to her.

―⁓―

The show opens in exactly a week. The cherry trees are crazed with blossom, which began falling even as they bloomed. Roses walks to the Barbican through drifts of petals caught against the kerbs. Eddies of petals are snatched up and harried in tight circles by the wind. Roses is living now with the constant tick, tick, tick of adrenaline in her blood. Her dreams are vivid cartoons: a Technicolor shipwreck, a pageant in her honour, public nudity, her father interrupting the first night to shout obscenities at the stage.

Rehearsal has moved to The Pit itself. She jogs down the stairs, swings into the space, greets Stefan with a kiss on each cheek.

'You're in a good mood,' he says, deadpan, a neutral fact.

'It's happening. It's fucking *happening*, Stef.' She feels jumpy and hungry and alive. An edgy state, like electrodes tapping against one another inside.

'I've got a good feeling about today.'

'Shall we have a little chat about *Macbeth*, while you're tempting fate?'

Roses smiles. 'I don't believe in fate.'

The performers arrive, Evita last. They warm up, and begin. From the start there's something wrong. Roses watches restlessly: the pace is off, the chemistry between the performers has changed, soured somehow. Evita is loud and brittle, cracking jokes, dissolving into breathy giggles mid-sentence.

At the heart of the play is a love scene: Evita and Marco, a shy dark-haired actor with whom Roses has worked on three previous projects. Marco is kind and softly spoken off-stage but mesmerising on it, versatile, thoughtful, with the latent energy of a basking alligator. The scene's been a high point, but today every word and movement drops flat and false in dead air.

Evita is speaking: 'But as all separate souls contain Mixture of things—'

'Several,' Roses says.

Usually she doesn't interrupt, saving notes until the end of a scene, but Evita has made this mistake so many times that Roses snaps out the word without thinking.

'What?' Evita stops the scene.

'The word is several, not separate.'

'But it means separate, right?'

'It does, in this context, but still: the word is several.'

'So why can't I just say separate?'

'Can you just say several?'

Evita raises her eyebrows, says something under her breath, turning away. Marco, the thread of the scene lost, has put his hands behind his head and is staring miserably at the ceiling. And something in Roses can't let it go.

'What did you say, Evita?'

The young woman turns back to her, eyes first, then her head, then her body. She licks her lips, raises her chin.

'I said: for fucks' sake.'

'Ok. Great. Thanks for sharing. Can we do the scene again from the top please?'

'Whatever.'

'And can you please use the word several.'

'Fuck you.'

The room goes still. The performers have frozen, knowing this is a moment of reckoning. All the grating tension in the past month, all the pressure of the week to come. Roses' skill and patience versus Evita's green and dangerous power. Stefan steps forward, spreading his hands, palms down, placatory. His look to Roses is an admonishment: rise above this.

'Evita,' Roses says. 'Can we talk for a moment?'

Evita stays where she is, in the middle of the black-painted room. 'Talk to me here,' Evita says, 'If you want to bully me, you can do it here in front of everyone.'

'*Bully* you?' Roses feels sick, like the word is something dead and rotting, flung at her feet.

'Everyone can see what you're doing,' Evita says, her voice rising in pitch and volume. 'You're *victimising* me because I'm young, because you think you're better than me. You think you're so fucking clever. You've been a total bitch to me since day one. You don't know how lucky you are to have me in this shitty second-rate play.'

Roses' head is reeling. She knows this is delusional. She can be tough on performers; some respond well to it. But she's treated Evita gently for weeks. Just at the edge of her certainty, something snags. Is it possible she's wrong?

Roses swallows down a hard lump of pride. A week to go. A week till opening night.

'I'm really sorry you feel that way, Evita,' she says. 'I didn't mean to embarrass you. I was just frustrated that the scene didn't seem to be working as well as—'

Evita cuts her off. 'Don't blame me if the scene's not working. You always blame me, never him . . .' she points at Marco, whose head snaps up, shocked. 'Oh, no. He's Mr Perfect. Well, newsflash, maybe he isn't? Maybe the problem is that he can't act for shit and I can't pretend to fancy a nasty little pervert.'

Marco takes a step back, like Evita's gone up in flames. His eyes are wide. Frightened.

And Roses can't do it any more. Can't pussyfoot, can't mollycoddle, can't stand it.

She walks onto the stage and stops a stride away from Evita. She stands to her full height. Evita's arms are folded tight, her lips are white. Roses feels a grim strength flow through her, like a captain at the wheel while his ship sinks beneath him.

'Call your agent,' she says. 'You're fired. Get your things, put on your coat, and get out of my rehearsal room.'

It feels good. It feels like suicide.

Evita smiles, lips pressed hard together so the smile reads as not a smile at all. A different look has come into her eyes, which Roses can't interpret. Then she understands it: a satiated look, like a big cat fed an easy meal it didn't have to hunt.

'Good luck with the play,' Evita says, singsong. She puts her head on one side and tilts up her lovely eyes. 'I wonder if anyone will come?'

A minute later, she's gone. No goodbyes, phone to her ear, though Roses knows that's a performance; there's no reception here, underground. In the aftermath she calls a break and tries to speak to Marco, but he just shakes his head like he's bewildered.

'Later. . .' he says, and wanders away.

Roses feels a presence beside her: Penny, the oldest member of the company. The two of them watch as Marco leaves, jacket on and hood up, hunched in on himself.

'They were fucking, obviously,' Penny says, gravelly and quiet.

'*What?*' Roses loud-whispers, wheeling towards her.

'You didn't know?' Penny raises her eyebrows. 'I thought everyone knew.'

Roses shakes her head. She's beyond surprised. She thought Evita – who is in a highly public relationship with another up-and-coming TV star – disliked everyone in the company.

'But . . . since when?' she manages.

'Oh, a few weeks,' Penny says, offhand, a smile in her voice at Roses' amazement. 'I told him to be careful, that she wasn't serious about him. But . . .'

She shrugs, palms outward and fingers spread, a gesture that reads precisely as *try telling young people about love.*

'So what happened?' Roses is trying to refit her memories of the past weeks into this new reality.

'Oh, she ditched him,' Penny says, pulling on a yellow mac, gathering her long grey hair into a knot on the top of her head. 'Turned it on. Turned it off. And then, it seems, turned mean.'

'So all that stuff about not being able to fancy him . . .'

'Yes, twist of the knife.' Penny gives a little shiver, like she's tasted something sour. 'Not nice. Not nice at all.' She pats Roses on the arm, looks into her face. 'So, good riddance. Well done, etcetera. Total nightmare now, obviously. But we'll get there, I expect.' She smiles.

Roses smiles weakly. Her conviction is at a very low ebb. It is her job to remain convinced.

'Thanks, Pen.'

'Coffee?'

'Yeah, milk and two sugars. I think I'm in shock. And will you check on Marco?'

'Oh, don't worry about Marco. Solid as a rock, he's not going anywhere. And this?' She makes another gesture with both hands, fingers fluttering: something, the entire existence of Evita, flying away. 'It'll go.'

Once all the performers have left the room, Roses sits in the front row. She feels the absent audience at her back.

'*Macbeth*,' she says. '*Macbeth, Macbeth, Macbeth, Macbeth, Macbeth.*'

'What are you doing?' Since the scene with Evita, Stefan has been tapping quietly at his laptop.

'Seeing if I can make it any worse.'

Stefan moves to the seat beside her, laptop on his knees.

'Yeah yeah,' he says. 'It is very bad.'

'Less than a week of rehearsals . . .' Roses begins.

'People will be cancelling tickets,' Stefan continues, as if Roses hadn't thought of this already.

'Fuck.'

'Don't worry about that,' Stefan says, but when Roses starts to protest he clarifies: 'You don't worry. I worry about tickets. You think about performers.'

He shows her his screen, tabs lined up, each one a CV.

'All the women we saw,' he says. 'You know who you want?'

The pictures spark memories. Roses focuses, takes the laptop.

'Yes.' She clicks through the tabs. 'Her. Esi Dunbar. She was stunning.' She clicks some more. 'If not, second choice is this one. Then her.'

Stefan takes the laptop back. 'Ok. I'll start calling.'

'It'll be a miracle if Esi's free.'

'I need to call Evita's agent too.'

'Yeah. God. Sorry you have to deal with this. Is it going to be bad?'

'Probably.'

'Call Esi's first?' Stefan nods, gets up to go above ground.

'Did I bully her?' Roses says. Bleak.

Stefan barely stops, gives a snort of laughter.

'She wanted to be fired,' he says. He throws on a jacket.

'Really?'

'I make these calls, you direct, ok?' Stefan says. 'We talk after.' He's gone.

In the quiet, as Roses waits for the performers to return, she looks into herself: a room with shelves. A dark jar knocked to the floor, cracked and seeping.

She gets up, faces the blank seats, and starts in her mind to plan the afternoon's work.

At the end of the rehearsal, Roses gathers the performers, Stefan, two of the designers who have come in to observe, and the stage-manager. They sit in a circle on the scuffed black floor: it will be painted before they open in a terrifying six days.

'Thanks for all your hard work today,' Roses says. She's aware she has to show them a calm she doesn't feel, to contain the potential chaos. Then she thanks each person individually, picking out something they did well, until only Stefan is left. 'Lastly, thank you Stefan for being unshakeable,' she says. He raises his hand in a dismissive kind of wave.

Esi Dunbar's agent said she'd get back to them. Evita's picked offended and self-righteous as his stance of choice. They've had no firm answers to their enquiries, have heard a lot of *We'll let you know by tomorrow*s. There's not much they can do but wait. Nevertheless, after everyone leaves – the performers quiet but not in obvious despair, the mouse-like stage manager freaking out, the designers stoic – Roses and Stefan spend another hour researching other potential performers. Then they part.

James is away, these three days, at a conference. She wants to call him, wants so much to tell him what's happened, to ask for his support. He hates speaking on the phone. Whenever he's talked to her about his dream, to quit his job and travel for months in distant places, she's let herself become excited with him. She's encouraged and imagined, and tried to tamp down the knowledge that if he goes there'll be nothing: no calls, perhaps an email or two; then silence stretching away, presumably, into infinity.

Roses walks away from the theatre, unfocused and without a plan. She takes out her phone, checks messages, hoping, and trying not to expect, that there will be a message from James. To her delight, there is, though it's thin in terms of detail or affection: *Conference is massive and boring. Might have to go and jump in a loch. Hope rehearsals are going well.*

No question mark. No hint at missing her. No kiss. Roses hates that she wants one, that a digital 'x' could make her feel special.

Clare, on holiday in Istanbul, has sent beautiful pictures with captions, lots of questions, many kisses. Two voicemails from her mother, asking her to call. She puts the phone away and walks northeast, not directly home, realising with a kind of outsider's wonder that it's Saturday night, and the throngs in the streets are in the midst of relaxed weekends. She crosses from Liverpool Street to Spitalfields, heaving with people and music, then Brick Lane, which is even more packed. Curry-house waiters tout, the street seethes with 20-year-olds, and every pub has a smoking phalanx. Roses takes a side street. Checks her phone, and thinks of calling James again. Her mind needs occupation, communication. She wants to smoke; to drink herself into a state where she can rest.

★

In the first weeks after they met, James took her to a lake. They had stripped and run, hand in hand, into its margins, and then dived, gasping with cold. Soon they were suspended, looking down through water absolutely clear and almost lifeless into slow-moving forests of black weed. It was the deepest lake in England, and Roses had felt those depths, mineral and massive, below her, and been afraid. They came out onto the bank together, whooping and red-skinned. She towelled herself off and dressed fast, but he stood, naked and dripping like the figurehead from a ship, looking out over the surface. Then he walked back in. Wrapped up and hopping from foot to foot, she watched him push through the water until he could strike out and swim. No wind creased the surface of the lake, and metre after metre she could see the smooth working of his shoulders and arms, the regular turn of his head from side to side. This is what he was designed for, she thought as she watched. This is the expression of all the certainty of his youth: the boy who won every race, the teenager who got up every morning to train, to travel miles to competitions.

She knew the story: his competitive career ascended further each year of his teens, distracting him from school, distracting him from the tension at home. And then, when he was seventeen, it faltered. Just happens to some people, he said with a shrug. You think you're cut out for greatness, but it turns out you're not. He was no longer the best. One shoulder began causing him pain; then his hips, his wrists. By nineteen he had finished one career and had to look about him for another. He was lucky: he was clever. His mother's only wish was that he try for medicine. James never talked about what he'd wanted, back then.

As Roses watched him swim the lake, she thought: this is what he is capable of. This directness, this level of quiet and precise action. The beauty of his swim took her breath away. She cheered when he finally emerged, ran into the shallows to kiss him. But, unable to express the awe, or the way it made her just-forming feelings for him more serious and less exuberant, she was quiet for the rest of the day. He dressed. They gathered wood and made a fire and cooked over it. They drank whiskey. They made love and fell asleep with rain falling on the tent's nylon shell. When she thinks about what James could do, she thinks about that moment. She wants a life for him that is as clear and as unswerving as the line he traced across the water towards the distant mountains.

Roses has hit Bethnal Green Road, leaving most of the bars and the money behind. No one is out walking here just for the pleasure of seeing, or being seen. She passes off-licences and betting shops, a taxi-company-come-social-club, places promising to unlock your phone, send money to your family half a world away. The jagged rip in the company left by Evita smarts and snarls. Roses tries to imagine Clare roaming the hot nights of Istanbul. James in Edinburgh, where it's always, in Roses' experience, raining. Thinks of the last time they were together in this part of London; that dinner which dissolved into a tangle of limbs. She takes out her phone and scrolls to *Cillian*.

Chapter Eleven

A great lake of blue carpet soaks up sound. There could be four hundred people at the conference, James guesses, but they make little impact on the huge space. He wonders if these places are designed to make people feel small.

James has a cup of coffee in his hands that was served just above room temperature. He's lost count of how many cups he's drunk, or mislaid, or abandoned if they were particularly sour and wretched. Another round of food has been produced to boost morale as the afternoon wanes. Young people who are probably actors or artists work the room with the inevitable pieces of slate. On some slates are blinis topped with smoked salmon, on others small towers of shortbread, whipped cream, strawberries. James has eaten many of each, alternating between fish and biscuit depending on which came his way. He checks his watch to see whether it could possibly be time to leave, but it's only 4.45 p.m. Though he's standing up, the possibility of falling asleep feels real. He closes his eyes.

He's greeted with a powerful flashback.

When James recalls sex it is always in fragments. He can't play an evening back from start to finish like a film on repeat, not even substantial sections of it. There are only images, and sometimes other sensory memories: a taste; the sharp out-in of a gasp. The image he sees now is soundless and comes from the night he and Roses spent with the other couple. He's seen it in his mind before, but each time it has power and each time it surprises him. It's an image of Cillian, naked and aroused, placing both hands on Hura's waist and pulling her towards him. There, the moving image ends, and James's mind spins for a moment in black space, before collecting itself in time for the image to repeat. He sees details: the tattoos on Cillian's arms and torso, a lock of hair falling across one eye; the way Hura's lips parted; the rapt expressions on their faces. But around it there is nothing, just a thick warm darkness like a moonless summer night.

'James ...' His eyes snap open. Emma, the consultant who arranged for him to come to this conference, and another woman, are standing in front of him.

'James, I'd like to introduce you to Meghan O'Connor, whose work I mentioned to you before.'

Emma says it as if she's noticed nothing of his distraction. James goes into mental paroxysms designed to erase any sexual signals from his face and make it entirely professional and alert. Emma offers a précis of the woman's work. James formulates a relevant question. They talk for several minutes, during which the image of Cillian disappears from his consciousness. Emma stays close and draws him into another conversation after the one with Ms O'Connor, and the next time he checks his watch it's 6 p.m.

'Dinner tonight?' Emma asks as they gather coats and bags from the cloakroom.

'I can't, thanks,' James says. 'Gotta make a call.'

It's difficult to find excuses not to spend more time with Emma. They're both away from their partners and he can't blame work, since they're also far from the hospital. He wants to be on his own, but also intuits that spending time alone with Emma, especially in the evening, is a bad idea. There's a mismatch in the level of intimacy they want. Emma has a husband, children, but he senses that she likes his physical presence more than is usual or even appropriate between colleagues. He hasn't told her yet that he's planning to leave his job; the booked flight whispers every time she alludes to future work.

James goes back to his hotel room, takes off the suit that makes him feel like a travelling salesman, pulls on a hooded sweatshirt, jeans, trainers. He sits on the bed with his phone in his hand, thinks about calling Roses, doesn't. She hasn't texted in the twenty-four hours since he left on the Edinburgh train. He starts a message in which he tries to explain the experience of turning a decorous, bland face outward while, inside, losing himself to memories of that night at Cillian and Hura's flat. He can't find the right words, and the text becomes unwieldy. He deletes it in favour of something short about jumping into a loch. He thinks about the time they went to Wastwater, and wonders if she remembers.

He puts in earphones and starts playing music from his phone. If he does run into Emma, he'll pretend to be on a hands-free call. The planned deception feels a little pathetic, but he ploughs on with it, pulling up his hood and striding fast down the hotel corridor, then the stairs, and out into the Grassmarket.

The evening weather is noticeably colder and wetter than down south. It doesn't bother him. Born in Newcastle, James rarely wears a jacket in spring, or a coat in winter. Cold and rain seem to him neutral, neither pleasant nor unpleasant; he finds extreme heat harder to bear. His hunger, usually straightforward and, by this point in the day, rampant, is confused by the hours of coffee and grazing. He feels puffed-up and foggy, an overfed fish in a lukewarm tank. He really would like to swim, but settles for a long, wet ramble, which does the job of tiring his body enough for him to stop. Finally, he finds himself gazing at every fast-food sign and sandwich shop and salivating. He ducks into a low-key Italian place with wood-and-wicker chairs and checked tablecloths. Still cocooned in music, he orders pasta and salad and red wine, then works his way through a basket of bread before the food arrives. The wine, the lulling beats and the warmth after dark streets wrap him in a velvety softness.

Now he lets the flashbacks come more gently. There is the back-lit tableau of Cillian and Hura. There is an image of Roses, head back and eyes closed, touched by other hands than his. He enjoyed seeing her like this with new people, was turned on by seeing her turned on by them. Their eyes meeting as these other bodies moved around them felt like the complicity of jewel thieves, or the mutual understanding of tightrope walkers. He wonders about his lack of jealousy. It feels to him like their togetherness negates that worry: if he is there, what is there to be jealous of? But then: could it be because he doesn't care enough what she does?

James's pasta arrives. It's badly cooked but he's too hungry to care, piling it instead with parmesan and salt. The salad is tiny, and he finishes it in two mouthfuls. His phone is on the table and he glances at it periodically, seeing no messages from Roses arrive. Once he's finished the pasta and mopped up the last of the sauce with the last of the bread, he pulls up the confirmation email for his flights. Heathrow to Buenos Aires. A seat number. A date. He's done this periodically since booking it, testing his reaction each time. Is this sensation, which feels like terror, actually excitement? Is there a difference? He has at least got used to looking at the words; they no longer flip his stomach quite so hard. It's still months away. He closes the email, and his eyes. The meal has left him with a sense of simple satisfaction that he's glad to savour while it lasts.

Another question, vague and hard to concentrate on, is skirting the edges of his mind. It has to do with that image: Cillian, the tattoos, Hura with her sweep of hair. What does it mean to him, what button did it press? He lets the image come, and holds it still in his mind. The moment didn't involve him. It was simple lust between two other people who knew each other well. It was sexy and romantic. He imagines himself as Cillian, about to make love to his wife. He imagines himself as Hura, feeling her husband's hands on her hips. He finishes his glass of wine, holding the liquid on his tongue before swallowing. The music in his earphones reaches a climax and then one chord hangs on and on, filling his mind with its pulsing.

Once he leaves the restaurant, a new phase of the night starts; one he's been dreading. It's late enough to go to bed, especially with an early conference start. If he does, though, he's fairly sure not to sleep. The hotel room, with its thick drapery and air-conditioning, feels claustrophobic, and he'd rather not be there if Emma should happen to wander down the hall and knock. Drinking alone feels unsavoury. He starts walking again. The sky is a deep inky blue, the streetlights pick out droplets in the heavy mist. Edinburgh's big sandstone buildings are handsome and closed, uncles in a sepia photograph.

So here I am again, James thinks. The pavements of a northern city at night. The smell of the stone tells him he is close to home. The precise temperature, the very feel of the place's air, is different from London – a taste more of the wild, of mountains and sea. His younger self walks close by his side when he walks like this. If Edinburgh had a principal river, he knows, he would go to it. Instead, even though his legs are beginning to tire and the weather's worsening, he heads towards the place that calls him: to Arthur's Seat.

Loneliness, which had loomed large when he imagined the carpeted and curtained Novotel, now takes on a different character – smaller, companionable, familiar.

The mist becomes rain. James walks. Pavement eventually gives way to a rougher path, and the shape of the Seat stacks above him. Before he begins the last part of the climb, James stops and takes out his phone. He turns it off so that it ceases being a conduit to the world elsewhere, and puts it in the driest pocket he can find. Then he sets off up the hill.

Gaining the top he sees the city below him as a pattern of light. The wind buffets him and the rain drives harder. James remembers a waterfall that he and Gull had found; one of their secret places. It was the summer before Gull died. The weight of water as they stood under it.

James takes off his hoodie, lets the rain, heavier still, beat against his skin. He stretches out both arms like a diver, raises his face to the sky. Roses' clavicle; Hura's hair; Cillian's chest tattooed as if his skin were a message to decode. James folds in on himself, and one hand seeks the back of his shoulder where he can feel a faintly raised edge. A date. A moment in time marked and gone.

★

Cillian buys each of them a second pint – Roses insisted on getting their first – and heads back to the table. Hura's away with Casimir visiting her parents, and he had been on his way home to an empty flat when Roses' text arrived, unexpected and brief: *Walking nearby, are you two around for a drink?*

Cillian likes company. He finds out what he thinks by talking, and also enjoys the companionable silence simply of being in the same space as another person. Hura, who loves to be alone – or, at least, alone with Casimir – finds this frustrating. One way they have discovered to keep their marriage working is to schedule regular times when they don't see each other: her walks in the woods, his runs in the park, or nights playing games with Dan at his flat nearby. More recently, dates. The two nights she's gone to spend with her parents are as much for space as they are for so-cialising. Her mother and father have busy lives. She will see them for dinner, for breakfast perhaps, but the rest of the time she'll be alone with her thoughts and plans in their beautiful garden and restrained, peaceful house.

As Cillian makes his way back to the table, he is able to ob-serve Roses for a moment before she sees him. She's looking at her phone, her hair falling across her cheek and hiding her eyes but leaving her mouth visible. Absorbed in thought, she chews her lower lip. He's pleased she texted, pleased she still wanted to meet, even though Hura's away. He didn't think she liked him much. There was that moment, with the four of them, when he had found himself biting her and she'd bitten him back, and they'd both felt the power of it and pulled back. But whether or not that was a real connection, he isn't sure. There should probably be no more drinks after this one, he thinks. Then he's at the table and puts the glasses down and she looks up at him, frowning.

'Everything ok?' he asks.

'Kind of,' she says. 'Thanks.' She sips the drink.

They had started out chatting about Eden, then other club nights that he's only heard about but she, it turns out, has been to. He's been asking, he hopes not too avidly, about her history with this kind of relationship: how has it turned out, in the past? In the last few weeks Cillian has begun experimentally arranging meetings with new people, and is finding the process fascinating. His friends in relationships have a fairly low tolerance for talking about the nuances of his and Hura's arrangement, and his single friends don't quite get it, so he's found himself jumping on the chance to discuss the new dynamics with someone who understands.

But now Roses changes the subject. Tearing a beermat carefully to shreds, she begins to tell him about the play. It takes him a while to grasp the severity of the situation.

'So you don't have anyone to play that part?' he clarifies.

'Nope.'

'And the play opens on ...'

'Saturday.' She says it precisely. The tabletop is now covered in mauled bits of beermat.

'That's terrible!'

Her head clicks up, eyes a hard bright blue.

'I'd noticed.'

'What are you going to do?'

'Get someone else. Someone brilliant.' Roses clenches her jaw. 'Know anyone?'

'Anyone as famous and fit as Evita McNeish? I wish.'

Roses shoots him a look, eyes half closed in disdain. Cillian kicks himself; he doesn't, in fact, really understand the hype about Evita McNeish. Still, while Cillian is enjoying spending time with Roses, something lofty in her manner keeps tempting him to tease her.

'Play the part yourself,' he says.

Her eyebrows go up. 'Oh, because I'm so famous and fit?'

'You're fit,' he says.

A quarter of a second while they look at each other. She looks away.

'No way,' she says. 'I'm not insane. You can't direct and perform. People always try and mostly it's terrible. Besides, I'm not ...' she stops.

'Not what?'

She shakes her head, doesn't want to share whatever complex pride, or insecurity, or both, she's feeling.

'Why did she leave again?'

Roses' frown deepens.

'She said I bullied her,' she says, her voice small. 'I don't think I did. I . . . she was difficult, I tried really hard to be fair, kind even. I thought I was being. But maybe something, I somehow . . .' she trails off.

Cillian resists the urge to offer empty reassurance. What does he know about her, really?

'I was in all the plays at school,' Roses says. 'All the main parts. I was "that girl", you know? Juliet, Lady Macbeth, Blanche DuBois, blah blah blah. My mum always came, usually more than once.'

Roses switches into a perfect French accent: 'Cherie, you look so *beautiful* up there, but the costumes are *terrible*, no?' Resumes in her normal voice. 'My dad never came, didn't "get" theatre, work was busy, etc. Then once he did come. *Who's Afraid of Virginia Woolf?* It's American, I told him, you'll like it. He'd moved back to Texas by then; he was only over for a week or two. Start of the second half, I looked out at the audience and his seat's empty. Those things were always packed, so this one empty seat was really obvious, you know? Like a missing tooth. I saw him in the bar afterwards – which was the canteen – two beers in. He didn't say he'd left. I didn't say I knew.'

She drinks from her glass, picks up a piece of flayed card between her finger and thumb. Laughs shortly.

'He wasn't a bad father. Not *bad* bad. He'd just rather drink warm Stella in a school dining hall than sit through another half-hour of me.'

She tries to tear a very small piece of card. Cillian takes the mat out from under his glass and offers it to her. She laughs, tired, perhaps relieved, and takes it.

'What's your dad like?' she asks.

'I last saw him when I was six,' Cillian says. Roses looks up at him. 'So there are two things I know. I know he left and never came back. And I know he had a lovely beard.'

He grins.

Roses tears the beermat down the middle, and gives him half back.

And then, in the warm seconds when neither of them speaks, Cillian feels her focus shift away to a place behind him, and her face falters, eyes wide. He turns to look.

There is a man standing in front of their table holding a pint of beer. He's about their age, not tall, and has a tattoo on one side of his head showing through the short brown hair. He looks furious: his face is pale but with high colour in the cheeks, his skin looks stretched over the bones. Cillian wonders if somehow he offended the man; were they at the bar together, did he push in front? But then the man speaks.

'You're Roses Green.'

'Yes.'

Cillian turns to look at her. She seems stricken, deeply embarrassed. Could this be an ex, he wonders, but then why would he check her name? His whirring mind fills in the blanks: perhaps she was meant to have a date with this guy, then changed her mind and invited Cillian instead.

'You don't remember me.'

The man with the tattoo isn't speaking loudly, but his voice is tight with emotion. It almost seems like he might burst into tears. Roses shakes her head.

'No, no. I do. It's just—'

The man doesn't let her finish; in fact he holds up a hand to silence her. She drops her gaze into her lap.

'You don't have to say anything,' he says.

Then his face cracks and he does, indeed, burst into tears.

'But I promised myself that if I ever saw you again I'd do this.'

Roses looks up at him again. The man gives one sob, and then he throws his entire pint of beer into Roses' face.

A group of people at another table, who Cillian hadn't noticed before but are obviously the man's friends, burst into cheering encouragement. Roses has leapt to her feet, Cillian stands too. The dark-haired man has tears running down his face, but now his crisis seems to have passed and he's almost smiling. He puts the empty glass carefully down on their table, pushing sodden pieces of cardboard out of the way.

'Roses Green,' he says quietly. 'Fuck you, Roses Green.'

He picks up Roses' own pint and throws that over her too. His friends cheer wildly, and now the whole pub has realised what is happening. All the clientele with a good view are watching in round-eyed eagerness. The bar staff have just noticed that something is kicking off, and are approaching.

Roses gasps as the liquid hits her for the second time, but to Cillian's surprise she doesn't try to protect herself, to retaliate, or even to move. She puts her hands over her eyes, wiping away the cold bitter liquid. Her black hair is plastered to her face, mascara streaked down her cheeks. The bar staff are just getting to the table when the stranger, almost laughing now, moves to pick up Cillian's drink. Cillian puts out a hand to steady it, which only succeeds in knocking it over, glass smashing on the floor. The stranger takes a step back and puts his hands in the air like a cornered bank robber.

'I'm sorry about the mess,' he says to the bar keeper. 'I'll pay for the breakages. I'll pay for the cleaning. I made myself a promise. You don't know what she did to me.'

He turns and walks out. His friends down their drinks and follow him, loud with support.

She's surprised by the cold; she's soaking wet. Her shirt is stiff with liquid and clings to her chest and stomach. Even her pants are wet with beer that's soaked through her thin trousers. Her hair is matted, and everything is sticky. She scans the street and starts to walk.

'You left your jacket,' Cillian says as he catches up with her.

'Oh.' She takes it but doesn't think to put it on. She's spotted the group ahead and speeds up in an effort to catch them.

'Where are you . . .' Cillian starts, then he sees them too. 'Ah. Is this a good idea?'

She doesn't have an answer. She's following an impulse and starts to run. The man and his friends are at the park gates when she catches up with them.

'Hey,' Roses calls.

Four heads turn, four pairs of eyes stare at her with absolute disgust. The man folds his arms across his chest, tilts his chin up, squares his feet.

'Yes?'

'Hi. Hey. I just thought, maybe – can we talk?'

'I have nothing to say to you.'

They turn to leave. Roses springs forward:

'Please. Wait. Just . . . one minute.'

The man stops again, friends close and defensive as an angry chorus.

'Ok then,' he says, turning to face her. 'Go.'

Now Roses folds her arms, conscious of her bedraggled state and the chill wind that's risen more since it chased the cherry blossom.

'Could we – I don't know. Go somewhere, sit down, have a drink?' she says haltingly.

'You haven't had enough drinks?'

She shakes her head, unsure how to proceed. The woody smell of hops is in her nose, the bittersweet taste on her lips.

'If you have anything to say you can say it to me here,' he adds.

She takes a breath.

'Ok. I know you must be angry about what happened. When we were at school. What we – the way I treated you.'

His jaw is clenched, eyes like hot coals fixed on hers. She forces herself to keep talking.

'More than angry. I was . . . awful. I made your life hell. I know I did. There was something wrong with me. I was so angry after my parents split up and I—'

'Don't you dare make excuses,' the man interrupts her. 'Don't you stand there and expect me to listen to how you couldn't help yourself because you were *just so unhappy.*'

'Of course, no, I'm sorry. What is your name, now? I mean, what's your name?'

He doesn't answer. Roses hugs her arms around her for warmth, for comfort. She wishes Cillian would go away, stop seeing this. She wishes James was with her, believing in her capacity for kindness, and at the same time is glad he's not witnessing it. The thought of him gives her a tiny hit of strength. She shivers; lets the knowledge of her culpability soak into her. She has, over the years, imagined this moment many times, though it was never anything like this. She has thought about the heartfelt apology she would make, the reconciliation that might result.

'What I did is unforgivable. I don't expect you to forgive me. But I promise, I've thought about it hard, I've had therapy—'

'Give me strength,' he mutters.

'. . . and I've even hoped I'd see you again so that I could say all of this. I was young, I was in pain, and I lashed out. That's not an excuse. But I've changed. Really, I have. I'd never, ever do that to another person again. Because I realised – after that summer I realised what I was doing. I terrified myself. I changed. Please tell me your name.'

She holds out her hands, not knowing exactly what it is she wants. A hug?

He turns his face to the side, and she's struck again by the familiar profile. She looks down at his feet in black trainers, then up at his jeans and shirt, buttoned to the top with the sleeves rolled up.

His arms are scarred with small cuts, healed but visible. She looks back up to his face, knowing his eyes are on her.

Roses swallows hard, sick with herself and with an overwhelming grief, for ruined childhood, and the children they were. When she played out this moment it never hurt so much. It had left her feeling relieved, to enact it in her mind. But there's no relief here.

It's ending. One friend has brought the man's jacket, like Cillian brought Roses', and holds it for him to shrug on. The others gather round, with protective arms and murmured words that Roses can't hear, that shut her out. It seems they're all about to leave without another word, but then he straightens, runs a hand over the tattooed side of his head, turns back to her, looks her in the eye.

'Try to be a good person,' he says. Then they're gone.

★

Cillian's flat is close and Roses needs a refuge. When they get through the door he points out the bathroom and she disappears into it without looking at him. He finds a towel and some of his own clothes: Hura's would be too small and it feels wrong to offer them. He tells her through the closed door that he's leaving the clothes for her outside it. He goes to the kitchen and calls Hura, but she doesn't pick up.

He's reading when Roses comes to stand in the doorway. She leans against the frame without speaking.

'I made you a sandwich,' he says.

Roses puts her hands in her pockets. 'Thanks.'

She's washed her hair and combed it straight back, flat against her head. She's removed all traces of make-up. Her face in the bright light has a scraped look.

She moves towards the chair opposite but doesn't sit. Stares down at the sandwich like it might attack her.

'They fit you,' he comments.

His jeans are the right length and hug her hips, his T-shirt drapes her contours differently to his but doesn't swamp her. There's a silence.

'I'm sorry you saw that,' she says.

'Don't worry about it.' She looks miserable. 'Who was he?'

She shakes her head like it's too much to explain. 'What's the time?'

'Almost ten.'

'Aren't you hungry?' she asks the sandwich.

'I already ate one. I was ravenous,' Cillian replies.

'I should go.'

When she doesn't, he turns on the kettle and starts to make her a cup of tea, hears her sit down at the table behind him. He hands her the cup and she takes a sip.

'I was bad at school,' she says then. 'Not like in films, not hanging out with the wrong crowd and getting mixed up in drugs or anything. I hung out with the *right* crowd. I was queen of the right crowd.' She's quiet for a moment and Cillian, thinking about Hura's recent experience, says nothing. 'I went to this exclusive girls' boarding school. Bourne High. It was like the Serengeti plains. There were the antelopes, the jackals. Everyone wanted to be a lion. And if you were, you spent your time lazing around – smoking by the rounders pitch – and every now and then you'd get up, stretch, and go hunting.'

She sits up straighter, looks at the ceiling. 'God, the things we did to each other.'

'Like what?'

'I can't tell you. It's . . . I was . . . I feel ashamed.'

She looks down into her tea.

'And that was . . . one of your victims?'

'She, *he*, got the worst of it. I . . .' Roses stops.

'Did you know, that now . . .?' He casts about for the right terminology.

She shakes her head again.

'I don't keep in touch with anyone from school. They were poison. Or maybe they were nice girls, and I was the poison. I've thought about – him, though. More, as time has passed. I keep thinking about the things we – *I* – did, and trying to work out how I could have behaved like that. Was it me? Was I me, then? Is that capacity for cruelty still in me somewhere?'

'So that whole thing with Evita and the bullying . . .?'

She nods, without looking at him.

'We used to surround people in the corridor and strip them. You'd have maybe ten people, they'd come from different directions. Suddenly you'd descend, pull off all of some poor girl's clothes, leave her there. Completely naked. She'd have to find her way back to her room without getting seen. We thought it was hilarious.'

She looks up at him. 'It's not funny.'

'No, no. I'm . . . Maybe I'm just smiling in surprise or something. I mean, I thought I had it rough going to school in Hackney, being the little blond kid who liked dancing instead of football.'

'You had it easy, trust me.'

'As easy as you?'

'No. No. It was eat or be eaten, so I just ripped everyone to shreds. We were so fucking repressed. About everything, but sex in particular. Like, we were *fascinated* by it, obviously, but also horrified. We teased people for having breasts, for not having them; for having periods, as though we weren't all going through it. Being "a lesbian" was, like, the worst crime we could think of. And, I mean, now look at me. It was all so fucking pointless.'

She closes her eyes, puts her hands against her cheeks.

Very quietly she says, 'Did you see his arms?'

Cillian saw. They're silent for a long minute.

Roses is very pale. 'When did you last eat?' he asks her.

'I don't know. It's been such a weird day.'

Gently he pushes the plate towards her.

'Come on, Tiger,' he says. Her smile is fleeting and sad.

He watches her demolish the sandwich. When she's finished, he gets out some packets of cereal and milk. They carry bowls of cornflakes over to the sofa and she curls up to eat hers, and gradually they start to talk about other things. Eventually they come back to the night they all spent there. With her knees pulled up and wearing his clothes, Roses looks like a tired teenager. She lets her angular body collapse out of the adult shape in which she normally holds it. Both of them slide down the sofa to rest their heads on the back, their feet on the coffee table. It's nearing midnight on a Saturday and they both feel sober and, now, strangely wide awake.

'Would Hura mind that I'm here?' Roses asks.

'I don't think so. I tried calling her. I'll tell her, obviously.'

'How have things been, between you two, since that night?' she asks.

'They've been better than ever.' He smiles a slow, almost private smile, eyes resting somewhere across the room; it's true.

'It's been really hot with James, too,' she says. Also true; except when he disappears.

'Will you tell him, about what happened tonight – with the person from school?' Cillian asks.

'No. I don't know. I think he thinks I'm a nice girl,' she says.

He turns to look at her and she turns her face towards him and their faces are very close. They move at the same moment to kiss.

Cillian had texted Hura, after trying to call, asking how her day with her parents had been. But he hadn't mentioned the drink with Roses, or the fact she was in the flat; had thought it would be better to tell her on the phone. Now he wishes he had; it would make what is happening simpler. His accountability to his wife, who would certainly ask what had happened between them, would imbue the acts themselves. But he didn't tell her.

The kiss is much slower than the first time. Like that time, they keep their eyes open. Their bodies are still relaxed, noncommittal. At every moment, it seems, the kiss is about to end. Then Roses lifts a hand and slides it up his arm and grips the bicep.

They move to touch more completely. Together they pull the borrowed T-shirt over her head; he didn't have a bra to lend her. She slides her hand up his stomach, and then his shirt is off too. Their skins meet along the length of torso and arm; hers is pale and cool, almost cold. Her limbs are long and strong, there is a faint saline taste to her skin and her mouth. Sudden and swooping, a sensation comes over him of wanting to consume her entirely and to be consumed in turn.

Roses wants him to bite her again, wants it almost more than she can bear. Ever since they got back here, since she stood naked and burning with shame in his shower and then dressed in his jeans, she's been finding his presence more and more bewitching. Maybe she wants him to distract her; maybe to punish her. Everything about him in the last hour, from the way he ate cereal to the way he ran his fingers through his hair to the tarnished-gold hair itself, has transfixed her. Now he's here under her hands and he's hard, and they are breathless, and there is nothing at all keeping them apart except for a couple of layers of denim and cotton.

'Shit, what are we doing?' he says, sitting up, away from her. She sits up too. They have been together before, here on this sofa, but their partners were there and it was agreed. This is something different and they both know it.

She's breathing hard, not looking at him, so her ruffled hair hides her expression. Roses hasn't checked her phone since she emerged from the bathroom. He knows because he planned to check his when she did. Did he forget, even for a moment, that he was married?

She turns and looks him in the face, a long look, her desire for him made plain; they are close, still, to the brink. They kiss again, hard this time and fast, like convicts, a kiss before parting. She has her arms around his neck and his hands find her breast, her waist, the place between her shoulder blades.

'Ok. We need to stop,' he says. He thinks he can taste blood, a lip cut on a tooth, or a lip bitten, or just the taste of her, or of them, of the dangerous moment.

'Yes,' she says.

He is the married one. He forces himself to touch, with his left thumb, the inside of the band on his ring finger. Thinks: so that's what it's for. He stands. He hands her the T-shirt he lent her and picks up his own.

'Keep the clothes as long as you need.'

She puts them on, and now they're business-like, dusting over the desire with a fine layer of practicality. They discuss cabs, they talk again about their partners, she thanks him for the food and shelter. She turns at the flat door to say goodbye. For half a second she thinks they might kiss again. But no, his glance has lost its complicity. She smiles too brightly and goes, surprised to find herself hurt by that lack of a final, closing moment to their intimacy.

In the taxi home she sinks back into the seat and looks at the passing lights. The blood buzzes in her thighs and hands. Her breath catches at the memory of how much she wanted something she has, technically, already had. The distance opening up between them is good, she tells herself. She needs to talk to James about tonight. She needs to not want it to happen again.

Chapter Twelve

Waking that morning, Hura is aware of light and silence. Her own bedroom is dim at this time but here, in the guest room at her parents' house, early light filtering through the white curtains promises a bright day. Air from an open window, wet with cut grass, is cool on her exposed arm. She turns and burrows under the covers for one more moment alone in a bed with fresh sheets and trees outside.

There was a dream. Some trespass committed by or against her. Her mind feels for its shape, large and amorphous and coloured a purple-black.

She was with Casimir in a landscape of canyons, rock walls looming and glowing as if struck by evening sun. She thought, I am in the desert and night is coming, and then it will be very cold. She didn't feel the cold yet, but she knew it would be mortal. There was someone else with her. Was it Cillian? No, she remembers now. It was James, and they were walking hand-in-hand. These canyons were made by rivers, he said, but the rivers dried up long ago. Then he put his arms around her and kissed her and as he did so she knew, without any doubt, that they would make love and stay too long, and lose themselves in the desert in the dark.

The feeling left by the dream is clouded and confusing. Perhaps James represented Cillian, she thinks, and the desert stood for the unknown future. Whatever it meant, it was unquestionably erotic. She strokes her hands down her body under the bedclothes, touching her own bare skin, thinking of Roses' hands. She slides both palms between her thighs and lies with her weight on them.

Rocking back and forth she thinks of the deep kiss, the purple mountains, the sense of wonder and transgression. She comes.

Later, showered and dressed, she walks downstairs barefoot to find Casimir in his own guest bed in the flagged kitchen. He tries to leap up with delight on seeing her, but he's less spry than he used to be and the leap has several stages. She strokes and feeds him, and checks the fridge. She's eating parathas and working on her laptop when tyres crunch over gravel outside. Hura's mother, Aisha, comes into the kitchen wearing sunglasses, vermillion scarf around her neck, carrying flowers, a shopping bag, a pile of news-papers and a takeaway coffee cup.

'I thought you were working today,' Hura says as she gets up to greet her mother.

'I am, but later. There's an evening clinic until nine.'

'Where did you go?' Hura pulls the papers towards her to read the headlines.

'Just into town, pick up a couple of things. I always wake early, you know.'

Aisha is a small and massively energetic woman with still-black hair cut short and neat, and very large black eyes. She finishes her coffee and throws the cup away.

'You know those cups are terrible,' Hura says.

'Ah, but it's such good coffee.' Aisha is unpacking the shopping, taking the cut flowers out of their cellophane and snipping the ends off the stalks. 'Also, I like them in that place, and I want to support a local small business. Right?'

Eyebrows arched, she glances at Hura, who concedes the argu-ment. Hura looks back at her laptop screen, the job advertisement she's been reading with a tight feeling of promise in her chest. It could be what she's looking for, the next step. A first, small step, but exciting. She wants to tell Aisha about it, and at the same time some contrary, teenage part of herself can't bring it up.

'How's Julia?' she asks instead, naming her mother's best friend and close neighbour: the roofs of Julia and Alan's house are visible now, through the kitchen windows.

'Ah, she is very good,' Aisha says. On some phrases, like this one, her accent is noticeable, at other times she sounds austerely English. 'You know Bella had a little girl?'

Hura had forgotten, though of course she did know about this latest grandchild.

'Yes, how old is she now?'

'Almost six months old now. So sweet. She's eating food and sleeping, my god. She sleeps through the nights! I have a picture.'

Aisha has her mobile phone in her hand and is scrolling through images. Hura mentally rolls her eyes, but who can refuse to see a picture of a baby? She looks: 'Very sweet.'

There is a small silence during which Aisha, putting away the last groceries, refrains from mentioning Hura's own fertility, and they both know she is refraining.

Hura, now annoyed and resistant to talking at all, summons her will and changes the subject.

'Mum, there's a job I'm thinking of applying for. I just found it, but the closing date is really soon.'

Aisha turns, bright-eyed and absolutely concentrated.

'A job in teaching?'

'No. Something else. I've been thinking about it for a while.' Hura takes a deep breath. 'It's at Westminster.'

'At *Westminster?*' Aisha says the word as if it were the name of a small Pacific island she was learning about for the first time. 'Doing what exactly?'

'Well, exactly, working at the department of energy.'

'What's the job title.'

'Researcher.' It is in fact Junior Researcher, but something makes Hura omit the first word.

'And this relates to your qualifications how?'

'Mum . . .'

'What?'

'You're not the one interviewing me.'

'I'm sorry, I'm trying to be helpful.'

Hura pauses, steadies herself against the frustration her mother so easily generates in her.

'Ok. So, first, I have a geography degree; that's a relevant subject.

Second, I have a deep and longstanding interest in climate change and the policy surrounding it, which includes energy. Third, I'm bright and good at research.'

'For so long I've been telling you you're wasted as a teacher.'

'Yes, I know you think that.'

'Can I?'

Before Hura has a chance to avert it, Aisha has stepped round to read her screen. Hura puts her hands in her back pockets. She sees the moment Aisha takes in the 'Junior' in the title and doesn't mention it. She sees her mother sit, and scan through the job description. Then Aisha leans back.

'This would be with a view to ...'

'A career in politics. Eventually. A chance to have an impact.'

Aisha narrows her eyes and nods, thinking. And again Hura is struck by her mother's complicated desires. She wants Hura to have a career. She wants Hura to have children. She probably wishes her daughter had married a different man, but, having accepted Cillian, she wants the marriage to blossom. For her that means money, kids, stability, a place in the world. Anything which makes that more precarious is to be treated with scepticism.

'A career change at this stage is no light thing,' she says.

'I know that.'

'And if you do it, a professional qualification is never a misstep.'

'Mum.'

'What?'

'Not this again.'

'What?'

'The "gentle" suggestion that I become a doctor.'

'I didn't say—'

'Like you. Or a lawyer, like Dad.'

There is a pause.

Aisha closes and rubs her eyes. For a moment she looks older, and tired.

'Hura, I don't know if you want my opinion or not.'

'Of course I want it,' Hura says, 'Just ...'

'So long as it aligns with your own,' Aisha finishes for her.

'No! Look . . .' Hura shuts the laptop, keeps her hands on it as she tries to explain.

'I want to make a difference. If I do have kids I want them to grow up in a world that isn't being destroyed one coffee cup at a time.'

Aisha exhales through her nose.

'Sorry,' Hura says, frustrated with herself; as if she's never used a takeaway cup. Her arguments with Aisha always bring out the worst side of her. 'I don't mean you're the problem.'

'Just part of it.'

'Teaching isn't working any more. Maybe you were right all along! But you have enough doctors to follow in your footsteps.'

Mir is a consultant now, Amin a surgeon. Aisha nods once, to the side, not conceding.

'And you have grandchildren.'

Aisha's large eyes flash. 'I have only one daughter,' she says.

'And I'm asking you to *listen* to me. Do I want children? Probably. Do I want them *instead* of doing something else with my life? I'm not sure.'

This fight is ridiculous, Hura thinks. In reality she is getting more and more certain every day that she wants children. But that doesn't answer the question of how to also find fulfilment.

'You think you have all the time in the world,' Aisha snaps.

Hura takes a breath to state, once again, that she's fully aware of the limits of biology. But something stops her. 'What is it? Mum?'

Aisha gets up and goes to the sink, fills a vase and starts stabbing flowers into it.

'I didn't want to tell you yet,' she says. Her voice isn't hard now. It's quiet and there's a faint tremor in it.

'What? Mum, what?'

'It's about Dad.'

'Oh god, what?'

'I don't want you to panic.'

'Just tell me.'

'They found a shadow. On his lung.'

Hura puts both hands over her mouth and looks at her mother with frightened eyes. Questions pour jumbled into her mind. She says: 'What?'

'It's ok. For the moment it's ok. They found a shadow on his lung. It's not clear yet whether it's a problem or not. For now we just carry on as normal.'

When Aisha leaves for work, Hura takes Casimir out into the surrounding lanes. Walking, she calls Mir, talks for a long time about the medical implications of their father's condition. She calls Haris, almost certain he won't pick up, and gets an international ringtone; he works for an NGO and she can't keep track of his schedule. She texts Amin, who replies immediately that he'll be in surgery for the next several hours and can they talk at the weekend.

She returns to the house energised and determined, and spends the afternoon writing an application for the researcher job. Her father arrives back just after 6 p.m. She bursts into tears as soon as she sees him, and he pours them each a whiskey, and they sit in the garden wrapped in blankets, talking about his health and her career until eventually they find they've moved on to books, her brothers, gardening. Cillian calls at some point and, not wanting to break the moment, she doesn't answer.

Late that evening – after they have waited for Aisha before eating dinner, and sat at the table talking afterwards – Hura lets herself out into the garden again. Her parents' bedroom light illuminates a corner of the lawn, but as she stands there it goes out, and the night readjusts. The dew has already gathered thick on the grass. She walks out onto it with bare feet. Casimir is asleep, well fed and fussed over by Ben. She checks the time on her phone, re-reads Cillian's message from hours earlier which asked about her visit. She sends him a text: *Awake?*

When he doesn't reply she puts the phone away. She misses him, his voice especially, his ability to find the right things to say to her in any crisis. She wants to tell him about the job and ask him to read her application. To talk through her mother's reaction to it.

Once she has told him about the shadow, she will be better able to cope with it. It will all have to wait until morning.

The whiskey and the wine they drank at dinner lend the night garden a weird clarity. She remembers her dream. The physical presence of James, his solidity bound up with that of the rocks and cliffs; as if the mountains were embracing her. She breathes in, all the way to the bottom of her lungs, and concentrates on that feeling. Then she tells herself to let it go. Be careful, she says silently, watch for the edge. Because where exactly, in the canyon-landscape of thought and action, is the border between fidelity and betrayal?

Roses is at the theatre with Stefan. The cast has Sunday off. None of the agents or casting directors they call answers the phone; no one is getting back to them.

They're in the big first-floor foyer, a place where the Wi-Fi works and phone signal isn't egregious. Stefan comes back with two cardboard cups of tea and puts one down in front of Roses.

'I thought you might want *this*.'

He places a tiny foil-topped pot of milk on the lid. Stefan thinks adding milk to tea is eccentric. Roses adds the milk, stirs the tea, tastes it. She already feels jittery with caffeine and nerves.

'I hate this. Waiting. Impotence. I can't stand it.'

'It's Sunday, nothing happens in this weird little country on Sunday.'

Roses rolls her eyes. Stefan spent a year in LA and thinks he knows just about everything about life as a result.

'And tomorrow is Monday. Which means *five days* until the show opens.'

Roses toys with the tea. She's uncomfortably hot. The space is gloomy, though it's a bright, warm day outside. Elsewhere in London, people are lying in parks and wandering around markets. That world seems far away, invented. Roses feels caged.

'Cancellations?' she asks without looking at Stefan. He's check-ing his phone.

'A few,' he says, also not looking at her. Then suddenly he stands, swipes his laptop off the table, and motions for her to get up with an upward flick of the chin.

'Come on. We go to the roof.'

Roses picks up the tea.

'Leave that ducks' piss,' Stefan says, striding away. Roses, smiling despite herself, follows him to the lift.

It's warm and windy on the roof, the flat heat of the sun laid on the skin for a moment or two, then lifted off by sharp gusts. After the dim interior the brightness is painful. Roses puts on her sunglasses; Stefan's already wearing his Ray-Bans and carrying his laptop under his arm. Since they're not rehearsing she's wearing a short dress, and the breeze is a relief on her bare legs.

She feels better in the open air, but the feeling is a fragile skin over terror underneath. The terror is made worse by exhaustion. Once home from Cillian's, she had lain awake for most of the night going over the events of the previous day. Evita walking out. Looking up in the pub to see that wounded, familiar face. The humiliation of her drenching. The deeper humiliation of knowing how much she deserved it. The surprising comfort of talking it through with Cillian. The kiss. The kiss.

'You are not going to like this,' Stefan says, stopping in front of a bench, turning his hidden eyes towards her.

'Oh shit, what?' Roses says. 'If you tell me you're quitting, I'll jump off the roof.'

'Don't be an idiot, of course I am not quitting,' Stefan says. 'You are not going to like it when I tell you to play the part yourself.'

'Oh god.' Roses sits heavily down.

'It makes sense,' Stefan says. 'You know the piece. You're a woman.'

'Great,' Roses says, 'Great reason. The right gender. I haven't performed in anything for ten years. I'd be a complete joke.'

Stefan sits beside her. His voice comes softer than normal.

'You're not a joke. I have been there, watching. Lots of times you fill in when Evita's not there. You're good.'

Roses shakes her head.

'Ok, so you have some complex, I don't know what it is and I am not going to talk you around it,' Stefan says, air quotes on the word *complex*. 'What I see is this: we have a fucking big hole in the play, and we have this fucking great hole-filler right here, who knows the part, who is powerful onstage, who is very beautiful blah blah. It is a solution staring us in the face.'

Roses is looking at him. 'A "hole-filler". Did you actually just call me a hole-filler?'

'Rose plural,' he says, the affectionate name he rarely uses but which makes her love him, in this moment, very hard, 'I will spend all the hours of my life searching for a new performer. I will do that. But I am saying now: you should play the part, because you are the best person to do it.'

James and Emma sit side-by-side at a table seat, rushing towards London. There was no excuse James could think of to travel separately. It's Sunday lunchtime and the weather, here in the north, is clearing, high white clouds with blue between replacing the uniform grey.

He's by the window and his shoulders, which are too broad for a standard train seat, touch glass on one side, and Emma's shoulder on the other. She could incline her body away from his and stop the contact, but she doesn't. She has a newspaper in front of her but isn't really reading it, just turning the pages to look at the headlines. James wants to read, but every time he picks up his book, Emma talks to him, and he puts it politely down. The journey is six hours long.

James rests his head against the glass and closes his eyes for a moment. The image of Cillian is there like a burn on the retina. He opens his eyes again, glimpsing a sheet metal sea across wheat fields, and then the tracks turn inland. He has his phone in his hand and, without thinking, he opens the image of his plane ticket.

'Buenos Aires?' Emma says. He immediately turns his screen face down. 'When are you going there?'

'I'm not,' James says, blindsided by what feels like an invasion of his mind. 'I mean, we're just planning it. A holiday.'

'We?' Emma says, smiling, eyebrows raised. She invites confidences about James's love life, tells stories about her own marriage. James evades, to the point where he's barely mentioned that Roses exists, a strategy which, even as he's pursuing it, he knows to be counterproductive.

'Yeah,' he says now, his voice brittle with the lie. 'Roses and me.'

'That's so romantic.' Emma says. 'I've always wanted to go to South America but Tony *hates* travelling and with the kids long flights are a total nightmare. I'm so jealous. When are you going? I can't do without you for long, you know.'

For a moment she puts a hand on his knee, then takes it away as if it didn't happen. An announcement tells them they will shortly be arriving at Newcastle.

'Your old stamping ground,' Emma says.

And James realises what he's going to do.

'Yeah, actually, do you mind,' he says, moving so it's clear he's trying to stand. Surprised, Emma gets up to let him step into the aisle, and James pulls down his jacket and weekend bag from the rack above her head.

'What are you doing?' Emma asks.

'I just realised, we're passing through, and I should go and see my parents, you know?'

He says it as if it's the most natural thing in the world as he shrugs his jacket on, talks over any possible objections.

'They're getting on, especially my dad. He's not well, like. So I'll just drop in and see them and get a later train.'

She starts to protest that he'll have to buy a new ticket, but he waves the point away.

'There are loads of trains on this route, I'll have plenty of time to get back tonight.'

He starts to walk down the carriage towards the doors.

'I'll see you at work, all right?'

'Ok,' Emma says. She's frowning, then makes herself smile. James gives her a wave and then turns away, and a few minutes later he's on the familiar platform, and the train has gone.

★

He doesn't call. They're either home, or they're not, and if not, they'll never have to know he came. He walks, taking the Redheugh Bridge, a slightly longer route that avoids the centre. Keeps his eyes down while crossing the Tyne. By the time he's in Gateshead the sense of weird familiarity is churning through him; the places he left so long ago. Things have changed, of course. The roads are smarter, the small brick houses look a little better cared-for. Shopfronts are brighter. He comes back so rarely, and yet – of course – every turning, every street corner is known to him. He's never homesick, unless he's actually here. When he arrives at his parents' street, he stands for a moment to look down the alley behind, where the houses back onto one another and the garages open. The kind of place you might see little kids skipping, teenage boys kicking a football or sharing a cigarette. There's no one in the alley today. James rolls his shoulders in an attempt to loosen them, walks round to the front door and knocks.

A blur of movement behind the frosted glass and then his mother answers and goes still. Her face is frozen, for a split second, as though she hasn't recognised him, or is afraid. Then the complicated emotions sweep across her features: pleasure and guilt, love, and something bleak and very old.

'Oh, James,' she says quietly, 'you should have called.'

He knows he should.

'Hello, Mam.'

He hangs back while she moves down the corridor, letting her get into the sitting room first, communicate something in the seconds before he appears.

When he does, it's to find his father struggling to his feet from the habitual armchair, high-backed, upholstered in faded check.

'Son,' his father says. 'You should have called.'

'It wasn't planned,' James says. He perches on the sofa arm. 'I was on the way down from Edinburgh, a conference up there. Decided when I was on the train.'

James's father sits again. He's shrunk. Or maybe it's just that James isn't used to being here as an adult, taking up the space of a tall man in this small, north-facing room.

'You've lost your accent then,' his father states. In London, James's accent sounds pronounced.

'I'll make the tea,' his mother says.

James says, 'I'll give you a hand.'

She busies herself with the kettle and the pot, a tray and cups, talking, filling him in on the recent activities of their neighbours and distant family. James, knowing she's talking to avoid silence, lets the sound wash around them for a few moments. But it's precious time, here alone in the kitchen, and when she reaches into the cupboard beside him for biscuits, he stops her with a touch to the arm.

'Mam, I need to ask you. You remember the Gullivers.' He sees evasion come into her eyes. 'Of course you do. They left town, after it happened.' Inwardly he calls himself a coward for this euphemism, but carries on. 'They split up.'

'They did, yes,' his mother says. Her eyes on his waver, like she's asking for a reprieve. 'They got divorced. He died, in the end, poor man. Stroke.'

'And she moved away. I heard, years ago.'

'Abroad. She went back to . . . wherever it was she came from. Brazil or somewhere.'

'That's what I heard. What happened then? Is she still there?'

'Sally?' James's father's voice. He must think they're taking too long.

'Coming, love,' she calls back.

'Mam,' James says. 'After all this time.'

Long ago, when Sally had to choose, she chose her husband. But James is still her son.

She presses her lips together, resolved. 'I don't know. But Auntie May knows everyone. I'll give her a ring.'

Cillian plans to tell her, at once and in person. It will be simple: he'll explain the circumstances of how Roses came to be in their flat, and tell her exactly what happened once she was there. He's so glad, now, that they didn't go too far. Sex would have been a real breach of trust, and the thought of having to explain that to Hura makes him shudder. This – a moment of accidental intimacy – is a contravention of what they agreed, and one he regrets, but it's just that: a moment.

She's been home some time on Sunday before he gets in. He calls her name and finds her lying on the bed.

'Holmes?'

He lies down behind her, his body along her back, and she turns to him, her face wet with tears. Oh god, he thinks, she knows.

'What's wrong?'

'Oh, Cillian.'

'Sweetheart. What is it?' He should apologise right now, before she says it. 'I'm so sorry.'

'It's my dad.'

'What?'

'My dad might be ill, they found something. Why are you sorry?'

'What? I'm sorry you're upset, what did they find?'

'A shadow. That's what they call it. On his lung. They don't know what it is yet, he has to have more tests. It could be cancer.' As she says the last word, her face crumples completely.

'Oh, shit, shit,' he says as he holds her. He likes Ben, really likes him. He's the best father Cillian has known. They lie in one another's arms and talk it through, and then they talk about Aisha, and about the job application, and Hura's plans and fears. Somewhere, what happened last night seems to become both irrelevant, and impossible to mention.

Roses asked what train he was on, so he told her, but neither of them suggested spending the night together. It's Sunday, after all. James has a long week of work ahead. Her show opens in a few days, and though he knows nothing about what's happened since he last saw her, he knows she'll be immersed in it. The time he spent in Newcastle has left him bone-tired. First his parents' house. Then walking round to Auntie May's – actually his mother's oldest friend – to hear a mixture of rumour and gossip and, perhaps, useful information. He feels like he's been living in a strange skin for days, a suit of some tough, unforgiving material that he wants to slough off, but knows that, when he does, he might collapse. His body feels bruised and held together by the performance of fortitude.

It's 9 p.m. when the train pulls into King's Cross, slightly late. James shoulders his bag and stomps down the platform, uses his ticket at the automatic gates.

And there is Roses. Her legs are bare and she looks cold, a cardigan wrapped round her but no coat, like someone who went out when it was sunny and hasn't been home. She's resting one shoulder against a pillar and has her bag slung round her, and when she sees him she gives him a hesitant smile.

He's so pleased to see her that he feels the sting of tears. She also looks tired. He wants to lie down with her somewhere, right now, and bury his face in her hair.

She comes to meet him slowly, and he drops his bag and, afraid his voice might shake, pulls her close and kisses her for a long moment.

When it's over she looks up at him.

'Evita quit and now I'm in the show, and I'm going to have to do nothing but work on it all week and I knew I wouldn't see you. But I wanted to see you. I can't come back with you. I need to go home.'

'You're *in* the show?'

'Yep.'

'That's . . .'

'It's awful. It's a car crash. I don't even want to talk about it.'

'Ok. Well. I saw my parents.'

'*Really?*' He hasn't seen his parents since they met. She used to ask him about them, early on. Then she stopped. 'How was it?'

He puts an arm around her shoulders and starts walking. 'Are you really not coming home with me?'

'No. I've got stuff at home I need for tomorrow. Are you hungry?'

'Bit, yeah,' he says with a smile that indicates he's more than a bit hungry.

'Come on.'

She takes him by the hand and leads him out of the station and straight to the McDonald's across the road.

'I thought you hated it here?' he says.

'Sometimes it's what you need.'

She tells him about Evita and the search for a new performer, the ticket cancellations, Stefan's suggestion, her eventual acquiescence.

'If someone turns up tomorrow, maybe there's still time to re-hearse them in,' she says. She's eating chicken nuggets and fries as if she hasn't seen food for days. 'Otherwise it's me.'

'I'd like to see you in it,' he says. She looks up at him from under her brows.

'I didn't even think you liked theatre.'

'But I'd like to see you in something.'

She takes the rare compliment without comment. Drinks some milkshake.

'Something else happened,' she says. She tells him the story of the drink, the thrown pint. She tells him she went back to Cillian's to change.

She tells him about the kiss.

Something fires in James when she says it, a primal kind of gasp. Jealousy, his mind names it. And yet who, in the story, is he jealous of?

James spent eighteen years practising to make sure his emotions don't show on his face. His mouth doesn't falter. His eyes are clear and meet Roses' without blame, without hurt.

'That's fine,' he says.

'Is it?' she asks. She sounds relieved, and something else.

'Of course, that's what we agreed. You're free. I'm free.'

She smiles at him. It's true; freedom is important to her.

'What about this guy, the one who threw the drink on you. What happened there?'

Roses leans back. She wipes salt and grease from her hands as if suddenly finding the food unpleasant.

'Someone from a long time ago. A past I haven't atoned for.'

There's a pause. James finishes his Coke. His urge to run away from the subject of the past is warring with how much he likes being with her. In the end he speaks without looking at her.

'You looking for forgiveness, are you?'

She looks at him for a long moment, then away. They are not only talking about her, and her past.

'Yes,' she says in the end. 'But I'm not sure I deserve it.'

James nods. She leaves a pause, just in case. Then:

'It's getting late,' she says. 'I've got to go.'

They kiss again before parting, eyes closed, falling through galaxies together while they stand on the street corner, the smell of hot oil caught in their clothes and in their hair.

Chapter Thirteen

'Tell me about her,' Hura says into his ear.

'Who?'

'Any of them.'

Cillian's racing heart re-finds its rhythm. It's been three weeks since Roses came to the flat, and the moment to tell Hura about it passed. He's all but forgotten it happened. Yet Hura's question still triggered the worry: that he should have told her; that somehow she already knew. But no. They're three months into the opening-up experiment, and in fact Hura is suggesting something else.

Back when they were purely monogamous, he'd often asked her to share her fantasies and she'd resisted. I don't have fantasies, she'd said, and thought it was true. For her, the very word *fantasy* spoiled the mood, conjuring images of faux-schoolgirls disciplined by stern teachers, or pointy-eared elves going down on one another. In truth, Hura's sexual self simply doesn't translate well into words. She knows what she wants to feel, but not how to express it. There are images and states that hold for her a sexual power: evening; the feeling of having climbed to a high place and looking out over open country; dark foliage pressing close in the heat of some tropical climate, the skin of the leaves beaded as if with sweat. But how can you explain, even to your husband, that you're turned on by a time of day? Who would understand the appeal of being ravished by a forest? Hura kept such details so private they were almost hidden from herself.

Now, the uncoupling of marriage and commitment from their

individual sexual lives has begun to give her a new vocabulary. Hura has been sitting, wide-eyed, in daytime talks about consent, and evening workshops on tantra. She's begun reading recent books with titles like *The Flexible Marriage Manual* and more ancient texts like the *Kama Sutra* ('How are you finding it?' Cillian asks. 'Impenetrable,' she replies, which he finds hilarious.) She makes friends online. Generally, this doesn't result in hook-ups the way Cillian's messaging almost invariably does. Rather, she begins conversations cautiously with people she finds interesting, and these turn into long, intimate dialogues. It feels daring, strange, subversive. She's instantly turned off by disrespect or anything explicitly sexual, and has terminated several chats that descended suddenly into unsettling realms. But a few interlocutors remain: a 68-year-old man in Oregon. A young mother in Islamabad. A trans man, and a woman who used to be straight but now lives in a gay collective in Wales.

Just once or twice, she's arranged to meet someone alone. The prospect has been thrilling, the realities a mixture of odd and anaemic.

One Thursday she meets a Polish pianist passing through London for just one night. She sees him play and falls slightly in love, then goes for strong martinis and ends up in his hotel room. As soon as they finish having sex, he rolls away and lights a cigarette, something she thought only happened in films, and then gets up and dresses curtly, as if he's planning to go out again even though it's past midnight. A strong sense of meaninglessness sweeps over her in the taxi home. They exchanged numbers, but a few days later she deletes him from her phone. One powerful memory persists: that of his fine, nimble hands.

The biggest change for Hura has been in her sex life with Cillian. The new vocabulary is shared; words become sexual between them in a whole new way. After the encounter with the pianist she tells him the story. She starts with the post-coital rudeness, moves on to the lyricism and lust of his performance. By the time she's describing him undressing her, Cillian is peeling off her top, and he continues to act out what she says as she speaks it.

Almost more than anything, she's enjoyed seeing Cillian happy. Her enjoyment of this blossoming has only been tempered by the faintest hint of worry, that his desire to be liked by new people veers too close to a need to be loved by everyone. His schedule also sometimes seems a little exhausting. But while she doesn't want to know details of Cillian's text messages or drinks arrangements, she does love hearing about moments of seduction.

'Tell me about her.'

'Who?'

'Any of them.'

'Ok.' He kisses her on the mouth where she lies beneath him, then takes the kisses to her ear and down her neck. 'So last week I met this woman who lives right by the river. Her place used to be a boathouse and has a big glass door that opens almost into the water.'

'What did she look like?'

'Long blonde hair. Tanned. Blue eyes, lots of freckles.'

'Are you making this up?'

'No. Why?'

'She sounds too perfect.'

'She was lovely, but not perfect. Not like you.'

'Stop it. Where were you?'

'In the room by the river. She opened the doors and turned off the lights, and then she came over to me and unbuttoned my jeans.'

He tells her the story as they kiss, as they touch. They swap who is on top, knot their fingers into one another's hair. She comes, more suddenly than he expected, and moves to lie beside him. There's a hiatus; maybe they're finished for the evening, maybe not.

'Would you like to see James and Roses again?' she asks in that sweet pause.

The mention of the name sends a twinge through Cillian, a skein of guilt wound with desire.

'If you'd like to, I'd be up for it,' he says.

'I'd like to,' she says. 'I really like them both.'

'Let's get in touch then.'

He should tell her now, about the drink, the drenching, the kiss. He rolls onto his side towards her:

'I—'

'We could have a baby,' she says. 'Then what would we do about all this?'

Cillian, surprised by the strength of his delight, hides it. 'This?'

'The experiment.'

'I don't know. Having a baby would change . . . a lot of things.'

'It's good though, so far, isn't it?' she says.

'I think so, yeah.' He smiles. He knows her jubilant post-orgasm moods.

'Why don't more people try this?' she says. 'You can have what you need, and I can have what I need, and then we can talk about it with each other. And have great sex.'

She smiles happily at the ceiling.

'Maybe this is what everyone does and we just don't know it.'

'Uh-uh, no way. Like Zahra; most people I've told are horrified.'

'Really? My friends think it sounds amazing.'

'Do they?'

'Some do.'

She sits up and strokes his chest, his stomach where there are fewer tattoos and which looks vulnerable without that armour. She takes his penis in her hand and holds it.

'Would you like to, though? Have a baby?'

'You know I would.'

'I know.' She runs her hand up and down the shaft absentmind-edly. 'I feel like I'm almost ready, too. It's just, this job change. I want to know what's happening with that. If I'm starting down a new road I want to actually be on it, before we try.'

'Mmmm.'

'And still renting isn't ideal. But that would be ok, I guess.'

'Holmes.'

'What?'

'Could you either stop touching me or stop talking about the five-year plan?'

'Oh, yeah, sorry.' She looks at him in her hand, fully hard again now. 'Which?'

'The talking?'

'Right you are.'

It's late when she turns her back so that he can loop an arm under hers and align his front to her back, their habitual falling-asleep position. She thinks, I love this person more than I ever thought I would love anyone. In the warm imperfect blackout she hears his breathing change from wakefulness to sleep. When her eyes are closed she sees purple mountains and a man who walks between them, his swimmer's shoulders silhouetted against the distance.

Cillian, on the edge of sleep, places one hand on her belly. She doesn't always let him touch her there, thinking it too soft, but he loves the difference from his own taut muscle-and-skin frame. He imagines their child growing inside her and the idea is so big his mind can't contain it. He begins to drift and thinks, in those final relaxed moments before sleep, about a woman wearing his clothes, and then removing them.

The next morning, Hura goes out early with Casimir, buys croissants and the newspaper while Cillian is asleep. She opens all the windows to let the outside world spill in: cars pass, a mother calls her child, a broken line of birdsong, sweet and then gone.

When Cillian emerges, he finds her cross-legged on a kitchen chair, a pot of coffee and a cup and the paper bag of pastries all on top of the spread-out newsprint.

'Look!' She holds out one of the segments to him. He scans it sleepily.

'What am I looking at?'

'The review. It's Roses' show!'

He finds it. 'Wow, five stars.'

'It's an amazing review. She must be so happy. I didn't know she was in it.'

'She's in it?' He's reading now. The review is indeed almost laughably positive. At one point it compares Roses to Sylvia Plath. At another, to Boadicea.

'We should go and see it! It's on for two more weeks.'

'Yeah. It's a busy time though.'

'Well, I'd love to see it. I can go on my own if you don't want to. Or maybe Zahra'll come,' she says, and goes back to her reading.

Cillian gets a cup, pours himself some coffee, finds that it's cold and puts it in the microwave. He's not sure why he evaded the idea of seeing the play. He finds sitting still for long periods difficult, and theatres are particularly demanding of silence and attention. But that's not it. He watches the cup slowly revolve, and it strikes him that he doesn't want a reason to find Roses more attractive than he already does. The realisation worries him, and he tells himself to face it down.

'I'd love to go with you,' he says, turning back to Hura, kissing her on the cheek.

'Cool.' She's not really listening now, immersed instead in a long piece of political analysis. He takes his coffee to the bathroom and balances it on the side of the bath while he showers.

Since they began the process of opening up, Cillian has been in touch with a lot of women and, more tentatively, some other people as well. Most of the interactions don't progress beyond conversation. But some do, and after years of intimacy with one person, albeit the love of his life, the latitude stuns him. He feels like an explorer on a new planet, thirsty for contact and knowledge and experience. He loves the chase, whether he's the hunter or the quarry. The sex itself, if it happens, is sometimes fantastic, sometimes merely fine. He would never bring anyone home, or stay the night. He returns hours after Hura has gone to sleep, showers, slips into bed beside her. She turns to him, hair a tangled mass and eyes closed, snuggles her head against his chest, and goes back to sleep. Sometimes there are a few words:

'You're back.'

'I'm back.'

'How was it?'

'Good.'

'Sex?'

'Yeah.'

'Nice?'

'Pretty nice.'

'I finished the lasagne.'

His work, though busy, is self-directed. He can easily fit in conversations with a few different people on any given day. The apps and sites and messages become an erotic backdrop to his workdays, his commutes, his exercise routines. Colours around him seem brighter and he notices things afresh: flowers on the reception desk at his building, a handsome stranger passing in the street. Presumably, he thinks, this has a time limit. Soon the new arrangement will be less startling and fresh, and when it is, he will slow down.

For now, however, the power of carnal possibility isn't diminishing. His mind is constantly firing up, and his body responding. It's pleasurable and destabilising. Will people notice? This week, buying coffee, he pretty much suggested a date to the tall barista. She raised a solitary eyebrow again, and looked at his wedding ring and then back at his face. He felt himself blush and didn't try to explain, with a queue forming behind him of curious, impatient caffeine addicts.

He's been scrupulous in telling Hura what he's doing, with the one odd exception of that drink with Roses. Hura is on her own voyage of discovery, which is fulfilling her in a different way. The period of stasis and knocked confidence that followed her dismissal seems to have passed. She's reading constantly, going to lectures, meeting people to talk about the state of the world over coffee, about body politics over wine. Cillian finds himself pleased, with just an edge of something else, like it's harder to recognise the Hura he knows in this whirl of new ideas and activities.

A couple of times in the last weeks, she's stayed out late at feminist or Queer groups, so late that he's gone to sleep, and woken to find her in the kitchen at 1 a.m., wired and eating toast, telling him about all the new thoughts she's having. She's talked about going on Vipassana, a ten-day silent retreat or – though she's fairly wary of drugs – taking part in an ayahuasca ceremony. It's like the responsibility of being a teacher, and all that entailed, has kept her in a chrysalis since she was twenty-one, and now she's broken free and discovered unfamiliar wings.

Hura is happier with his prolific dating than if he was seeing one other person. He understands why. He is careful not to encourage attachment in anyone he meets, not to promise, not to seem too keen or too available. He always tells them immediately that he is married, and mentions Hura, their home, their dog, early in the interactions.

It doesn't always work.

On a Tuesday night he meets up with Teiko, a photographer, for the third time in as many weeks. As he chains his bike outside the restaurant he can see her through the glass, glaring straight ahead. He rushes in and sits down, apologising for his lateness. They order bottles of Sol and bowls of noodles but conversation doesn't immediately start to flow. When the beers arrive she takes a photo of the lime wedged in the neck, then a photo of him pushing the lime in with a finger, then one of him while he drinks.

'Come on, stop it,' he says.

'Why?'

She holds the bottle up and takes a selfie with it, then puts it down without drinking and begins tapping the picture with her thumbs.

'Are you posting it? Where?'

She flicks her eyes up to him, he thinks, a little coldly. Then she scoots round the table and leans towards him, holding up the phone with one hand and smiling up at it.

'Say cheese!'

He leans away, out of the frame. 'Teiko.'

'What? You don't want to be in a picture with me?'

'No, it's just—'

'You don't want anyone to see?'

A waiter places bowls in front of them, steaming with coriander and seafood.

'What's up?' he asks.

'Nothing's "up". What's "up" with you?'

She slides a pair of wooden chopsticks out of their paper case and snaps them apart.

'Um?'

'You've been ignoring me.'

'What? When did I ignore you?'

'Five days. We meet, we have sex, and I don't hear from you for *five days*.' Her voice is low. She picks up a prawn and eats it angrily.

'I don't understand.' He runs through their interactions in his mind. They had messaged, met, and slept together; then messaged and met again. Was there a sudden cooling-off after that second time? Not in his mind. She had seemed light-hearted, to him; full of confident abandon.

He apologises profusely and she thaws a little. Eventually she laughs at something he says, and begins to chat more easily. She tells him about her students at a nearby community college.

'Hura used to say about teaching that – what?' He stops because she rolled her eyes.

'You always have to mention her, don't you?'

'What?'

'Your little wife.'

'Do you . . . not want me to mention her?' Cillian swallows with some difficulty.

'I just don't see why you always have to.'

'But, I mean, I live with her. I love her. Why wouldn't I talk about her?'

'Oh, you love her. Men are all the same, they have affairs—'

'*What?*'

'. . . but they love their wives.'

'Teiko. We're not having an affair. Hura knows about you, she knows about every . . . We have an – I thought you understood?'

Teiko looks at him in a way that makes him feel he doesn't know anything about her.

'Oh yes, I understand. Just sex. It's always just sex with you.'

He doesn't know whether she's talking about him specifically, or men in general, or even, he's horrified to wonder, white men. Then, bafflingly, she smiles as if she might just be joking, and carries on eating her noodles.

When the waiter brings the bill she is looking at her phone. Cillian pays. They walk out together and she waits while he unlocks his bike. As he straightens, she turns and begins walking towards her flat.

'You coming?' she asks over her shoulder.

He starts walking with her. It's close, and when they arrive she asks, not quite meeting his eye, if he's coming up.

'Teiko, I don't get it,' he says.

She kisses him. Surprised, he kisses her back, and his mind is filled with sudden, searing memories of her body, her hands, her feet, the ropes she owns.

'Come. Up. Stairs,' she says.

He cycles home fast, taking too many risks, lungs straining. It's complicated, god it's complicated. The warm London air is sweet with barbecue smoke and tarmac. The night around him crackles and hums.

On Wednesday Hura meets her father on Huntley Street, outside one of University College Hospital's many buildings.

She's wearing shorts and sandals, and is cold: the weather is changeable. She's listening to bouncy, summery pop music through big headphones, trying to distract herself from the building behind her, the Cancer Centre. Couldn't they call it something else? Though what, she doesn't know. All the euphemisms she can think of – Wellness Centre, Centre for Hope – sound like an Orwellian nightmare.

She spots Ben walking down the road. His gait seems slow, his tall frame slightly fallen-in on itself. But it could be an illusion. He may be no different to a year ago, or to the last time she saw him before the 'shadow' came into their lives. The sun comes out from behind a cloud, and he spots her, and waves.

'Hi Dad.' She hugs him hello. 'Urgh, this place.' They push the revolving doors and enter a bright atrium.

'It's actually a very beautiful building,' he says.

It's warm and high inside, light-filled. The Centre of Light, Hura thinks, then discounts it as abjectly terrifying. Ben gives his name to the receptionist, and they're ushered into a separate waiting area. Everything is pristine. Sound is hushed and gentle. It makes Hura tempted to scream.

They sit side-by-side on clean plastic chairs. Hura takes her father's hand, something she never does in normal life. 'Are you worried?'

'Not particularly. We won't get the results today. Maybe I'll feel worried waiting for them to arrive. But there's not much point in worrying, really, is there? I might as well not worry, and wait to see what they say.'

'Yeah, great. Great if you're a robot,' Hura says. She turns her back, speaks over her shoulder. 'I forgot to set my Worry Switch to off, could you just do it for me?'

He laughs. She smiles. She wants to cry.

'Do you want to come and see a play with me, after this?'

'A play?'

'A friend's play. At the Barbican. It's at two-thirty.'

In the end, Cillian and Hura couldn't find an evening when they were both free. Zahra read the blurb and said she'd rather spend an evening performing colonoscopies, or trawling Tinder, or both. Hura decided she'd try to catch a matinee – that she might as well enjoy the luxury of being unemployed. She's heard nothing back about the energy researcher job, and her hope that she'll hear is fading.

Ben checks his watch, the same watch he's had since she was a child. She remembers picking it up and playing with the metal links, feeling its surprising weight. It looks loose on his wrist.

'I'm afraid not. I'd like to, but I've got a conference call I need to be on.'

Of course he has work. She can't imagine him ever stopping.

'It's weird not having a job,' she says.

'What are you doing with the time?' Ben asks.

'Looking for jobs. And experimenting. Meeting lots of new people, trying to . . . I don't know how to explain it, it always sounds like I'm joking. Broaden my horizons, or something. Get beyond the limits of my own mind.'

'That sounds dangerous.' He smiles. Then: 'But I think I know what you mean.'

'Cillian and I are . . . we don't have a totally conventional marriage,' Hura says. She had no idea she was going to tell Ben this. But here they are, and she's saying it. He's looking at her with a calm, questioning gaze.

'We see, sometimes, other people, a bit,' Hura says, struggling to frame it in a way that sounds non-explicit. 'We're not totally . . . monogamous. Any more.'

Ben nods slightly. 'And how is that?'

'It's good! I think it's good. It's part of this whole . . . experiment. That sounds stupid. But it's really interesting.'

'Hm. Interesting,' Ben says. 'And is Cillian also finding it "interesting"?'

'Dad, don't worry. It's totally mutual. Cillian isn't cheating on me. And I'm not cheating on him. It's consensual.'

Ben gives a little cough. Hura is embarrassed that she's embarrassing him, happy that they can talk like this.

Ben says: 'Well, that sounds very modern.'

'Dad!'

'What?'

'I'm OK! Really.' She smiles at him, her warmest, most reassuring smile. 'I'm having a pretty amazing time.'

He smiles back, then turns slightly away. 'Could you just check, I thought the Worry Switch was off, but I think I got the setting wrong.'

Hura laughs.

'Mr Holmes?' A woman with a clipboard, standing in front of them.

Ben gets up, smiles down at Hura. 'Won't be long.'

'See you after.'

When she's alone on the plastic chairs, Hura takes out the book she's reading, a big history of the Middle East. But she doesn't open it. The sun goes in, outside the glass walls, and all the contrast disappears. The Centre of Light and Shadows.

She doesn't have a ticket, and when she arrives at the Box Office there's a queue. It moves fast, and she's almost at the front when the person before her has a problem. She tunes in, hearing the guy laugh wryly that he's forgotten his wallet. The man has dark hair shaved short at the side so that a tattoo shows through, though she can't make out what it is. There's something about the side of his face, the angle of his neck, that she likes without knowing why.

'I can pay for you,' she says.

The man turns. Very dark eyes with long lashes.

'What?'

'I can buy you a ticket, if you've forgotten your wallet. You can send me the money.'

The man frowns, rubs the back of his neck. He looks up at her through his lashes.

'That's really nice of you. But I don't mind. Not seeing it.'

'No, come on, you're here,' Hura says, not sure why she's trying to persuade him. 'It's meant to be really good,' she adds.

He grins at that, but the grin isn't a happy one. 'Yeah. Ok,' he says. 'Thank you. I promise I'll send you the money. I should have set up the thing on my phone . . .'

She buys them tickets, and now there's barely time for Hura to get to the loos and then find her place before the show starts. The man is in the next seat, arms folded, looking ahead. She sits beside him.

'Always a queue for the ladies,' she says. He nods and smiles, his expression inscrutable. The lights dim to black.

There's no interval. To begin with, Hura finds the narrative style confusing. Then she ceases to care. Roses is familiar but quickly becomes a stranger, magnetic, moving now smooth as a cat, now frenetic, now light as an insect as she embodies different moments and moods. Everyone in the cast is extraordinary in their own way. The intense male actor locked into a love story with Roses'

167

character. The grey-haired woman who sings, without warning and into a sudden silence, a tune so sad and ancient it makes the hairs stand up on Hura's arms. When the show ends an hour later Hura has tears coursing down her face. She brushes them away, embarrassed because she's not quite alone. It seems socially awkward not to talk to the man whose ticket she bought, but that feels like a long time ago, and she doesn't want to talk.

'What did you think?' she asks, the most boring of questions. She searches her bag for a tissue, pointing to her own tears and rolling her eyes, self-mocking.

The man doesn't answer. She glances at him to see that his face is thunderous.

'You didn't like it?'

He shuts his eyes tight. Keeps them closed while he answers.

'It was fucking incredible.' His voice is quiet. It's light, pleasant, the accent impossible to place. He puts both hands over his mouth and nose, stares bleakly at the stage. Drops his hands into his lap with a thwack.

'I need a drink.'

'It's only 3.30 in the afternoon,' she smiles.

'Shit, you're right. Anyway, no wallet. Jesus, what a day.'

He stands, holds his phone out to her.

'Can I have your number? I'll send you the money. I promise.'

She taps it in, calls herself so that she has his contact.

The emotions of the play are running high though her. Love and loss. Sex and deceit. God and the body. Somehow she doesn't want this person to go, but he's already leaving.

'What did you think it was about?' she asks as he turns away.

He stops, looking down at himself, rather than at her. She thinks he won't answer, that her question has once again been dull.

'I think it was about wanting to connect, and it being impossible. Thinking you are close to someone. Realising you will always be apart. Because of biology. Because of death.'

He looks at her, and holds out his hand. Hura puts her hand in his.

'Thanks for the ticket,' he says. It's not a handshake; he just holds hers for a moment and there is something powerful and strange in the contact. His bones are fine and his hand cool. She stays in her seat as he edges out of the row and trots down the stairs, collar and shoulders up, not looking back. She stays as the whole house empties. Until it's nothing but a black-painted room full of chairs, facing an empty space.

That summer, Sam's friends seem always to go to the same bar. It's on the roof of a multi-storey car park, with the city below them and the sky above, light for hours in the long evenings. Their close and noisy group expands and contracts around old friends and new partners. It contains a spread of ages and has an easy way with pronouns. Sam's preferred pronoun, for the last six years, has been *him*.

Sam orders a lime and soda, and sits quietly at the end of a picnic table. It's good to be with people, but he's habitually quiet in any configuration bigger than a two. Eventually he wanders away to the concrete parapet, wishing he smoked because that would give him an excuse to stand alone in the warm dark and look out over the lights of south London. He wishes Saul, who has been deep in conversation in the middle of the group since Sam arrived, would join him so they could talk here, apart from the others.

Saul must have intuited Sam's thoughts, because he comes over with his half-finished drink – something sweet-looking in a tall glass with a paper umbrella – and a cigarette, and leans against the wall.

'What's that?' Sam nods at the drink.

'A mocktail. I think this one's called a Daylight Robbery.'

Saul takes a sip, makes a face, offers the glass and the straw. As Sam drinks, Saul says, 'Let me know if you plan to throw it over anyone. I wouldn't mind, only it cost eight pounds.'

Sam grins, gives it back.

'Her show's on at the Barbican. She directs and performs.'

'Of course she does.'

'I went to see it today.'

Saul lights the cigarette. After exhaling he says: 'Good?'

'It was excellent.' Sam puts his elbows on the parapet and his face in his hands. 'I hate her. It's eating me up. Why should I care if she's successful, or what she does? I thought it was over. It's so long ago. And then that night, seeing her in the pub, it all came back. What should I do?'

'How about not torturing yourself by following her career and going to see her plays?'

'Easy to say. Hard to do.'

'Throwing the drinks didn't help?'

'A bit at the time. Now it seems kind of childish.'

'Could you try to ruin her life?'

'Don't tempt me.'

Saul turns to him. 'Look, you're happy, right?'

'Yeah. Pretty much.'

'Ok, life's not perfect, but you had shit to deal with and you dealt with it. You're at peace with the choices you've made?'

'Absolutely.'

'You've got a nice family. You've got fabulous friends, if I do say so myself. You've got a good job, you perform, you've got the activism thing going on. Ok, you don't have a partner, whatever. It doesn't *matter* what she's got. Think about what you've got. That's what matters.'

'I know, I know.'

'Would it help to talk about it more – what went on back then? I can listen.'

Sam thinks for a moment. 'Did I ever tell you about the night they came to the farm?'

'Nope. You haven't told me much.'

Sam turns his back on the view and looks towards their friends. They're talking over the music, laughing together.

'Another time maybe,' he says. 'You're right. This is what matters.'

'What are you drinking?'

'Lime and soda.'

'Oh, please have something more interesting.'

'Surprise me.'

'One overpriced juice blend, coming up.'

Saul finishes his cigarette and goes to the bar. Before Sam joins the group he takes out his phone and sends a text.

Thanks for that ticket. Send me your details and I'll pay you back. Also, I'm curious: why would you do that for a stranger?

It's late. If Roses is coming over tonight, which has been rare since the show opened, she might be here soon. Sometimes he hides a key and she lets herself into the warehouse after he's gone to bed, climbs in beside him, and falls immediately asleep.

James is holding a piece of paper in his hands, a small pale-blue square with flowered corners, printed with the word *Notes*. On it, the name of a town and – the triumphant result of Auntie May's network – a phone number. A number from years ago in a town far away. He double-checks the time in Argentina, confirms that it's 7 p.m. there. He's sure the number won't work. He calls it.

After the sixth ring: '*Aló?*'

'*Hola.*' James is wrong-footed by the young, male voice. He explains in halting Spanish that he's looking for a woman. A woman called Maria Gulliver.

There's confusion on the other end, people speaking rapidly to him or to one another. In the background he hears a television, a high-pitched child's yell. A shout to someone in another part of the house. The receiver covered, a muffled conversation. Now a woman's voice speaking to him, a string of words he fails to grasp.

'*Lo siento. Puedes repetir, por favor?*' James says.

'*La señora no está acá. No por tres, cuatro años.*'

'Do you know where she went?' James tries in English, his grammar failing him.

'*Al lago. Lago. Entendés?*'

To the lake.

'What lake? *Qué lago?*'

He tries to scribble down phonetically what the woman says, but she's padding the name with so many other words that he's not sure he's got it. She's trying to explain something else, but perhaps just that she needs to go, because abruptly the line goes dead. He will call back several times, in the next days, but no one ever answers.

He goes online, searches the map for lakes near the town. Did they even say it was near? He trawls the internet hopelessly, with no idea how he will ever locate one woman, now in her seventies if she's still alive, who may have moved back home, to Argentina, years ago.

He checks the time again and realises it's too late for Roses to come now; the stab of disappointment he feels is mitigated by knowing he has an arrangement to see her the next night. He's suddenly dead tired. He lies down in his clothes and the next thing he knows it's 4 a.m. He's sure of the time before he even opens his eyes because if he wakes, which he usually does, it's almost always at four on the dot. James rolls onto his back and begins waiting until he can reasonably get up, put on his running clothes, and leave for work.

He saw the play on opening night when, Roses says, nerves threw the pace into disarray. James isn't sure he'll be able to tell the difference, but he's happy to go again since she asked him to. He liked watching her. The slew of great reviews mean every night is now packed, but she has put aside a ticket for him. It's a particularly manic day at the hospital and for most of it James forgets everything but the tasks in hand. He surfaces once for a few breaths of air and a terrible sandwich in the dirty courtyard where the smokers go, then plunges back into a day that seems it will never end.

And then, somehow, at 6.30 p.m. he's free. The next shift arrives, the acute cases are handed over. He walks out into a still-bright day, dazed and ravenous and without time to eat dinner.

At the theatre he picks up the ticket, then buys a plastic half of lager and pulls from his pocket the Cornish pasty he bought at the station. He's trying discreetly to wolf it down, leaning against the corner of the bar in a fog of low blood sugar, when he sees a flash of familiar gold hair through the crowd. Cillian turns in his direction, sees him, grins, heads over.

'I'm an idiot,' he says by way of greeting. 'Didn't book. It's obviously sold out.'

James wipes his mouth with the back of his hand, which then feels too greasy to extend in a handshake.

'Ah, yeah. It's really popular. Do you want some of this?' For some reason he's offering Cillian the pasty.

'Thanks, I'm fine. Hura'll kill me, she said I had to see it.'

'I can ... try and talk to them? If you like. Or you could take mine, I've already seen it, like.'

'Hura said it was incredible.'

'It's good, yeah. I think. I don't know much about theatre, to be honest.' James shrugs.

Cillian catches the barman's attention. 'You want another drink?'

'All right. Same again,' James holds up the glass. 'I'll check about that ticket.'

There is another ticket. Somehow there always is, if you say the right name. James files into the theatre behind Cillian, and they sit together in two strange side seats with restricted views, Cillian's a little in front and both of them turned sideways towards the stage. As they sit, Cillian swivels round and leans to speak quietly into James's ear, putting a hand on his shoulder as he does so.

'Hura was totally blown away by this,' he says. 'She said afterwards she might divorce me so she could marry Roses.'

The hand on his shoulder seems, to James, to thrum; like leaning against an idling car. When Cillian removes it and turns away, James blushes in the dark. Two drinks and too little food have made him drunk, he thinks. Cillian is being friendly, not flirting with him. And yet. The easy touch. The allusion to their intimacy contained within his comment about Hura.

Watching the show a second time, James thinks he understands what Roses meant about pace. This time the action rolls cleanly along, moment following moment in a way that seems eminently logical, like the audience is in safe hands. The poetry hits him more clearly this time, as though the actors are surer of their emphasis; or maybe it's just easier to absorb at a second hearing. Roses is very good in her part, and he feels proud of her, at the same time as feeling like she is someone else, not his girlfriend but some professional performer he oddly recognises. And there are long moments when he zones out of the story, and watches, instead, the lit cheekbone of the man in the next seat. The shoulder-blade close enough to touch.

After the show Cillian tries to leave. James persuades him to stay, at least say hi to Roses. He shifts from foot to foot while he waits. Cillian has spent an hour in a state of arousal which started the moment Roses came onstage and was only enhanced by the passionate storyline. Other than that aspect of it, he has little idea what happened in the play, and doesn't have anything ready to say about it.

When Roses emerges there's an immediate relief. She's a person again, glowing with exertion, but not illuminated from the inside as she seemed onstage. Not mythic in her proportions. Just happy, in hastily thrown-on clothes and smudged eye make-up.

She puts her arms around James and kisses him for a long moment on the lips. Then she turns to Cillian.

'It's so nice of you to come.'

'You were great. And Hura told me I had to. She came the other day, to a matinee. Said it was one of the best things she'd ever seen.'

'Wow, ok. I didn't know she was here.'

'I'll get drinks,' James says. 'If we're staying here?'

'I'd love a red wine,' Roses says, then quietly: 'It's weird, I'm the director, so most of the time I'm outside all this . . .' she gestures to the rest of the cast, all emerging and greeting friends. 'But now I'm in the show, I get to be part of the "cast" thing in the evenings. Then the next day we get together for notes and I'm outside again.'

James says to Cillian: 'A beer?'

'I won't, thanks. I should get home.'

'Ok. Let's all meet soon, yeah?'

James heads to the bar and Cillian shrugs his jacket on. Roses' attention keeps getting called away by people waving from various parts of the bar or smiling as they pass.

He says: 'I feel like we just had this intimate experience. But it was one-sided. I mean, I was watching you, but you didn't even know I was there.'

'It's not like that,' she says. 'It's intimate for us as well. The audience is part of it.'

They look each other in the eye, then away with tiny private smiles. It's the first time they've met since she left his flat.

'So . . . are we doing it again?' She looks back at him quizzically. 'The four of us?'

Cillian is suffused with pleasure at the thought of it; and with relief that such a meeting might overlay and erase the small transgression of their last.

'I'd like that,' he says.

They kiss once, cheek to cheek, and he leaves.

Chapter Fourteen

Hura doesn't believe in God, but there are times when she feels closer to understanding belief. The summer which pours like molten gold over London that July is one of them. A few sunny days, in England, is pleasing. But this, morning after morning blue and bright, the days cloudless and perfect, feels to Hura's sun-loving body and her buzzing mind more like a blessing than weather. She craves heat. Her skin shines, her muscles unknit so that her very limbs feel longer. Her unemployed status is a delight, but also a curse. She feels guilty most of the time, as Cillian gets up and leaves for the office; as everyone else races around the capital with important places to be.

But she's emerged from the uncertainty of her first reeling weeks and is now making a concerted effort to find out what she wants to do next. The initial shock of Ben's illness has softened into a more everyday concern. For hours each day she forces herself to ignore the sun that calls and calls her from outside, and to sit in front of her laptop writing emails, searching listings. She knows the job sites so well now that she can spot a new posting almost instantly. She's eclectic about what jobs, courses, and other opportunities she researches, but picky about those she actually applies for. She's still hopeful that something perfect will come up, and that when it does she'll know what she's been searching for. There are regular pangs of angst: she is going about this all wrong; she is bound to fail. She suppresses them by going outdoors, letting the sun burn away her doubts. The city shimmers with an exuberant joy that halos long-haired lovers in the parks, and sun-stripes the playgrounds, and sounds like an ice-cream van playing its siren song just round the corner.

Once she's done as much job hunting as she can bear, Hura rewards herself by reading. First the news, online and in print, focusing on all the pages she used to ignore or didn't have time for. She reads about healthcare and banking, education and boxing, about kidnappers and peacekeepers, about films, about the migration of birds. Once the news media starts to addle her brain, she reads books: history, political biography, philosophy, fiction. Hura finds herself amazed and scared to discover that, while she spent years teaching, at some point along the way she stopped learning. She feels parched for knowledge; reading is like slaking a thirst.

Today, a couple of weeks after her trip to Roses' play, the city is heady with warmth and the coming weekend. Hura takes her laptop to one of the dog-friendly cafés, and sits outside under a flowering lime tree, struggling to see the screen. She opens her email and finds, to her surprise, a message from an old teaching contact offering her work at a summer programme, kids cramming for re-takes. The campus is miles away but the pay is excellent, and it starts immediately. She replies to ask a couple of questions, then sits back and takes a sip of her drink. To be offered something, even teaching, after so long outside any system, creates a pleasant glow of being wanted. The money would be useful. Maybe she and Cillian could go away after all, a few days in Cornwall once the posting ends . . . Her mind quickly fills in the fantasy. At the same time, she's already pining for what she has now, this hot freedom, which had briefly seemed infinite. The course director writes back, confirming the salary, but Hura delays replying. Until it's certain, she can maintain the illusion that every day will be like today: wearing sunglasses, her legs in the heat and Caz tucked into the shade. Drinking coffee, expanding her mind. And anticipating tonight. A pleasurable tug inside her, low in the pelvis; after she insisted Cillian see Roses' show, they quickly arranged another date. For a few seconds Hura closes her eyes. Remembers the breadth of James's shoulders and the gloss of Roses' hair. There is a fluttering sensation surrounding the images, which she recognises as nerves.

She's wide awake, distracted, jumpy. She shakes herself, writes an email accepting the position. Hits send.

Her phone rings and she turns it over to see the screen: *Sam theatre,* it reads. Casimir lifts his head and looks at her. The heat pulses around her as she answers.

'Hello?'

'Hey, are you sitting outside a café near Victoria Park?'

'Er, yeah, why?'

'I'm on the other side of the street.'

She looks up. Across the road, Sam waves with his mobile phone as he hangs up.

Hura and Sam have been texting ever since they met. Sometimes there have been hours or days in between messages, sometimes flurries of many texts in a few minutes, but never an end. His opening gambit led to a conversation about what constitutes a stranger, and when does an acquaintance become a friend, during which, they later noted, they forged the beginnings of a friendship. Recently they've been talking about work. Hura has found in Sam a smart interlocutor about the things that most concern her, namely climate change and how best to 'make a difference', that amorphous goal which seems to her both naive and consuming. They've never arranged to meet.

Now Sam checks for traffic, hikes his shoulders up and puts his hands in the pockets of his baggy shorts. He's wearing a baseball cap and vest. He gives her a quick smile but then lets the peak of his cap half obscure his face as he talks.

'I wasn't sure it was you, that's why I rang.'

'Not to check if I'd reject the call?'

'Ha, no. Did you think about it?' His eyes flash from under the brim, dark and amused.

'I'm teasing, it's great to see you.' Hura gets up, holds out an arm for an embrace. Sam ducks towards her for a brief hug. His cheek against hers is smooth and soap-clean.

'Sit down! Do you want a coffee?'

Sam squats instead and strokes Casimir's ears.

'You must be Caz. I've heard all about you.' The dog nuzzles
Sam's hands, sits down and holds up a paw to be shaken, pants with
a pleased look on his face.

Sam looks up at Hura from the pavement, smiling wider now:
'It's great to see you too.'

He holds her eyes one second longer than friends normally
do, she thinks, but then looks back at the dog. His arms are slim
and muscular and, she notices, marked with scars he seems to be
making no attempt to hide.

'I've been thinking about you,' he says. 'All your questions about
what to do next. I have an idea.'

'An idea for me?'

Bumping into Sam after all their textual contact feels both surprising, and somehow right. She knows now that he was assigned
female at birth. So far, she's stopped herself asking more questions
than that.

He takes the opposite chair, watches with mild disdain as a sports
car with its roof down cruises by.

'All the chipping away behind the scenes isn't the right approach.
You can do something bolder.'

'Oh, can I?' His familiarity is presumptuous, and also flattering.

'You can. You can be more direct.'

'I've told you though, I'm not an activist.'

'But that's perfect. What we need is decision-makers taking the
right decisions. No one's going to get into those positions unless
they run for them. So we need credible, clever people trying to do
just that. Getting themselves elected.'

Hura frowns, recalling Roses telling her something similar.

'Elected as what, or to what though? And how would I even
start? I mean, you need money for that, right? Don't you need
backers or something, sponsors. A private income. Supporters.
How do you even go about starting to do something like that?'

A waitress in dungarees and a crop top comes out and picks up
Hura's empty cup:

''Nother coffee?'

Hura smiles at her.

'Yeah, go on. Sam?'

'It's too hot for coffee.'

'It's never too hot for coffee.'

'I'll just have a sparkling water, please.'

The waitress leaves and he shrugs with one shoulder: 'Caffeine does weird things to me.'

They talk until the shadows stretch away down a golden road. Though everything Sam suggests – starting out with a political party job, much as she has been thinking herself, but then quickly moving on to finding support for her own campaign and soon getting elected to parliament – seems highly theoretical, she's also intrigued. It is bold, as he suggested. It's exciting.

'Come with me to a meeting tonight,' he says suddenly. 'It's a group I've been part of for a while. Climate change activism, the X-rated version.'

'Climbing power stations?'

'Much more disruptive.'

'It's just not my way,' Hura says.

'I don't mean come to get converted. Just to understand, meet some people. You'd get on with them, honestly, they're cool but also really serious. About changing the future. The only thing is, it's also *seriously* secret.'

'Why?'

'Because the police try to infiltrate groups like this—'

She starts to laugh but he leans forward, firm.

'I'm not joking. We meet in a different place every time. And we don't just invite anyone.'

'How do you know I'm not an undercover cop?' She smiles.

'The fact that we met by chance. No one knew I was going to the Barbican that day, I didn't even know until I found myself walking in. I was suspicious when you offered to pay for my ticket, which is why it's taken a while to get to this point. It might have taken longer, but running into you like this, by chance . . . It would be hard to stage if you were one of the Feds.' Sam is smiling, wry, but Hura knows it's the truth.

Intrigued, she remembers.

'I can't. Not today. I, we, have a thing. But I'm interested. Next time?'

Sam nods, and Hura notices the time.

'Oh, shit, it's almost six! Where did the day go?' She starts to search for her wallet.

'I'll get these, you go if you need to.'

'No, no, I had three coffees and you only had water, I just need to . . .' She rummages in her bag.

'Please.' Sam puts his fingertips lightly on her arm so that she glances up at him. 'I'd like to. A thank-you for the theatre thing.'

She smiles: 'Ok.'

A beat. He removes his hand.

She only just has time to hurry home, change, and leave again, dropping Caz with a friend on the way.

She stands: 'It was really nice to run into you again.'

'I'll message you,' Sam says. He gestures with his chin: Go on.

Hura wraps the lead around her hand to keep Caz close and strides away. The park is full of children, the late light drenching it like amber yet to set.

The long windows meet the grey carpet, so that if Roses stands very close and looks down, there's a vertiginous sense of the building falling away beneath her. The East End is a long swathe of low-rise buildings – Aldgate, Whitechapel . . . Wapping? – and beyond that the Isle of Dogs. At Canary Wharf, the tallest tower is topped with a tiny red eye, and the others shoulder up against it like gangsters round the boss. From this angle, and in her current mood, that big rearing building recalls an obscene salute. She places her own hand on the glass and gently unfurls the middle finger, her silver ring clicking the quietest of all possible Fuck Yous.

The show ended a week ago.

'Rose?' A peremptory voice from the room behind her. She drops her hand, the gesture shielded from view by her body, and turns.

'Rose, we need everyone switched on right now, ok? We need you not to be standing around.'

Denise, Roses' tiny South African superior on this gig, waits for an answer; she's a woman who likes to know she's been heard.

'Roses,' Roses says.

'What?'

'It's not Rose. Ros*es*.'

Denise looks at her for a moment, and then begins to bustle purposefully around the table in a show of busyness. It's laid already: white cloth, heavy napkins, glass and silverware. They finished prepping ten minutes ago and there's nothing to do until the guests arrive.

Roses turns back to the window. If her body can't be elsewhere, at least her mind is free. She was thinking about her father; the two hormone-ravaged and pugilistic years when Roses lived with him in Texas, between the ages of sixteen and eighteen. Today is his birthday. He'll still be asleep there, under the endless sky.

Tutting loudly at a smudged tumbler, Denise leaves the room. Roses takes the opportunity to slip her phone from the pocket of her black slacks, hoping Clare has replied to her last message. She hasn't even read it. Four hours, Roses says to herself, just four hours and then a whole afternoon of freedom. And this evening, more freedom still.

'Excuse me.' Denise has returned, so silently Roses has to assume she tiptoed. 'No phones, Rose.'

'It's Roses.'

'Hand it over, please.' Denise holds out her hand.

'I'm not giving you my phone,' Roses says, almost laughing with incredulity.

'We can't have staff checking phones all the time, slouching around, staring out the windows.'

Roses stands to her full height, raises her chin. She's easily eight inches taller than Denise.

'*Slouching?*'

Denise still has her small, manicured hand extended. Roses has been working for this outfit for four years, one of her steadiest money jobs. It's menial, but they pay a reasonable hourly rate, and she gets on with most of the other employees. Only Denise, a recent addition, treats the team of students, artists and immigrants like underlings. Over the other woman's shoulder, Roses sees the first of the guests arrive in the lobby. Tomasz materialises to show them in.

'They're here,' she tells Denise. They stare one another down for a moment longer, then Denise purses her lips.

'Right. Chop chop,' she says as she turns.

'Chop fucking chop,' Roses says, loud enough that she knows Denise will hear. As the group of men and women in suits and smart florals begin to file in and take their seats, Roses tries to get her adrenaline under control. Her face is flushed, she can feel, but so long as she keeps it passive no one will even notice what she looks like. She goes to the sideboard to retrieve a bottle of mineral water, and begins to work her way around the table.

At 2.45 p.m. she flings herself out into the street and walks rapidly away. Denise had not addressed another word to her for the remainder of the shift. She'll have to stop this shit, Roses tells herself. This mindless work and the way it saps time and energy from what she loves. She's thirty-three, for god's sake. The crushing expense of living in London. The fact that the show, success though it was, is over. The simple fact of her dad, who of course didn't come, with his new young family and his nonchalance. She pictures him, handsome and hangdog in the doorway of his home, that baffled expression that pisses her off so easily.

'He's the fucking sloucher,' she mutters to no one.

She leaves the City, passes St Paul's and walks up through Holborn, then Bloomsbury, even though it's too hot to walk this fast or this far. Her father isn't the problem. She can hardly blame him for not flying from Texas to see a small-time play in some London theatre. Her mother came, perfumed and effusive, already half-cut by the time Roses emerged into the bar. Ghislaine insisted on taking her for an expensive dinner at which her mother barely touched the food and Roses ate both meals and left feeling ill.

And now it's over, and even though it was a 'big success', it seems to have left almost no trace on her life. Just lots more doors to knock on, and threads to pull that will probably unravel into nothing. Just the sense that she made something good, and now it's gone.

Her walk has taken her close to the back of the hospital where, somewhere she's never quite pinpointed, James is working a daytime shift. She doesn't even consider letting him know she's outside. If she wanted any attention from him during work hours, she grimly thinks, the best way would be to step in front of a bus, get herself taken to A&E. James's relationship with his work impresses and confounds her. He's if anything more dedicated, more self-sacrificing, because he hates it. There's a complicated history there: some pressure that made him study medicine in the first place. Some doggedness, or fear, or both, that makes him stick with it. A deep sense in him that, despite the appearance of doing good, he is in fact causing harm.

James. Even the cadence of his name, common as it is, now has a power over her. Despite herself, she realises, she's stopped in her tracks looking up at the hospital. The big, unknowable building seems suddenly like such a perfect metaphor for James himself, so closed while she scrabbles around looking for a way in, that she almost laughs. He is hiding things from her, that much is obvious. But why? And how much?

Since the Eden weekend, neither has had much time for other lovers. The sex they've had has been red hot but somehow freighted, almost panicky; as though every time might be the last.

She feels itchy, like her skin is too tight. Perhaps the meeting with Hura and Cillian tonight is making her nervous. Usually, she can handle nervous. It comes with the territory, and there's even something pleasurable about it; about being pushed into the unknown. The problem, of course, is that since Cillian saw her humiliation at the pub, since the kiss which he so clearly stopped, something has shifted between them. She wants him more than he wants her, perhaps. She thinks about his body, lean and taut, the fine contours under her hands so different from James's.

By the time she gets to Tottenham Court Road she's thirsty and exhausted. She buys a tray of ready-made sushi from one of the chains. At a grocery, on impulse, a bottle of white wine. Something is still nagging at her. She cuts through towards Fitzroy Square, its garden green and inviting and locked, and eventually crosses Euston Road, thick with traffic. Regent's Park is ahead of her, though she has to walk past high white mansions and more locked gardens to get there. And then, finally, she's inside.

Her legs are shaky now with the distance she's walked and with hunger. She keeps going until she finds a private spot under a big plane tree, flops down, and unscrews the wine. She takes a long gulp, knowing it's a bad idea to quench her thirst with alcohol, enjoying it anyway. She eats the sushi. She lies down to look up at the tree.

Roses began researching 'Janice Sheldrake' the week the play opened, found nothing but irrelevant social media profiles. She remembers the first name associated with that picture on the app: Sam I am. But he never did tell her his name, and she doesn't know where he works or lives, or how he spends his time. She searches for 'Sam Sheldrake', hits walls and dead ends. He's disappeared from the app.

While the show was in full swing and she was acting every night, giving notes every day, trying to find moments to see James in between, she'd put the meeting, and the memories, to the back of her mind. Habit helped keep them tucked away from scrutiny. But since the play closed they've flooded back, in every quiet moment, and with a vengeance. Things she didn't even remember she'd done crowd her mind. She drinks more wine. Gazing up through the overlapping leaves, she lets herself remember. An address on a flimsy sheet of paper, indented where the biro had dug hard into its surface. God help her, she can still remember the name of the farm: Castlebrey. She remembers what they did there.

—⁓—

Summer, 1996

They drive to the farm in the first week of the holidays. It's a long drive, but they've persuaded one of their brothers to take them and he – Milo, seventeen and freshly through his test – couldn't resist a chance to show off his driving. They're high on newfound license: to go out alone, to flirt with risk. They wind the windows down, put their bare feet on the dashboard, drink cans of warm cider, sing. They haven't made a plan. They're pushing at something, pushing, seeing what gives.

Ro, in the front seat, reads the map. They arrive at the start of a long, intoxicatingly beautiful evening. They park in a lay-by and climb a gate, lie in a meadow. They smoke weed, and at some point she and Milo walk down the hedgerow and when they're out of sight they kiss.

They only close in on Castlebrey once it's dark night. Milo stays in the car; he's tired and stoned, has scared himself quiet by smoking and driving, and is not even really curious as to what they're doing here. The three girls – Roses, Aradia, and Francesca – holding thin jackets around them now there's a nip in the air, run across a field, gasping and giggling. They tell each other about guard dogs, about dangerous bulls. They still don't know what they're going to do; pop up at a window and make a scary face? Write a message in the grass with weedkiller (they don't have any weedkiller, but it's a farm, right?) The reality of the situation is unfolding as they live it. They don't plan on doing real harm, though what is real, and what is harm? Roses is sure, always, afterwards, that they don't plan to kill.

In bed, Janice lies and listens. She does so every night, and her watchful, chronic sleeplessness isn't going to suddenly be cured because of a temporary reprieve from boarding school. Her parents have noted in their uninvasive way that she looks thin (she laughed; she's the size of a house), that she's quiet. She is aware of an adamantine resistance to telling them anything, but also feels it might eventually crack. She hopes it might. Each night she lies awake and thinks about that address, drawn out of her stiff and shaking hand like a bloodletting.

Now she hears something; a shuffling on the gravel. Of course, it's a farm, there are shuffling noises all the time, but somehow she knows this is different. Her whole body is rigid and listening, her armpits prick. There is nothing. Then she thinks she hears another sound, a stifled laugh, close to her window. She can't move, she can only painfully listen. Then, closer still and unmistakable: the exclusively human sound of a zip.

She's out of bed in a second, bare feet cold on the floorboards, desperate and naked-feeling in her thin pyjamas. Her room is on the ground floor. Her brothers' rooms, nearby, are empty; they're both away. Her parents are upstairs. Could it have been her father, outside to tend a sick animal? She can't twitch back the curtain for fear of being seen. Even opening her own door makes her reel sickly, remembering every *Point Horror* book she's ever read, imagining what might be on the other side. She does open it though, and there is nothing there, and she pads upstairs to her parents' room and puts her head round the door. Two sleeping forms do not stir.

She retreats back to the corridor and waits with her back to the wall. She wants to wake them, but how can she justify that? A 15-year-old can't climb, crying, into her parents' bed complaining of a nightmare. She listens, but from here it's much harder to hear anything happening in the yard. There are a couple of small sounds, some clucking from the hen coop beside the barn. But animals make sounds, and this is the countryside, not some sterile waste. She slides down the wall, puts her head on her knees. The points of her spine are visible through the skin; she has indeed grown very thin, though she doesn't see it. Maybe she falls briefly asleep.

Sometime later she raises her head and then stands. She's aching and very cold. She pads back downstairs, glad she didn't wake her parents. In the hall she stops again to listen and then, suddenly decisive, walks to the front door and opens it. Like the bedroom door, she thinks. She'll prove to herself that there's nothing to fear.

Outside, the yard is moonlit and blue and still. She didn't turn on a light, so no glow spills out. She breathes in the cool night air but there is an iron scent in it that she knows well and doesn't want to recognise. As her eyes grow used to the dark, she sees that there is a small shape lying on the ground in front of the door.

She takes one step closer and the stone under her feet is wet. She doesn't scream aloud. It's only a chicken, after all. They're kept for the eggs and sometimes her father kills one to cook that's past laying. He didn't kill this one, though. This one has had its head snipped off with a pair of shears that also lie beside it, and its blood has sprayed across the paintwork of the door, the letterbox, the brass knocker, and has drained into a pool on the step. This one is a message.

The Ethiopian place is unprepossessing. Housed at street level in a concrete block of flats, it looks out onto a paved area with slab-sided beds where nothing grows. Kids on bikes make slow circles, watchful and bored. It's hot and airless in the restaurant, which has polaroid film on the windows and large plants blocking some of the sunlight but none, it seems, of the heat. As they enter, James senses Roses tense. She'd prefer a terrace overlooking water, he thinks, with a breeze blowing across it and drinks full of clear ice in thick glasses. Things he can't give her.

At a plastic table alone, Hura gets up to greet them. Each has forgotten how much they like the look of the others, and attraction is enhanced by familiarity. Hura has caught the sun and her shoulders are a deep brown, her piled-up hair glows with red tints. She smiles apologetically.

'I didn't realise how hot it would be.' She kisses each of them on the cheek. 'The food's great though. Cillian's late again. I'm actually going to have to kill him if he ever arrives.'

Roses, glad Cillian is not yet there, relaxes. She looks around the place curiously, as James and Hura talk about the weather; compares it briefly to the world of yachts and highballs and broad-brimmed hats that she grew up in; thinks with satisfaction that neither of her parents would have any idea how to behave if they suddenly walked through the door. The restaurant doesn't have a licence, so they drink cold bottles of beer bought from the newsagent next door. They're dehydrated, the alcohol quickly hitting their bloodstreams, and the place is so hot it starts to feel like they're on holiday abroad. There are only two things on the menu, *Meat* and *No meat*.

'Let's order,' Hura suggests. 'He can't be that far away.'

James nods. His stomach feels small and knotted, so that he can't imagine being able to eat much. He wants Cillian to arrive, and at the same time feels even more nervous at the prospect that he soon will. Under the table, his ankle touches Hura's. He places a hand on Roses' leg.

Cillian arrives, apologising, at the same moment as the food: huge, hot, sour pancakes with different dishes piled on them at intervals, spicy and complicated. They eat with their hands. Conversation, lubricated by the beer and the warmth of the evening, and by the food which seems all the better for appearing from such a tiny kitchen, flows lightly over a taut undercurrent that is sexy and mostly pleasurable. They are individual animals; they are a new-formed, febrile pack.

They finish and begin to walk, as planned, towards James's warehouse; it's empty tonight. Cillian drops back a little with Hura, and takes her hand.

'Are you ok?' he asks softly, feeling like some atmosphere has rippled between them during dinner.

'Yeah. Mostly,' she says. Then, after a couple of steps: 'Why are you always late?'

'Sorry. Was it awkward?'

'No, it was fine, just . . . I don't know. It's a bit embarrassing.'

'Ok, I know, I'll try.' They walk for a few moments in silence, letting the tension pass.

'It's great about the work, though,' he says.

'Yes! And do you know what? I bumped into that guy again, the one from the theatre. Whose ticket I bought?'

'Oh, right, where?'

'Near the park, I was just sitting outside a café. It's weird, to meet again like that. We've been texting loads.'

'Have you?' He looks at her.

'Well, not *loads* loads.'

They arrive. As they head up the stairs, into the big space, Hura squeezes Cillian's hand. James gets drinks. Roses opens the windows and puts on some music, and because they're drunk and they can, and it's summer, all of them start to dance.

James feels Hura move towards him and, more relaxed this time, opens his body to her approach. She dances close and he runs his hands down her back. Over her head, he watches Roses and Cillian. Not looking at one another, they seem in that moment to be attending to the music, each dancing alone. Moving in this way is revealing, like sex. Cillian dances well, James thinks, looking at his back, the graceful shifts of weight and the muscles adjusting under his T-shirt. And, as he watches, James is overturned by a big wave of lust. It hits him in the groin and in the throat, makes him lose his balance and lean more heavily against Hura. Her body, pressed hard against him, is pleasant, but the source of that powerful sensation is the Cillian who is here, and also the memories of moments in their two previous dates, condensed.

Then something blind and muscular rears up in James and is angry. Look, it says. Touch, maybe. But don't feel too much. He dips his head and kisses Hura on the mouth.

Roses watches James kiss Hura, and the thrill it sends down her spine is like the thrill of his lips on her own. Before the kiss becomes too consuming the two of them break apart and laugh and James glances quickly at Roses, a check-in. She smiles a private smile just for the two of them, dances. Ever since dinner ended, and maybe during it, Cillian has been avoiding eye contact. Roses is sure by now that it's deliberate. They dance close, but without touching. His eyes, the brown and the blue, focus inconclusively somewhere over her left shoulder. Look at me, she wants to say, and can't. She can't say anything. All this freedom and yet actually putting what she's feeling into words is beyond impossible. Touch me, she wants to say. Don't make me touch you first. He does not touch her.

Later. Hura has shed all of her clothes except a thin, gold chain. Her long hair is down around her shoulders. The dream she had of James has changed the way she relates to him. He is no longer a new friend, nor a man she met on the internet. There's some connection, deep and strong, some seam running through their interaction like agate in bedrock. It's this idea driving her now, as she straddles him and guides him inside her. Moments ago she used her tongue to trace a line up Roses' thigh, and tasted her, and then, transported by the very idea of what she was doing, had to stop before she came. Now, still, as she begins to fuck James, she wants to hold the climax at arm's length. She doesn't want to come too soon, perhaps not at all tonight. She doesn't want it to be over.

There is a moment when the women take a break. James, standing by the table wearing only boxer shorts, is mixing a Cuba Libré.

'Want one?' he asks as Cillian leans beside him.

'Thanks,' Cillian accepts.

James hands it to him and their eyes meet. To Cillian the look is unreadable, questioning.

Cillian feels light-hearted, experimental. What else are they doing, after all? He puts a slim, tattooed arm around the other man's neck and pulls him close, lip to lip and tongue to tongue. He doesn't know that this kiss will pick the lock to a cage of wild memory.

James closes his eyes and feels himself fall off a ledge into dark air. He waits for an impact, a body hitting water, counts to five in his mind, and pulls back. His hand is flat against the other man's chest in a gesture that could be read as defensive. He feels the heartbeat under the skin and it reminds him of mortality. He wants to be kissed again. He wants to cry. He wants release, but whether it is an orgasm he craves or the launching of a punch he isn't sure. The women join them and the moment is gone. The group heightens some experiences, dilutes others. Cillian, feeling he might have gone too far, takes a step into the background for a while. He doesn't initiate contact with James again; he never lets himself get carried away with Roses. He tries to centre Hura, and the pleasure of seeing her transported.

★

It's getting light, the thinning blue of an English summer dawn. Birds are singing. Where do they even live in the hard city, these starlings and blackbirds, Roses wonders? She's read somewhere that urban birds sing a different song from those in the countryside. A song of loss.

Out on the fire escape, Roses sits on a window ledge, balances her bare feet on the rail, drags on a cigarette. She's taken too much coke and is humming with overstimulation. The night has been characterised by moments of euphoria, by head-spinning eroticism, by vague paranoia and hurt, giving way again to swooning pleasure. Part of her wants to be alone now, quiet in her cool bed or curled against James in all his singular solidity. Part of her isn't yet satisfied.

'Can I join you?' Cillian asks as he climbs through the window onto the metal structure. Since he's already there she doesn't reply. They sit side-by-side and watch the brightening rim of sky where the sun will eventually appear. Wordlessly he holds out his hand. She passes him the cigarette. He offers her a glass and she takes a sip, and wrinkles her nose: something alcoholic, flat and warm.

'The others have fallen asleep,' he says.

'Together?'

'Hura's curled up in an armchair. James is on the floor. It doesn't look like the most comfortable place to sleep but he seems pretty determined about it.'

'James is an insomniac. If he's asleep, great, don't question it.'

She feels him look at her profile. Their partners have departed into another realm, and for the second time since they have known one another, they are alone. For hours they have been in the most intimate contact, touching one another, kissing, a shifting but constant intercourse. Yet this moment has its own particular and separate charge.

'What?' she asks, her eyes on the horizon.

He moves to stand in front of her; she has to take one foot off the rail to let him, but then she puts it back. She's wearing a long cardigan against the morning chill, and nothing else. He puts his hands on her shoulders and pulls it down, and then, to stop her shrugging it back on, he holds both her arms in place. The balcony is overlooked by a hundred windows, if anyone is awake to see. Her skin goosebumps and she sucks in her breath.

'Cillian, we're outside. Let me go.'

'Really?'

'No.'

He tightens his grip, now he has permission, and leans forward. Their faces are touching. He whispers: 'Are you ready?'

'Yes.'

'Don't move.'

He lets her go and takes a step back and looks at her, mostly naked on the window ledge. She stays still, letting herself be seen. Cillian undoes his jeans and lets her look at him too. He takes a condom from his pocket, slides it on.

'You are so fucking beautiful,' he says.

The compliment, unexpected and heartfelt, turns up the dial of her desire to a high ache. He moves towards her and pushes into her, his whole length in one slow, smooth movement. For a few moments sensation transcends thought. There is no complexity; only completion.

And then, a rustle from inside the room breaks their rhythm. Frozen, joined, they look at one another.

'Awake?' she asks. He looks into the far part of the room.

'Yes.'

'We should stop.'

'Yes.'

They break apart, reassert their separateness. He gives her one smile, one look from under his eyelashes, no kiss. He climbs back through the window. Roses wraps the cardigan tight around her body and breathes in, forcing herself to fill her lungs slowly, slowly, right to the top, and let the breath out just as slow. An old exercise from drama school. A way to make the body quieten and obey.

Chapter Fifteen

The trip happens every year, at the start of the summer term. It's a reward, almost mythical, like a grail. It is the year Cillian turns six, and he is going to the zoo.

The June day dawns with the soft, hazy light that will burn later into intense heat. Cillian is wide awake, eating Rice Krispies alone at the kitchen table. He's been doing this most mornings for the past year. His mother leaves cereal and a bowl out, milk in the small fridge.

When he's finished, he climbs onto a chair and rinses his bowl and spoon. Then he lifts the kettle, puts it in the sink, opens it, and watches the water flow in. Too much and he won't be able to lift it when it's hot. He places the kettle on its stand, switches it on, and gets the cup ready: a tea bag and cold milk together. When the kettle boils, he holds the handle with both hands, lifts with concentration. Some spills and steams on the counter but he manages to fill the cup. He stirs it and waits. Then he lifts the hot teabag out with a spoon, slides the cup to the edge of the work surface, and climbs down from the chair. This is the most difficult part. He reaches up to the high counter, takes hold of the cup, and lifts it down. Now, taking slow steps, he carries it out of the kitchen and up the stairs to Joy's bedroom.

He remembers, or thinks he does, that when he was smaller his mother was different. His dad was still around then, and would sleep heavily into the mornings. But sometimes, the best of days,

Joy would wake early and come to his room. They would play, whispering, with the curtains closed, laughing into the covers to stifle the sound. Later, downstairs, she made toast and once or twice, magically, pancakes. Every day she made tea, and carried a cup up for his dad, and when Cillian learned to do the same for her, she beamed. He is a fast learner. What he wants more than anything, now, is to make her smile like that again.

She has the covers drawn up to her mouth and seems to be sleeping, her face clear and small against the pink of the sheets. She sleeps so much now, and when she's awake there seems to be a haze around her like early morning. As though the sun is trying to rise, but can't.

He whispers: 'Joy. Joy.' Using her name means she responds quicker than if he calls her 'Mum'. She stirs, frowns, opens her eyes a crack.

'I made tea for you,' he whispers.

'That's great,' she says, and closes her eyes again.

'It's the zoo day,' he whispers, in case she has forgotten. They are often late to school. But today he must not be late.

When he arrives, the classroom is in subdued frenzy, kept in check but ready to break into chaos. Cillian takes his place and waits. He is good at waiting. All the complicated organisation takes place, the register called, the children counted and paired and processed, and they are on their way. They arrive at the zoo gates in the middle of the morning.

Inside, Cillian is immediately aware of a pungent smell, alien to a boy who has spent most of his life in the city. It's like a mown verge, but also like a sweat-soaked shirt, and like fruit that's gone brown in the bowl. It is fierce and strange. Cillian, who has never had a pet, finds it unsettling. Also unsettling is the mood of the class, high-pitched and off-key. As they begin the predestined trail through the zoo, he tries to hang back, to find moments alone. To look, without being told what he is seeing.

Most of the boys are paired with boys, the girls with girls. But Cillian's partner is Amy, dark-haired and half a head taller than him.

He adores her. She treats him with patronising affection, as though he were a baby, or her younger brother. Impatient, Amy pulls on his hand to hurry him along, then lets go to join the others, then returns to chivvy him. They pass through the Insect House, then a dark Reptile House, the snakes in camouflage, the lizards still as stones in their lighted tanks.

It is at the monkey enclosures that things start to go wrong for Cillian. First are exquisite, small spider monkeys and lemurs, eating fruit and gazing with black and orange eyes at the children gathered below. The class is getting more raucous, and there aren't enough teachers to keep them in line. They laugh, tease, shout at the animals and are told off, and shout again. Cillian notices a marmoset with a baby slung around her flinch at the noise. She climbs away into a corner where, still exposed, she strokes her infant like a human mother might. Cillian begins to feel sad. He is angry with the rest of the kids who can't keep quiet. Angry that he can't escape.

There are chimps next, faces wrinkled and clever, and solemn. Cillian sees the bars and the wire. He sees the worn places on the floor that the animals have scuffed again, and again, and again. The dead branches are shiny with use. The lights are an artificial glare. Around him the kids shove and argue, and a rage starts to build in him that he can't name. By the time they get to the gorillas he is close to tears. Here they are, two of them, huge in their blackness. One reclines near the back of the enclosure, apparently exhausted. Cillian thinks about his mother, how tired she has become, how often she sleeps late in the morning and goes to bed again after she collects him from school. She has tried to explain that she feels tired and blue, that she's taking medicine to make it go away. But he wishes the medicine would work faster. He wishes it, or he, could stop her from crying so often.

The other gorilla is very close to the glass. His stare is defiant, but his body sags and he seems, in all his power, defeated. The school party is running late, and the teachers hurry them along. Cillian hangs back. He's looking at the bleak, strong face of the gorilla. He's trying to picture his father's face. He doesn't know how long it's been since his dad left, one night while Cillian was asleep. But when he tries to focus on the face in his memory, like in a dream, it slips away. Amy comes back, grabs his hand, and pulls him after the group. And Cillian, who loves her, brings the hand to his mouth and sinks his teeth into it.

Joy doesn't come to the school gates. She has phoned and asked Amy's mother to walk him home; Amy who isn't talking to him. Miss Hayworth, his form teacher, had been waiting to talk to his mum and now tells the story – the zoo, the bite, his exclusion from seeing the rest of the animals – instead to Amy's. The walk home is frosty.

When they get to his door, Amy's mother pushes it open and calls inside: 'Cillian's here.' Neither mother nor daughter steps in, as they normally might.

From upstairs, Joy calls down: 'Thanks so much. Sorry not to come down, don't want you to catch this flu.'

Amy ostentatiously turns her back. Her mum relents. She crouches, smoothes Cillian's cropped hair and looks into his face.

'Will you be ok?'

Cillian doesn't know if he'll be ok. But he knows she wants him to be, so he nods and manages a smile. She smiles back, and closes the door.

Upstairs Joy's room is dark and hot. Cillian takes off his shoes and, still in his uniform, climbs into the bed. He wonders if she has been there all day. Joy has a job in a shop, but sometimes now she doesn't seem to go.

'Hi little man,' she says, putting an arm around him. 'I'll get up soon. I don't know what we'll have for tea.'

There's a silence, while Cillian tries to listen to her breathing and match his to it. The bed is uncomfortably warm, and he is hungry, but he doesn't move for fear that Joy will take her thin arm away.

Cillian gathers himself. Very quietly, he whispers: 'Is Dad still in Ireland?'

There is a long silence, during which he half-hopes she hasn't heard. If Cillian has been to Ireland, he has no memory of it. In his mind it is a single green mountain rising from a single cloud. He has almost given up hope of an answer when it comes.

'I don't know.' More silence.

'Are you tired?' Cillian whispers after some more time has passed.

'Yes, Sweetpea.'

The question seems to recall her, though, because Joy suddenly pushes back the covers and reveals her face, flushed, so familiar it's impossible to know whether it's beautiful, though many have called it so, in the past. Hundreds of strands of her white-blonde hair, which is tied back, have come loose and halo her face. She is twenty-four, Cillian knows; quite old. Copying the gesture from earlier, he reaches up a hand and smoothes them back.

'Oh my goodness, how was the zoo?' she asks, remembering. 'Was it wonderful?'

For a quarter of a second, Cillian's mind is flooded with frozen reptiles and anxious lemurs, the gorilla's dead stare and the scream Amy gave when he bit her. He had sat, with a disgruntled teaching assistant, on a bench near the entrance for the remainder of the trip.

'Yes,' he says. 'It was wonderful.'

Joy smiles a wide smile that seems, somehow, bright with tears.

'Tell me about it.' She lays her head on her hand, looking at him.

And, happy at last to be making her happy, Cillian begins to talk. He invents monkeys that laughed and threw bananas. He describes tigers and wolves he didn't see. He conjures a giraffe, an elephant. Joy closes her eyes, but the smile or at least its shadow stays on her lips. He doesn't think about whether the school will telephone; whether Joy will talk to Amy's mother or Miss Hayworth; whether a letter will be sent. The menagerie unspools from his imagination, and everything is all right.

On the interminable journey back from Hertfordshire, where the cramming school is located, Hura and Sam text back and forth, continuing a conversation about how having kids might fit, or not, with her current lifestyle.

Maybe it can still be part of our lives, she writes, *but I think a stable home is more important to me, once we have children, than being free.* It's a couple of weeks since they bumped into each other. The secretive meeting is happening again tonight, and this time Hura is going.

The message sent, she turns to stare out of the bus window from her seat on the top deck. The glass is grimy, and beyond it the city is a grey, sluggish urban porridge. Is this the right place to raise a child? She has an idea, embedded deep in her psyche, of family life: carrying a baby out to lie under the spreading boughs of a tree. Watching her children run across a field, or clamber over a mossy woodland floor to discover hidden streams. Yet here she is, working and planning to work in the very heart of the city.

There's a long delay before Sam replies, and she is lost in thought and takes a moment to connect his message to their previous conversation.

Stability vs freedom. Classic dichotomy. What does C think?

Sam drops the phone back into his gym bag, then clenches and unclenches both hands, cramped from the weights. On the back of the left is a tattoo of a jay; that flash of blue, a hint at the sublime. He's pumped after the workout, pleasantly tired, looking forward to the steak and greens he'll cook for himself when he gets home, and strangely nervous about the evening ahead. He zips up his hoodie and shoulders the bag, waves goodbye to Kate, the gym receptionist, runs up the stairs and out into the throng.

Brixton high street is hot and packed. Teenagers in school uniform or tracksuits or a mixture of the two call to one another. Early-evening drinkers wander between pubs. Shoppers and parents with pushchairs cast thirsty eyes about them. Sam walks through a cloud of ylang ylang smoke from the incense-seller, past the mouth of the Tube breathing in hordes of people and exhaling even more. The pavement is sticky with ice cream and spilled Coke and chewing gum and spit. The clouds are warm mud.

Brixton has changed so much in the ten years he's been living here. Its covered market has become a trendy hang-out. Artisan coffee joints have replaced greasy spoons. Though the Jamaican shops, the fish vendors and vegetable stalls are still there, the texture of the place has altered. It's whiter. More monied. He's acutely aware of being part of the transformation.

At the foot of his building, Sam taps in an entry code and takes the lift to the twelfth floor. The corridors and lift doors are graffitied; he'll have to talk to the kids again. He unlocks his front door and when he shuts it behind him there's a sudden cooler quiet. His body, alone, fully relaxes.

He sheds his hoodie, then walks in singlet and shorts through to the main room of the flat, big windows facing north and tiny balcony. He fetches a glass of orange juice from the kitchen – he never drinks during the week – opens the doors and steps out. There is a breeze this high, but the clouds feel closer, like palms pressing downwards.

He thinks about the text conversation. This place – his own flat, hard won – is both stability and freedom to him. Living alone, making the little space just so, fills Sam with a deep sense of fulfilment and joy. Just sometimes, though, arriving home to its perfect emptiness is bittersweet. His friendships are plentiful and intimate, but there's no one person; not since Alex, and that ended three years ago. You can't have everything. Sam has become adept at managing his own emotions, and his ability to reason through problems makes him a sought-after giver of support and advice in his social group. He heads back inside, puts some broccoli on to steam, and calls his mother.

She's still up on the farm, though he's not sure how long that'll last. She's become frailer since his father died. Both Sam's brothers, with their wives and children, live nearby, so she gets plenty of visits. He's taught her how to use the video call function on her mobile phone, even if she still handles it like a prop in a sci-fi film, and they speak almost every day. 'My boys,' she sometimes calls him and Paul and Stephen, the phrase sounding self-conscious, but so sweetly meant it brings tears to his eyes. 'My sons.'

★

He cooks the steak rare. As he eats, he has the distinct sense that power from the food is flooding directly into his muscles. He finishes the meal slowly, a book propped open in front of him. It is ok, it is good, this measured life he is leading. Healthier than the turbulence of his twenties, when clubbing and drug-taking, dancing and alcohol defined his existence, making his night-times blur into the following days, eating up whole weeks, ruining his ability to concentrate. Infinitely better, of course, than the misery of his teenagehood. Extensive therapy has helped take some of the sting out of those memories, but he still finds himself back there sometimes.

When he had spotted Roses Green it came searing back. He was glad it had been early in the evening and he'd only had one drink, giving him courage without making him too clumsy or inarticulate. He had raised his eyes and seen her across the room, a decade and a half older yet disastrously familiar: the distinctive black hair, the long limbs on which clothes hung so beautifully. He knew her at once and a shockwave coursed through him like he'd stuck his tongue on an electric fence – a dare he and his brothers used to issue to one another back at Castlebrey.

He's replayed the moments over and over again: the drinks he threw over her, the words they exchanged, the proximity of her beer-soaked body to his. It still disturbs him. There was satisfaction of a kind, but it was messy, and made much worse by going to see her perform in her stupid, wonderful show. Now, feeling alert and vital and strong, with more than an hour before he needs to dress and leave, he takes out his laptop and does something he's never done before: he enters the name Roses Verier Green into a search engine.

Pages of theatre credits appear, her name associated with the production at the Barbican, as well as others at the King's Head, Trafalgar Studios, the Chocolate Factory. He clicks through photographs: Roses in a rehearsal room, dressed in black and cross-legged in a circle of actors. Roses, in a black-and-white image, looking straight into the camera without a smile. Each of the images gives him the same sensation: a sickening jolt, a jab to the stomach. He keeps looking, thinking that maybe he can get used to the pictures, that if he looks for long enough they will become familiar and lose some of their power. Eventually he glances at the time and sees, with surprise and some self-disgust, that he's in danger of being late. He closes the laptop with a snap, jumps up and goes to his room to throw on clothes. He pockets his keys and phone, and slides the glass door shut. The pattern of criss-crossing streets like a giant net; the city that caught him and saved him from falling.

The small Islington flat where the meeting takes place this month is stifling, its living-room window open to a warm starless night. The close-packed bodies are leaning forward and very quiet, listening to the speaker's final words. Hura's back is pressed against the knees of the dreadlocked woman sitting two steps higher on the stairs. Sam is sharing her step, and they are trying not to touch one another, out of politeness or because it's hot or for some other reason.

The speaker makes a final point and rakes her blonde-and-grey hair back from her face, while the audience members, disciplined and near-silent, raise their hands, fingers extended, and rotate their wrists in a show of consensus and appreciation.

'And on the subject of warming, this must be the hottest meeting we've ever had. Well done everyone, especially new people.' She nods at Hura. Her voice is deep, with a hint of the south coast. 'I think there are some cold – don't cheer – beers at the back there, so let's try to have a drink. I'm around to carry on the discussion, but since we've promised the owners of this flat not to annoy the neighbours, we can also do that online after we're done here tonight, ok?'

Hura and Sam rise and flatten themselves against the wall as people go up and down the stairs in search of the bathroom or beer or air. She turns her face to his.

'She's incredible.' Hura's eyes shine.

'Let's go and talk to her.'

'I'll be starstruck.'

'Come on. She knows people. If anyone can help you get to the heart of things quickly, it's her.'

They begin pressing through the small, thick crowd, and Hura, looking at the well-cropped hair at the back of Sam's neck, wonders why he thinks she wants to 'get to the heart of things quickly', and then wonders whether she does, and is surprised to find that that's exactly what she wants.

The speaker, Anne Brady, the founder of the militant climate change movement planning major disruptions to London, is deep in conversation with a grey-bearded man. Without looking in Sam's direction, she uses a cigarette lighter to flip the top off a bottle of beer and hands it to him. Sam passes it on to Hura, who takes a long grateful swallow. And then, suddenly, Brady's focus has switched to them. Hura, taken by surprise, almost chokes as Sam introduces her. Brady's eyes on hers are steady as a falcon's.

'Let's chat,' she says, with calm decision. 'But I have to pee. Come with me.'

Now they make their way back through the room and up the stairs, and the crowd must part for Brady because it takes all of twenty seconds before Hura finds herself wedged between sink and door in the small bathroom while Brady sits on the toilet, so unembarrassed that Hura forgets to be.

'Sam's a great friend. He's told me all about you,' Brady says.

'That's nice of him, though I don't know how well he knows me yet.'

'He says you're passionate, up for fighting for the cause from inside. Government.' Brady tears off two squares of toilet roll.

'Do you think that's a good idea? I don't even really know how to go about it.' Having been mesmerised by Brady's poise as a speaker, Hura is continuing to find her presence powerful and crave her opinion, despite the situation.

'Absolutely it could work. It will. Do you know what a SPAD is?'

Hura shakes her head. 'No.'

'Special advisor. Like a civil servant but more rock and roll.'

Brady washes her hands and dries them, and Hura expects they'll leave the cramped bathroom, but instead the other woman sits on the edge of the bath and takes out a pouch of rolling tobacco.

'If we go out there we'll only get interrupted,' she says. 'Go, if you need to.'

'I'm fine.'

Brady rolls a thin liquorice cigarette.

'They're recruiting now. You'd meet the secretary of state, maybe the PM. If they like you, you're in.'

Hura decides she definitely also needs to pee. She sits on the loo.

'But why would they like me? I don't know anything about—'

'Why wouldn't they like you?' Brady interrupts, and then answers Hura's unfinished question. 'And you do know, a lot. I've seen your CV.'

Hura is taken aback, but Brady waves a hand to indicate 'don't worry about it'.

'You're the right person, Hura. And with the right kind of support you'll be amazed at what's possible. Now if you're finished we need to climb out of this window so I can smoke before someone else tries to have a conversation with me.'

She's pushed up the sash and Hura sees it leads onto a small flat roof. Brady swings a leg out and disappears.

'Unlock the door on the way out, we don't want to hog the bathroom,' she says from outside.

Hura slides the small bolt and opens the door a crack, then turns to follow.

Zahra picks up the phone on the second ring: 'Hura.'

'Hey, are you at work?'

'No, just got home from climbing. I'm not working till this afternoon.' Zahra gets a glass and wedges the phone under her chin while she opens a bottle of milk, pours it. She takes the glass and a bowl of almonds out to the table on the balcony.

'I've got to tell you something,' Hura says, and without waiting: 'You know that woman I met last week?'

'The activist? The one who made you climb out of a toilet onto a roof?'

'She didn't make me but yeah. Anyway, she said she could get me a job interview and she bloody has. I'd be working for the secretary of state for environment.'

'What?!' Zahra coughs, gets a piece of almond down her wind-pipe, keeps talking hoarsely over the problem. 'That's fucking crazy, what do you mean? That's amazing. You're meeting them? When? What are you going to say?'

Hura's laughing, incredulous: 'I know, right? It's in a couple of weeks. I've got no idea what I'm going to say. I have to just spend every waking second researching and becoming a genius between now and then, but I've got this teaching thing in Hertfordshire and we really need the money and it's—'

'You can read on the train. And in the evenings.' Zahra warms to the idea, gets up to lean on the balcony rail.

'Yes. Cillian will have to have Caz all the time—'

'He'll cope. This is brilliant. This is what you needed.'

'Thanks, doc.'

'Isn't it?'

'Yes.' Hura's smiling. 'I can't remember feeling this positive about work since . . . I don't know. Marching into those schools after training. Thinking I could change the world one geography lesson at a time.'

'You'll be great. Oh my god, you're going to be the prime min-ister. My friend *the prime minister*, I'll have to call you. Oh yeah, my friend *Hura Holmes the prime minister* is coming over for dinner tonight. Shit, you won't be allowed to come over for dinner, will you? I'll have to come to Number 10 and be frisked by some big dude with a gun . . .'

'I think I'll still be able to come for dinner, Zahra. Mostly be-cause this isn't an interview *to be the prime minister*.'

They talk about the job for a long time, during which Zahra showers, shouting, with the phone on speaker, and gets dressed for work. Hura, at her flat, wanders around looking out of the various windows without really seeing what's beyond. Absentmindedly she picks up and inspects each of the birthday cards, hers from the previous week, on the mantlepiece. When they've also talked about the tricky dynamics of Zahra's medical practice, the conversation shifts gear. Each has less they need to immediately talk about and it becomes slower and more contemplative.

'How's Cillian? Hang on, I'm just looking for my keys and then I'll keep talking while I walk.'

There's rustling at the other end, then jingling: 'Got them.'

'He's good.' Hura hasn't told her about the date that ended at James's flat. Something tells her it makes Zahra uncomfortable; that, despite their intimacy, the discussion of this sexual exploration upsets and destabilises something delicate in their friendship.

'He gave me the most beautiful thing for my birthday. A book of our life together. It must have taken him hours.'

'Nice.' There's a pause, maybe Zahra negotiating traffic. 'He still seeing other people?'

'We are, yes. It's been interesting,' Hura says. 'I guess it's on the back burner a bit now. And I've been thinking more about kids.'

'Really?' Zahra's voice is more surprised than Hura expected.

'Only thinking about it.'

'Just when you're about to make a bid for the big job?' Zahra's voice has an ironic tinge to it, or something like irony.

'I don't know. I had my birthday and everything.' Hura laughs lightly. 'It could be a good time. As much as it's ever going to be a good time. Which feels like never.'

'I didn't even think you wanted kids that much,' Zahra says. Their solidarity over this ambivalence has been strong for a long time.

'I know, I'm still not sure. Am I ever going to feel sure?'

'How's your mum?'

'You mean is she still asking me every fifteen minutes? Yes. How's yours?'

'My mum is actually talking about arranged marriage again. Seriously. I mean, what am I meant to say to that?'

'Are you ever tempted?'

'Shut up, Hura,' Zahra says affectionately. 'No no, it'd have to be the sperm bank for me. Whack it up with a baster.'

'Zahra!'

'What? I'm just arriving, ok. Talk soon, yeah?'

'Bye!'

Hura hangs up and looks out of the window for a few more seconds. A group of homing pigeons swoops past like certainty. She gets out a pad of paper and a pack of coloured pens, and starts work on a schedule.

Cillian shakes himself: he's opened the site again. There in front of him are the message icons and lists, the wide-eyed faces photographed from above, the heavy-lidded faces photographed from below. He closes the tab. He closes the next as well, the site of a surf school for their possible end-of-summer getaway. He closes a dozen more: shopping pages, maps, the litter trail of his unfocused mind. The last is the site, now live, for his mother's paintings. He looks at it again for one appreciative moment. This morning he woke to a thrilled message from Joy, telling him that someone had bought a painting through the site for the first time. He pushes his T-shirt sleeves up and grips his upper arms. It's all displacement, he knows; a way to stop himself from worrying.

The summer school was already taking up much of Hura's time, but since she began prepping for this interview, every waking moment is packed. He tells himself he's being ridiculous, needy. He had got used to her being so present, since she lost her last teaching job; to relying on him more than ever. Neither of them would have wanted that to last forever. But at the root of his worry is a suspicion: that this is the shape of things to come. Hura is embarking on a new way of life, one that will entail irregular hours and demand both intense commitment and constant effort. The idea of having children, which seemed to have recently come closer, will recede again. He wants to talk to her about it; will do, if they ever get a moment together.

Meanwhile his desire to meet new people, to court strangers and feel that electricity pass through him, has crept up like a fever. He meets people at lunchtime, even for breakfast. Last week he brought someone back to the closed office and ended up having sex with them in the toilets. At the time it felt dirty in a good way. Now, in the post-lunch slump of an ordinary Tuesday, it feels dirty in a bad way. He misses Hura. Even when they lie next to each other in bed, at the moment, she feels far away.

Sometimes, late at night, he tells her in whispers about his encounters, hoping to elicit a reaction. This worked at first, after all; their individual exploits fuelling their desire for one another. Hura's response now is to laugh, or fall asleep, or silence him with a light kiss and turn away, like she's left the project and moved on to something new. He tells himself this aloofness is a blip in a long marriage, but her retreat hurts and makes him feel alone. That it stems from a deep and passionate interest in work seems, sometimes, to contain a reproach at Cillian's lack of engagement with his own career.

He wonders how many times she's met this Sam now. Just three? It feels like more. Cillian has suggested that they all have a drink; he'd like to know the person who seems to have taken such an interest in the trajectory of his wife's life. Hura says she'll arrange it for when the interview is over, once they all have more time. He's never asked to see a picture and Hura hasn't taken any, but in his imagination Sam is tall, with a curl of the lip and, for some reason, always dressed in a polo neck. Cillian would never look at Hura's phone; but he sometimes wonders how often they text.

As Hura's bedtime has moved earlier, Cillian has begun to stay up very late. In the mornings he needs more caffeine than usual to function. Because none of his managers seems to notice his threadbare concentration, he does even less work, half-hoping they will pull him up on it, and that will somehow lead to a change, a new direction.

His phone buzzes and he grabs it from the desk, but it's a survey sent by his bank and fails to deliver even a tiny hit of pleasure. He should drink some water, he thinks. But before he gets up to fill his glass, an internal message pings onto his screen, and he spends the next hour discussing a particular shade of green with colleagues. While he does so, he begins scrolling on the phone. Swiping his thumb this way and that across the faces of strangers.

Chapter Sixteen

After the success at the Barbican, Roses and Stefan form a company, Unruly Sun.

But every new project is a voyage in the dark, and Roses finds herself, that August – a bad time for theatre, with London emptied out in favour of the Edinburgh Festival – at a tiny space near Euston, about to open a show that's failing to come together. It's a one-man adaptation of Franz Kafka's *The Metamorphosis*, wordy and bleak, full of psychological musings intercut with segments of interpretive dance. Even describing it makes her want to curl up, much like the beetle at the centre of the story, and die. She took it on at the urging of the actor and writer, a friend from drama school called Webster Samson. She has since come to realise that he is a talented man, but also a maniac. He takes personally the coincidence of his name with Kafka's main character; *Samsa/Samson* is the name of the show. Roses soldiers through the extremely short rehearsal period, trying to believe problems can be solved by careful work on Webster's delivery of text, his movement, his engagement with the audience. During the dress rehearsal, they practise a curtain call. Even the way he bows feels wrong.

On opening night she sits at the back of the audience. Her recent success, perhaps, and the smallness of the venue mean that the place is full. James isn't here; she told him not to come until later in the run, but really she'd prefer if he never came. Things have gone off-kilter again; perhaps since the foursome at his flat, she's not sure.

Stefan has been called back to Leipzig for a funeral. Most of the people in the seats must be strangers, or Webster's friends and contacts; she barely recognises anyone. Then a woman with blonde hair takes a seat in the front row, glances round, spots Roses, and winks. It's Clare. For a moment the sight of her friend distracts Roses from the sense of impending doom. Then the lights go out.

'Are you hiding?'

'Yes.'

After the performance Roses went straight back to the tiny dressing room to congratulate Webster, and salve the raging neuroticism that makes him so unpredictable both onstage and off. She found him in full post-show mode, hyped and loud. He was furious about a lighting cue that had gone wrong, bombastic with pleasure at his own performance, craving praise, and angry with what he called the 'zombie' audience. Roses limited herself to quiet support, and said they'd go through notes in the morning. Then she went back to the empty auditorium and, unable to face the noisy foyer bar, stayed there.

Illuminated by plain hanging bulbs, the black paint of the walls and floor looks dusty and chipped. The pieces of set resemble a junk-shop window. She sits in the front row and, for a moment, indulges the urge to put her head in her hands. It's in this position that Clare finds her. Caught in an attitude of despondency, Roses pushes her hands through her hair and attempts a quick, bright grin.

'Not hiding from you, though. Just thinking about the performance.'

Clare sits beside her. 'How did it go?'

'You saw it, I should ask you.'

'I thought there were some really good moments. The transformation was good.'

Roses smiles a grim smile. The transformation is the only part of the show she can watch without cringing.

Roses stares at the objects on the stage, all rickety and wrong.

'There's a fire escape at the back,' she says. 'Run away with me?'

★

Once they're outside, Roses sets off walking north and Clare falls in step beside her. They don't speak for a few moments.

'First nights can be rough,' Clare says eventually.

Clare started out in theatre, quickly quit in frustration. A series of disparate jobs has eventually led her into the amorphous world of consulting. Clare gets well paid, and has a fiancé with whom she owns a house. Sometimes Roses senses her own life and Clare's could diverge utterly, if the bonds of long intimacy didn't hold them together.

'Seeing a show you've directed for the first time, with an audience,' Roses says. 'It's like having your diary read aloud. It's like having your mind turned inside out for judgement.'

'Was that a good reflection of the inside of your mind?'

'No! I mean, my ideas were in there. But a lot of it was Webster, and a lot of it was compromise, and a lot was just *stuff*, things that happen, things that get said. That's the problem with this show, maybe. There's no vision. It's just a morass.'

'You're not happy with it?'

She gives a short bark of laughter. 'I wish the ground would open and swallow me.'

Clare links arms with her. 'That would be a shame,' she says.

It's a warm night and the bars in Camden are packed and loud. They keep walking and talking, thinking they'll stop and never quite doing so.

'James didn't come?' Clare asks.

'I asked him not to. But I think he was relieved. Theatre's not really his thing.'

'Does that matter? To you, I mean. It's so much your thing.'

'No. I don't think that's the problem.'

There's a beat.

'Is there a problem?'

Roses blows a long stream of air through her lips.

'I love him. That's the problem.'

Clare stops, smiling widely. 'Ro, that's not a problem. It's wonderful!'

'Not if he doesn't feel the same.'

'But I think he does! I've seen you together. The way he looks at you.'

They walk again.

'Thanks. But you don't know. You're just biased because you're my friend. There's something in the way. Stuff he's not telling me. Maybe, I've been starting to think, he never will.'

'What kind of stuff?'

'I don't know. About his past, or . . . or something else. Sometimes it feels so good. Magical. And then there are moments when he just . . .'

Roses makes a gesture with both hands, a sound like a quiet detonation: something exploding, dispersing.

'. . . he just disappears.'

They're getting close to Clare's place in Belsize Park. Roses marvels, as she always does, at the beauty of the buildings, asks herself how anyone manages to live this way, remembers that both Clare and her partner Tim have family money. Roses' father would give her money, if she asked. She's not sure how much, but he's in the oil trade so probably plenty. Tainted, utterly, for her: by its origins, yes, but mostly by their relationship. Guilt money. Since she turned eighteen, she's refused to take anything.

'Come and sit on the roof,' Clare says now and, when Roses hesitates for a half-second: 'I have pink wine and, wait for it . . . *crisps.*'

It's cooler on the roof terrace than down in the streets, and there's a view over towards Hampstead and back down to the city. Roses can smell the bricks giving up their heat, sage from the pots around the terrace and, beyond that, an edge of decay, rubbish left too long somewhere in the street below.

'Maybe he's scared,' Clare says, coming up the steps, the words slightly distorted by a packet of salt and vinegar crisps which she's holding between her teeth. She balances two glasses on the parapet, unscrews the cap of the wine and pours.

'Don't knock anything off. We'd probably kill someone.'

Roses eats a crisp. It's the first thing she's eaten since lunchtime.

'He's definitely scared. I've almost never known someone so afraid. He thinks it's hidden but it's not. This big strong man, this doctor, and he's frightened all the time.'

'What of?'

'Spiders. Death. Being discovered. Love. Getting stuck here. Leaving.'

Roses drinks some wine and it burns her stomach – she's thirsty as well as hungry. 'Can we make some pasta?'

'Sure,' Clare says. Neither moves.

Roses asks: 'Is Tim scared of things?'

Clare laughs. 'Tim is deeply and desperately terrified of one thing, and one thing only.' She sips her wine. 'Fatherhood.'

'Oh god,' Roses says. 'We haven't even got near that one.'

Now Clare looks at her with a sidelong smile.

'So is there anyone else on the scene?'

Roses remembers the balcony at dawn, the precise feeling when Cillian was inside her, like their bodies were built for one another, to fit together in that way, at that moment.

'There is someone else. But he's not on the scene. He's . . . on some other scene. A different scene in a different play about someone else's life.'

James struggles out of a dream of drowning. He opens his eyes to check the clock: 4 a.m. Roses is sleeping soundly beside him. The new show has been on for almost a week, and she still hasn't asked him to come and see it. The previous evening was her one night off. They'd tried to watch a film but hadn't been able to agree which one, had started two and eventually given up. James came close, several times, to bringing up his booked flights, but didn't. The unsaid thing sat between them: a figure that James could see clearly, and Roses sensed without comprehending. He watched her trying to feel out its shape, failing. When they got into bed he read frustration into the curve of her spine turned towards him, and lay bathed in guilt until he finally fell asleep.

Now he gets up, dresses as quietly as he can, picks up his backpack.

He puts on his trainers by the front door, closes it silently behind him, and sets out running.

His insomnia has got worse in the last few weeks, since the long hot night that started at the Ethiopian place and ended, for him, at dawn when he had suddenly and unexpectedly fallen asleep. He'd woken with a feeling in the pit of his stomach, something like excitement and something like dread, which he hasn't been able to shift since.

He runs, and tries not to think about that night; attempts instead to concentrate on the rhythm of his moving limbs, the blue air, the surreal sense of being the only person on the London streets. The flight is now two months away. He's done almost no more research – hasn't found a trace of Maria Gulliver, has barely thought about the places he might spend time. He's arranged a whole change of life for himself. But even though, intellectually, he knows it's going to happen, until he shares it, it still feels like a fiction.

He arrives at the hospital drenched, leans down, hands on his knees, to catch his breath. When he straightens up, Emma is standing in front of him.

'You're very early,' she says, smiling. It's more than an hour before his shift.

'Yeah, well.' He wipes a hand over his face, shakes drops of sweat from it onto the paving slabs.

'Do you run here every morning?'

'Not every day.'

'Most of the young doctors are so unhealthy, getting smashed every weekend, taking god-knows-what. I'm impressed.'

She lets her eyes move down over the T-shirt, stuck to his body, before turning to walk in. He doesn't have much choice but to follow her.

'It's not that far,' he says, omitting the loops he made around the parks, the fact he's run more than ten miles that morning. 'And I'm not that young.'

'And you have a shower here?' Emma asks.

'Yeah. They're bad, but it's better than nothing.'

They turn together towards the changing rooms.

'I just find it so hard to motivate myself to run alone,' she says. 'Maybe I could meet you on your route sometime? Head in together.'

There's no way to politely refuse, so he makes vague noises of agreement.

Alone in the locker room he tears off the T-shirt and drops it in a wet heap on the floor, kicks his trainers under the bench. In the weak shower he closes his eyes. He's thinking about Cillian again. It's got to stop, he tells himself. He dresses fast, but not in scrubs – he still has time and doesn't want to see Emma in the hospital canteen. He jogs out of the building into a morning that's suddenly bright and bustling, walks fast to his favourite café. On the way he tells himself there's no way Cillian will be there this early; that the possibility of bumping into him is no part of the reason he's going to this particular place. No part of the reason he got to the hospital with so much time to spare. Of course he won't be disappointed if Cillian isn't there, because Cillian won't be there.

When Cillian turns from the counter and spots James at the door, his first reaction is a rush of unexpected happiness; like seeing a long-lost friend. Their shared intimacy seems to punctuate the previously mundane scene; the scent of the coffee richer, a tune in the background hitting a major chord. He smiles and sees James's answering smile, and takes a step towards him.

Before they've even greeted one another, other thoughts have welled up. Cillian remembers James pushing him away. And he remembers the balcony. The soft-boned clouds and kingfisher colours that made him wish he still painted. The cold skin and the fire inside that made him wish – for what exactly? A more perfect freedom, if only for a moment. A sublime singularity. It was just a moment, though, and one that shouldn't have happened. No one has mentioned it since.

The men hug hello.

'What are you doing here?' Cillian asks, cup in hand, moving aside to let another customer past.

'Oh, I work down the road. Getting a bit of breakfast,' James says. 'Anyway, don't let me keep you.'

'No, it's fine,' Cillian says. He's made an early start and isn't in any hurry to get back to his desk. Maybe, he thinks, this is the moment to clear the air, if it even needs to be cleared. He spots someone rise from one of the tiny outside tables. 'Why don't you get a coffee and I'll wait there?'

The back of James's throat is dry. He waits in line with his back to the door, and to the pavement tables visible through the large window. He wonders when he last felt this nervous. Not his first date with Roses, and certainly not with keen, earnest Heather, who opened her eyes too wide whenever she listened to a point he was making. Cillian seemed a bit on edge too, he thinks, but James finds him hard to read. He orders coffee and a roll, then goes out to sit. It's almost a relief to find that the other man is an ordinary person with slightly crumpled clothes and no visible aura. But as they talk James feels lumbering, slow, compared to Cillian's glimmering grace. He moves his eyes diligently between his cup and the people passing in the street.

'How's Hura doing?'

'She's ok. Good, I guess. She's got this really important interview tomorrow. So I'm staying out of the way. Letting her concentrate. I miss her though.'

James's food arrives and he takes a bite, glad of the focus.

Cillian says: 'It's silly. It's selfish. But I feel like she's gone to this place where she doesn't need me.'

'Do you normally tell each other everything?' James asks.

'Pretty much. Do you and Roses?'

James swallows the mouthful with some effort. He forces himself to look up, and directly into the other man's eyes. If he can hold this look, James thinks, he'll know. It will be clear if there is an answering feeling in Cillian to the thing he feels in himself.

'No,' he says.

They look at one another for a long minute. The eyes of different colours, pale-lashed. People pass by, looking at phones, pushing prams. A car playing its bass so deep their bodies all reverberate, together, for a moment.

Then Cillian laughs gently and looks away. And James thinks: it isn't there. It isn't mutual.

'No,' James says softly again. 'We don't tell each other everything. I'm going away. To South America. Leaving my job. I haven't even told her that.'

Cillian thought a reckoning was coming: Roses had told James about the sex on the balcony, and now he'd have to explain himself, explain it to Hura. Terrible timing, with the interview tomorrow, but somehow a relief. He waits, looking into his eyes, for James to say it.

When he doesn't, Cillian is wrong-footed. That intimacy on the balcony was almost sanctioned, but not quite. Maybe he should bring it up himself? But if Roses hasn't mentioned it to James, that would be a kind of betrayal too. Maybe, Cillian thinks, he should talk to James about their own kiss. But James's long look at him was ambiguous, and he's not sure. Probably it's too early in the morning for this kind of conversation. James is talking about visiting South America and Cillian, distracted, missing the significance, starts to tell a story about a long-ago trip to Peru.

Two women, walking down the street, greet James as they pass the table. He gives them a closed-mouth smile, and Cillian notices him sit straighter, less relaxed than before.

'From work,' James explains.

Cillian watches as the women walk on, and one glances back. He wonders whether James sees himself in the way many others might: tall, broad, handsome, successful. He suspects not.

'Do they know about your . . . lifestyle?' Cillian asks.

'No.' James looks up sharply, surprised. 'Do your colleagues know?'

'They do actually.'

Cillian, with so many dates taking place near his office, had mentioned his and Hura's openness to one or two workmates, and in a few hours the whole small office clearly knew. He doesn't mind. He's striving to be honest in what he does; it's just often a challenge.

He opens his arms wide to loosen the tension of the difficult conversation he thought he might be about to have. It's a beautiful morning now. He closes his eyes and lets the sun play on the lids.

In James's mind there is a buzzing that drowns out much of what Cillian says, an intensity that slowly subsides. It's good, he tells himself, to have an answer. Eventually, like an old-fashioned radio, he's able to tune a part of his mind out of the conversation and into the frequency of a sensation, or maybe a memory, that he's been trying to grasp since he walked into the café and was winded by the sight of Cillian there.

He locates it: a swimming pool changing room. He is fourteen, and has recently joined the club and doesn't know anyone. He's tall and too thin, and ringing with distrust.

Sitting at the flimsy table, that atmosphere comes powerfully back to him. The smell of chlorine soaking wet hair, the mineral scent of the shower and the animal tang of the boys. The feel of skin that has recently been dried and then enclosed in layers of clothing. Even the clunking sound of the lockers closing, his and Gull's side-by-side, is there in his mind as if he never forgot it. Even the padlock he used. The metal smell it left on his hands, and the feel of the key, which he wore on a string around his neck, cold against his heart.

Sunset on the same day, and Roses is in Regent's Park again. It's only a ten-minute walk from the theatre, but she needs to leave now or she'll miss the show. Perhaps, she thinks as she looks up at the late-summer sky, that's what she wants.

She has spent the whole day trying to prep for her next project, but mostly being distracted by whatever is going on with James. Last night, arguing over what film to watch, she'd felt herself becoming more and more upset, irrational, snappy. She was certain, all evening, that something was very wrong. By the time they gave up on their second film choice, she had convinced herself that James was about to break up with her.

Once they were both in bed, and the blow still hadn't fallen, she began to despise herself for thinking it. She didn't recognise herself: where was her confidence, her lightness of heart?

She woke this morning, opened her eyes to see the edge of a dark-blue rug on concrete, and was flooded with pure joy: she was with James. She turned towards him, and he wasn't there.

Now she lies in the long grass and talks to herself. You've lost your way, she tells herself. You're losing your strength. She needs to get up, leave the park. She doesn't.

The day darkens with infinite slowness. Every few minutes she notices a shade more indigo in the air, like water in which a calligrapher occasionally washes a brush. But this is summer dark, London dark. Regent's Park can never disappear, only become more indistinct, purpler, apparently more limitless. The red and yellow flowers in the beds become monochrome; the blue flowers glow. And the park takes on an aspect less ordered, as if remembering that once, so long ago the fact seems almost impossible, thick forest grew here. Back then there were no arboretums, no rose gardens. Just pathless trees and the plants that grew in their shadow; mushrooms and moss, lichens laid across the fallen branches like a blanket. Back then there was no city all around with its veins of light, its bar rooms hot with the press of bodies, its abundance of duvets and the sleeping forms beneath them. Just rivers and gentle hills, and then greater hills and moor and scree, and sandbanks and mudflats and eventually, in every direction, the sea.

Roses has not planned to get locked in the park. But when she rises on one elbow, feeling the chill at last of the night that is almost upon her, she realises the keepers are probably long gone. She is alone. For the first time in her life, she's missing a show she directed and planned to attend.

From inside a lit room, she knows, this state would look like true darkness. But outside and with her accustomed eyes, the trees are still distinct shapes against a sky that hasn't yet lost its hold on

CASSIE WERBER

daytime, and into which the light of thousands upon thousands of bulbs is pouring. The grass, growing long at this spot, is becoming an indistinct fretwork. But there is the path not far away. Here is the fence that forms part of the boundary of the zoo.

Roses stands, brushes dry grass from her slacks, shakes out the sweater that has been rolled under her head and puts it on, then follows the black palings southeast. On the other side of the railing, the zoo, long closed, is empty of people. She thinks of James; his spider, and all the other animals involved in demonstrations, back in their aquariums and enclosures. She imagines them, after their handlers are gone, levering open their pens and gathering to debrief.

But then Roses stops, dead still. She is passing the place where the zoo cafeteria opens into an area of wooden tables. Something moved, she thinks, there among the bins and benches. Something large. She steps a little closer, but even though her eyes are used to the dark it's hard to focus on anything specific.

There it is again. A picnic table has taken a half-step to the left, unfurled and changed shape. 'It must be a dog,' Roses thinks. A dog left sleeping by a careless owner and unnoticed until the zoo closed. Or a guard dog, a legitimate inhabitant left to keep watch over the other animals.

It is not a dog. As Roses watches, the creature – she's now sure it's a creature – turns and stretches, and then it takes a step and raises its head. It is a wolf. Roses is acutely aware of her own heartbeat, hard as a fist beating against a door. She wants a cat's powers of sight in the still-thickening gloom. She wants a hound's sense of smell. Between her and the cafeteria are the fence, and a dip like a small moat with a steep bank of grass either side. The wolf is perhaps twenty or thirty metres away. It moves two paces into deeper shadow and she almost loses sight of it completely, its grey-black form nothing more than a dark smudge on darkness. She waits. She is motionless. She barely breathes. She has her phone, of course, but who would she call? The police, is the only answer she comes up with; imagines explaining the situation to a raddled call dispatcher and gives up on the idea. Besides, she has begun to doubt herself, peering ever harder at a patch of night and thinking, is that the outline of a snout, or a paper cup fallen on its side? After long minutes she gives up, cold now and distrustful. She huddles her arms around herself and turns to walk away, and only after a few paces does she turn to look back.

The wolf is standing in the open, and it's watching her. There are dim lamps in the zoo at rare intervals, and it has paused crossing a pool of cool light, silhouetted. The instant she looks back it moves off again, a silent swift trot. And it's gone.

Roses' phone is in her hand to take a picture but the moment is over long before she has the chance. Then she thinks again of calling the police. But alone as she is, with this predator close, she suddenly feels afraid. She turns instead and walks away, not quite running, but fast, deciding she'll call once she's out of the park. She climbs a low gate, gains the road, and keeps going; once she's indoors, in the nearest pub perhaps, she'll call.

But as she walks under the orange streetlights, on the familiar tarmac now, her heartbeat returns to its habitual undetected rhythm. And when she gets to a pub, and goes in and orders a whiskey to calm her nerves, her nerves no longer feel so jangled. She takes the phone from her pocket again, but she doesn't place a call. Already she's losing trust in the memory. Can she really be sure of what she saw, there in the dim park? As the whiskey threads its way through her bloodstream she becomes even more uncertain. Hears in her mind others' incredulity; who would believe her? She'll tell James, she'll tell Clare, and the way she'll tell it – the insistence she'll manufacture to amuse them – will make both her and them doubt the experience and its veracity. And yet, that classic outline. The silent lope so like yet so unlike a dog's. She saw it.

The adrenaline and alcohol spark wildness in her. She wants to fight someone, to fuck, to be chained and break the chains and find the edge and lean over it. She downs her drink and sends a text message, three forbidden words. Then she bangs out of the door into the night.

Chapter Seventeen

Hura books the whole day off for the interview, tipping the permanently annoyed course coordinator into fury. She wishes she'd phoned in the morning, feigning illness.

Cillian isn't at home, the night before, and she's glad. Her mind feels sharpened to a point that interaction will blunt. Cillian has Casimir with him, and the flat feels empty, clean and quiet when she arrives home. She peels off her restrictive teaching outfit, sticky with commuter sweat, climbs into the shower and sets about washing her thick hair. The washing itself feels like a ritual, a preparation. As she rinses away conditioner, she realises that she is ready. She doesn't need to pore over notes tonight, to rehearse answers or read news. All she needs to do it rest, and the feeling is delicious. She cooks a meal she never eats unless alone, and would never admit to: white rice, peas, cheese, mayonnaise. She drinks one small glass of white wine and watches a cooking programme while she eats. Then she dries her hair and goes to bed, stretching out happily between clean sheets.

She wakes with a sudden pang of fear. Aquamarine figures on the digital clock by the bed read 2.23. She's alone in the bed and in the flat; she listens and hears only silence. Cillian almost never stays out this late on a weeknight. What was it that woke her? It seemed like there was a sound, but now the silence is heavy. There is not even the usual noise from the road; it's almost eerie. Hura checks the phone by the bed, but there's no message from Cillian. She closes her eyes again but her heart is beating fast, and there's a sense of foreboding somewhere deep inside she can't identify.

Her mind begins cycling through worries, looking for the fear's root. It's late. Cillian should be back by now. Where is he, and who is he with? Perhaps he has fallen asleep somewhere by accident. Or perhaps he's planned this: to stay the night somewhere else, with someone else. The idea brings with it a swarm of anger, sudden and stinging, that shocks her with its power and makes her open her eyes. They agreed this wasn't part of the deal: no lying, no falling in love, and, she had said, jokingly but serious, no falling asleep. The edict had a literal and a more symbolic meaning. She didn't want him to have that sweet and vulnerable moment with any other woman, when two people surrender together to the unregulated territory of sleep. But also, she had meant, stay vigilant. Be on guard not just for your own behaviour, but for the safety of the marriage. She's suddenly furious. The anger is fuelled by missing important sleep. She picks up her phone and sends a quick message asking his whereabouts, lies back and stares at the ceiling.

Casimir is with him. This also infuriates her. Casimir is her dog, or was originally. How dare he deprive her of the animal's companionship, and at the same time confer that companionship on someone else? Part of her knows she's being irrational – that without Cillian looking after Casimir, Hura herself could never have worked and studied as she has done. But it's the middle of the night, and rationality is a distant possibility.

When he doesn't reply immediately to her text she starts a new train of worry. Maybe he is dead.

For a few minutes she keeps her eyes resolutely closed and tries to think about relaxing things like rivers and flowers. She attempts not to imagine the blind-side of an articulated lorry crushing her husband against asphalt as he cycles, or a bomb on the Tube, or a drunken attack in which a knife-wielding thug takes against Cillian's dress-sense. Then she switches on the light, sits up, and calls him.

The phone goes straight to voicemail. He's turned it off. Or he's underground. He's probably, almost certainly, not dead. She thinks about her father.

The aqua numbers read 3.35 by the time she hears the key in

the lock and the scuffle of claws on floor. She hears Casimir pad straight to his bed and lie down, and Cillian drop his keys on the table and head towards the bathroom. She gets up without switching on any lights. Cillian is brushing his teeth when he catches sight of her in the bathroom mirror and screams.

'Oh my fucking god, you scared me!'

He's reeled round and has his hand on his heart.

'*You* scared *me!*' she cries. 'I thought you were dead!'

'What? Why?' He washes the toothpaste out of his mouth and turns to hug her but she pushes him away.

'Where were you? Why were you so late, and why was your phone off? I've been imagining all kinds of things. I . . .'

She stops because he's managed to get his arms around her and is squeezing her face against him.

'Holmes. Sweetheart. I'm sorry. I didn't know you were worrying. I thought you'd be asleep.'

'I *was* asleep. I *need* to be asleep. But then I woke up and I didn't know where you were. Or who you were with.'

'I was at Dan's,' Cillian says, one of his best friends, a single man with money, an enormous flat and a stack of the latest consoles. 'We were playing games.'

'Why was your phone off?'

'It ran out of battery. I didn't realise, and then when I came to leave it was out of juice and I didn't want to hang around and charge it. I'm really sorry. I thought you'd be asleep,' he repeats.

'Why can't you even manage to charge your phone?' she asks. 'You're hopeless.'

It comes out more unkind than she means; she sees Cillian flinch.

In that moment she compares him to Sam, who seems to pack so much into his life – work, creativity, activism – and never drop the ball on anything. Who always answers her messages quickly and with enthusiasm, who meets her ideas with ideas of his own. Then she shakes herself. Cillian's eyes are red, and the laughter lines around them are more pronounced than usual. They have known each other such a long time that she normally doesn't notice that he has changed from the boyish 23-year-old she first met.

'I kept thinking about you with someone else,' she says, her tone much softer. 'And I was so angry with you. But then I thought you'd been in an accident. And then I started thinking about my dad . . .'

They hug, and are silent for a while.

Eventually she says: 'I'm going to fuck the interview up completely if I don't get some sleep.'

'Come on, let's get to bed. It's at noon, right? I'll tiptoe out.'

Before she goes back to bed, she passes by Casimir's basket, strokes his sleeping head. His paws twitch, like he's dreaming about running.

'Good boy,' she whispers.

In bed, minutes pass. The aftermath of Hura's anxiety is empty, dry exhaustion. Unsure if Cillian is asleep, she murmurs: 'I imagined your whole funeral.'

'I hope it was a good one.'

The interview is near, though not at, the Houses of Parliament. Hura arrives ludicrously early. She walks up and down the embankment, around Victoria Tower Gardens, back up to Westminster Bridge and halfway across it. She'd dressed smartly in the grey morning: a skirt, silk blouse and jacket. But the day, though overcast, is warm, and walking makes her uncomfortably hot. On one side of the river, the London Eye turns, imperceptibly slow. Like a clock, she thinks. Look away for a minute and it's moved on. Big Ben, beside her, says there's still half an hour to go. She is seeing things differently in this hyper-aware state. Last night's broken sleep hasn't yet caught up with her, probably because of the amount of caffeine she's consumed. Her mind flickers with light.

She identifies the entrance to the building where her interview will take place, walks again around the block, and finally buzzes and goes in. Part of her expects lofty halls and expensive suits. Instead, up a flight of stairs covered in institutional blue carpet, is a small outer office with a few people working quietly at desks. A very young man, blond hair, grey suit, comes to meet her.

'You must be Hura Holmes?' he asks, in a voice he could only have acquired at public school.

They shake hands and he shows her to a seat and offers coffee. She declines, her veins flowing with the stuff, and asks for water. The young man returns with a small plastic cup of warmish water and sets it down on a table next to her. He hovers, seeming unsure about whether his role is to leave her or to chat.

'Have you come far?' he asks.

'Just from Bethnal Green.'

'Oh, brilliant,' he says. 'So you're a Londoner?'

'Yes. Well, I am now. My parents are in Essex.'

'And where are you from originally?'

That question. She maintains eye contact and replies: 'Essex.'

The boy reddens deeply in his fair cheeks.

'Oh, of course, sorry, I meant your family,' he stutters. She feels guilty.

'My mum's from Pakistan. My dad's English.'

'Oh, Pakistan!' he says, beginning to regain his composure. 'Brilliant. I went to India in my gap year.'

'Oh, really, what were you doing?' she asks politely.

'I was working in an orphanage, and then also in an elephant sanctuary. It was really amazing life experience,' he says.

'I'll bet.'

'Anyway, it's so great to have a BME candidate for this role,' he says earnestly.

Hura takes a sip of water. 'It is?'

'Yeah, so great. I mean, there aren't quotas really, but it's just really good for diversity?' He looks at her, nodding. 'Diversity is really important,' he says.

Hura, at a loss for how to respond to that, nods back. She feels so much older than this boy, world-weary. It seems unfair to take advantage of his insouciance, but she can't help fishing for information.

'So have you had many other candidates?' she asks.

'Quite a few,' he says. 'Though not as big a range as we'd have liked. I think we had one LGBT candidate, which is brilliant.

226

But we also have to be really careful, you know, because it's, like, government? We always check, you know, people's online perso- nas. I do that, actually. So this one candidate, I was looking at his Facebook, which was completely public, and there were pictures of him at what was basically a sex club!'

Hura sits still. Is this all a precursor to something? Is this tall, indiscreet child going to tell her he knows about her private life, about her marriage and its unconventional rules? For the first time, she truly links the last months of experimentation with a possible life of public service. Has she been a fool, to think she could do what she wanted and no one would ever know?

'So have you vetted me?' she asks, innocently.

The young man laughs. 'Oh, no, not yet!' he says. 'But, I mean, I'm sure I wouldn't find anything incriminating. Are you religious, by the way?'

'I'm not religious, no.'

'Of course, cool.'

Hura wants to concentrate, to go through the ideas she's plan- ning to express, the parts of her experience she hopes to highlight. She smooths her skirt down with her palms.

'So are you married?'

The young man, apparently desperate to keep up his end of the unnecessary conversation, is gesturing to her hand, the ring.

'I am, yes.'

'And is your husband also, does he also have, like, Muslim heritage?'

Hura laughs, she can't help it. But at that moment another door opens and a woman with a steely bob and a red skirt suit comes out. The young man jumps to introduce her:

'Oh, great, Miss Holmes, this is Sandy Carmichael, the private secretary,' he says. The woman holds out a hand. It grips Hura's like a mousetrap while she introduces herself. 'I hope Will's been looking after you?'

She turns away without waiting for an answer and begins to lead the way down a corridor, clicking away on the small heels of her court shoes. Hura grabs her bag and follows. Speaking over her shoulder as she walks, the private secretary says, 'I imagine Will's been banging on to you about diversity?'

'He did mention it.'

'That generation, honestly,' Sandy says. 'Pious little shits. Wait.' She's stopped outside a door, her hand on the handle and eyes like gun sights turned on Hura. 'How old are you?'

'Thirty-five.' Hura finds herself almost proud.

'Now that,' she says, showing Hura into an interview room, 'I can work with.'

On the day of Hura's interview, Cillian gets up quietly, dresses in the living room. Before he leaves he goes back to look at her. She's an early riser, and he barely ever sees her asleep in the light of the morning. Her chestnut hair flows over the pillow, one bare arm outside the covers, and on her face a small frown, like a child concentrating. Risking waking her, he takes a step into the room and bends over the bed, kissing her on the shoulder.

'Leaving?' she says, not opening her eyes.

'Don't wake up. Good luck today.'

'Thanks.'

'You're going to kill it.'

She doesn't reply, just frowns harder and gives a tiny, determined nod.

He's not going to the office. A client meeting, somewhere in the vicinity of Gatwick Airport, means he's driving out of the city, taking Caz with him. He collects their battered Mini from its residents' parking bay on the road and notices a fresh scratch on the driver's side. The car is always getting damaged, and recently they've used it so little it doesn't make much sense to keep it. He loves it though, and resists the environmental and financial imperative to get rid of it. Caz jumps into the front seat, and Cillian winds the window down so the dog can put his head out.

Before they pull away from the kerb, Cillian again opens the message he received from Roses last night, and stares at the words.

I want you.
He hasn't replied. He starts to drive.

After the coffee with James, Cillian had gone back to work, but at the end of the day he'd felt lost. He'd sensed that Hura wanted to have the flat to herself for the evening, to prepare and focus, but arranging a date simply for the purpose of having somewhere to go felt a little desperate. He'd called Dan, a friend who was usually single and rarely stressed about work, and quickly received an invite to join a group eating pizza and playing computer games at Dan's flat. He'd been standing on the doorstep holding four cans of lager when his phone had buzzed with the message from Roses. Simultaneously he'd been shocked and pleased, turned-on and wrong-footed, worried and confused. The door had clicked open and he'd gone up, greeted everyone. The next time he'd looked at his phone, the battery was dead.

Unusually, he's the first to arrive at the meeting. Waiting for his colleagues in the foyer of a characterless office, he looks at the text again. There is no context, no explanation. They haven't been in touch for weeks. The rawness of the message makes his head spin with sudden desire. The others arrive and they're ushered into a meeting room, and Cillian sits down at the wide wood-effect table gratefully, hard and glad to hide it. He accepts a cup of coffee and exchanges the usual small talk: discussion of traffic and routes to this inconvenient office; mention of the muggy weather.

'Who's this?' asks one of the clients, a middle-aged woman with large glasses, bending down to stroke Casimir's head.

'Casimir. He's very friendly and old. He'll sleep through the meeting.'

'Aren't you nice?' the woman says, stroking Casimir's ears. The dog closes his eyes in long blinks, blissfully.

'We'll never get any work done at this rate,' the woman says, joking, but unwilling to stop stroking.

'Cazi, time to lie down,' Cillian says softly. Immediately Casimir walks slowly to a corner, lies carefully down, and falls asleep.

The meeting begins with a long PowerPoint presentation, which Cillian tries to listen to. In his mind, interfering, sexual energy buzzes like static. Its power is both generative and destructive; it's difficult to ignore. He tells himself to wait until the meeting is over before replying to the text. But everyone has their phones out, checking messages, tapping out rapid emails. He cradles the screen so that it can't be seen, types.

I want you too. Where and when?

It's a game. A playful nudge at the boundaries. A careless thought, with no plan behind it, no meaning. Perhaps she won't reply.

He drags his brain back to the room, answers the clients' questions with sentences in the language of his profession. He turns his phone face down, and only succumbs once to the temptation to check whether a message has come back; tells himself he really hadn't expected one. The meeting ends. They get up, shake hands, and fuss over Casimir who, aware of a change in the atmosphere of the room, has climbed delicately to his feet. As Cillian says his last goodbyes and promises to incorporate the new ideas and send drafts in the next days, he feels a tiny vibration in the palm of his hand.

Some need to test himself means he doesn't look at the phone until he's parted from his colleagues, walked Casimir down to the car park, and let him loose to pick his way slowly around the bank that borders it. Low clouds brood. Leaning against the car, Cillian takes out his phone, telling himself the message probably isn't from Roses.

I'm free this afternoon. Not at your place or mine though. Can you think of anywhere else?

It is becoming real. Cillian stares into the middle distance. In front of him Casimir noses across the short grass enclosed by wire mesh, which holds at bay a stand of thick, dark fir trees. Cillian thinks of Hura, her interview, all the careful work she's done to get ready for it. He thinks of his own office and the computer on his desk, and how little interest he has in getting back to it. He thinks of Roses sitting on that window ledge at dawn, and of her running down the road soaked in beer, determined, and to blame, and brave. He thinks of his marriage vows, and the license he and Hura have granted each other. He doesn't see the fence or the trees. He sees a pattern of interlocking lines, connections between one thing and another, and the intersections and dependencies seem to him endless in that moment, and unclear.

He replies.

Dan has a spare studio flat. A ludicrous luxury in central London. He rents it out some of the time, and uses it to host guests and visiting family. It's a bright, barely furnished single room, with a kitchen at one end and a bed at the other, and a minuscule bathroom behind a curtain. The flat is in Kensington, a part of London which Cillian barely ever visits. As he drives into the area, even the people seem different to those he usually sees. They are blond and dressed in pastel colours, in fabrics that seem, even from a distance, richly draped. It's almost lunchtime, and the sky has lightened a couple of shades, from London-pigeon to a mistier dove colour. He doesn't know exactly what he'll tell Hura; he certainly isn't going to check in with her now, minutes before her interview. He's stopped thinking, and is only acting. He pulls up to the kerb, runs in to collect the key from the newsagent that looks after it, gets back into the car and begins to search for a parking space. Parking is extortionately expensive, and everywhere is full, but eventually he finds a tight gap between shiny, smoothly contoured cars. He checks his phone again: he sent the address to Roses and she didn't reply, so he doesn't even know if she's coming. He says to himself that this is a very stupid thing to do. It's not worth it, for some brief thrill.

A message pings: *See you there, 12.30.*

It's almost 12.30 now. Perhaps the message was delayed getting through. He pays for an hour in the parking space, and then looks at Casimir. Suddenly, he realises that taking him into the flat is an impossibility. It is entirely open, and the bathroom doesn't even have a door. Could he leave him at the shop where he collected the key? He should have asked, but he didn't, and the likelihood of managing to negotiate such an arrangement while time is ticking away seems remote. Cillian gets out of the car and opens the door for Casimir to climb out onto the pavement, pours water from a bottle into his hand so that the dog can lap it. He looks at the clouds. Then he opens the door for Casimir to jump back in. He lets down the window a little, and shuts the door.

'Good boy,' he says. 'I'll be back soon. You lie down and rest.'

So now they are in a room together, alone. The fact of aloneness thickens the air, the word – alone, alone – seems to bounce around in the space. None of their actions, not the sex parties, not the groups, nothing, seems transgressive compared to this moment. This is it, Roses thinks: the edge. It is almost palpable, this crossing point, this change. Her heart is beating heavily. Her skin prickles with expectation. She hadn't thought he'd say yes.

The room itself is white and almost featureless. There are long windows that let in a lot of light, floorboards, and a futon with white cotton sheets. There are a few personal possessions – a rack of clothes, a guitar, a desk with books stacked on it – but nothing adorning the walls, no ornamentation. It feels – but maybe this is a trick of the mind – temporary, a stage set. A blank canvas.

On the other side of the room, near the door where they came in, Cillian removes his jacket, drapes it over the back of a chair. He's not looking at her. He seems to be in his own world, as if listening to music she can't hear. He drifts towards the windows and she says, 'Open one.' The radiators are on as if it's already winter, and there is a slight smell of hot dust. As Cillian opens the window, a tongue of air laps into the room. He closes the curtains, casting the room into an unnatural twilight. Obscuring a sky that is beginning to whiten.

Roses, in black boots and a leather jacket, feels caught by her clothes, overdressed. But any move to disrobe – even taking off her jacket, as Cillian has so casually done – seems freighted with meaning. If she removes one item, she will end up removing them all. Of course, that is where this is going. But to start the process is a commitment. The not-starting is moreish, painful. They have very little time.

Roses didn't see James the previous night and has spent the time since the wolf, since the message she sent to Cillian, in a state like a fever. Thinking about this other man – his eyes and his body, not his plans for the future or his secrets – has been a sweet relief, and she's indulged it. Last night, she'd let a hundred fantasies play out in her mind as she caught the Tube home, lay in bed, brought herself to a stunning, stilling orgasm. He hadn't replied; she thought that fantasy was all it was.

Since he texted back this morning she's tried not to think: not about James, not about Hura, not about the kind of person she wants to be or whether there might be any sort of fallout. Whenever a worry has threatened to rise she's had the same answer ready: it's one hour. What can really change in an hour?

Meanwhile she has a theory about her and Cillian, the thing that seems to pull them together. It's like an infection, she thinks. She doesn't want it in her system, but without treatment it's taken hold, it's in her blood and her tissue. The treatment is to satisfy the craving she has to touch him, to be touched by him. Just once, but fully.

Cillian leans against the window frame, then turns away from it in what is almost a pirouette and sits down in a metal and leather armchair. His decision to sit, to delay, reads as a kind of teasing. She adopts the same game; she turns her back and walks away to the far end of the small room. At the kitchenette tap she fills a glass of water and drinks. When she turns back, the atmosphere has shifted again. Cillian now seems poised, a gathering-point of energy which before had been scattered. He looks her in the eyes. She puts the water down on a windowsill.

'Tell me to take my clothes off,' Roses says.

Cillian waits. He doesn't smile, and barely moves, but they keep looking at one another. Then, clearly in the very silent room, he says:

'Take your clothes off. Now.'

When Roses turns away, Cillian watches the spiky-smooth way she walks, like a panther, like a member of a biker gang, like the

CEO of a brutal firm. He slides his hand into his pocket, finds the off button of his phone, holds it down. Time is condensing around him, slowing. The last hours have been an assault of concerns both large and small, an emotional and administrative ticker-tape parade of the mind. Guilt and worry about Hura and about Casimir. Flashbacks to moments with Roses and flashes forward to this, their stolen hour, imagined. The charge for driving into central London, the parking, the possible fine for overstaying. The fact that he's meant to be at work. More guilt. Self-justification. Excitement.

But now everything is becoming quiet. His racing mind slows. The phone no longer strives, with its invisible feelers, to connect elsewhere. His thoughts are only here, as his body is only and can only ever be in one place at a time. He feels it. He feels the blood course through him. He breathes deep in the bare room.

Now she begins to undress. He forces himself not to move. She doesn't smile, doesn't seek a smile or any reassurance from him. It is as if he is not there – almost. She takes off the jacket and drapes it over his. She's wearing a black dress, and as she turns away from him he sees that it plunges low, revealing her whole back, spine indented between the strong muscles either side. With her back to him, she removes the straps and lets the material drag itself off her body and fall to the floor. Then she turns and looks at him.

Her form, which he has seen before, amazes him again against the emptiness and silence. Tall in nothing but boots and black pants, long-legged and broad-shouldered, dark and angular. He takes in her silhouette, which reminds him of a stylised painting from the 1920s, and her details: the curved belly, the dark hair under her arms, the small silver earrings that shimmer just below the hard line of her hair.

He says, 'Come here.'

She doesn't. Instead, she stoops and picks up the dress, lays it over the back of the chair. Then she looks back at him, puts her thumbs under the waistband of her pants, slips them down, and takes them off. She walks over, not to the bed, but to the table. She leans back against it, hands either side of her body on the surface. She puts one foot, quietly and deliberately, on a chair.

In a single quick movement he's standing and has moved across the intervening space, and has her body full-length against his. She leans into him, skin against his clothes and hands under them. He pulls her close, hard, with both hands. Their mouths meet, and they kiss deeply, and Cillian is overcome by that feeling which he knows well, and always seems to be seeking, and is always so brief: the depth-charge of desire, thudding and spreading in him, somewhere so far down it feels like it must be at the root of his being. Time, which has become so sluggish that it has almost halted, now ceases to exist, in that room.

Outside, bright rays finally break through the stubborn clouds and, triumphant, burn them all away. The day, which had begun only sultry, becomes hot, dazzling. One long, last, resplendent afternoon; as if the summer, having sunk its teeth into the sun one last time, can't bear to let go. News bulletins this evening will cheerfully list record highs in parts of Surrey, East Anglia, London. Climate scientists will be called on to give judgement. The parks fill with sunbathers, rice flung onto green linoleum. Windows become sheets of reflected fire.

Chapter Eighteen

Roses and Cillian say goodbye in the street outside the flat. Something has already gone from them. It's as though an elastic band that pulled them together has loosened: without the tension, the connection is less. They hug goodbye but don't kiss. They have sated the need.

Roses walks away. The street is wide, with large pale houses raised above street level, short flights of steps leading to the front doors. She takes long strides, feeling big, and happy, and at home in this great city. As if she is being filmed, and the film is about her own life. The time in that flat with Cillian is fibrillating in her memory, and, as she replays it, the details send pleasurable twinges across her shoulders and into her core. She thinks of his hands closing around her face, pulling her mouth against his. She remembers the smell of him, the taste of his sweat, the look in his eyes as he held her down. She closes her eyes for a moment, even as she walks, and revels in the memory. She opens her eyes and lopes along.

She doesn't have anywhere to be for hours, and the day has become gorgeous. Her phone is still off and she leaves it in her bag. She doesn't want to check for messages. She wants to walk; she is young, and brimful of freedom.

She reaches Hyde Park. The beautiful day is already declining. How long did they spend together, after all? She doesn't know what time it is; doesn't know what happened in a car parked a few streets away from the borrowed flat. The grass here is thirsty for rain after a long summer. The green is patchy, the plane trees beginning to shed leaves across the paths. And as Roses walks her mood falters. The last days of summer always give her a peculiar feeling, of endings but also beginnings, a strange low murmur of anticipation, or trepidation. She thinks of the winter nights that are coming; more work, as the theatre season truly kicks off; a whole slate of possible projects to focus on.

She passes the Albert Memorial, the dead man burning gold in the afternoon sun. Looking up at it she thinks about the ostentation of love, of possession, that could give such a public cry of loss. Rollerbladers weave up and down the broad swathe of tarmac at the memorial's foot, legs criss-crossing, oblivious. She keeps walking until she reaches the Serpentine, and stops to look down its length.

There are swimmers in the water, circling slowly. It is beginning to be difficult not to think about James. She thinks of that lake she watched him cross, and his past of training and missing out on glory, which he doesn't like to talk about; understandably, she's always thought. Now she wonders why she hasn't asked him more about it. His lack of enthusiasm for his work now, his restlessness, the desire to travel and simultaneous fear of doing so, she sees as all connected to that success and disappointment, encountered too early, before he had a mechanism to cope with it. She will talk to him about it again, she thinks, suggest they work through it together or even that he has some kind of counselling. Then she remembers again the afternoon just passed. Was it a serious betrayal? If she doesn't tell James about it, it will become one. Roses closes her eyes and thinks about the moment when Cillian lifted her onto the table and went down on her, the sensation so intimate it took her breath away, made her almost want to escape, and at the same time satisfied something deep in her; something that had little to do with her mind or even her heart, something more difficult to explain in words.

And now, for the first time since reading Cillian's reply to her text, she truly thinks about Hura. A stab of disquiet. She frowns, takes out her phone, turns it on.

It rings almost immediately. Cillian, sobbing and frantic at the other end, saying he'll have to tell his wife everything.

*

Hura emerges from the interview building baffled, thirsty, smelling of tension. Answering questions in three separate interviews – they hadn't told her beforehand that there would be three – she'd begun to feel the prick of sweat under her arms. Fearful of it showing through her shirt and already overdressed, she had kept her jacket on, compounding the discomfort.

Now, in the suddenly hot afternoon, she shrugs it off as she walks, dazed, towards Trafalgar Square, not yet sure how she'll get home. She has a strong desire for a drink, a cold pint, and considers stopping for one, before deciding that it's possible she'll be spotted by someone who just interviewed her. She can drink at home, with Cillian. A celebration. If she travels now she'll have time to shower, change, and possibly even nap before he gets back. She takes out her phone to text him and stops. There are five missed calls from him and a message, asking her to phone. Her heart is suddenly cold: it's her father, she's sure of it. She wasn't available so they must have called Cillian. Hura taps the number and he picks up immediately.

'Oh my god, what is it?' she asks. 'Is it my dad?'

'No, no,' he says. 'Your dad is fine. As far as I know. Yes, he's fine.'

She blows air out of her lungs. 'Oh, thank goodness, I was so scared for a second.'

'I'm sorry,' Cillian says. His voice fails to reassure her.

'What? Something's happened, hasn't it?'

'I can't do this over the phone. Can you come straight back?'

She's walking fast now, passing Downing Street on her left without a glance.

'I'm on my way. Are you ok?'

'I'm – I can't talk about it on the phone, ok? Please just come back.'

'Cillian, this is terrible, can't you just tell me what it's about?'

There's a pause. Then he says: 'Hura, please. Just come home. I'm sorry.'

'Ok. I'm coming. I love you.'

She puts down the phone, runs to the Tube station, down the

steps and onto the train. As the doors close, she remembers he used her first name instead of calling her Holmes.

After Cillian's call, Roses runs all the way back to where they parted, round the corner to the street where his car is parked. The Mini points towards her, the front door wide open, and on the windscreen a bright-yellow parking ticket is affixed like an insult; Roses wonders briefly if the traffic warden noticed the dog. Then she rounds the open door and finds Cillian in its shade. He's kneeling on the pavement, holding Casimir in his arms, weeping, wordless. Roses crouches beside him and puts an arm around his shoulders while he cries. But it isn't comfort, from her, that he truly wants, and certainly not her forgiveness. She strokes the dog's long, smooth side, which no longer rises and falls under their touch. Together they move him to deeper shade and, with the sun still merrily shining, she runs to buy bottles of water. Watches as he pours it gently over Caz's mouth, wets his head and body. Both knowing it's too late. She makes Cillian drink some water, then downs a litre herself in long, desperate gulps. She offers to drive him to the closest vet, but isn't insured. She offers to go with him, but is grateful when he insists on going alone. Gently they place Casimir's body into the back seat, and she watches the car drive away. No, thank you, she doesn't need a lift.

Hura unlocks the door and runs to him, as he gets up from the table, and puts her arms around him. She is so used to their relationship: the touching, the reassurance, the care. He has been crying. He looks awful. Her mind has been churning through possibilities ever since they spoke: that, despite what he said, one of her parents is ill or dead. One of her brothers. That Cillian's mum is sick. That he himself has a terminal condition. A sexually transmitted infection. That he's lost his job. That he's leaving her. The uncertainty has made her angry – with him, for keeping her in the dark – but the fear has also made her desperate to see him and hold him close. Now she does so and he puts his face in her shoulder and sobs. She strokes the back of his neck and whispers reassurances, not yet aware of what's happened, but sure, now they're together, that they'll be ok.

After a minute he pulls back and rubs both eyes with the heels of his hands, worsening the look of them considerably. He can't seem to look at her.

'What is it, please tell me.'

'It's Cazi. Hura, he's gone. He died. Because of me.'

She looks around the flat. Of course: now she knows she felt his absence, but pushed it out of her mind because of the more pressing need to comfort Cillian. She looks back at her husband with wide eyes.

'It's the worst thing I could have done,' he says. 'I – I left him in the car. I can't believe it, I can't believe I did it. I'm so sorry. I'm so fucking sorry. The day got so much hotter, so quickly, and – it was so, so stupid. I know you can't do that, I know. Everyone knows.'

He watches her eyes, uncomprehending at first, cloud with realisation: not only that Casimir is dead, but that he is to blame. He sees pain and fury, mixed together, take her breath away.

'In the *car?*' She almost gasps. She is too angry, too stunned, to cry. 'You left him in the *car?* Why? For how long?'

Afterwards, Cillian will spend hours and weeks wondering why he gives the answer he does. Because the betrayal on Hura's face is already too much to take. Because losing her has never felt possible until this moment. Because, so many years ago he can barely remember it, he learned to soothe pain with stories.

'I was in a meeting,' he hears himself say. Then quickly, frightened by his own words: 'I thought it would just be a few minutes. I left the window open. But then I came back and he was slumped in the seat, and I couldn't wake him up.'

Self-blame wells up with such violence that the last word is choked in a sob.

Roses makes her way automatically to the theatre. The place is still locked and she feels shaky, like she has a temperature. Probably it's low blood sugar, but the idea of eating makes her feel sick.

Tickets are sold out again tonight; she has no idea why people keep coming to see this fucking play. The success of it, even though it's her success, disappoints and upsets her. She's been involved in so many better pieces of work that played to a handful of people, charitably spread out to make the house seem fuller. What's almost certainly made the difference, of course, is that unaccountably positive *Time Out* review, now pasted across the billboards in front of her. Hyperbolic words separated by ellipses. She suspects the reviewer is a friend of Webster's, though he insists not. And then, with an inward blink of surprise, Roses thinks: maybe I'm just wrong. Perhaps the problem isn't with the show; perhaps I'm not seeing what other people are seeing. Roses is used to trusting her own judgement; it's the cornerstone of her career and much of the rest of her life. But right now it feels frail; like it could rub away between her fingers into a fine, gritty dust.

She wanders back onto Euston Road and sees the glinting glass of the hospital over the road.

She climbs the steps into the foyer, looks up at the signs pointing to radiology and neurology and, there, accident & emergency. She doesn't know what she'll do if she sees James. All she really needs, she thinks, is thirty seconds, perhaps a minute of his time. Not a conversation, not a cup of tea and a tearful explanation and kind words. Just to see him. Perhaps, if possible, a single silent embrace. When she reaches A&E it's oddly quiet; she'd expected flashing lights and shouting and the rush of trolleys down hallways. Instead, there are a number of people who don't look particularly ill or injured, sitting in padded chairs. Many of them are old, though there are also some children with tired-faced parents by their sides. One man cradles his arm in his lap, the hand wrapped in bloody cloth.

At the desk a nurse in blue scrubs is typing at a computer while another talks into a white phone, twanging its spiral cord with a biro. Roses waits for one of them to finish. The call ends and the nurse replaces the phone. Immediately it rings, and he picks it up again. Neither of them looks at Roses. Perhaps they can sense, without so much as a glance, that her emergency isn't medical. Another woman walks up to the desk. Smart civilian clothes, a badge on which she glimpses the first name Emma. Roses leans across the desk.

'Excuse me, sorry to bother you, but I just wondered if James was here. Doctor Alston.'

The title sounds like a joke to her; she's never said it seriously before.

The woman looks up. She's in her forties, Roses guesses, with a delicate nose and freckles that make her look younger, dark hair expertly swept up, sharp eyes.

'He's with a patient. Can I help with anything?'

The woman comes round the desk. She's wearing heels, which Roses imagines must be hard during the hours of standing.

'No, thanks,' Roses says. Next to this neat woman, compact and firmly on her own territory, Roses feels suddenly clumsy, ridiculous in the slippery dress she wore on some impulse that now seems inscrutable. Her head has begun to ache. 'I just ... I was passing. I'm just a friend. It's not important.'

'Are you Rose?' the woman asks. 'Or, what was it?'

'Roses. Yes.'

'Roses! Such an unusual name.' The woman, Emma, smiles. She has very straight teeth. 'James has told me so much about you.'

Roses touches the back of her neck, which is starting to feel raw. She must have got sunburned during this endless afternoon.

'Has he?' She doubts it. She glances beyond Emma's shoulder, hoping James might step out of one of the rooms down the corridor.

'He's such a wonderful doctor, you know. You're a lucky woman.'

Roses smiles and knits her brows at the almost-compliment. This has been a mistake. Better to leave before James even knows she came.

'And you must be so excited about South America.'

Roses, who has been angling her body to walk away, turns back. 'What?'

'Your trip to Buenos Aires. James showed me the tickets, on the way back from a conference. We end up spending a lot of time together.'

Roses can't find anything to say. A cellar door has opened and she is staring into its dark mouth.

'My husband hates travelling, and we have a place in France, so we just always end up going there,' Emma says. 'I said to James, if she can't go, I'll come with you!'

She laughs.

'I've got to go,' Roses says. She turns to walk away.

'I'll tell him you came by,' Emma says.

'No, don't,' Roses says, a beat too quickly. She needs to get outside, speaks over her shoulder in the approximation of a cheerful key. 'No need to disturb him. It was lovely to meet you.'

She walks towards an exit sign, which leads her down corridors forever. Of course Emma will tell him. Finally, Roses sees a glass door with daylight on the other side, flings it open. She finds herself on an unfamiliar street. Hot concrete and blue sky between the big buildings. Cars beginning to gridlock. The sun shining on and on.

Cillian tells Hura that he couldn't wake Casimir up. That he drove hopelessly to a vet's surgery, and eventually home again. He tries to put his arms around her but she takes a step backwards.

'Where is he?'

Cillian nods in the direction of the bedroom. Hura goes to where Cillian has laid Casimir on the bed, and shuts the door behind her. He doesn't knock, doesn't ask if he can be with her. The closed door is clear: she wants nothing to do with him right now. He paces the living room.

He curls into a ball on the floor, suppressing a howl.

He will not leave her, but has to exert all his self-control not to run out of the door, run anywhere, preferably into fast-moving traffic.

He pulls his own hair, grabs the flesh on his arms and twists, the pain inside expressed in physical pain.

Later. Cillian makes Hura a cup of tea, considers pouring the boiling water over his hand, knows deep down it would be a self-indulgence; this isn't about him. He adds milk and two spoonfuls of sugar to the tea, opens the bedroom door enough to put the cup through and place it on the floor. The sun has long set, and though he resists looking into the room, he can tell that Hura hasn't turned on any of the lamps or closed the curtains. When she comes out, if she'll talk to him, he'll tell her everything.

The only practical thing he can think to do is cook for her, even though he himself can't imagine eating and he's sure Hura won't want to either. He makes the simplest nutritious thing he can think of, pasta sauce with fresh tomatoes, basil. Can't bring himself, yet, to boil spaghetti he knows his stomach would reject. When he's finished, he opens a bottle of wine, pours a glass and takes it to the bedroom door. He listens outside for a moment: silence. He puts the wine through the door. He carries the cup of cold tea to the sink and pours it away.

He sits on the sofa and sips his own glass of wine. The sensation is the first relief of the day. He drinks the glass fast, feeling wretched even as the alcohol dissolves some of the sharpest corners of his grief and guilt. He lies down on the sofa and closes his eyes.

When he wakes, he's disoriented by the lights, has no idea what time it is. Hura is sitting beside him; her presence must have woken him. He sits up fast and throws his arms around her, unable to stop himself trying, even though he expects that she might push him away. She doesn't; she lets him hold her, for a moment, then wraps her arms and legs around him, tight as she can. They are both crying. She puts her mouth beside his ear and whispers:

'I forgive you, I forgive you.'

For James the day has been steady and stifling, not frantic, but full of the unsettling pain of others. Broken hips, crushed fingers, toddlers gasping for breath. The unexpected heat has made it worse for everyone, and towards the end of his shift he finds himself writing rapid notes in a small windowless room and sweating through his scrubs.

Emma looks round the door, watches him for a moment until it seems she must have something to say.

'Hi,' he says, writing. She waits to reply until he looks at her.

'I've got a meeting with The Man,' she says, gesturing upwards with her eyes. 'Anything you want me to bring up?'

'Tell him we need air-con,' James says, writing again.

Emma laughs, silvery.

'Sure. I'll insist they give us air-con, and build a pool on the roof.'

'Great. I'm going to the lido as soon as this is done.' He's not really thinking and as soon as the words are out of his mouth he regrets them.

'Really? That's weird, I was planning a swim tonight too. Mind if I come?'

He does mind. The open-air pool at Gospel Oak is his favourite place for time alone, for re-setting himself. The idea of being there with her, the intimacy of it, makes him feel almost panicked.

'All right,' he says, unable to think of any other response. 'I'm leaving at eight.'

By the time they reach the pool, the day has finally begun to cool and the light is taking on a bluish tinge. James changes quickly on the men's side and swims two lengths before he sees Emma emerge and walk to the deep end. She looks confident in a swimming costume, and when she sees him she dives expertly and comes up for air beside him. He wants to swim, not talk, but the situation is strange and he doesn't know how to navigate it.

'You like swimming?' he asks, politely.

'I love it. Don't get to do it much any more. But I was on the swimming team at school. I was pretty good.'

'Great. You want to do some lengths?'

'Sure,' she says, but makes no move to leave the side. 'You were a swimmer, weren't you? A child prodigy?'

'Not a prodigy. Or a child. I swam till I was nineteen.'

'How far did you get?'

'Olympic qualifying.'

She whistles to signal that she's impressed. 'And?'

'I didn't qualify.'

She reaches out and puts her hand on his bicep. 'I bet you were great.'

As naturally as he can, he turns his shoulder so that her hand drops away.

'What's that?' She's indicating his tattoo, normally hidden under his work clothes. Not just pointing: her fingertips on the dark marks, the date.

'A friend. He died,' he says, pulling the goggles down over his eyes.

'What happened?'

'We went out and got drunk. Said goodbye to us in town, walked home. He fell into the river.'

'That's terrible.'

James puts both arms behind him and grips the pool edge.

'I'm going to do twenty, ok?' He doesn't wait for an answer; he puts his head down, and swims.

The pleasant ache in his arms, the coiling post-swim hunger, are reminders of a past life, a former self. He waits on the steps outside the lido, fully dressed and glad of it. He'd like to head straight home, but politeness dictates he say goodbye to Emma.

Roses hasn't answered any of the texts he's sent her today. He looks at his phone to make sure he hasn't missed a message.

'I'm starving,' Emma says as she comes up beside him. 'Do you want to get something to eat?' Looking at her, James tries to remember how old her kids are. Twelve and fourteen, he thinks. He wonders why she doesn't want to get back to them. James has never come close to having kids of his own but, somewhere deep down that feels strangely simple, he knows he wants them. That when, if, they ever exist, he will love them with all his might. He will make amends.

'No, thanks,' he says. 'I'm really tired.'

'Are you seeing Roses?' she says, teasingly, like the name is in inverted commas.

'I don't know.'

'I've got to tell you something,' Emma says. 'She came to the hospital this afternoon. To see you. It was so sweet. You were in that complicated pelvic thing and she couldn't wait. She told me not to tell you.'

Emma smiles like it's a conspiracy.

'She's very striking, isn't she? Not very chatty though. I asked her about South America and she kind of blanked me. What?'

For a moment, James realises, he has looked at her with unveiled dislike. Then his phone beeps.

At last, Roses has replied: *I'll be at yours in half an hour. Please come.*

He leaves Emma where she's standing, and runs.

James arrives home, throws the bag with his wet towel and trunks down by the door, grabs an apple from the communal bowl, and heads to his room. Roses is sitting on his bed, arms wrapped around her knees. She looks up as he comes in.

The look in her eyes is one he's never seen before, half angry, half broken. He wishes it were all anger. Carefully, he puts the apple down on the desk. He takes a step towards her like he's going to sit on the bed beside her, lie down, hold her in his arms.

Before he can do it she speaks, and it stops him. Her voice is changed too. Normally deep and resonant, it comes out thin and metallic, like someone speaking from inside a cell. She says:

'Steve let me in. I don't know where to start. I think it might be over.'

James pulls a chair away from the desk and sits down. His limbs feel heavy. The tension, released by the swim, cinches again into the small of his back.

She tells him about the text she sent to Cillian, about his response, about their plan to meet. She tells him about the sex they had; about how good it was. Having begun, she forces herself onward, determined not to slip into half-truths or excuses. She tells him that the recklessness of the plan only hit them both afterwards. As she describes it, she remembers: lying in Cillian's arms in the afterglow, knowing as the minutes ticked past that soon they would get up, and walk away. Putting their clothes on, practical and only slightly awkward. Kissing once, long and deep, in the flat. Knowing they had transgressed. Not yet knowing by how far.

She tells him about walking away, and the phone call, and running back, and Casimir's warm dead body in Cillian's lap. She stares down, dry-eyed, at her hands in the dark skirt of the dress he bought her. Eventually she pauses and looks at him.

'You're not saying anything.'

'Have you finished?'

'No. But you can talk too.'

'Ok. Why didn't you tell me you wanted to meet up with Cillian alone?'

'Because it felt dangerous.'

'Dangerous how?'

'For us.'

'You like him that much?'

'It's not that. It's not that I wanted to be with him instead. We had something that was hard to explain. But so strong. A chemistry.'

'I don't mind if you sleep with him,' he says.

'I know. That's not the point.'

'Isn't it?'

'No!'

The forcefulness in her voice flicks both their eyes up and together. For a long moment they hold each others' gaze, until she breaks away.

'It wasn't about the sex. I've had sex with him before. You were there. I've had sex with other people, and you knew.'

She frowns and shakes her head, like she doesn't know how they got here.

'So if it wasn't about the sex, what was it about?' he asks softly.

'Maybe . . . maybe the betrayal,' she says, also quiet.

'You wanted to betray me?'

Her face is angled towards some shadowy corner of the room, in profile. 'I think so.'

'Why?'

Finally she looks back at him. Her eyes are fiery now, big and black and hot.

'Because whatever we do, however close we get, there's a place in there I can never get through to. You're so reasonable. You're so calm, on the surface. Get underneath that and it's seething, all fear and doubt and confidence mixed together. And I loved finding it all, being let in. I was stupid. I thought you would let me in all the way. But you never have. There's something in the centre of you that you won't ever share. And I don't know what it is. And now you're going to leave.'

'I'm sorry I wasn't there today to—'

'I met Emma. I'm sure she told you, she seemed to be loving it. But you know the worst thing? As soon as I understood – you booked plane tickets, you're going, you're not planning to come back – I wasn't even surprised. It's like I knew this was coming. It's always been coming.'

'Why do you think I'm not planning to come back?' he says.

'Are you?'

He pauses, which itself is an answer, drops his eyes.

'I don't know.'

There's another silence, during which James tries to work out where to begin explaining. He needs to tell her about his plans in South America, his reasons for going. But before that, perhaps, he should tell her about Emma, his job, the certainty that he has to leave, and his inability to do it. And yet he knows he needs to go further back, right to the beginning, if they're to have any hope of getting through this.

Getting through this, as an idea, surprises him. And he knows that, despite everything he's done to prevent it being possible, in his heart he's always hoped that they – he and Roses – wouldn't have to end.

She breaks into his thoughts with a dry question, like she's trying to tie up loose ends:

'Have you actually resigned?'

'No.' James's voice sounds strange to him, a sandy croak, and he clears his throat. 'Emma does think I'm just going on holiday.'

'With me.'

'Yeah. With you.'

He thinks about Roses and Cillian together this afternoon. The idea, despite the deep pain of this moment, isn't itself painful. It's almost as though Roses, who James is so close to, brought Cillian closer by her intimacy with him.

The silence has begun to ring, like the silence after a glass smashes. Then into it, Roses says in a voice more like her own:

'It's stupid, but I feel like this is a punishment. Because I'm always the one who doesn't get drawn in, who doesn't commit, who doesn't care as much. But this time I did. I cared so much. I love you.'

She looks up at him and the fire has died, her eyes are ashy and lost.

'I love you too,' James says.

It's the first time.

Silence again.

Then Roses says, 'But you're going to leave. And we won't survive it. Maybe there is no "we". There's just you, me, and the person inside you who I've never met.'

They stare at one another, until Roses closes her eyes.

Then James closes his and tries, for the first time in so many years, to focus on the parts of himself and of his past that he never lets himself see. There, in the blue-black inner world, is a great cave, and inside the cave an animal slumbers. It is huge. Its shoulders and haunches scrape the cave's rocky walls and its neck is bent around its body. It breathes and sleeps, a depthless and determined sleep. Can he wake it? Roses, watching him now, sees him sigh, and gather himself. The animal shifts against the walls. It begins to unfurl. The pressure that has kept it still is James's work and his uneasy relationship with Emma; his confusion about the feelings he's had for Cillian; his desire to travel, and his terror of leaving. It is his love for Roses and his fear of loving her. It is the look his mother gave him when she opened the door, like he was lost and found and lost again all in the same moment. It is his father's hands on the arms of the habitual chair. It is kisses so long ago he can't remember how they felt. It is himself, on a hillside, digging into the peat and stone with the savage determination of youth and despair. It's all the things he has never said: not to his parents, not to his friends, not to anyone. As the animal stretches, the cave walls strain. A crack of rock breaking. And, finally, James starts to speak.

—⁓—

Winter, 1997

James and Gull leave training together, as they often do. It's a Friday, gone 9 p.m., when they part from their coach on the pool steps, promising to go straight home to bed. They're in the lead-up to a big competition, on a strict schedule of practice, sleep, and carefully planned meals. They're serious, both of them, and usually observant. But tonight is special. Gull's parents are away for the weekend and his house empty. Tomorrow is an unusual practice-free Saturday. Instead of heading their separate ways, they aim for the centre of town.

When they're well on the way, far from the pool and from any-where people they know frequent, they duck down an alley. Gull's done the prep: from his training bag he pulls two smart shirts and two pairs of shoes. James kicks off his trainers and steps into one of the pairs, black and pinching. He looks over as Gull performs the same action and stifles a laugh.

'What the fuck are those?'

'Piss off, they're my dad's.'

'Is your dad gay or what?' The shoes are shiny and two-tone.

'They're his wedding shoes. Now shut up, man, cos without these we're not getting in anywhere.'

Gull pulls his T-shirt over his head and stuffs his arms into the sleeves of a shirt, puffing as the freezing air hits his skin. Their hair is still damp and the ends have gone crisp with ice crystals.

James pulls off his own T-shirt, but before he can pick up the shirt, he's been grabbed and held tight and Gull's mouth is on his. He pretends to fight back but then submits. When they break away from the kiss, both check the alley, right and left, then laugh and play-punch each other and James gets dressed. It's like this, their love. Snatched moments in hidden places. No one knows. Their coach would cut them without a word, if the team didn't lynch them first, they think. And then there's James's dad, who they both believe might very well kill one of them, or both. Their shared sport and resultant close friendship provides cover enough, so long as they're careful. They've always been careful.

Gull bundles the discarded clothes back into the bag and pulls out a bottle of Coke, takes a swig and offers it to James. He drinks and manages not to cough; it's eighty per cent whiskey. They share it as they walk the rest of the way into the city, eating chocolate bars in lieu of dinner, and by the time they arrive at the pub they're both halfway to being hammered. They're seventeen but look older, and they buy pints and tequila shots. The memories of this time will always be bright disjointed pictures, and James will drive himself close to madness by running through them over and over again, searching for clues with inadequate information. When did it all start to go wrong? Were they too loud or, god forbid, flamboyant? Did he knock over a pint; did Gull push past someone in a corridor? He'll never know. Perhaps the two of them could have pieced it together, good team-mates as they were. But by the end of the night Gull is gone.

There is the pub, more pints, more cheap tequila with its engine-oil rasp. There's the walk to the club, and a queue, and then darkness with strobe lights, everything soaked in smoke and heavy with music and pheromones. At some point they stumble outside, perhaps leaving, perhaps just for air, too drunk to know whether or not they're having a good time. Outside they prop one another up and prop themselves up against walls and don't notice the cold. They meet a group of young men who seem familiar but only vaguely so. Have they met already that night? James isn't sure.

Then there's a moment that sticks.

'Look at these two,' says one of the lads. 'Couple of homos, aren't they?'

He walks up to Gull and speaks into his face. 'Having a nice date, are you?'

Gull shouldn't rise to this. But he's drunk, and anyway he's always been easier with the situation, and periodically rebellious against the tight secrecy on which James insists.

'What if we are?' he says, and James feels himself go as still as a hare that feels the hawk's shadow.

'If you are?' the lad says, closer still. 'That's fucking disgusting.'

Gull's head goes back an inch as if in mild surprise, and then his forehead crashes into the other man's nose. It's a bad, drunken headbutt but produces a crunching sound and a spray of blood. And then all the boys are on him like a pack of hyenas and James, in uncoordinated horror, rushes into the fray and gets hit and blacks out.

The next moment of clarity is James opening his eyes and staring at a flickering streetlight. Realising he is lying on the ground. Getting up and seeing Gull hunched on his side and still.

James propels himself up, fighting through the protest in his cold limbs and bruised stomach and back. He rolls Gull towards him and gasps at the state of his face. Then Gull groans and feebly moves, and relief floods every painful sinew of James's body.

The club is near the river, not far from a warehouse where the boys go to smoke spliffs and drink cans, after school or on weekend nights if they can't get served. James and Gull have been there a couple of times. Now they hobble and drag themselves, James carrying Gull's bag and neither with a jacket; they must have left the rest of the stuff in the club. Like normal, the warehouse is locked at the front but abandoned, the door at the back only held shut by a rock. Inside there's fractured darkness and the smell of piss and old fires. James listens at the entrance, teeth on edge, but it's quiet. He helps Gull in and they slump together on a torn and taped sofa brought here once, long ago.

James opens Gull's bag and pulls out all the extra clothes, which aren't many, and helps Gull to put them on, then hugs him close from behind. Gull is trembling. One eye is swollen shut and there's blood on his face and neck.

'How you feeling?' James asks.

'All right. Head hurts.'

'That was fucking stupid, man,' James says. He's angry and the anger, compared to everything else, feels good.

'Yeah.'

'Look at the state of you.'

Gull half turns his head towards James, to try and see him with the unclosed eye.

'You're not much better yourself. How are you going to explain that to Mike?'

Silence, while each contemplates with horror how they'll ever explain this to their coach.

'What should we do?' James asks after a while. 'Go to the hospital?'

'Nah, I need to sleep. We'll see tomorrow,' Gull says. 'You never know, maybe I won't look so bad in the morning.' He tries to smile but his lip is split.

'Reckon you can walk to yours?'

'In a bit. Just let us rest for a while, all right?'

James helps Gull take off his shoes and lie down. Some instinct towards protection, remaining alert, makes him keep his own shoes on. He arranges himself against Gull, who is turned to face the back of the sofa with his eyes squeezed shut. For a long time, James lies there, cold and so angry it feels like he has to physically contain it or he'll scream. He holds Gull close and feels him breathe in sleep, and eventually the anger leaches away and is replaced by an agonised loop of what they'll do next. Eventually he forms a plan that calms him. Get back to Gull's and clean them both up. He's pretty sure his face isn't too bad, and anyway, a couple of bruises, on him, aren't likely to start anyone talking. Gull will just tell his parents, and Mike, that he got beaten up. Happens all the time. No one needs to know why. No one needs to know they were together. Somewhere in the rehearsal of the plan, James falls asleep.

When he wakes it's in the absolute dark of 4 a.m. The warehouse is full of a terrible stillness, and he knows the boy in his arms is dead.

Chapter Nineteen

Roses' face is wet and she realises now that she's been crying silently. The tears are for those boys, years ago, the living and the dead. They are for James, in all the time since, ashamed and alone. They are also tears of confusion and fear. Everything is falling apart.

'What did you do?' she asks, trying to keep her voice level, gentle.

James isn't near enough for her to touch him. He seems on purpose to have positioned himself on a hard chair in the middle of the room, like a man confessing during an interrogation. He rests his elbows on his knees and stares at the hard floor.

'I held him in my arms for ages. I was so scared. I thought about calling an ambulance, the police, course I did. There weren't any mobiles or anything. I thought about carrying him, you know, to try and get help. I thought about leaving him there.'

James's voice breaks and he stops, takes a deep breath.

'But the idea of it all coming out. And having to face it, alone. Because he was dead.'

He swallows.

'I picked him up. He was heavy, but I was strong. I carried him outside. Maybe I was still drunk. I thought someone would help us, like, take the decision away. There was no one around. I knew I couldn't get far. The river was right in front of us. And I had a clear thought at last. I thought: we'll go in together.'

He stops, steadies himself. He doesn't look at her. She wills herself to stay silent.

'I got him to the rail. Over the rail. And. And he just fell away into the darkness. He was gone. I couldn't believe what I'd done.

All I wanted was to have him in my arms again, even dead, even just for a moment. I hadn't kissed him goodbye. What if I was wrong, and he wasn't dead, just unconscious? I went to dive in after him. And then something stopped me. I didn't dive. My mind said, do it, jump. But my body wouldn't go.'

She has always known the story from here on, the one that everyone believed to be true: that James lost his best friend when they were seventeen. That they parted on a drunken night out and afterwards, somehow, Gull fell into the river. The blow to the head which killed him must have been sustained as he fell, the inquest had found, since the autopsy had discovered that he hadn't drowned. The working assumption was that, confused by alcohol, he'd decided to dive into the freezing river for a swim and hit his head as he jumped, and that his body had then been battered by the flotsam and the fierce current.

Their minds have arrived simultaneously at the same point.

'I went back into the warehouse for the bag. Somehow that's the worst part, that I remembered to do it. We left stuff at the club but no one ever noticed. When I got home I realised I was still wearing Gull's shoes. I put them under my bed. For weeks, while they looked for him and found him, during the autopsy and after, the bag and the shoes were just there. I liked having something of his. I thought maybe I could keep them. But I was too scared. A few weeks after the funeral I went out into the Pennines and buried them.'

With a sob she gets up and goes to him and wraps him in her arms, and then they are on the floor, him curled and weeping, her holding him as best she can. She's no longer thinking about what any of this means for them. All she does is hold him and shush him and rock him like a boy as he cries. She tells him in whispers that she loves him, that it's ok. Eventually they make their way into the bed in all their clothes. They are on the brink of sleep when their bodies find each other. They make a reckless kind of love that feels like the fusion of nuclei in the core of some reactor, bigger than them, not quite of this world.

★

When dawn filters through the glass bricks, it finds them, still half-dressed among the twisted covers. James has been sleeping for a long time, a dense, exhausted sleep from which he hasn't stirred. Roses is awake. She watches the ceiling solidify into a more certain shelter. Her body, her mind, perhaps her soul, seem to her like high chambers in which the light is slowly increasing.

—⁓—

Winter, 1990

Roses sits on the stairs and counts the fleurs-de-lis on the wallpaper, hundreds of them, blending into one another in their repetitive pattern so that she always loses track.

Her mother's voice from the sitting room, raised in that way adults have that also indicates they are trying to be quiet: 'You can tell her. You will have to tell her.'

There's a murmur in response: her father's voice, octaves lower, and quieter. His voice is always low and even, a gentle drawl.

Now there are the sounds of someone moving around the room, a chair being scraped across the parquet; a drink being poured. Some words she can't make out and then again her mother, with clarity:

'You say that but it is not true. You don't love her like I love her. You don't love her enough.'

Roses strains to hear. Her body is tense: she can't be discovered here. The moment she sees the door move she'll have to disappear noiselessly upstairs. In the last year she has worked fiercely at blending in, at becoming invisible. She's still failing at it though, she tells herself, cruelly. She's still the newcomer, the one who doesn't get it. Raw; vulnerable. The stair-carpet is rough under her bare feet, very different to the deep pile in the rest of the house. She is listening so hard for the answer her father makes. But when it comes, after a silence, it is once again muffled by its own cadences and by the expensive drapery, the almost-closed door. Did he refute her mother's words? Did he agree?

Then there's a sob and the sound of a glass banged down on a table and Roses, suddenly afraid, bolts up the stairs and into her bed, the purple linen that she chose herself from Harrods. If they move again, where will they go? Back to France? Will her father – tall and loose-limbed, with his dark moustache and his easy Texan gait – stroll gently away and be lost to her in the glare of some movie-bright American sunset?

'You don't love her enough,' her mother had said. You don't love her enough.

———

Hura drives. It will be her last trip in the Mini. Cillian, they have agreed, will take the car back to London alone and then arrange for its sale. She never wants to see it again.

Hura keeps both hands firmly on the wheel and her eyes on the road. In the rear-view mirror she can see Casimir's dark head lying still where it emerges from the white of the bedsheet that wraps his body. Cillian's face beside her is angled slightly away as he looks out of the window at the passing road. They drive to her parents' house and, at the bottom of the garden where the shrubs grow tall and the grass is interwoven with tendrils of moss, they dig a grave.

They don't speak much during the work. Aisha is out at a clinic. Ben greeted them at the door and showed them to the shed where they collected two spades, but then left them together and went back to his office, sensing that what they needed most was silence. For hours there is little sound but the chop of the spades and bird-song, crows, pigeons, feathers of wind, and they lose themselves in the leaves-and-water smell of the earth, the rhythmic movement.

When the grave is long enough and deep, they collect Casimir from the car. Cillian offers to help carry him but Hura wants to hold him alone. He is heavy. She sits on the edge of the hole with the body on her lap, then climbs into the grave so that she can lay him gently down. Cillian holds her hand to help her out, but she turns away before he can try to comfort her with any other touch. She picks up a handful of earth and sprinkles it onto the bright sheet.

Cillian, knotted inside by the words he has spoken and those he hasn't, waits to see if Hura wants to say anything, a eulogy of any kind, a farewell.

Hura, meanwhile, would like to say goodbye, to tell Casimir what he meant to her. But the only person to hear it would be Cillian, and she is angry with him. Last night, when she emerged from their room, she and Cillian had been able to share the loss, grieving in one another's arms. His desolation had been so great that it had drawn sympathy from her and even a desire to comfort.

But as the hours kept passing and she dwelt more on Casimir's death, the loneliness of it and the lack of care kept surprising Hura like little wounds; cuts that stung, were briefly painless, and then stung again. She has accepted Cillian's explanation of the work meeting and the unexpectedly hot afternoon. She has accepted his apologies. She even feels bad for how upset he seems. But when she looked at his sleeping face last night in the light from the street lamps, she saw a man who had failed to protect something precious. Even now, on this gentle early-September day, he looks very slightly different to her. His eyes seem to slide away from hers a fraction of a second too soon.

Once the grave is filled, they turn and walk back to the house. They put away the spades. They wash their hands carefully and hug for a long moment before he leaves. But her kiss on his lips is dry and brief.

'How long do you think you'll stay?' he asks.

'A couple of days. The school called; they don't want me to come back for the last week.'

Cillian nods, though he didn't know this before.

'And you think you'll get your dad's results tomorrow?'

They are talking to each other like strangers, he thinks.

'Hopefully. Do you want to say goodbye to him?'

They always say goodbye, warm handshakes and one more cup of tea for the road.

'No, don't disturb him, if I go back now I might miss the traffic.'

He gets into the car. Before he pulls away he winds down the window.

'Farewell, my brave hobbit,' he says in a very bad Gandalf impression. She smiles, shakes her head, stands watching as he pulls away. He cries as he drives, tears he barely notices and doesn't bother to wipe away. He tells himself that he will do whatever it takes to build up her trust in him again.

The next day Hura marks the grave with a circle of stones and plants a white winter rose, a hellebore.

Just as she finishes planting, her phone rings, a perky and incongruous sound in the hushed garden. She takes it out expecting to see Cillian's name, but it is Sam. The name recalls many things at once: Sam's physical presence, dark and sure and filled with something, a latent energy, a promise. The bird on the back of his hand, the line of hair at the temple. The interview, and all her excitement and preparation. Half-forgotten in the last two days, it now surges back and surprises her with its power. She answers the phone.

Sam asks about the interview, but she tells him about Casimir. It's a relief to tell the whole sad story as she paces around the garden, keeping warm in the patchy sun-and-cloud afternoon; overnight, it seems to have become autumn.

'He was old, you know,' she says after a while. 'It was close to his time; I just wasn't ready. But also there's this undercurrent of what's going on with my dad, which is so much more important than . . .'

For a moment she can't go on.

'They're both important,' Sam says.

'Anyway. I do want to tell you about the interview. Interviews. There were three . . .'

They talk, and talk. The shadows lengthen. Eventually Hura, who isn't wearing a watch, asks the time.

'Hang on,' Sam checks. 'It's nearly five.'

'Really?' He called at two. 'I need to go. Think about getting home . . .' she trails off. She doesn't want to go back to the flat yet, she realises. 'I feel like I've just talked at you.'

'Not at all. Welcome distraction. I'm meant to be practising for this performance, but I don't have much energy today; and I'd rather talk to you.'

'What's the performance?'

'It's hard to explain in words. But you could come and watch me rehearse, if you want? It would help, to show someone.'

'I don't know how much I'd help. But I'd love that.'

'Be warned, it's not really ready for public consumption,' he says. Then, a smile in his voice. 'And I do take some of my clothes off.'

'Is it about ... your body?' she ventures. They've talked about his gender before, but she's tried never to dwell on it, not to pry.

'Partly it is. About how we take care of ourselves, how we have to, in order to survive; but at the same time how we can be quite violent with our own bodies. Run risks, you know? Imagine we're immortal. Court pain.'

'Does it have anything to do with your arms, the scars?' She swallows, afraid; maybe she mistook the intimacy of this phone call for a license she doesn't have. 'When did that happen?'

Gently, Sam replies: 'They're from school. I was really unhappy.'

'Why?' Hura asks softly. She holds her breath, unsure if he'll answer.

'It was a cruel place. I was a long way away from the people who loved me. And surrounded by a lot of mean girls who didn't.'

It's the first time he's mentioned a girls' school. She thinks about her brothers, her own turbulent teenage years, how much worse it would have been if she'd had to go through it far from home. She thinks about all the young people she's known, fragile and determined; about her brush with the force of Jenna's teenage venom.

'I'm sorry,' she says.

'It's not your fault. But yes, to answer your question, the scars are part of the story I want to tell.' They're silent for a few seconds. Hura has wandered all over the garden during this conversation, and now finds that she's left the grave behind and is standing on the lawn looking back at the house. A light in the kitchen goes on. Her feet are cold and she badly needs to pee.

'I was meant to spend the day with my family, they're going to hate me,' she says.

'No one could hate you.'

There's a shout from the house, her mother's voice, uncharacteristically raised. The test results.

'Sam, I'm sorry, I have to go. I think it's about my dad.'

★

261

The day after James tells Gull's story, he doesn't go to work. Even with the insomnia, he's never taken an unplanned sick day before. He knows the likely consequences will be an understaffed department, longer waiting times, other doctors inconvenienced, and the guilt propels him up several times and has him searching for clothes. Roses doesn't try to stop him. It is something else that pulls him back to bed each time: an extraordinary lightness, such as he never remembers feeling in his life before. You are shirking a duty, say his own internal thought police. Yes, the lightness breathes, but it's my choice. A choice I'm free to make. The word – free, free – flutters around his mind like a breeze

And so, half-dressed and striped by sunbeams, they talk. Roses wants to know, in minute detail, all about what Gull was like. At first James is taken aback. The memories are so private he barely lets himself revisit them. Part of his reserve is a fear that he's forgotten most of what happened, half a lifetime ago. But as he talks he remembers: Gull's accent, and the long words he had used, which James had teased him for – *You're an oxymoron* – and then started to adopt. Practising swallow dives together, watching one another and offering pointers, then counting down on the high board and launching themselves, synchronised, into space. The first time he'd known there was something between them, something different. He still tingles at the memory: the two of them watching TV one night in the Gullivers' empty house. James had returned from getting an Irn-Bru and thrown himself back onto the sofa, where Gull was already sitting with one arm along the back. Gull hadn't moved his arm. James had felt its presence, the hand close to his head. His breath got shallower and he tried to keep it quiet, expecting every second that Gull would move the arm away. And then he did move it. He dropped the hand so that it rested lightly at the neck of James's T-shirt. Both pairs of eyes still trained on the television, some show made up of home videos in which kids fell off swings and men walked into plate-glass windows. Still, the hand could be a mistake, meaningless, James told himself. And then Gull had lifted his thumb, and stroked the nape of James's neck. And nothing was ever the same again.

'So, did you think you were gay?' says Roses and then, con-fused: 'At that point? I mean, did you know you liked boys, or girls too . . .?'

'I didn't know anything, tried not to think about it,' James says. 'I couldn't be gay. Gay was an insult, a daft thing we called each other at school. The team would've . . . Or, we assumed they would. And my da. It wasn't like now, here. This was the nineties in Newcastle, and I was seventeen and I didn't know what the hell was happen-ing, but I knew that my dad would kill me, or him, or both of us.'

'Actually kill you?' Roses says. Her voice is small and serious.

'Maybe. I don't know. It sounds crazy now.'

'Did he hit you? Your dad?'

Her voice is even smaller. They're lying side by side, and the question is directed to the ceiling. She's never asked before but now, she realises, she'd always assumed something like this was behind James's distant relationship with his family.

'Hit us, no, not really. Not like, punches. He didn't beat us up or anything.'

'Us?'

'Me and Mam. But slaps, yeah, a lot when I was little, less but harder when I was bigger. He'd push us around, you know, let us know he could. It was more the power thing, I guess.'

'Fear,' Roses murmurs.

'Yeah.' James's voice is light. He half-laughs as he says: 'He threw me over a car once.'

'He threw you over a *car*? What? How?'

'I'd pissed him off, been out too long mountain biking, I think. He was furious, and we were outside on the pavement, and he kind of picked me up and threw me at this car. It was parked, like, not moving. He threw me and I hit it and slid over the bonnet and fell off the other side into the road.'

'How old were you?'

'Eleven? Maybe ten, since he could pick me up.'

Roses swallows hard. None of this is helping her detach, as she had thought she must, the filaments of herself that she's allowed to grow towards James and tangle with his own.

'And your mum?' she asks. 'What did she do?'

'She picked me up and dusted me off and told me not to provoke him,' James said. 'That was the worst of it, in a way. That she never stood up to him for us. By the time I was a teenager I knew she never would. It wasn't her fault, he was a frightening man. But I always thought ... There were two of us, you know? If we'd been in it together, we could've ... I don't know. Even just left. We'd've managed.'

'Did she never talk about leaving him?'

'Oh, no. She'd never leave him. Now they're getting old and it's just the two of them, and for all I know he still slaps her when the tea's late.' James puts one arm across his face.

They lie for a long time, bodies lightly touching, silent. Finally James checks his phone for the time.

'I think the coast's clear,' she says. They've been listening for movement from the flatmates; neither wants the day diluted. James turns and they look into one another's eyes.

'Can we make a fry-up?' he says. 'I could eat a fucking horse.'

They talk about Emma. James has complained about her before, in the way people complain about a difficult boss, but Roses is only just beginning to realise that the problem is deeper than that, another power game that's no fun at all to play. The more she hears, the angrier Roses gets.

'Is this why you can't just resign? Do you feel like you owe her something?'

Roses is slicing mushrooms and making a pot of coffee. James is cracking eggs into a pan, and there's bacon under the grill giving off its smell of savoury smoke.

'I don't know. I don't want to have to explain it to her.'

Roses turns to him.

'You don't have to explain anything to her. You *don't*,' she adds, when she sees resistance in his face. 'Do you like her?'

'I respect her, as a doctor.'

'But do you like her, like a friend?'

James frowns as a yolk breaks. 'No,' he says slowly. 'She makes me feel ...' he stops.

Roses waits. When James doesn't go on, she says, 'She's your boss. She's sexually harassing you. If I were you, I'd feel afraid.'

James lets out a long sigh, rueful and fast.

'Oh, great,' he says. 'Another thing I'm afraid of.'

She puts her arms around him and hugs him tightly, kisses him on the most accessible part, which turns out to be his ear.

'You don't have to feel ashamed of it, James,' she says. 'She's a bully. Your dad was a bully. Bullies are terrifying.'

Roses hears her own words. She leans her forehead against James's shoulder for a moment and then, suddenly chilled, looks around the room for her sweater, for anything she can wrap herself in. There's an anonymous cardigan on the back of a chair and she pulls it on, the material scratchy on her bare arms. James is cooking the mushrooms. She pours them both coffee and, carrying her cup, takes a couple of steps away to look out of a window. A bit of car park; a day pallid with pervasive cloud.

'I bullied someone, at school,' Roses says. She doesn't look round, but feels James glance up at her.

'More than one person. But one in particular.'

James gets out plates, puts them in the top oven to warm.

'Who?' he asks. His voice is neutral.

'Someone called Janice Sheldrake. It was really bad, what we did. What I did. And then, a couple of months ago, I saw them again. Do you remember that night when you were in Edinburgh, someone threw a drink over me? I was ashamed, I didn't want to explain. They've changed a lot: gender, look, everything. I almost didn't recognise . . . him.'

James makes a short sound that avoids, for the moment, explicit judgement.

For a while neither speaks. James is buttering toast and transferring the rest of the food to plates. Roses is fifteen again, remembering the horror of their escape from the farm. Running across fields in the dark, gasping, sick with fear. Wiping blood from her hands on wet grass.

'It's ready,' James says, and they sit down and start to eat. But there's something hard stuck in Roses' throat, like concrete poured and suddenly set. She takes a bite of toast but it's dry in her mouth and swallowing feels like a distant possibility.

James puts down his fork, reaches over and holds her hand until she looks at him.

'Last night I told you about a murder I've been covering up for twenty years,' he says. 'If you've got shit to exorcise, I'm listening.'

—◦◦◦—

Summer, 1996

The headlights illuminate two girls in a field. Milo and Francesca are huddled inside the car, where she is crying quietly. They want no part of this. It has gone much too far.

Roses and Aradia face one another, blood on their hands and thighs and shorts and tops. Their breathing ragged and painful after running from the farm faster than they have ever run from anywhere.

'What the fuck. What the *fuck.*' Roses stoops to put her hands on her knees, sees that they leave bloody prints, and kneels down, trying to wipe it away.

Aradia has both hands over her mouth, her eyes are round. Roses looks up at her. Ra removes her hands and Roses sees that she is laughing.

'It's not funny. What were you *thinking?*'

'It was your idea,' Ra says.

'I said we should leave a chicken on the doorstep.'

'We *did* leave a chicken on the doorstep.'

'You know what I meant! I meant put it there, ring the doorbell, run away. I didn't mean . . . oh my god.' On all fours, she retches. Her arms are shaking violently.

'Stop being so *dramatic,*' Ra says. 'You're not even a vegetarian.'

'I can't believe you . . . What's wrong with you?'

It was true: it was Roses' idea to open the hen coop. It was she who crept in, selected a bird and held it by the wings, warm against her body. She hadn't seen the shears, though. Not until it was too late.

'I wanted to see if it would run around, you know: like a headless chicken,' Ra says.

She has also wiped the blood off her hands, and now she gathers up her long soft hair and starts to secure it into a ponytail.

'You're insane,' Roses murmurs.

'Come *on*, Ro,' Aradia says. They're a twosome, the most popular girls at school. Ro and Ra. 'It was just a chicken, you're acting like we killed someone's baby or something. I can't believe *you* think *this* is going "too far".'

Roses understands the emphasis. She's been the ringleader of so many of their attacks, less gory ones, for sure, but maybe no less savage.

She gets to her feet, walks to the car door, opens it.

'Give me my stuff,' she tells Francesca. The other girl snaps to it, hands out a bag and a cropped denim jacket. Roses slams the door.

'What are you doing?' Ra is standing on the other side of the car, her hand on the handle.

'I'm not getting in a car with you.'

'Roses. We're in the middle of *nowhere*. It's *the middle of the night*. What are you going to do, walk back to London?'

'If I have to.' She folds her arms. She has a credit card without a limit in her bag, but even so, she truly doesn't know what she'll do here, alone in the dark.

Milo starts the car and winds down the electric window.

'Come on, get in the car,' he says, mechanically. She knows all he wants is to be gone.

'Roses! We can't leave you here!' comes Francesca's thin voice from the back seat.

Roses and Aradia stare at one another over the bonnet for a very long moment. By the end of those seconds they will no longer be friends; will never share anything like this intimacy again.

'Fine.' Aradia accepts it. 'Stay here, get murdered by a serial killer, get raped, see who gives a fuck.'

She gets into the front seat.

'Drive,' Roses hears her say through the open window.

'Aradia . . . !' Francesca tries, ineffectually.

'*Drive.*'

Milo turns the car in a loop over the grass. Roses sees his face briefly through the window as he passes her, his jaw set, the lips she kissed, his eyes facing front. She sees the tail lights, red as embers. She waits, standing very still, until the sound of the car driving away down the lanes has completely faded.

She shivers violently. The stars are holes in the sky and the moon a knife blade, and she puts the jacket on with trembling hands. For the first time, the future seems as empty as the alien countryside around her. She is more alone than she has ever been in her short life. She puts her bag over her shoulder and starts to walk.

—*⁓*—

Three weeks after the interview, Hura stops expecting to hear back.

It is also, of course, three weeks since Casimir's death. The period immediately following that day was a haze of grief, and it wasn't until the following Monday that Hura, unemployed once again and too alone in the too-quiet flat, had started seriously hoping to hear back. For a few days, each morning commenced with hope buoyed up by confidence. A whisper of excitement on waking – *this will be the day* – was enhanced by the belief that if she were to be offered the job, it would be deserved. She would rise to the challenge.

The pain of losing Casimir and the resultant coolness in her relationship with Cillian co-existed with this excitement, and with the relief engendered by Ben's test results: not conclusive, but promising. The shadow has receded into the background of their lives, perhaps nothing more than a phantom after all.

By the second week of silence, Hura still woke with excitement, but it was no longer pleasurable. A void developed beneath it, a hollow she felt, obscurely, as being within herself. She picked apart the answers she had given in each interview, remembering the same mistakes every time, and burning with embarrassment. The days were long. She dreaded 6 p.m., because it meant that another day had passed, and also looked forward to it, because at that point there would be no chance of hearing anything until the next business day.

In the third week, Hura begins to develop a low-level sense of self-loathing. Of course she messed up the interview. She shouldn't even have hoped. (And yet there it is each morning, hope, like a bird slicked with oil but still trying to fly.) Moreover, she should never have set so much store by one job, one interview. It's a numbers game, she tells herself. Everyone has to apply for twenty, thirty, a hundred jobs before they get one. She sits in front of her computer and makes lists of possible positions, none of which are quite what she wants. She opens her CV to edit it, changes nothing, and closes the document again. Missing Casimir is a sharp-toothed ache.

The school term is well underway, and she hasn't been called about any teaching work. She is exhausted by the idea of chasing it. Guiltily, because they're relying heavily on Cillian's salary, she lets the days pass without calling her contacts or trying to temp. The final payment arrives for her summer job, less the week she didn't teach because they asked her not to return. She begins to wonder if it was just that day of leave she took for the interview. Was there something else about her that they sensed; that they didn't like?

The one thing that seems worthwhile in this moment is fixing up the flat, which also has the benefit of being distracting. She enlists Cillian and he seems only too happy to join. He's working in the days but devotes evenings and weekends to the project. She thinks, when they're working in separate rooms on some individual task – applying masking tape to skirting boards; finally repairing that lamp – that both of them are keen for the noise and the work because it distracts them from the absence of Casimir. Often she automatically prepares to walk him before she remembers he is gone. And each time, though she tries to quell it, she feels a stab of keen anger. He is gone because of Cillian.

Over the three weeks Hura has entirely repainted the bedroom, replacing the yellow with a cool grey, and built shelves in the alcove, as they've been meaning to do for years, and painted them too. She's bought and installed blackout blinds behind the thin curtains, so the streetlight no longer compromises the dark. She's chipped the dirty-blue tiles from the wall behind the kitchen sink, sanded down the surface, and replaced them with new green tiles for which she spent many late-night hours scouring the internet. Together they've cleaned and re-oiled the wooden floors in every room, filled rogue holes in the walls, fixed broken frames and installed new hooks from which to hang the pictures: their wedding; a print they bought together on a trip to Rome; a painting by Cillian's mother of the sea at Aldeburgh. Cillian has photographed and listed and sold the car.

Throughout the process their treatment of each other has been careful, almost polite. Cillian asks how she is feeling about work, but not too often. Their conversation is mainly practical, the discussion of paint colours or plumbing techniques. They take turns to make dinner and usually eat while watching television. Sometimes they go out alone. Hura to see a film with Zahra, a quiet dinner with friends. When Cillian goes out, she often doesn't ask where.

On the Thursday of the third week, Hura is waiting at a clinic not far from home. She's reading a women's magazine, a mixed pleasure she indulges in waiting rooms. In fact, she is not really reading but skimming, flicking the pages and taking in a glossy ad here – three stony-faced models holding lion cubs – a nicely cut jacket there, a piece of advice on how to spice up one's love life. A nurse calls her in, and she sits in the wipe-clean chair and thinks about coming here, five years ago, to have her coil put in. She had been thirty. The procedure was more painful than she expected. Cillian had come with her, she remembers, and while she lay pale and nauseous on the recovery table, he'd run out and bought her a cheese sandwich and a surprising bunch of flowers, big orange lilies and yellow roses and freesias all mixed together.

'So,' says the nurse, clicking with her mouse and watching the computer screen, 'this one's coming out. Did you want us to pop another one straight in?'

And although she knew, until this moment, what her answer was going to be, Hura hesitates.

Chapter Twenty

For James these are extraordinary weeks. There is something new in him, something growing and budding and spreading, sending out shoots in all directions. He has fully accepted, now, that these are his last weeks as a doctor, and is consequently enjoying the work more than he has ever done before. His interaction with patients feels more immediate, his interest in them more genuine. He has changed his stance with Emma, making it curt to a point where he feels extremely awkward and rude, but it's working – she's stopped initiating conversation, suggesting out-of-hours meetings, touching him. He's emailed the leader of his training programme and given himself a deadline of the end of September for telling everyone that he's leaving. That's now a week away, but it doesn't fill him with dread any more. Having made the final decision, it feels less epic. Who knows what the future will hold, he tells himself, he who has long seen it clearly as a dark map leading soon and inevitably to the shores of a country that no one leaves. He has been enthusiastically emailing conservation charities in bad Spanish, and getting some positive, welcoming responses.

He and Roses are talking about everything. To James, it's like he's tapped into a whole new kind of conversation, or discovered that he can speak a new language. He had thought, when they began experimenting sexually, that that was openness. Now he knows it was just a chink, a glimpse of what was possible. They discuss their childhoods and the things that formed them, talk about past relationship patterns, psychoanalyse themselves and each other, and make each other laugh. They make love and give each other massages and discuss their sexuality, individually and together. For the first time, James uses the word 'bisexual' in connection with himself, turning it over like a curious crystal to let its facets catch the light. They talk about Hura and Cillian. They imagine, in terms both keep deliberately fantastic, their own wedding: in a hot air balloon, in Vegas, at that campsite in the Lakes they both liked.

The one thing they don't talk about, by tacit agreement, is what will happen to them when he leaves. Roses never suggests he shouldn't go. He has strong reasons to travel in that part of the world, and no reason, apart from Roses, to stay.

For her, he knows, the opposite is true. London is the epicentre of her work. She has a jigsaw of forthcoming projects, few absolutely settled, most contingent on something: funding coming through, or a venue being secured. Roses has always found it extremely difficult to take holidays, and has often had to cancel them last minute. Protracted travel is anathema to her career choice. If he were to ask her to come with him, he'd be asking her to give up a fundamental part of herself, James thinks – perhaps the part of which she is proudest. Added to which, he's pretty sure that at this precise moment she's on the cusp of something, some big step forward. Job offers and interest in her work have never been so intense. Of course she can't leave now.

In this new atmosphere of confronting the past, Roses makes a decision. One beer-soaked apology in the street isn't enough. She needs to try again, and find out exactly what she can do to make amends. Maybe she can get an address and write a letter. Roses worries that Sam, if that's his name, will feel hounded by her contact, even, god forbid, bullied, but forces herself to keep looking. She has the idea that if she can only show him how much she's changed, that the ogre he's been carrying in his head no longer exists, it might help. She knows there's something else in the search too, something more selfish; some need to be forgiven or know she's tried to earn forgiveness.

She tries their old school, the tiny handful of people for whom she still has any contact details. She trawls the app on which he once, briefly, appeared, other apps, social media, and of course the great dim forest of the internet. She gets nowhere.

One day, checking theatre listings for the coming week, she stops and stares at a picture. It's small and dark, showing a man's shoulder and his face in profile, some dark clothing, blue-lit. She scans the listing, for a cabaret in Vauxhall the following week, but there's little to go on, just the names of some acts she's never heard of. That profile, though, is deeply familiar: Roses thinks she stared at it from the back of a classroom, for years, years ago. She calls the theatre and asks if anyone knows who is behind the weekend's acts, but the person she's speaking to sounds like a mystified intern, or someone who works behind the bar. She books a ticket.

In the nights leading up to the show, Roses begins to dread going. The summer is truly over, but each night her sheets are drenched with sweat. She moves to the dry side of the bed, turns the duvet over, lies looking at the ceiling of her room. Something seems very wrong. She searches her mind for what might have happened in the last days to trigger this sensation, akin to despair. Despair that hasn't yet taken full hold but is worrying at her, scratching, needling.

Roses' period is due, maybe even overdue; she's not particularly regular. She tells herself that the sadness is probably the result of some rogue hormones. But thinking that doesn't make it go away. Lying in the dark, wakeful for the third night in a row, she becomes convinced there is something she needs to work out, a problem that won't take on an exact shape. Is it about Hura? Roses hasn't been in touch with either her or Cillian since the accident, giving them all the space they could need; imagining she's the last person Hura wants to hear from. Her body aches with a deep tiredness, but her mind is restless and anguished. Perhaps there is something physically wrong with her?

She begins to dwell on Casimir's death, and can't stop. Her mind latches on and starts imagining it in incremental and evolving detail, adding, iterating. Now she is in his body, lean and furred and starting to be stiff in the joints. Now in the car, her claws digging into the fabric of the seats, experiencing the preternaturally acute hearing of a dog. The rising heat. She knows that Cillian, who was responsible for the dog, is culpable for his death. But the guilt she feels about it is growing, twisting. It was her that suggested the meeting.

If she can only imagine it all, she thinks, it will be better. It's a penance, a task to complete. In her mind, her Casimir-self dies, and she hopes that will be the end, but the process just begins again from the start. Something is wrong with her. The sensation of discomfort is so strong it makes her coil up onto one side in bed and press her face into the pillow, squeezing her eyes tight shut. Then she uncurls and stares at the ceiling again.

She picks up her phone and writes a text: *Clare, what is wrong with me? I feel like there's some huge problem somewhere that I have to solve, some kind of doom approaching . . .*

She stops typing. Not even Clare wants to hear about her existential crisis at 3 a.m. She leaves the text unsent and puts the phone away, then lies there for another two hours, and falls briefly asleep at five. When her alarm sounds she feels like she's been run over by a truck, exhausted by the idea that she has to get up and face the day.

The Royal Vauxhall Tavern is packed and stuffy, smelling of lager and people, music loud and conversation shouted. There's a small stage at the centre of the pub with space for an audience to stand or sit in front of it; around the edges, a raised section with tables. To the right, a bar.

Roses sheds her outdoor layers, buys a large glass of white wine and searches for a dim corner. In a room that's roughly circular, it isn't easy. She ends up with her back to the wall directly opposite the stage but outside its circle of light. She takes a swig, the wine acidic and barely cold, and surveys the crowd. There are men in shirts, women in sleeveless tops and jumpsuits and dresses. People in lace and fur, a feather boa or two, glitter. Two young women with multi-coloured hair and elaborate make-up wear carefully home-made unicorn costumes. A tall man is made taller by platform shoes and latex. The first act has recently finished, and the performer is chatting and resting against the edge of the stage wearing a bolero adorned with doll-heads, Barbies and other brands, sewn on by the hair. They're holding a blonde Barbie wig, and their body is not the body of a doll. They lounge against the stage near two fully dressed friends sitting in bentwood chairs, laughing over cocktails.

Then the compere comes out. She quietens the room, announces the next act and names its performer as Sam Sheldrake.

'Sam,' Roses says to herself, very quietly.

Sam's routine appears to be very different to the one which preceded it. The music is loud and electronic. He doesn't smile, his stage persona is intense rather than teasing or coquettish. His costume is black and complicated, with make-up and a wig that recall Edward Scissorhands. A couple of minutes into the wordless act, he produces, with a flourish, two large pairs of pattern-cutting shears. A dance ensues in which he threatens audience members from a distance, eliciting laughter when he mimes chopping off a shock of hair or a penis, but refusing to break out of his serious demeanour. Then he begins to cut off his clothes.

There's a change in mood from the audience at this point. They, like Roses, had probably hoped that the shears weren't sharp. Now, as the blades chop precisely through straps or slide down an inner thigh, parting fabric, there's a sensation of menace and worry. The performer might hurt himself, the audience thinks. That might be what he wants.

Slowly, the body beneath the costume is revealed. It's slim but muscular, with a small amount of body hair, a scatter of tattoos. Sam, who has shredded his top, now returns to the clothing around his legs, closer and closer to the groin, until all he's wearing is a couple of tight bands of fabric, and large black boots. Finally, gazing out at the audience, he places one foot on a block, high up and well-lit. Then he cuts the boot off, shears severing the leather so easily it makes the audience wince. As the music reaches a climax he cuts off the other boot, destroying it also. The track peaks and ends. There is sudden quiet. Sam gestures to the technician, who switches on all the lights. In the absolute silence that follows, he drops the shears to the floor with a clatter, one, then the other, two. He stands, almost naked, facing them. On one thigh, a tiny rivulet of blood runs from an invisible cut. Applause breaks out, and he bows, and leaves the stage. But as he looked out, his eyes met Roses', and so she knows he has seen her.

She waits. One or two people make attempts at conversation, but any capacity for friendly, polite chatter seems to have deserted her. She sees Sam emerge from backstage, low-key sportswear and no make-up; sees him keep his eyes averted from the part of the room where she sits and go over to the bar. He's greet-ed enthusiastically with hugs and pats on the back, all of which she watches in pantomime, too far away to hear over the sound of the crowd. Eventually, there's a break in his conversation. He turns round, leans against the bar, and surveys the room until his eyes come deliberately to her. They look at one another, and he raises his chin in a quick, unsmiling greeting. She makes a gesture, eyebrows raised, pointing to the bar with her empty glass: shall I come over? He gives a tiny shrug, an inclination of his head to the side: sure.

When she gets to the bar he's leaning with both elbows on it.

She leans beside him and speaks to the barman: 'A glass of white wine, please, large. And what are you having?' she asks Sam. There's a moment when she thinks he'll refuse the offer. Then he addresses the barman: 'A ginger ale. Thanks.'

'That was a great performance,' she says. She wishes he'd asked for alcohol.

'Thanks.'

'I'm a theatre director . . .'

'I know what you are.'

'Sorry, I just meant: I see a lot of shows. And that was really gripping. The ending was amazing.'

'Well, thanks, but I didn't do it for your approval.'

Their drinks arrive and she pays.

'What are you doing here?' he asks.

Roses takes a moment putting her card in her wallet, the wallet in her bag.

'I wanted to apologise. Again. Better. Would you like to sit down?'

'Not really, no.'

'Will you sit down with me anyway? Just for five minutes. I'd really, really appreciate it.'

Roses takes a hopeful sip of wine, watching his face over the rim of her glass. His eyes scan the room wearily, as if looking for an excuse to refuse. Then he blows out his cheeks, resigned, and gestures to an empty table.

They sit. Sam slides his spine low in the chair, extends his legs, and examines one of his trainers from a distance. Roses sits straight and drinks some more wine. Her stomach is tight with nerves. She takes a breath to speak, finds her throat constricted, takes another sip instead. Several opening sentences come to her mind. She discards them.

'How did you find me?'

His voice is level, almost casual.

'It was hard, there's barely a trace of you on the internet—'

'Deliberate,' he murmurs.

'In the end it was chance. I saw a picture alongside the listing for the act. I wasn't sure it was you, so I came anyway. It's a great venue . . .' she stops; she's gabbling.

'So you found out my name,' he says thoughtfully, tasting his drink.

'Only just now, for sure. I'm so glad it's you. I think it was important to see you again.'

'Important for you or for me?' Sharper, eyes on her for a moment and then away.

'I've been thinking a lot about what you said, about being a good person,' Roses says. 'I've been thinking about it, and failing.'

Sam laughs shortly. 'How am I not surprised?'

A man stops beside their table, back to Roses, and puts his hand on Sam's shoulder. Sam looks up and his face softens into a smile. He puts his hand on Saul's and nods: I'm ok. Saul glances over his shoulder, looking Roses up and down for two hostile seconds, then turns and leaves.

'Protecting you from the wicked witch?' Roses says, watching Saul walk away.

'Friends,' Sam says. 'Who'd have thought, I got myself some in the end.'

Roses swallows hard. She scans Sam's face, though his eyes are averted from hers.

'I have thought long and hard about those years when we were at school,' she says. 'About what we did to you. What I did. For a long time I think I tried to pretend it was normal, or at least normal for a toxic girls' school. Now I know how laughable that is. When I think about it now, honestly, my blood runs cold. It appals me. That I could do those things.'

Sam looks up from his shoe and raises his eyebrows a fraction: he has nothing to add.

'I guess, until I saw you in the pub that night, I'd managed to make it abstract. I was ashamed, deeply ashamed, but I didn't have to do anything about it. I *couldn't* do anything about it. I'm not in touch with anyone from those days. None of those people were real friends—'

'Poor you,' Sam interjects.

'I just mean, it was like I locked the past away and thought it would stay there, and that I'd changed. When I saw you—'

'You realised you hadn't.'

'It came roaring back. The memories. That night we came to your parents' place.'

Sam seems to shiver, very slightly. She goes on.

'I thought: I need to do two things. I need to face up to what I did, see if I can make it better in any way. And I need to make sure I don't cause any more damage.'

The last word sticks in her throat and she looks down.

'How's that going?' Sam asks.

She shakes her head, presses the edge of a fingernail against the tabletop. Someone has carved a jagged love heart into the polish.

'It's not going that well.'

★

Sam looks at the bowed head and tries to keep his hands still, resisting the urge to rub his palms dry. There's always a mixed high after he performs, mostly elation but with a scattering of something like shame, or discomfort. The elation is draining away fast tonight and the discomfort surging. He's almost sure he shouldn't be spending time with this person, allowing old hurts to open, but not completely sure. While most of him wants to throw another drink over her and possibly throw the glass as well, get out of there, surround himself with friends, something makes him stay. It might be the hope that his old anger can at last find an outlet. But it might be something else.

'So. What?' he says. 'What's "not going well"? Your career's obviously fine, you've always had money, you're probably married by now, right? Let me guess, he works in finance slash corporate law but he just *loves* "the arts" and so he's bankrolling your shows, and you have had slash will have two perfect kids, and send them to boarding school because it never did you any harm, and because it means you can keep going to dinner parties?'

To his surprise, Roses laughs, a genuine though despairing laugh, and puts her head in her hands.

'Not exactly,' she says through her fingers.

'Go on then. What? Problem with the trust fund?'

'I'm seeing someone who I love,' she says. 'But he's leaving the country and probably not coming back, and because I love him I have to let him go. I've always been in control and now I'm not. I tried to hurt him so he'd show me he cared, but I ended up hurting other people instead. I can't sleep any more. I wake up in the night and these images play over and over again like vicious little films.'

She looks up and meets his gaze, then looks away.

'Interesting,' he says, 'Roses Verier Green has problems too. Why exactly did you want to share them with me?'

'I just . . . I don't know. Really I want to hear about you. How are you? What's your life like?'

Sam thinks about his flat, about work and getting lost in the

279

flow of writing code. He thinks about Saul and the others laughing and dancing, about Sunday mornings running in the park, about Hura turning to smile over her shoulder as she walked away on that afternoon of golden light, about her voice on the phone, about the passion of his fellow activists and the terrifying vision of the future they're trying to avert. He thinks of his mother, her sometimes-bewildered but constant kindness. He thinks of how his father died before he had the chance to really explain how he wanted and needed to live. He thinks of a warm summer night years ago when he scrubbed blood from the doorstep, alone in the dark, rather than wake his parents and their questions. He thinks of other blood: a stall in a bathroom at boarding school where, after his periods started, he pressed clean sanitary pads to the fresh cuts on his arms.

'Me?' he says. 'I'm fine.'

Roses nods sadly. Why should he trust her?

'You won't believe this,' she says, 'but back at school, I liked you. I didn't like anyone, really, but I always felt sort of drawn to you. I don't know why it got so twisted out of shape.'

'If that's what you do when you like someone, God help the guy you're seeing.'

'Ha. Yeah.' Roses gestures vaguely towards Sam's scarred arms. 'Look what I do to people.'

As soon as the words are out of her mouth, Roses knows how wrong they sound. There's no taking them back. She sees the muscles work in Sam's face, the fury that sweeps through him.

'Fuck, no, I'm sorry. That wasn't what I meant. That was such a stupid thing to say.' Tears of frustration sting her eyes. 'I only meant that I've fucked so many things up.'

'You think I'm your fault?' he says, very low.

'No.'

He swallows, finds his voice to carry over the music. 'You think the way I am, everything I've chosen in the last fifteen years, my body, the conversations I've had with my family, the life I've built, are *because of you?*'

'I'm – no. I don't think that. I just don't know how to explain what I was—'

'You were a psychopath!' Sam almost shouts, people at nearby tables turning to look. He laughs, suddenly, anger replaced by incredulity.

'I didn't know how to love people. Or, or, be kind to them. Maybe that is the definition of a psychopath, I don't know, or maybe just a teenager. But I want to stop hurting people, you and James and Cillian and Hura and their fucking *dog*—'

'What?'

'I'm just so sorry.' Tears run down her face. She feels drunk and sick. The crushing night-time anxiety, the hot shame of this whole conversation. Cillian weeping on the pavement. James booking that flight. A departures lounge long ago where she waited to see if her father would turn back and look at her one last time.

Sam's eyes are wide, his nostrils slightly flared. He's sitting bolt upright now, jaw clenched, fingertips on the table edge. But as the seconds tick by she sees him make an effort and lean back. A look of dawning realisation has come over his face.

'I think you want me to absolve you. To say it's ok, I'm not broken, you didn't do anything that bad. I'm not going to. But I can tell you this: where I am is exactly where I want to be. I suppose that means I accept your apology.'

Roses closes her eyes and lets the words sink in and settle.

'You know what's funny,' he says. 'Until this moment I've always thought I knew exactly why *you* picked on *me*. You were perfect, and I was different: it was my fault. But actually, since you're here insisting we talk about it all, you can answer that question for me: Why? Why me?'

Roses opens her eyes.

'Because it was your turn.'

Sam laughs on stunned out-in breath: 'Oh, like you had a turn?'

But as he says it, he sees from her face that's exactly what she means.

'After I moved to England,' she says. 'The last three years of primary school.'

They sit with this for a moment.

'It doesn't make what you did ok,' Sam says. But something has shifted, very slightly, between them.

'I know. I know.' She presses her lips together hard. 'Before I moved to Bourne High, I made the decision. I had to reinvent myself. To become invincible. I had to be . . .'

He finishes the sentence for her: '. . . the hunter.'

She laughs, then bites her lips to press them together. Puts a hand up to shade her eyes from the light, or from view.

'Tell me about the dog,' he says.

Roses is tired, suddenly, far too tired to find the question surprising.

'Casimir. He died,' she replies. 'He belonged to our friends. Lovers. Whatever. They're called Cillian and Hura. The four of us had been seeing each other a bit. But I met up with Cillian alone and Casimir was in the car, and the sun came out and we lost track of time.'

She takes the hand away from her eyes and searches for an anchor: her empty glass. A wave of nausea, hot and cold at the same time, rushes over her and recedes. She's so thirsty, but can't imagine asking Sam to wait while she gets water. She looks up at him and sees that something profound has changed in his expression.

'What?' she says. 'What is it?'

'I'm not the one you need to apologise to.'

Hura is washing her face when her phone, balanced on the side of the sink, starts to ring. She grabs a towel, hoping the phone won't vibrate itself into the basin, dries the droplets from her eyes and looks at the screen. To her surprise, it's blank. Then the ring comes again, not from the sink but from the side of the bath: Cillian's phone. She smiles at the fact they'd both pointlessly risk dropping their phones into water, and looks at the screen. Frowns in mild surprise, answers the call.

'Hi, it's Hura. I just found Cillian's phone here, he must have forgotten it.'

'Oh. Hi,' Roses says.

'How are you?' Hura asks. She glances in the mirror as she talks, a quizzical expression creasing her own brows.

'I just, I needed to talk to Cillian about something. I wanted to check something,' Roses says.

There's a lot of background noise, music. It's late, Hura sees, looking at the time on her own phone. Thinking: if Cillian's phone is here, he can't get in touch with me.

'Do you want me to ask him? When he gets back?' she says.

She carries both phones to the bedroom and throws hers onto the duvet. She leans against the headboard. The dove-grey walls are calming around her, the smell of fresh paint still lingering.

'I can't, I don't know. I need to talk to him, I think. I'm sorry,' Roses says.

There's a long moment where all Hura can hear is music, something with a niggling, too-fast beat, like a heart murmur.

'Are you ok?' she asks.

More beats, background laughter, a fumbling sound and some breaths.

'I'm sorry,' Roses says again.

'What's wrong?' Hura asks. She can tell Roses is crying.

'Hang on,' Roses says. Voices, moving past the microphone now, then a change in the quality of the sound, quieter, the scratch of traffic.

'Ok. I'm outside. I just, um, I just, oh shit,' Roses says.

'Roses,' Hura half laughs. 'Come on, I'm getting worried here. I've got no idea what this is about.'

But as Hura says it, a tiny bell is ringing somewhere, and getting louder. Neither speaks for a long moment, still as an engine stall before the plane starts falling. The bell rings. Maybe, Hura thinks, it has been ringing for weeks.

'It's about Casimir, isn't it?' she asks. She pulls the covers over her, cold. 'Was Cillian with you?'

There's a sob on the other end of the phone: 'Yes.'

For a few seconds that feel like minutes, neither woman says anything. Then, more muffled, Roses swears again and there's a sound of footsteps. Then nothing for a moment. Then another voice, very clear, familiar, and cut through with pain.

'Hura. I'm so sorry about this.'

'*Sam?*'

'I know, I know. Roses just handed me the phone and ran off, I think she's being sick. You shouldn't be finding out like this.'

Roses has no hope of making it back inside to the bathroom. She gets as far as a corner of the building and throws up on the pavement, the awful inside-out feeling of internal revolt. Surely, she thinks as she retches, all she had was three glasses of wine. Her whole body feels clammy under her clothes. She partially straightens, one hand on the cold brick wall, the other on her cramping stomach. The area between her navel and her pubic bone. And there, in a moment of wretched clarity, she knows exactly what is going on.

Two thoughts hit her at the same moment: she has to find James and tell him what she's just realised. And: there is no way she can see James. She needs Clare, a cab to Clare's. She prays Clare is at home. She searches her bag and pockets for her phone, remembers where it is and wheels round.

Sam, her phone at his ear, looks at her across the intervening space.

They look at each other for a long moment. Sam is listening and talking softly; she can't hear the words over the traffic, or the external smokers and drinkers who, she now realises, have edged away from her. He gives her a questioning look. She spreads her palms at either side, indicating her abject state. He nods, turns away and finishes the call. She takes two steps towards him but keeps her distance, waiting. When he finishes he looks at the phone for a minute as though it's his and then, decisive, walks to her and holds it out. She takes it. Closes her eyes, hangs her head. She has nothing left to say.

'Are you going to be ok getting home?'

His kindness is unexpected. It almost makes her cry again. She looks back at him.

'I'm not going home if I can help it. I'll go to a friend's.'

He nods.

'What about you?' Roses asks. 'Will you be ok? Getting home, and everything?'

'Yeah, I just live over there,' he says, indicating somewhere vaguely west and south.

'How did you meet her? Hura?' Roses asks.

'We met at your play.'

'I didn't know you came.'

'Yeah, I came.'

'And Cillian?'

'I've never met him. You should get going. To your friend's.'

'You mean I look like shit and smell of sick.'

For the first time in the evening, Sam smiles at her: a sad but genuine smile that makes him look suddenly young.

'Night, Roses. Take care.'

They turn away but he calls after her: 'Roses?'

'Yes?'

'I also liked your show.'

Chapter Twenty-One

Roses settles back against the synthetic blue seat fabric and turns her face to the window, with its impossible view of the tops of clouds. She is a good flyer. Her carry-on bag fitted neatly into the overhead compartment. She has a warm wool wrap against the air-conditioning. In the net pocket on the back of the seat in front are her travel essentials: a bottle of water, a novel, an eye mask, headphones, moisturiser. She had walked confidently onto the flight with a couple of minutes to spare, one of the last passengers to board. Flying is familiar, even comforting, she thinks wryly; it's just everything else that's up in the air.

She closes her eyes and tells herself to be patient. She's ravenous, but it will be a while until a meal is served and in the meantime she will just have to distract herself. She's still not used to this: a new kind of hunger that makes her legs weaken and her mind fall to pieces. A burning, animal need. The sandwich she ate less than an hour ago seems to have been vaporised by the furnace inside her. But furnace is the wrong metaphor, she thinks. The kiln.

How did I get here, she wonders? Life has taken a series of such unexpected turns the past year and now this: a child she didn't mean to conceive; a journey she didn't plan to take.

Beside her, in the middle and aisle seats, sit a couple in their fifties. The woman, next to her, has short dark-grey hair, handsome aquiline features, glasses on a string of amber round her neck. Her husband – Roses noticed the rings when she noticed that they were holding hands – is too tall for the restrictive seats. He's bearded, bearlike, kind-looking. They could be professors, she thinks;

probably of psychology. They are, she imagines, parents. Where are they going together, these people in another chapter of their lives to hers, but one she can now, suddenly, picture more clearly than ever before. Are they happy? Settled? Are they faithful?

The cabin crew come by with drinks and tiny packets of pretzels. Roses asks for extra and the steward, with a purse of his lips, gives her three more packets. She eats them all.

'Would you like mine?'

It's the woman beside her, looking over the tops of her glasses with laughing eyes.

'Do you mind?' Roses says, and then, surprising herself: 'I'm pregnant.'

'I guessed,' the woman says. 'I've been there. How long?'

'Twelve weeks,' Roses says, and bursts into tears. Emotion rinses and swirls through her in these days. The terror and bleakness she felt at first seems, just in the last week, to have been replaced by a lifting sensation, as if she had been sitting up through a dark night and suddenly seen the sun begin to rise.

'Almost no one knows,' Roses says without meaning to. She sniffs, wipes her eyes with the square napkin that came with the snacks. 'I haven't told my mother yet. We have a complicated relationship. I'm on my way to see my dad now, to tell him.'

'He's in Austin?' the woman asks.

'Yes. He lives there. He has other kids.'

'Right.'

'He moved back when my parents split up. I was ten. It was messy. I tried living with him when I was a teenager but I was so angry with him. I felt like he didn't really want me around. He was going out with all these younger women, just a few years older than me. Anyway, he ended up marrying one of them and having two children and I've barely ever met them. Now, I don't know why, it feels important.'

'Oh, wow,' the woman says.

Roses smiles. 'That's complicated too,' she says.

They lapse into silence, then, because even in her mood of sudden over-communication Roses is aware that it's too much for someone to take in at once, especially a stranger. And how could she put the rest into words? The discovery that she was pregnant and the cataclysm that preceded it; the roles played by Sam, Hura, Cillian. The fact that she didn't know for a long time whether to keep the baby. The question of its paternity.

Roses puts on her headphones and turns her face to the window again. Now the clouds have a soundtrack and everything feels like it's happening in a film. The physical distance from home and from her destination, the enforced stillness, the need for distraction combine, and she starts to replay the last weeks in her mind, starting with that night in Vauxhall.

———

She calls Clare from the cab. The phone goes straight to voicemail. She continues the journey anyway, slumped against the door for the duration of the long, expensive ride. Trying to think about nothing except the hope that Clare will answer the door. The street, when she steps into it, is echoing, cold, and deserted. She presses the buzzer and waits for a long time. Hopelessly, she presses it a second time. They're clearly not there.

Then the intercom crackles.

'Hello?' Tim's voice, very curt and hard.

'Tim, it's Roses. Is Clare there? I'm sorry, I know it's late . . .'

'Come up.' The door clicks open.

By the time she's climbed the stairs, Tim is nowhere to be seen and Clare is standing in the dark doorway, legs bare, eyes slitted against the hallway lights and hugging a beige jumper around herself.

'What's up, Bunchie?' she says sleepily as Roses ascends and then, getting a better look at her: 'What's happened, are you ok?'

She holds her arms out and Roses hugs her.

'I'm sorry I woke you up.'

'Come in, you idiot.'

They walk down the corridor quietly and into the sitting room, where Clare turns on a lamp and Roses burrows herself into a corner of the familiar sofa and puts a cushion over her face.

288

Clare comes to sit with her. 'What is it? Ro?'

'I'm pregnant. Also, I'm a monster.'

'Oh my.'

Clare takes her hand and holds it.

'When did you find out?'

'About forty-five minutes ago while I was throwing up three glasses of wine in Vauxhall.'

'Ah. So James . . .?'

'Doesn't know. Will probably skip the country as soon as he finds out. Oh, no, he's doing that anyway.'

Clare, Roses knows, is wondering how this happened, did they use protection, is she sure who the father is? She peeps over the edge of the cushion into Clare's eyes, made black and serious by the news and the dim light.

Clare says: 'Would you like a cup of tea?'

'Yes, please.'

'And a biscuit?'

'Yes, I would like a biscuit.'

'Anything else?'

'Can you please make a decision about what I should do and then inform me of it?'

Clare smiles: 'Sure.'

She gets up and puts the kettle on.

'You should have some tea and then get into the spare bed. Maybe have a shower first.'

'I got puke on me.'

'No, really?'

'Should I call James?'

'Do you know what time it is?'

'Only kind of.'

Clare brings over two cups of mint tea and a packet of pink wafer biscuits.

Roses looks at them with suspicion.

'Why have you got these?'

'Tim likes them.'

'Such a dark horse.' She eats a biscuit. It's perfect. She eats five more.

'Wow,' says Clare.

'You see?' Roses says, her mouth full.

Clare stretches her arm along the sofa back, rests her head on it.

'Are you sure? You should do a test.'

Roses nods. 'Yeah, I will. But I'm sure. My period's really late. And it feels exactly the same.'

She looks up to meet Clare's eyes.

'Does it?'

'Exactly the same. Sickness and dread, chills, night sweats, everything. I can't believe I only just realised.'

Back when they were twenty-three, it was Clare who bought the pregnancy test. Sat in the bathroom with her while Roses did it, while she stared at the two blue lines. Five days later, she'd gone with Roses to the clinic.

'The difference is, I knew exactly what to do then,' Roses says. 'I didn't question it. Chris was – well, you know. And I was just starting out, there was no way I was ready to become a mum.'

'And . . . now?'

Roses puts the cushion on Clare's lap, her head on the cushion, her hands over her face.

'What the fuck? Clare, I think I might be too bad to have a baby.'

Clare strokes her hair. 'You're not that bad, babes, really. You're sometimes quite a nice person.'

———

David Bowie is singing about space. Roses notices the lyrics differently in this familiar song, now it has a backdrop of the upper air. Like the man says, everything does look different today.

Recalling that night has shaken her again. The sickness has passed, thank god, but its memory is so recent that her stomach clenches. And the bleak terror has not entirely lifted. When Roses confirmed she was pregnant, she had felt like her life was over. There was no way she was going to keep the baby. And yet, so unexpected it took her breath away, the decision to end the pregnancy brought no relief; only a yawning sensation of loss she never thought she'd feel. With Clare, she had been able to rage and sob out her frustration with herself – how could she have made such a stupid mistake, how? – and voice her darkest feelings about the future: she would lose everything she loved. Her work. Her freedom. Eventually James, since she would grow to hate him for wanting them to have the child.

Because that was the biggest surprise: James did want it. A baby. With her.

After fitful nights, the days had been, if possible, worse. Nausea rolling over her like great breakers that left her rinsed and abject, wanting nothing except silence and stasis, and not to have to choose.

Roses shivers, pulls out the inflight magazine as a distraction, opens it. A symmetrical, familiar face gazes at her from the feature spread. *Flying high,* reads the bold text beside the photograph. *Can anything stop the incredible rise of Evita McNeish?*

Roses doesn't even try to resist reading the story, a breathless jumble of admiration for its subject's acting, her humility, her eyebrows. The stylist has gone to town with white draped dresses and what look like swan feathers. It leaves the lasting impression that Evita, at twenty-two, has the world at her feet. Roses closes her eyes, leans her head back. She is thirty-three and has six more months to work before her professional life, which truly felt like it was moving into a new gear, is changed forever. It will be all right, she tells herself, trying to sound convincing. They will share the load. James will teach their child kindness. She will keep working. It will be different, but possible. A lot about this baby's upbringing will be different.

It's not what she planned for her life; not what any of them planned. But despite that, glimmering around the edges of her very rational worry is a brightness she can't name. Something is aflame, or astir.

She remembers Sam, then, and his exhortation the night he drenched her with beer. Try to be a good person. Ok then, she tells herself once again. Ok.

'Give me five minutes,' says Hura, fingers clicking fast across the laptop keys, eyes on the screen.

Sandy looks theatrically at her watch. 'You have three minutes,' she says.

'I'm going as fast as I can!' Hura smiles, typing even more swiftly.

'Two-and-a-half,' Sandy says. 'Come on! I need coffee before this meeting.'

Hura likes Sandy, the private secretary she met that first day, a brusque Scottish woman with wiry hair and spectacles, who looks much more like a teacher than Hura herself ever did, and who talks like a squaddie. They began to form a bond a few weeks ago, on Hura's first day, Sandy introducing her to the whole office in a quick-fire burst of names that Hura tried hard to memorise, and managed to, after years of classroom practice. She'd never know if she'd been hired because of some diversity quota, but once she got the email, she put the question out of her mind. The job meant so much to her: a new light to aim for, pulling her through the darkness. She was going to give everything to it, learn as much as she could, progress quickly. She concentrated on it with all her might, in part because it felt like the decisive beginning of a new chapter in her professional life; in part to block out everything else.

Meetings follow meetings, papers are written and re-drafted, speeches are tweaked, fat reports have to be sifted and responses given. The activity is constant, and Hura barely has time to think, let alone eat. Everyone seems to survive on a terrible diet of coffee and vending-machine snacks, and the finger-food served at early-evening functions. There's one such drinks party tonight in a small House of Commons reception room, and Hura accompanies Sandy and chats for two hours before it finally breaks up and she heads home.

Home, right now, is the tiny second bedroom in Zahra's lofty Canonbury flat. Hura lets herself in and calls a greeting, then wanders into the open-plan living room and kitchen to find a note on the counter: 'Gone dating. Pray for me. Eat leftovers.' For the twentieth time since moving in, Hura is grateful that Zahra is a great cook, and grateful that she's often out. She wants to be alone.

It's not yet late. Hura washes her hair, surprised again, pleased, very slightly dismayed, by how easy this is since she had it cut short. She changes into comfortable clothes, finds an aubergine dish and salad and chickpeas in the fridge and makes herself a plateful, sitting down at the table to eat. She doesn't want to drink any more alcohol, after several glasses of bad wine at the function; she doesn't listen to music. She eats slowly in the quiet flat, not seeing what's in front of her, but letting her mind range over reality as it now appears, and the future, bare as bone.

Hura can see herself growing into her new role, doing well, getting ahead. She has a good connection with the minister, a woman ten years older than her who, Hura thinks, could become a mentor of sorts. Where could she herself be in ten more years, or even five? The possibilities seem huge and genuine: a parliamentary seat in a by-election. The front bench one day, even the cabinet. Her brain is whirring, in such different and more intense use than for the past several years, and ideas are sparking in a hundred new directions at once. She could have so much, she senses, if she wants it.

Hura sips from her glass of water, and thinks about Cillian. Of course, she thinks about him all the time. The photo-book of their life together is under the second pillow on her bed; opening it a sweet torture she inflicts on herself only sometimes. Her phone is on the table, switched to silent. They're still in touch, but less so; she asked for space. She is getting used to the idea of a future without him.

Without him, the man with whom she thought she was about to start a family, means without the family. Hura looks, clear-eyed, at herself: a woman in her mid-thirties, at the start of a new career, who has just broken up with her long-term partner. She had been getting used to the idea of becoming a mother. Now that image – herself with a baby in her arms, Cillian beside her – has begun to blur and fade. It was to have been her reality. Perhaps she won't become a mother at all. The sense of loss is intense, abstract, baffling. She wonders, just a little, how much she is grieving for her own loss, and how much for the loss of the thing she and Cillian, together, imagined. Because, though the thought is new and raw, it's there: she doesn't *have* to get used to the idea of mother-hood, now.

After she'd put down the phone to Sam and Roses, she had sat very still on the bed. More than once, she'd reached instinctively for her phone to call Cillian, then remembered his phone was sitting there beside her on the quilt. She didn't know where he was, and it had never truly mattered before, because she trusted him. Now she knew he had lied to her. Casimir's death had not happened because of a business meeting. It had happened because of a pointlessly clandestine liaison. Cillian was meant to be protect-ing something precious. Instead, he had sneaked behind her back when he didn't even have to. She'd twisted the sheet between her fists. He wasn't a man to be trusted with the vulnerable. He wasn't a man of his word.

If Cillian had been there, or if she could have called him, who knows how things might have been. The thought still chafes at her, the what-if. But then she tells herself: What if the sun hadn't come out that day? What if Cillian hadn't lied, when he'd first given her the terrible news? The what-ifs cancel each other out until all she's left with is reality. It doesn't matter what could have been done, or said. Only what has.

Her phone lights up, and she sees without touching it that the message is from Sam. She waits to read it, but notices the sensation it gives her: a tiny nudge of pleasure; a shifting of wings. She doesn't know what is going on with Sam, except that he is still in her life and she wants him there. They text often and sometimes speak on the phone. She's heard the story of his childhood, all the details of Roses' part in it. Both Roses and James have messaged her. So far, she hasn't been able to bring herself to reply. No one from work has met Sam; she hasn't yet tried hard to engage her brain with that particular dynamic.

She is in mourning for her life with Cillian; it will be a long time before she can contemplate another relationship with any-thing like the seriousness needed to begin all over again. She isn't sure how she feels about monogamy; about so many things.

With Sam she's been to a classical music concert at lunchtime, to Kew Gardens in the frost. These could, she supposes, be called dates. Nothing physical has happened, except perhaps a hug at parting. The occasional light touch of hands.

That terrible night of waiting, six weeks ago – she's stunned it's so recent, it feels like years – Cillian had eventually come home, telling her his bike had been stolen and he'd had to walk. That was in the moments before he'd realised she was still dressed, and then why. Only days later, she'd gone to stay with Zahra. He had offered to be the one to leave; but it was partly the flat she'd wanted to escape from.

There had been a moment on waking, that first morning at Zahra's, when she had been absolutely certain that she and Cillian would pull through. Sick with sadness, she'd opened her email just to have something to look at. She'd waited so long to hear anything about the job that she'd given up hope, but there, at last, was a message. She almost laughed at the grim timing: a belated *thanks so much for coming in* to top off the chaos of the previous days.

She opened the email, but couldn't bring herself to read the words in order. To be ambushed by rejection, lying in wait at the end of an apologetic sentence. Instead, she scanned all the text at once, saw her name – *Dear Ms Holmes* – unfamiliar because for-malised. Sought the words, *we're sorry*. Unable to find the phrases of rejection, she forced herself to read in sequence.

Then she put the phone down on the covers and stared across the room at a black-framed Japanese print, long boats and their grim-faced crews menaced by a beautiful sea. She heard a move-ment elsewhere in the flat and was sure, just for an instant, that it was her husband. He was here; she could tell him her news, their news. Then there was another sound, a sigh or a cough, and Hura realised it wasn't him. Of course, it couldn't be him. She'd picked up her phone, and begun writing a text to Sam.

★

She gets up, washes her plate carefully at the sink. Heartbreak, she thinks, doesn't happen all at once, a decisive crack. It happens again and again, a tap-tap-tapping, so slow you almost get used to it. She thinks, as she has done every day since she left: perhaps this isn't really the end. But the thought of going back to where they were, of trying to rebuild, fills her with a sense of impossibility. She thinks about her new work. She thinks about the grave at the bottom of her parents' garden. She thinks about Cillian's arms around her, his voice warm against her ear, the way she trusted him, blithely and completely. No, she thinks; there is no going back. Only forward.

Since his bike was stolen, Cillian has been walking everywhere. This takes hours, but he has a deep aversion to going underground to get the Tube, and besides, the walking takes up time, gets him outside, and provides a rhythm that makes his thoughts more bearable. He thinks about Casimir every day. He thinks about Hura constantly, an unproductive loop that includes nostalgia, anger, pain, and hope, and that usually ends in a smaller, more unhealthy loop of self-flagellation.

It's Saturday, and the weekend lies ahead like an echoing corridor. Cillian has no plans, and is only out on the Marshes this morning because he has nowhere else to be. The flat, without either Hura or Casimir in it, is unbearably quiet. It's cold now they're into November, but the sun is an intense autumnal gold. It hits the low trees and faraway buildings, the scattered people and horses and even cows from a steep side angle. Shadows are long and black.

He takes out his phone and thinks, for the tenth time that morning, about texting Hura. He forces himself not to, to respect her request for time to think. Instead, he opens an app and cycles through messages, communicating about a few potential group meet-ups and arranging one definite liaison: with the woman by the river – Sadie – who has become an occasional and as yet uncomplicated lover.

He knows that one thing he's doing with all these people is distracting himself: seeking comfort, looking for a way to see himself that is more positive, stronger, more hard-edged and highly coloured because it is filtered through someone else's eyes. But there's more to it than narcissism, or escape. The experience of his lie and its consequences has convinced him that he will be scrupulously open in every aspect of his romantic life. There will be no secrets, and no blurred lines. Finding himself, unwillingly, in the role of solo adventurer, he will push the spirit of adventure to its limits, exploring what it is truly like to have no commitments. He's very aware this might have a time limit.

Though straight-up sex is still part of the picture, he's much more interested in groups, parties, a community of which he's just beginning to feel a part. He is not seeking to replace his and Hura's intimacy with any single other person. He has always craved the hurly-burly of a family life less quiet and solitary than his own and he's finding something like it, surprising even him, among the kinder, more congenial members of the kink scene.

Hura retains a special status: he would be willing to try almost anything, give up almost everything, if it meant they could find their way into a future together. He's angry with himself for hoping, against all the odds, that their story isn't over. But he can't quite bring himself to give hope up.

Turning south, Cillian passes under a bridge, then crosses the river. He reaches an open circle of concrete and rusted iron, part of the old Victorian filter beds. Above him, the sky is an immaculate blue, as if freshly painted all over. He watches a plane draw one perfect chalky line across it and wonders if Roses might be on it; he knows she's flying today. After Casimir died, he had thought he would probably never see James and Roses again. He'd ignored her calls in the first unbearable days after Hura left. But she'd called again. She'd asked him to come and see a painting.

She's standing in front of Henry VIII – Roses suggested the National Portrait Gallery because she's researching a new project about the Tudors.

When Cillian arrives, he understands: they can talk without looking at one another, directing their attention to the pictures instead. They're not entirely alone, not sitting pinned to some pub banquette or squirming on a coffee shop sofa, and he's grateful for it. She's there first; he sees her silhouetted against the brightly lit painting, hands in the pockets of an oversized coat. He comes to stand beside her, and she looks sideways and smiles at him but they don't kiss on the cheek, don't touch at all. They look at the painting together.

'Nice outfit,' he says after a moment.

'Great, isn't it? All the rubies. And the tights; men should wear tights more often.' She seems more nervous than he's seen her before, edgy and pale.

'How are you?' he asks.

'I'm . . . ok. How about you?' She flicks a glance at him. 'Are you ok?'

He pulls his shoulders up to his ears and lets them drop.

'My favourite part is the cape,' he says. 'Is that ermine?'

They move on, towards a portrait of Elizabeth I, all pearls and precision and power.

'I'm really sorry. About you and Hura.'

He's given her the basic facts by text. He looks around, superstitious; the last thing he'd want is for Hura or one of her friends to see him with Roses right now. Small groups mill around the gallery, all apparently anonymous, but it doesn't put his mind at ease. He thinks about Sam, who one day gathered the threads of their lives together in a neat handful; for Cillian, disastrously.

'You and James – you worked it all out?' he asks.

'Um, not exactly.' She pauses. 'I'm so sorry about the way she found out. From me, not you.'

He drives his hands deep into his pockets and looks at the floor.

'It's not your fault. I should have told her. I knew it. I meant to. I was waiting for the "right time". But the right time was in the past. It kept getting further away.'

'How are things now?'

'I'm giving her space.'

She whispers, as if to herself: '*I could be bounded in a nutshell, and count myself a king of infinite space.*'

Then she turns to him: 'Cillian.'

'Yeah?'

'Come and look at this a moment.' She nods towards a corner. They cross to look at a painting of a dark-haired woman, skin stark white, mouth closed like she's holding her breath.

Roses swallows.

'I got pregnant,' she says. 'I am. Pregnant.'

He looks at her sharply.

'Ok. Wow. Congratulations.'

A frown passes over her face and he adds: 'Or . . .?'

'Yeah, I don't know. It was an accident. I still don't know how it happened.'

'You were, you and James were . . .'

'We used condoms. I always used them with everyone.'

Anne Boleyn's eyes are on them, knowing. Roses adds: 'Including you.'

She looks at him, and he looks at her.

'Are you saying . . .?'

Her gaze is level and serious. 'I don't know.'

Cillian puts his hand over his eyes and rubs them with fingers and thumb, then uses the same hand to rub his mouth. His mind is full of Hura, the way her face faltered when she understood that Casimir was dead. He thinks about her hearing this news, and closes his eyes tight. Roses, and the unblinking paintings, disappear. Even the decorous indoor sounds of the gallery seem muffled as he stands there, and Cillian is back in the future he used to imagine, so clear it was as though it actually existed somewhere, and he'd one day simply arrive there. A gang of wild-haired children. Hura, crouching among them, inspecting something they were showing her, and him beside them, among them, never leaving them to fall asleep or wake up alone.

He opens his eyes. Roses has hung her head, so her expression is hidden by her hair. Maybe he should reach out to her in some way, but how? A pat on the arm? He clears his throat.

'And what are you, I mean . . . what do you want . . . do you know what you want to do?'

She takes a moment to gather her answer. Then she wipes a hand upward over her face and pushes her fringe back, sniffs.

'When I found out, I thought it was obvious: there was no way I could keep it. I don't want a baby. Didn't want a baby.'

Cillian nods, finding he is acutely aware of her use of tenses.

'And now?'

'James is delighted. I was amazed. He's up for it. He says he's always wanted kids and why don't we just go for it?'

They're standing near an austere, polished bench.

'Can we sit down?' Roses asks.

The lunchtime crowd seems, mercifully, to have drifted away from this room, where light makes pools in the gloom. They sit, and she twists the silver rings round her fingers.

'So, James is happy,' Cillian says. She doesn't look happy. 'What about you?'

'I'm surprised. By a lot of things. The fact James is so sure; that he wants this with me. The fact that I *feel* pregnant, different. I can tell something is growing inside me. And in some ways that seems horrifying, like an actual horror film. But in other ways . . . It's hard to describe. I'm even surprised to discover I'm not twenty any more, and the decision isn't . . . obvious . . .'

She trails off. Unsaid words beat moth-wings around them. Cillian, regardless of whether there is anyone left in the gallery to hear, has to ask:

'Is it possible the baby's mine?'

She sighs. 'Yes. The dates make it possible.' Looks down at her hands.

He exhales a long breath. He's surprised by the mix of emotions: shock, mostly. Fear. Something, keen and singing, an arrow in flight.

He puts two steadying hands either side of him on the bench. Seconds pass or minutes. The arrow, loosed, doesn't strike home; it hangs there vibrating as though time and space have become elastic and are stretching, the past away from the present and the future away from both.

A touch rouses him and he looks down. Roses' hand is beside his, the edge of her finger against the edge of his.

'I have no idea how to even say this,' she starts. He has no idea what she'll say either, and can't help, so stays silent.

'If it did turn out – I mean, even if it didn't, or if we didn't know either way. Could you imagine. Would you ever want to, like, be involved?'

The arrow hits. The pain so sharp he almost gasps, and with it a blood-like gush of joy.

'Would I . . .?' he starts, not sure what he wants to say or how he'll continue. 'How would it . . . I mean . . . what do you mean?'

She looks into his face, and hers, for the first time since they met today, is completely alive. The tip of her nose is damply red, her lips and cheeks flushed, her eyes liquid and bright.

'I don't even know.' A tense half-laugh. 'I know it's not . . . normal. It's hard to imagine. There's you and Hura, which is probably the most important thing to you. But if it – this baby – was yours, and even if it wasn't, somehow, I think both me and James could imagine . . . doing things differently. I mean, I love James. I really love him. But everything I've said is still true, for me. I don't want to have kids if that means some kind of total collapse. If it means signing up to become this little separate unit that never allows another person in.'

There is a Cillian who, still very much married, and still certain he can and will forge ahead in that unit, gets up and leaves the gallery. There is a Cillian who stays.

'How would it even work?' that Cillian asks. He listens to his own voice, surprised it's formed a rational-sounding question.

A small incredulous smile flickers around Roses' mouth: 'I have no fucking idea!'

Suddenly the frigid stillness of the bench and the gallery's calm hush is overwhelming, the dark walls press in. Cillian jumps up, hands clenched, eyes flicking nervously from paintings to gallery-goers to the illuminated exits. He takes a step away before he's realised what he's doing, that it looks like he's running. He wheels back to find that she's also on her feet.

'Listen,' she says, very serious again, 'you don't have to decide anything today. Of course you don't.'

'I need to leave this room,' he says.

'Of course, go.'

'No, I mean, come with me.'

She follows him out of the gallery and down the stairs, neither speaking as they dodge art-appreciation groups and school kids in neon tabards and scarf-wearing ladies and tourists. They push through the heavy revolving doors and Cillian turns left and marches on, Roses keeping pace with him, until they find themselves on a side-street somewhere near Leicester Square.

He stops and puts his hands flat against the wall, pushes like he could push it over.

'I need a cigarette or a drink. Or both. Several of both.'

'I know the feeling,' Roses says. 'Now try resisting that urge for the next eight months.'

They look at each other. He puts his hands in his hair and finds himself smiling.

'What the fuck,' he says.

'Yeah.'

'Do you want the baby?' he asks. He hopes, suddenly and very hard, that she does.

Roses puts out a hand, takes the fabric of his open jacket between her fingers, as if she's interested in the weave.

'I'm terrified,' Roses says. 'It feels too soon. For my work. For me and James. There's so much I want to do, and can do, and sometimes I think about *this* and I can see all that crumbling. The future I thought I was going to have. You know?'

He nods, because just at that moment he can't speak. She doesn't let go of his jacket.

'But yes,' Roses says, and now she looks at him and also smiles, though her eyes are full of tears, 'I think I do want it. At first it felt like a terrible mistake, but now – I don't know. Now it's starting to feel ok.'

Without planning to, they kiss.

The kiss is long and deep, and tastes of salt. It is a kiss that might be an ending, or a beginning.

★

When the kiss ends, Roses puts her arms around Cillian and holds him tight. She knows they will leave now, they must, but she wants to remember the sensation of his chest against hers, his cheek, the way he seems to smell of bonfires and rain. Something happened in the last months, in the borrowed flat that day, inside them, inside her. A mistake, almost certainly. She closes her eyes and sees, as clearly as the moment it happened, a wolf outlined in the light of a lamp.

Still walking, Cillian realises he's getting light-headed with hunger. The meeting at the gallery was a month ago. Passing a shop he buys bread and canned soup, and heads home to get warm.

While he's eating his phone rings: 'Hi, Mum.'

After years of serious ups and downs, hard graft in jobs too menial for her intelligence, and harder graft as a single parent, Joy finally left the capital a couple of years ago for a cottage on the Suffolk coast. This man Daniel, who she's been seeing, owns a boat. Cillian dismissed him for months before realising he was becoming a real part of Joy's life.

After a few preliminaries Joy asks: 'Have you heard from her?'

'Not since I last talked to you.'

'And have you tried to be in touch?'

'Not since she asked me not to.'

'Just don't let her forget you love her,' Joy says. She has always adored Hura.

'Mum . . .'

'I know, none of my business, I'm sorry,' she says. In fact, he suspects, she is angry with him, her anger struggling with her affection, and affection just about winning. She knows some of what brought about the calamity, but not all the details.

'Are you keeping warm?'

'Yes,' he shivers. 'I mean, no. I'm . . . it's cold.'

'It's bitter here. We've been having lots of good open fires though.'

'We?'

'Me and Dan. He's moved in, you know. For a bit.'

'I didn't know.' Cillian finds himself bristling. He's only known Joy alone, for such a long time. He tries to remind himself that he likes Daniel. He pictures the two of them walking on the beach, Dan's craggy face cracking into a smile. Joy's hair, so blonde it has always bordered on white, flamed by the wind.

'Please come down and see us. See me,' Joy says. 'I want to look after you.'

'I will. Soon. I promise.'

Cillian will go; there are things he needs to tell her, including plenty he doesn't know how to put into words, and certainly can't say on the phone. But right now he isn't sure he could handle being looked after; feels that particular kind of gentle pressure might shatter him to pieces.

'What are you doing with yourself?' she asks.

'Walking,' he says. Dating, he doesn't say; navigating an unknown country in the mist.

From where he sits, eating soup on the sofa, he looks across at the dining table, which now can't be used for meals because it's completely colonised by painting and drawing equipment: oils, solvent, a pile of small canvases, jam jars and mugs full of brushes. A box of pens, and packs of pastels and charcoal, all stored in the attic for years. On the floor are several reams and pads of paper, and a large drawing board is propped against the wall.

'And I've started painting again,' he says. He's weirdly reluctant to tell his mother, feeling that her approbation, her knowing about it at all, will jinx it. He hasn't made any art for years, outside his work, which he strongly feels does not count. Sensing that she shouldn't be too enthusiastic, Joy almost lets it pass without comment.

'That's great, Sweetpea,' she says. Then adds: 'Suffolk's very good for painting, you know. Good light.'

'Thanks, Mum. I'll remember that.' Suddenly he says: 'Do you love him? Daniel.'

There's a pause. When Joy answers it's quiet, considered, surprised.

'I think I might. Yes.'

Cillian nods, a pointless gesture since he's on the phone. Once he's gathered himself enough to sound normal he smiles.

'That's really great,' he says.

'After all this time,' Joy says. 'I didn't see it coming. I didn't see it coming until it was here.'

Chapter Twenty-Two

'So she's gone? Le Bouquet Toxique?'

Saul is lying on Sam's sofa, diligently colouring in a pattern of seashells.

'Gone for now,' Sam says.

He's working at his laptop, but it's relaxed weekend work. Saul's occasional interruptions are only slightly annoying. He glances over at his friend.

'What's the point in that, exactly?'

Saul doesn't look up. The coffee table beside him is strewn with coloured pencils, as well as a gin and tonic, a pack of rolling tobacco, cigarette papers, and a small bag of weed.

'The point is, it's incredibly fun,' Saul says. 'Tell me you don't like colouring.'

'I've never tried colouring.'

'You haven't lived.'

They're both silent for the next twenty minutes, during which the only sound is the soft tapping of Sam's fingers on the keys and the almost-imperceptible swish, swish of Saul's pencil. It's a grey, still afternoon, and the lights are on in the warm flat.

'Been to any good plays recently?' Saul asks innocently.

Sam holds his hands still a moment, then resumes.

'A couple.'

There's a long pause.

'Forget your wallet at any of them? Have to ask any nice young ladies to pay?'

'If you're asking whether I've seen Hura again, yes. Couple of times.'

'Interesting,' Saul says.

Sam shoots him a look and Saul gazes back at him with wide eyes and a smile of perfect sweetness.

'Stop it.'

'I'm not doing anything except colouring.'

'Stop it anyway.'

Saul gets up, examines his drink, wanders over to the big window.

'What about when she gets back?' he asks over his shoulder. 'Is it still bothering you?'

'What she said?'

'All of it. Her existence all tangled up with yours.'

Sam gets up too. Maybe he's done enough work for the weekend. He opens the fridge looking for the tonic water, for something that might eventually be made into dinner.

'No,' he says, getting a glass out of the cupboard and pressing ice cubes into it from a plastic tray. 'I think maybe she has changed. Once we talked and stuff, eventually. I don't know. I kind of, maybe, liked her.'

The place James picks to stay for the first few nights is on La Defensa, overlooking a small square with trees, and lamp posts painted green. He's been enthralled since he got to Buenos Aires by its archaic prettiness, reminiscent of Paris or Madrid, nothing like the rugged, alien city of his imagination. He's barely left the immediate area since arriving two days ago. In that short time he has developed a routine he loves: walking around the streets in the early morning, taking a book to a café and drinking coffee, and watching people go by. The morning of the third day, he buys a newspaper and sits with it at his favourite café, a corner place with striped awnings and sky-blue tables. He orders coffee and enjoys the newspaper's physicality, its fonts, the look of the text confettied with accents. He reads carefully and slowly, speaking the words in his head. His Spanish is limited, but he's determined to persevere.

The morning is still cool, his shirt a little too summery, but the sun is warm. Most people are going to work, stopping to drink a *cortado* and continue on their way. The only other people sitting in the café are two young Chinese tourists and a few older men. At the next table, one of these men has the same newspaper, one hand resting on it but his eyes far away. The man wears a good, faded suit and a fedora, and is smoking a thin cigar, its smell luxurious in the fresh morning air.

James finishes his coffee, drinks his glass of water, folds his paper. He goes inside to the corner where he has already identified an old-fashioned payphone. He takes from his pocket the telephone card he bought yesterday from a kiosk. He dials a number. His heart thumps as he listens to the unfamiliar dial tone. Then a woman answers:

'*Sí, diga.*' Tell me.

'Señora Gulliver?'

'*Sí?*'

'This is James. Gull's friend. James.'

There is a long pause, so long he thinks they've been cut off and suddenly panics, searching his pockets for coins in a reflex he didn't know he possessed.

'Are you there?'

'Yes, yes. I'm here.' The voice is strong and hybrid, Argentine with a drop of Newcastle mixed in.

'I'm in Buenos Aires. I said I'd call when I arrived ...'

'Yes,' she says, and pauses again. 'Are you coming here?'

'If you say I can.'

'I think that would be best,' she says. They arrange that he'll book his travel and arrive at Lago Puelo in two days' time.

When the call finishes, James walks out of the dim interior into the shade of the awning, feeling his pulse return to normal. The man with the fedora has finished his cigar and is getting ready to leave. As he stands he looks at James from under his hat brim.

'Beautiful morning,' he says in English.

'It is,' James says. The man's gaze is direct and he's almost, but not quite, repressing a smile. His eyes are the colour of water reflecting the sky.

'Full of promise,' the man says. He folds his newspaper and puts it under his arm, touches his hat, and turns away. As he watches the man walk across the square, James realises his heart has speeded up again. He smiles, draws a hand over his mouth.

The bus takes twenty-five hours. James tries to sleep but the dilemma of what to do with his legs, which barely fit into the space behind the seat in front, keeps him constantly shifting and unable to relax. In the window seat beside him a young woman with a full, smooth face and melancholy eyes arranges a scarf as a pillow between herself and the glass, turns from him, and seems to fall deeply asleep. James tries to fidget as little as possible, in deference to her composed presence, but it's torture. Through the long night he listens to music and audiobooks until his batteries die, and thinks, with his eyes closed, about two people: Gull, who is dead, and Roses, who is carrying a new and unknowable life.

Until the night when he told Roses Gull's story, James had been swimming face down, like the survivor of a shipwreck, blind in a trackless sea. After their conversation he raised his head and saw land. Still far off, but solid and real. He knew he had the strength to reach it.

James is aware, intellectually, that the baby might not be his. It doesn't matter. Ever since he found out about the pregnancy, his certainty hasn't wavered. He wants to be the child's father. He wants her to be its mother. His resolution remained intact through Roses' real and deep uncertainty, during which he tried as best he could to support without pressuring and hoped, fervently and mostly in silence, that she would choose to keep it.

Cillian's involvement in any potential future creates a sensation in James that he's tried to articulate to Roses, but can't even quite explain to himself. It is like a warm stone nestled in the palm of his hand. There is something comforting about it, a sense of private rightness. Maybe all Cillian will ever be is a friend, someone who sends a thoughtful present to the kid every now and then. But maybe there will be more. The three of them are talking, tentative and careful; feeling out the shape of something none of them can yet describe.

In the end, perhaps, it was his most practical conversations with Roses that had made the decision. Come to Argentina, he said. Ok, she agreed, but who would look after the baby if he was off travelling and she needed to work? And so James had had to face the fact of his freedom, so hard won and new, being curtailed. And still it didn't matter. He would come back. He'd have to think seriously about how to make money, if they were going to remain in London. But in the meantime there were his savings. Roses was earning, and he'd be at home.

He began in earnest to search for Gull's mother. He knew Maria had gone to study in Newcastle as an undergraduate, then married and stayed. From his mother's friends he'd heard again that Gull's father was dead, and the same rumour that Maria had gone back to Argentina. From somewhere, Auntie May had even dredged up a maiden name, Torres, though she didn't know which name Maria used now. No one else seemed to have kept in contact.

Searching online for the names in different combinations was dispiriting. There was so little to go on – no job that he could remember, no address in Argentina, no other living relatives. When he reached his wits' end, he booked another train to Newcastle, thinking that just being there again might possibly spark something. It was only once he'd booked the ticket that he remembered the swimming club.

Once he'd recalled it, it seemed incredible he could have forgotten it for so long. Gull was a brilliant swimmer but it didn't come from nowhere: his mother had taken him to the pool since he was a baby, and she'd done so because it was her own great love. Now James remembered: a black-and-white photograph of Maria, at about fourteen, in swimsuit and cap, poised on the diving block. She'd been a prodigy too, back home, long before she became a foreign student, a wife, a mother. She'd given up serious training, but every single week she swam with the same group of women, a hardy, laughing mob that headed out to inhospitable waters without wetsuits.

It must have been so hard for Maria to believe that her only son had dived, drunk and deliberately, into a freezing river. Like a slap, James realised: maybe she'd never believed it.

This was in those strange weeks before he asked Roses to come with him on his travels, before they knew about the pregnancy. He was surprised when she said she wanted to come with him to Newcastle.

'Where are we?' Roses asks.

'That was my grandparents' house,' James says. He's not sure why they're here, standing in front of a small semi-detached prefab, the top half white and the lower half pebble-dashed, a square of patchy grass in front. His grandparents have been dead for years. 'They had a greenhouse in the garden,' he says.

Roses takes his hand quietly and he looks at her.

'You ok?' he asks. She's paler than normal, dark patches under her eyes.

'Really hungry. Or maybe I just need a coffee. But fine.'

He nods, looks back at the house.

'We don't have to stay. I just wanted to see the place.'

They don't move. There's a pink child's bike on the front lawn, tumbled on its side.

'If they hadn't died, I always thought, it might have been different,' James says. 'For Mam. But then they both went, within a couple of months of each other. And after that there was nowhere else to go.'

Roses squeezes his hand.

'Come on,' he says. 'If the corner shop's still there we can get you some crisps.'

That afternoon, they track down a secretary of the swimming club which, incredibly, is still running. She knows someone, who knows someone, who knows someone. After many calls, delays, and dead ends, James finds himself holding a piece of notepaper, on which are written, at an angle to the lines, the name of a town, and an email address.

★

A couple of weeks later, he asks Emma to step into the empty staff room with him and shuts the door. She leans with both hands behind her against the table and puts her head on one side, smiling a conspiratorial smile, his coolness of the past weeks apparently forgotten.

'What's on your mind?'

He tells her that he's handing in his resignation.

'That's not how this works,' she says. 'You're on the rota, for months.'

'I know. It's done though.'

Her lips are hard and bloodless.

'If you do this, there's no coming back,' she says. 'You're breaking a contract. You're destroying everything.'

He goes to the door, opens it, holds it for her to walk through.

'I expected more from you, James,' she says. 'Ever since I met you—'

'You've never met me.'

He looks her in the eyes, then. A long look, after which they both know that this is over.

She walks past him, out of the room. She never looks him in the eyes again.

The bus arrives in El Bolsón early in the morning. It's hours before his meeting with Gull's mother, but now that he's so close to actually seeing her he finds himself dry-mouthed and tense with worry. He'd laid out some of the facts he told Roses in his email, but there's so much more to explain. What does she already know, or guess?

Despite his exhaustion, he climbs into a taxi. The car drops him at the end of an unmade road, and the driver points to a gap in the mesquite bushes:

'*El lago, por ahí.*'

'*Gracias.*'

James hoists his backpack onto his shoulders, wishing he'd left some of his stuff at a hostel before coming here. He heads in the direction the driver pointed, finding that a neat walkway of planks leads through the vegetation. He follows it for a while, then stops to take a drink of water. Behind and in front of him the boardwalk disappears into low foliage, and he has no idea how far he is from the end. There seems to be no other human presence for a long, long way in any direction, and the only sounds are the chirrups and calls of birds and insects. He starts walking again.

The tramp of his feet on the boards, the hum of crickets, become a mesh of sound around him; there's no wind, he realises after a while, here among the dense, sheltering scrub. After what seems like a long time the path rises and he can see, at the end, a brighter gap. He reaches it, and emerges onto the shore of Lago Puelo.

The sun is high now, and there are white clouds piled up above low mountains. The lake stretches away, huge and quiet, edged on every side by slopes dense with trees. After the long enclosed path, the sudden visible distance seems unreal, like a painting of mountains. Far beyond the lake there is snow on the peaks of the San Lorenzo range, with the Chilean border beyond them and, beyond that, the sea. Some distance away to his right is a seam of beach. To his left the andesite is stacked into cliffs.

He has emerged onto a large, flat rock that serves as a lookout point. Beneath him a fall of boulders and smaller stones leads down into clear water. Picking a path through the rocks, James makes his way towards the still margin. Before he reaches it, he unclips and shrugs off his backpack and nestles it into a hollow. Then he takes off his clothes and piles them neatly on his bag. Without them or his weighty pack he feels light, as though gravity has been turned down a notch. Fingertips of breeze make him shiver.

James has never been someone to imagine other lives he could have lived. But here and now, naked and unmoored and far from home, he is surrounded by a shimmer of possible realities. Gull is alive somewhere, with a business and a boyfriend and a cat, coaching swimming at weekends. Seeing Roses, as James first did, in the corner of a bar, he turns away instead of looking at her for the one, two, three seconds it takes for her to raise her eyes and meet his. He is a boy again, walking bruised but triumphant down the street in just one shoe, his mother's hand held tightly in his own. He, a father, holds a child in his arms, and makes her a promise.

James walks across the scree until he can stand looking down into the green shallows. Light is running in patterns over the lakebed, and he takes a step into the water, the cold of it like a blank white fire against his skin. He takes another step, and another, wading out until he's submerged to the waist. He raises his hands above his head, ready to strike out. He thinks: this is the beginning.

Acknowledgements

Thank you to Sareeta Domingo for believing in this book and making it better, as well as for all the astute ideas and patience along the way. Thank you to Sam Eades and all the speakers in our Debut Writers' Academy, and to all the authors I met through it for sharing your questions and wisdom.

Great thanks to Francine Brody, Jo Roberts-Miller, Donna Hillyer and Jo Whitford for your editorial acumen. Jessica Hart, Jake Alderson, Paul Stark, Liam Iliffe, Helena Fouracre, Francesca Pearce, thank you for all your incredible steering of the design, audio, press and marketing of this book. To Carina Bryan, and everyone at Trapeze who has worked tirelessly on this book, I appreciate you all.

To my agent, Emma Finn, whose combination of a critical eye with true warmth has given so much to me as a writer, and to this novel. Thank you for your encouragement, and for being with me on this journey. Thank you to Saida Azizova and everyone behind the scenes at C&W.

Charlie Castelletti, thank you for one of the most important conversations I've had about this book, for agreeing to read it, and for your kindness.

Also for the kind, early steer on my clumsy questions about trans cultures, thank you Thomas Page McBee, and the writings of CN Lester and others towards which he pointed me.

Thank you to Rosie Seddon and Bill Seddon, for everything, but specifically for the time you have given me to write by looking after my children, and for believing that was important. To all the people who have looked after my children while I wrote, including but not limited to Abbie, Amie, Georgina, Lacey, Ramadu, Deniz, Ines, Jackie, and Nich. To everyone who has cleaned my house, for doing your work so I could do mine: Iryna, Karen, Aidee, thank you.

To my colleagues at Quartz, an invariably brilliant group of journalists and the nicest, smartest people I could have hoped to work with. There are so many of you, so I will limit myself to some of the editors who supported my choices and helped me do too many things at once over the course of many years: thank you Kevin Delaney, Heather Landy, Indrani Sen, Jason Karaian, Jackie Bischof, and Samanth Subramanian.

May Abdalla, whose positivity after early reads of unready, flawed work made me believe in myself, and that I could do better. To the earliest readers of this book in its entirety: Theo Brown and Georgia Platman, thank you so much for the time you took, the insights you gave me, for treating it like it was a real book. To Katherine Kingsley and Alan Macdonald, thank you for your detailed, generous readings and the time spent talking about them.

Isolde Godfrey, Joe Wild, Jason Bower, Sonya Cullingford, Nich Galzin, and Ti Brown, thank you, love, respect, always.

To people who helped me in so many different ways, either with this book, or the ones before: Juliet Brooke, Tim Martin, Kevin O'Loughlin, James Harrison, Ben Clement, Clemmie James, Anna Hope, Lara Pawson, Aro Angelique, Anoushka Warden, Llywelyn ap Myrddin and Joe Dunthorne. Thank you to Sam, Jo, and Simon Wren-Lewis, who gave me a physical space for a week, at a time when that was so valuable. Sarah Cunningham, thank you, just because you are wonderful.

To the staff of all the many cafés in which I have written, and overstayed the time one coffee buys you, particularly E5 in Hackney and Bakers and Co. in Bristol: you do an important and wonderful job.

Ellie Bard. None of the novels I read before we met hinted that such a friendship was possible; none I've read since have come close to capturing it.

Valerie Irving and Lawrence Werber, thank you, for more reasons than I could ever list. If I had to pick one: for teaching me about freedom.

To my children: you didn't exactly help me get this done, but I love you more than words can say.

David Seddon. Thank you for your unstinting support, your never-failing encouragement, and your ability to remember, and remind me, that it's about love not glory. In a galaxy of bright planets, you are the sun for me.

CREDITS

Trapeze would like to thank everyone at Orion who worked on the publication of *Open Season*.

Agent
Emma Finn

Editor
Sareeta Domingo

Editorial Management
Jo Roberts-Miller
Jo Whitford
Carina Bryan
Jane Hughes
Charlie Panayiotou
Lucy Bilton
Claire Boyle

Copy-editor
Francine Brody

Proofreader
Donna Hillyer

Audio
Paul Stark
Jake Alderson
Georgina Cutler

Contracts
Dan Herron
Ellie Bowker
Alyx Hurst

Design
Nick Shah
Jessica Hart
Joanna Ridley
Helen Ewing

Finance
Nick Gibson
Jasdip Nandra
Sue Baker
Tom Costello

Inventory
Jo Jacobs
Dan Stevens

Production
Sarah Cook
Katie Horrocks

Marketing
Helena Fouracre

Publicity
Francesca Pearce

Sales
Jen Wilson
Victoria Laws
Esther Waters
Tolu Ayo-Ajala
Group Sales teams across
Digital, Field, International and
Non-Trade

Operations
Group Sales Operations team

Rights
Rebecca Folland
Tara Hiatt
Ben Fowler
Alice Cottrell
Ruth Blakemore
Ayesha Kinley
Marie Henckel

About the Author

Cassie Werber is a writer and journalist. She studied English at Clare College, Cambridge, and holds Master's degrees from Central School of Speech and Drama and City University. She lives in London.